HADAMAR

THE HOUSE OF SHUDDERS

JASON K. FOSTER

First published 2019

Big Sky Publishing Pty Ltd
PO Box 303, Newport, NSW 2106, Australia
Phone: 1300 364 611
Fax: (61 2) 9918 2396
Email: info@bigskypublishing.com.au
Web: www.bigskypublishing.com.au

Cover design and typesetting: Think Productions
Printed in China by Hang Tai Printing Company Limited

A catalogue record for this book is available from the National Library of Australia

For Cataloguing-in-Publication entry see National Library of Australia.

Author: Jason K. Foster

Title: Hadamar The House of Shudders

ISBN: 978-1-925675-86-3

HADAMAR

THE HOUSE OF SHUDDERS

www.bigskypublishing.com.au

JASON K. FOSTER

CONTENTS

Dedicated to my Mutti, for giving me the strength and conviction to see the world in a different light, and dedicated to the forgotten children of Hadamar.

The following story is based on true events.

BERLIN, DEN 1 Sept 1939

Reichsleiter Bouhler und Dr. med. Brandt
sind unter Verantwortung beauftragt, die Befugnisse namentlich zu bestimmender Ärzte so zu erweitern, dass nach menschlichen Ermessen unheilbar Kranken bei kritischster Beurteilung ihres Krankheitszustandes der Gnadentod gewährt werden kann. (Signed, A. Hitler)

BERLIN, 1 Sept 1939

Reichsleiter Bouhler and Dr. Brandt
are charged with the responsibility to extend the authority of designated doctors, so that they may decide whether those considered incurably ill, as far as can be judged, after the most careful evaluation of their condition, may be granted a mercy death. (Signed, A. Hitler)

As World War II loomed, Hitler authorised the implementation of *Aktion* T-4, a eugenics program designed to rid Germany of unwanted and undesirable citizens. The program's headquarters were in Berlin, at number 4 Tiergartenstrasse, but its day-to-day operations took place in various institutions around the country, including in the southern town of Hadamar. When the truth of what happened within the asylum's walls became known, the people of Hadamar gave the institution a nickname.
They called it the House of Shudders.

PROLOGUE

5 May 2017

My grandfather never said anything about Hadamar. I pushed and pushed him, but he refused to say a word. The rest of the family simply left Opa be, but I always wanted to know. Only in his final days did he reveal anything, and all he told me was her name: Ingrid Marchand. I asked him where I could find her.

He said he hadn't seen her since the end of the war. At a guess, he said, she would be in America, possibly Long Island, New York, as that is where she has always said she would go. Her kindergarten teacher had moved there, and she had said she would go there one day too. Maybe she had become a teacher, he said, but he didn't know. Opa spoke about her with love, such as I had never seen from him – not even for Oma. It only intrigued me even more.

I researched the name Ingrid Marchand online.

There she was: a teacher in Long Island, rewarded for her charity work. It took a little more digging and a few emails and phone calls, but soon I found out where she was.

Hadamar was fast becoming an obsession.

I rang the nursing home and spoke to her. At first, I didn't tell her who I was; I just told her I was interested to learn more about Hadamar. She hung up. I rang again and got one of the receptionists, who told me that Miss Marchand did not want to speak to me. I asked her to tell her that I was Johan Kapfler's granddaughter.

The phone went silent. I waited and waited.

'Miss Marchand says she will talk to you, if you wish, but not over the phone.'

I caught a plane from Berlin to New York that evening, not knowing what to expect. Perhaps she had agreed to see me, thinking I would not make the trip across the Atlantic Ocean. If what Opa had told me was correct, she was ninety-three. Would she even remember that she had agreed to meet me? Would she remember much about Hadamar at all?

I arrived in New York, caught a yellow taxi that soon pulled up outside the nursing home. It was bigger than any I had seen in Germany, with several wings. It looked like a large hotel with thousands of residents. Walking into the reception area, I encountered a middle-aged nurse busying herself behind the counter.

'Can I help you?' she asked when she noticed my presence.

'I'm here to see Miss Ingrid Marchand.'

'Is she expecting you?'

'Maybe. I'm Johan Kapfler's granddaughter. She said she would talk to me if I came to see her.'

'One moment,' the nurse said before she disappeared down the corridor and into the nearby lifts.

I sat in the reception area and waited. Several minutes passed before the nurse returned.

'Miss Marchand says she will see you. Follow me.'

I followed the nurse to the lifts and along the corridor until we came to a room with number 18 on the door. The nurse opened the door and led me inside. Sitting facing the window, looking out at the distant ocean, was a frail old woman. She had a red and blue crocheted blanket across her lap. She was fingering a gold ring.

'Ingrid,' the nurse said. 'The young lady I mentioned is here to see you.'

The old lady slowly turned her head towards me. Her deep blue eyes immediately drew me in. Her face was wrinkled but her age perhaps came more from the hardships she endured than the weariness of years. She had become an old woman long before her time. Above her blue eyes she maintained a full head of snowy hair; the brightness of both were accentuated by her chocolate-coloured skin.

'*Guten tag, Fräulein,*' she said warmly as she pointed to a chair beside hers. I sat down as the nurse departed.

'You came to ask me about Hadamar, *ja*?'

'I wanted to know more about my Opa's life, but *ja* – I came to find out about Hadamar.'

'The House of Shudders, that's what the townspeople called it.'

'The House of Shudders?' I asked.

'You know,' she said, 'you are the spitting image of Fräulein Rothenberg. When I was young, I was convinced that my kindergarten teacher was a real-life princess. She was the only teacher at my school who ever cared about me, who defended and protected me against the worst the world could offer. I can still remember the waft of her vanilla perfume. I remember her eyes, bluer than the summer sky, her

China-doll skin, and her tight black curls. Why do you want to know about Hadamar?'

'Because Opa never talked about it.'

'Never?'

'*Nein*, not until his last days – and all he mentioned was you.'

'Johan is dead?'

'*Ja*, he died last month.'

'That hurts my heart to hear. Yet I'm surprised he managed to live this long,' she said as she looked longingly out the window towards the bay. 'I've only ever told other people pieces of what happened to me, and only when someone asked – which, as the years went by, happened less and less frequently. I didn't mind. I've tried so hard to forget. My time is short and I find myself longing for death. If there's a Heaven, I think I deserve a place in it. If there's a Hell, it couldn't possibly be worse than where I've already been. If there's nothingness … then at least I will be able to forget, and finally find some measure of peace.'

'I was thinking about writing a a book about yours – and Opa's – experiences. It seems the people of Germany have forgotten about the suffering of people like yourself.'

'I've thought long and hard about how much I should tell. At first, I thought my story should die with me, but if you say the people of Germany have forgotten about the horror, then maybe you should write down what I have to say.'

'*Danke, Fräulein*,' I said politely as I retrieved a tape recorder from my bag. 'So, you called Hadamar the "House of Shudders".'

'*Ja*, the House of Shudders, but that name does not do that place justice. I was a prisoner of Hadamar for six long years. By the end, when the Americans came, it was too late: Hadamar had stolen my soul.'

She continued to stare mournfully out the window as the memories of Hadamar played over in her mind.

'They stole everything from me: my chance to have children, my chance at love, my innocence, my *soul*.' Her bottom lip trembled as she turned the ring on her finger. She stayed silent for so long that I wondered if she would speak again. 'When I say they took my soul, I mean exactly that. I've only ever truly loved one man: your Opa. After the war I found it hard to let another man touch me. Perhaps, when my story is done, you will understand why. Do you think a long life is a blessing or a curse?' she asked as she pulled her gaze from the window and looked at me. She wasn't crying, but her eyes had become watery.

'Fräulein Marchand, I'm only young. I wouldn't know.'

'People say my long life has been a blessing, but sometimes I wonder if it has been a curse. Soon enough, I will meet God, if He even exists, but if He does exist I will demand explanations from Him. Most of all, why was I allowed to live? Why was my life more valuable than others? I have been given the "gift" of a long life but am I worthy of that gift? I don't think so.'

'But, *Fräulein*, you were a teacher. Surely all those years of educating children count for something?'

'Miss Kapfler, I can see it in your pretty blue eyes. They're filled with hope; hope and optimism for the future of humanity. That hope was taken from me when I was very young. Don't mistake me, I've tried to see the good in the world – I have! But I have seen humanity at its most evil. I am ninety-three years old. I've seen beautiful things, had wonderful experiences. I've tried to convince myself that the beauty outweighs the evil, but I'm not convinced it does. If you had seen what I've seen, I wonder: would you still have hope? My life plays through my mind like a disjointed movie, all the events, all the people. Perhaps I *have* lived a fortunate life. I've spent my life teaching; it's a noble profession. I tried to give back to society, in debt and gratitude to God for sparing me, but it never seemed enough. Perhaps there is hope. I've seen it in the faces of the children I've taught. Maybe it's just because I can't escape my past. Still, at least I'm not one of the unlucky ones.'

'The unlucky ones?'

'*Ja*, the unlucky ones. The survivors of the death and concentration camps who have dementia, the ones who have Alzheimer's, the ones who re-live every day believing that they're back in the camps. I've only ever seen a few come and go in this retirement home, and I have always been glad I'm not one of them. My memories force me to re-live my time in Hadamar, but some days I can push them aside at least long enough to keep my sanity.

'In recent times, America has become in many ways like Nazi Germany. The politicians have used mass media here in the same way the Nazis did – and an unpredictable man has come to power.

'I don't understand this new "social" media or how it works,' she went on, 'but when I hear some of the grandchildren of others' talking about Facebook, Snapchat and Instagram, it reminds me of the movies, the radio and the newspapers that Hitler and the others used to lie to the German people and to teach them to hate. I've heard it on the TV, the way people in this country talk about Muslims. It's the same as how they used to talk about the Jews. I didn't think people would forget, but they have! Perhaps my memories need to be preserved so history does not repeat itself. I know the Americans kept legal transcripts and I'm sure there is mention of Hadamar in textbooks and academic journals, if you wish to learn more, but none of that would ever give the true picture of what happened there – not in the same way that someone who lived through it can. With your Opa gone, I doubt there are any other Hadamar survivors left. If what was done to me and others like me is forgotten – then *they* win. The world needs to be reminded of what can happen when pure hatred is allowed to run free.'

I reached out and took her hand in mine. I looked down as my smooth, blemish-free hands wrapped around hers, contrasting starkly with her wrinkled and withered black hands. She squeezed tightly before she looked up at me again.

'If we remember the past,' I said to her, 'perhaps we can create a better future?'

CHAPTER 1

THE PREVENTION OF MISCHLINGE

2 March 1938

I remember the exact day they came for me.

It was Ash Wednesday, the beginning of Lent and the last day of the *Mainzer Fassenacht,* a time of great celebration that marks the blooming of the flowers, the greening of the leaves and the coming of new life. The squares and streets were filled with revellers and there were parades every evening. In years gone by the floats and costumes had revolutionary undertones, with a particular hatred directed at the French, something that had taken on even greater significance after the National Socialists had consolidated their power. Mutti thought it best that we – more specifically, I – stay indoors. So we stayed at home and drank Glühwein.

It was mid-evening when a hefty knock came at the door. In the dappling firelight my eyes found Mutti's and, despite the heat emanating from the hearth and the wine in my hand, I felt chilled to the bone. Everyone hated me and, by proxy, my mother, so company was a rarity. Brushing it off as drunk revellers falling upon the door, we returned to our wine, but when the knocks intensified I felt my skin crawl. Mutti ignored it, choosing instead to stare at the flames. I stood up, moved beside her and put my hand on her shoulder. She felt ice cold.

'Frau Marchand!' a voice bellowed. 'We know you're in there! Open up now or we'll break the door down!'

'Don't answer it,' I said to Mutti. 'If we ignore them long enough, they'll go away.'

Suddenly, Mutti stood, placed her wine glass on the mantelpiece above the fire and strode to the door.

'Mutti! What are you doing?' I cried.

'Ingrid,' she said, looking back at me. Even in the firelight I could see her face was drained of colour. 'We have no choice.'

Upon reaching the door she opened it, revealing two black and red–clad Gestapo *Unterscharführer*. My throat constricted, my heart pounded. They stepped aside, revealing two doctors dressed in white coats, *Obersturmführer* insignia hidden beneath their collars.

'What do you want?' Mutti asked coldly. 'You already took my husband.'

'We have not come for your husband,' the closer, older *Obersturmführer* said as he stepped inside. 'We have come for your daughter.'

Mutti looked at them. Her legs began to quiver. Her knees wobbled beneath her. Her left hand shook as she grasped in vain for the doorjamb. I only caught her moments before she hit the floor.

With the help of the older *Obersturmführer* we got her back in her chair. I retrieved her wine glass from the mantelpiece, topped it up and gave it to her. She shook so badly; she could barely hold it. It was only when I held it to her lips that she could finally drink. After the first few sips, she wrapped her hands around the glass, drained what was left and placed her hands on the armrests of her chair. She stared into the fire for several moments before she stood up, walked to the table and retrieved the bottle. She refilled her glass, drained it, and filled it again before she returned to her armchair.

'Frau Marchand,' the older doctor said as he moved from the doorway and laid out some papers on the table. They were covered in writing, signatures and official stamps, the only one of which I recognised was the official black eagle of the Reich stamped at the top of the page. 'Are you aware of the Committee of Experts for Population and Racial Policy?'

At first Mutti ignored him staring absently at the flames.

'Frau Marchand, *are you aware of the Committee of Experts for Population and Racial Policy*?'

She gave a quick, almost imperceptible shake of her head.

'In March 1935,' the doctor announced, 'the Committee of Experts for Population and Racial Policy met in Berlin and decided that *Mischlinge*, like your daughter here, were an affliction on the purity of the Aryan race that needed a resolution. Hence, we at the Gestapo created Commission Number 3. The role of this commission is to document all the *Mischlinge* in the Rheinland area and in other parts of Germany.

'We thought we had dealt with all of the *Mischlinge* in this region but, until we seized the records of one Dr Oborwitz, we were unaware of the existence of your daughter. This, taken with the testimony of a —' he paused as he retrieved a notebook from inside his jacket, flipped it open and read, 'Herr Waldheim, who confirmed that Ingrid was a decidedly mentally disabled *Mischling* child.'

My stomach sank, my legs felt weak. Herr Waldheim, my former school principal, was desperate to be the model Nazi. But no matter how hard he tried – no matter how much of their dirty work he did – he would never quite meet their 'lofty' ideals. He was not Aryan and Mutti had always said that he preferred the company of men, but no one had ever been able to prove anything. When the Gestapo pressed him about me, I imagined, he would have gladly told them whatever they wanted to know. Eager to impress or to deflect attention away from himself, he would have embellished and signed off on any lies that they fed him.

My courage wavered. I wanted to be strong for Mutti, but hearing that Herr Waldheim had denounced me made me terrified of what was in the papers on the table.

'Hundreds of other Rheinlander bastards like your daughter, have been designated as biologically inferior and of possessing extensive negative traits,' the Gestapo doctor continued. 'A panel consisting of myself and my companion here as well as a judge have reviewed Ingrid's case and decided she will be taken to a local hospital to have several special procedures performed. Do not concern yourself. There will be no harmful consequences.'

CHAPTER 1

Mutti snapped out of her trance-like state, her voice ferocious as she leapt from her chair. 'You will not take Ingrid from me!'

She snatched the papers off the table, howling and screaming as she tore them into tiny pieces and flung them into the air. I watched as they floated to the ground like tiny white feathers. She cried, 'You will NOT take my daughter – not the way you took my Guillaume!'

Unperturbed, the Gestapo doctor reached inside his coat, retrieved a duplicate of the documentation and placed it in the same place as the originals.

'Frau Marchand,' he said coldly, 'I did not come here to debate this matter with you. The law states that I have the right to take Ingrid. Her special treatment will not take long. She will not be gone more than a few hours.'

Hatred burned in Mutti's eyes as the two *Unterscharführer* marched towards me, grabbed my hands and arms and forced them behind my back. My shoulders burned as if they were on fire.

'Leave her alone!' Mutti cried as she tried to pry their arms away. 'She is not a common criminal!'

My head swam. The torment of school, the hatred of the townspeople, the coming of the Nazi Party. I thought all of that had made me grow up. I was wrong; I was a scared little child. The fear engulfed me. It took everything I had not to wet my pants. I thought back to the moment they had taken Vati – how Mutti had fallen to pieces; how I almost had too. Despite the tenderness of my age, I'd taken everything in my stride. I had taken care of Mutti. I had nursed her back to health, brought her back to relative normality. If I could handle that, I could handle anything the Gestapo could do to me.

That is what I tried to tell myself.

'Mutti! Mutti! Don't let them take me!' I wailed as they forced me out the door.

'Ingrid! Ingrid!' Mutti yelled, throwing all of her body weight into one last attempt to free me. It was futile. One of them brushed her away as if she were an insect, while the other *Unterscharführer* blocked the doorway.

Waiting in the street was a black Mercedes, identical to the one that had taken Vati. The *Unterscharführer* holding me let me go and the younger of the *Obersturmführer* doctors forced me into the back seat. Through my watering eyes I could see Mutti's arms, stretched out, searching, feeling, like two tentacles as they reached around the *Unterscharführer's* torso and grasped at thin air.

'Get in there, you black bitch!' the younger doctor growled as he threw me into the car. The door was open and I contemplated trying to escape, but I was not quick enough; the older *Obersturmführer* had slid in beside me. I fumbled at the door handle. Managing to grasp hold, I turned it and opened the door, only to find the other *Unterscharführer* blocking my way. He slipped in on the other side of me. The crushing weight of the two men made it hard to breathe. I struggled to get air into my lungs. I felt as if I would pass out at any minute.

Then I heard banging.

'Give me back my daughter! *Give me back my daughter*!' Mutti cried as she pounded the windows with her fists. They paid no attention. The *Unterscharführer* in the driver's seat turned the key in the ignition. The engine sparked to life and we pulled away from the curb. My breathing was quick and short. I tried to turn my mind to what they were about to do to me but, starved of oxygen, all I could think about was taking my next breath. Time lost all meaning. Had we been driving for ten minutes? An hour? I didn't know.

Suddenly, the car came screeching to an abrupt halt, making all three of us lurch forward.

'*Aussteigen*!' the *Obersturmführer* doctor in the front seat ordered while the other doctor wrapped his arms around me to keep me from escaping. The two *Unterscharführer* got out of the car and stood beside it. They had cut off all avenues of escape.

The older doctor grabbed me painfully by the right biceps and wrenched me from the car. I barely had time to steady myself before they were pulling me towards a small fountain in the centre of a well-manicured lawn that was surrounded by a clipped square hedge. Running toward and beyond the fountain was a pebbled pathway. I contemplated kicking my legs, flailing my arms – anything to break free, to run away – but where would I go? How far would I get? They had said it themselves. I was one of hundreds. They must have done this hundreds of times. They would pre-empt anything I could do. All that remained was passive resistance. I let my body go completely limp. It didn't deter them. They simply dragged me towards two rows of elm trees that guarded either side of two enormous entrance doors.

'*Halt*!' the senior *Obersturmführer* doctor ordered. He turned around and looked down his nose at me. Then he coldly said, 'Walk properly or I will order these men to shoot you here and now. Your diseased black blood will spill on the stones beneath your feet.'

I did as he had ordered and walked 'properly' towards the entranceway. There was a large golden crucifix above the doors. Once, the sight of it would have filled me with hope. Now, however, I got the distinct feeling God had forgotten me. They led me inside.

Everything was white. White walls, white linoleum floors, and white uniforms on the doctors and nurses bustling up and down the corridors, some of them with arms full of clipboards and medical equipment. The whiteness was only broken by brown wooden crosses that sat at equidistant points along the walls. My heart felt as if it was gripped in a vice. Inside, I was numb. The two *Unterscharführer* stopped in front of the first door we came to and shoved me inside. I looked around blankly for a moment before noticing a long table covered in a white cloth.

Seated at the table were three Gestapo men wearing white coats. Looking closely underneath their collars, I guessed them to be *Sturmbannführer*. To the right of them sat the older of the two *Obersturmführer*. Only one spare chair remained, the single one on my side in which I was ordered to sit. A man with tightly clipped grey hair and smallpox scars on his face sat across from me. The mere sight of him filled me with dread. My frequent trips to Herr Waldheim's office paled into insignificance as this man opened a leather-bound file and perused it.

CHAPTER 1

Then he said, 'Ingrid Marchand, you have been brought here to decide whether you are a candidate for sterilisation.'

I stared blankly back at them. I was fourteen. I didn't know much about sterilisation. I'd only heard the word a few times in science class and all I knew was that it meant to cleanse something. The townspeople of Mainz often taunted me, saying that Germany needed to be 'cleansed' of people like me, but I didn't really comprehend how sterilisation came into it. I felt like I was on trial, accused of a crime I didn't commit, nor even know about. But this was no trial. The people in front of me were my judge, jury and, in a sense, my executioners.

'Ingrid Marchand,' the grey-haired man said in a deep voice that made me shiver. 'You fulfil the necessary criteria for sterilisation. Based on your biological inferiority, disharmonies in the phenotypic appearance, and your preponderantly negative character traits, it is in your best interests, and those of the Reich, that you do not and will not have children in the future as they will carry the genetic weaknesses you possess with them. If you are permitted to marry another undesirable, these weaknesses would only serve to multiply. We cannot allow this to happen. We have a sacred duty to the purity of the German people to prevent the poisoning of the entire bloodstream of the Aryan race. You will, therefore, immediately be taken to have the sterilisation procedure performed.'

I sat there stunned. I looked at their faces, hoping to see a trace of sympathy. They remained cold and distant. I contemplated escape but I was stunned, too confused to protest or resist as two burly nurses with plaited blonde hair, broad shoulders and square, heavy jaws appeared. Standing either side of me they placed their hands under my armpits, lifted me up off the chair and took me away to an adjacent room. Inside, there were medical stands with hanging bags, and metal trays bearing all kinds of silver tools. In the centre of the room was a bed. At the end were two leg clamps that resembled horse stirrups and on either side there were two more belts. The nurses threw me down heavily onto the bed and attached a black leather strap across my chest, forced my arms along the outer parts of the bed then fastened my wrists into place.

I tried to move my arms. I tried to flip my chest from side to side. It was useless. I went to kick my feet, but the nurses had a tight hold of them as they fixed them into the stirrups and strapped them into place. The two nurses covered their faces in white masks and gloves as the two *Obersturmführer* appeared. The older doctor paused over my abdomen as he pressed his fingers down on either side of my belly button. He turned around and reached for a large knife.

Hovering above me, the blade glinted in the artificial light as he twisted his hand. With his left hand he retrieved a small square of white bandage. Momentarily placing the knife beside me, he picked up a brown bottle, placed the bandage across the top and tipped it. After dabbing my belly with the bandage, he put the bottle down and picked up the knife once more. I watched on, utterly helpless.

He plunged the knife into me.

At first I felt nothing but the pressure of the scalpel as it drove its way in. I remember thinking that my blood was the same colour as anyone else's. Then came the most excruciating pain I had ever felt;

as if someone was driving a hot poker into my sides and twisting it around and around. I scrunched my eyes closed, but I could still feel the doctor's careless cutting as he carved me up like a butcher hacking up a carcass. I begged myself to pass out but I couldn't. Instead I opened my eyes, lifted my head as high as I could, and watched as he reached for another tool that looked like a pair of scissors. Unable to raise my head any higher I couldn't see what he was doing, but I heard a loud clicking sound. Then I felt a needle being threaded through me.

He cut me again, on the second mark he had made. I felt the same sensation: the scalpel penetrating my skin, the same jagged slicing, the clicking sound.

'Nurse! Stitch these back up,' he ordered as he wiped his gloved hands clean of my blood. The nearest nurse retrieved a needle and ream of blue thread and began sewing up the wounds. At every rough entry, I felt like I was being stabbed with a thousand knives. Each time she pulled the thread tight it felt as if I was being lifted towards the ceiling.

'Finished,' she said distantly as she untied the leather straps and indicated for me to stand up. Still reeling from the pain, I sat up, wobbling back and forth as I tried not to fall off the bed. I put my hand out onto the bed to steady myself as I stared down at the two jagged and zigzagged rows of clumsy stitches running down either side of my stomach like a pair of railway tracks.

'Get up!' the doctor ordered, tossing his gloves into a nearby bin.

The pain was unbearable but I was determined not give them any further excuse to hurt me. I gingerly lifted myself off the table, trying to stand, but I was too nauseated from the pain. I grabbed the bed again, while my other hand held my stomach, my fingers tracing the coarse stitches.

'You can go,' the nurse said as she nodded in the direction of the door and handed me a piece of paper. 'One of the soldiers outside will take you home.'

I took my hand off my stomach to take the piece of paper. Pain pulsated through my body as I tried to place one foot after the other. I was dizzy, weak, in shock. Breathing slowly and deeply was the only thing keeping me from falling unconscious to the floor. I made it to the door, but I had to hold the wall for a moment before I could continue. Recovering enough to shuffle out into the hallway, I found one of the Gestapo *Unterscharführer* waiting for me. His imposing frame made it impossible to see anything else – until he stepped aside and allowed me to pass.

I was sure I was hallucinating. Up and down the corridor were lines of people waiting beside different doors. Mine was only the first. Most of the people were white – whiter than most Germans I knew. But amongst them were mixed-raced children like myself. Clearly, many of them did not have all their faculties, and few of them dared to look at me as I staggered away.

As we reached the exit, the other *Unterscharführer* joined us. Each step, each crunching of the pebbles beneath my feet, echoed inside my head as my torment intensified. Several times I stumbled. I don't know how I kept my feet. The two *Unterscharführer* reached the car long before I did; the bigger one of them tapping his foot impatiently as he held the rear door of the same black car open and waited for me to catch up.

'If you don't hurry up – if you fall down – we will leave you here to die,' he said.

Fighting through the pain, I made it to the car, collapsing into the back seat as the *Unterscharführer* slammed the door shut behind me. He sat in the front before his comrade set off at speed. I lay in the back holding my stomach, writhing in agony; every bump, every jolt in the road sent shockwaves of pain through my body.

The car came to a screeching halt outside my house. I was flung forward into the rear of the front seats. I grabbed at my stomach. It felt like the clumsy stitches had ripped open.

'Get out,' the *Unterscharführer* in the passenger seat said.

Looking down at my blouse, I expected to see pooling blood, but only a few specks had seeped out from the stitches. But my blouse was soaking with sweat, as if I had been drenched in a rain shower. My vision was blurred as I fumbled around for the door handle. Impatiently, the *Unterscharführer* exited the car and opened the door for me, grabbing me by the hair as he pulled me from the car and tossed me onto the curb.

'Here,' he barked. 'Don't forget your piece of paper.'

It floated into the gutter as the car sped away. I picked it and myself up, terrified that if I did not have that piece of paper, they would come for me again. I knew I couldn't stay outside so I mustered my last ounce of strength and headed for the house. Each movement sent searing waves of pain through my body. Several times I thought I would collapse in the front yard.

Finally, I reached the door and attempted to compose myself. I did not want to worry Mutti. Since the night they had taken Vati, she had been fragile. If she knew what had been done to me it would break her, pushing her over the edge to a place from which I didn't think she would ever return. As a child I had hidden so much from her. I could hide this too. I hobbled inside. Mutti was sitting in the kitchen, a glass of wine in her hand, a bottle resting on the table beside her. At first, she did not notice me, but then she slowly turned her head.

'Ingrid!' she exclaimed as she drained her glass. 'I cannot believe it! I cannot believe it! When they took you I thought I would never see you again!'

Feeling myself beginning to sway, I smiled, trying my best to remain steady on my feet.

Enraptured by my return, she smothered me with hugs and kisses. I winced with each hug.

'Ingrid,' she said as she stopped abruptly. 'Your skin is clammy, and —' she pulled away and inspected me, 'you are so pale. Are you okay?'

'I am fine, Mutti,' I lied before I collapsed, conscious only long enough to hear her crying, '*Gott in Himmel!* God in Heaven! What have they done to my beautiful girl?'

I awoke to find myself lying in my bed. My forehead felt scorched with fever. I tried to sit up but even the slightest movement caused me unbearable pain. Out of the corner of my eyes I could see that my curtains were drawn, making it impossible to tell if it was day or night. I thought I could hear Bach playing in the background. Maybe my mind was playing tricks.

'Thank you, Herr Schuster,' I heard Mutti say.

'You are most welcome, Frau Marchand. I have seen how the townspeople cross the street when you and your daughter walk by. I have heard what they have said about you but, my good *Frau*, not all of us are like Hitler and his cronies. I fought in the war too. I am ashamed of what Germany has become, but I dare not say what I think too loudly. Hitler promised to make Germany great again, but Germany is far worse than she has ever been. Times are tough for some. I will try to do as much as I can to help you.'

'Herr Schuster, I know how highly respected you are in this town. I would never ask you to put yourself at risk.'

'Mark my words, no good can come from any of this. National Socialism will bring Germany to her knees.'

I heard heavy footsteps going down the stairwell.

'Mutti,' I whimpered.

'Ingrid.' Mutti's voice was sweet but melancholy as she sat on the side of my bed and cried. 'Herr Schuster was just here. He helped me bring your Vati's old radio up to your room. I thought the sound of music might help you recover.'

Fighting the pain, I propped myself on my pillow. The radio sat beside my bedroom window. For a moment, Bach soothed my soul and eased my suffering – until an emergency broadcast interrupted.

Mutti looked at me; I at her. Herschel Grynszpan, a seventeen-year-old Polish Jew, had shot a German diplomat, Ernst vom Rath, two days earlier. Vom Rath had just died from his wounds.

'I don't want to listen to this!' Mutti declared as she got up and spun the radio dial – but not before we heard the last words of a past speech by Goebbels about how the 'World Jewry' was conspiring against us. When the speech stopped the presenter said that, according to Goebbels, a seventeen-year-old was not capable of acting alone; he must have been forced to do this as part of a wider Jewish conspiracy.

'Turn it off, Mutti. I'm tired of hearing about hate.'

She switched the radio off and came back to my bedside.

'How are you feeling, *meine Liebschen*?' she asked as she reached for a towel, moistened it in a bowl and patted it on my forehead.

'Every part of me hurts,' I replied.

'The only doctor that would ever see us was Herr Oborwitz, but, like many of the Jews, he has disappeared.'

'It's okay, Mutti, I'll be fine,' I mumbled before I drifted back into unconsciousness.

My dreams were as vivid as they were disturbing. I relived my childhood, all the torment inflicted upon me by those children who didn't think for themselves, blindly following what their ignorant parents told them, repeating Nazi slogans and ideologies word for word as if they had thought of them themselves.

When I woke, Mutti fed me a weak broth made from whatever vegetables she had managed to scrounge. As the days passed, I began to regain my strength; as the pain lessened, I could sit up and let her feed me. As I ate, I examined her face. She was becoming gaunter with each passing day. It broke my heart that she was sacrificing herself for my benefit.

Despite her best efforts my wounds became infected, rimmed in red scabs and filled with yellow pus. Frau Dreyfus, my best friend Sarah's mother, brought some drugs around for me which she called 'sulfa', apologising that, due to the economic difficulties the Jews faced, she had only been able to secure one bottle. It helped heal my wounds, but the nausea remained. Rashes developed on my skin.

Knowing my love for reading, Mutti brought me any older newspapers she could find. All the papers could talk about was *Anschluss*: the unification of Austria and Germany. Of more interest to me was that they were sending more and more Communists to concentration camps such as Flossenbürg and Dachau. They'd said Vati was a Communist, so I spent my waking hours scouring every photograph for any sign of him. Surely he would not be hard to find; a black man in a world of white men.

For all the hours of looking, I never did find him.

Then, one night in early November when I finally felt well enough to get out of bed, I heard shouting and chanting outside my bedroom. '*Juden* pigs! *Juden* pigs! *Juden* pigs!' I rushed to the window just as the street outside echoed with the shattering of glass. Mutti hurried from her room and joined me at the window, the two of us watching as Nazi troops, dressed in their shiny leather boots and grey uniforms, goose-stepped along the street. Either side, their companions systematically targeted Jewish shops; a group of soldiers were smashing the front window of Hubermann's laundry store. Suddenly, as the last of the soldiers passed by, a gang of men sprinted down the street. The lead man tossed a fiery bottle through Hubermann's broken front window as they ran past the store.

The explosion filled the street, the force of it knocking Mutti and I backwards.

'Sarah!' I cried as I got to my feet.

'Ingrid! Where do you think you're going?' Mutti shouted as she followed me downstairs. 'You've only just become well enough to get out of bed!'

I ripped my coat from the stand, putting my arms in the sleeves as I paused at the doorway, and turned to her to say urgently, 'Mutti, I'm okay. I have to make sure Sarah is all right!'

'Ingrid,' she said as she pulled me back inside. 'Look how worked up they are! It's not a good idea to go outside right now.'

'Mutti,' I said, lifting my shirt. 'What can they do to me that they have not already done?'

'Kill you!' she cried. 'That's what! Ingrid, I forbid you to go!'

I ignored her. Sarah had always been there for me. Always.

I'd only just reached the front gate when Mutti caught up with me, pulling her coat on. She looked me in the eyes and said, 'I cannot stop you, but you're not going alone.'

The scattered fires around the city illuminated the streets, but there were pockets of darkness in which Mutti and I could hide. Scores of Jewish shops had their windows smashed, the destruction worsening as we approached the *Domplatz*. Some stores smouldered, others still burned; those remaining intact had '*Juden*' or the Star of David painted on the windows. Mutti and I reached Sarah's house. The window of Herr Dreyfus' shopfront was broken, anything of value looted. Above the shop, thick, black smoke billowed from the second-storey windows.

'*Mein Gott*!' Mutti cried. 'The world has gone completely mad.'

I started to cry. My only friend, my defender and protector at school, must be dead. Then Frau Dreyfus appeared, walking down the stairs. Sarah was walking behind her, struggling to carry two suitcases. I had never been so relieved to see her.

'Hello, Frau Marchand, Ingrid,' Frau Dreyfus whispered.

'I'm so glad you're all alive!' Mutti exclaimed as she embraced Frau Dreyfus. 'Is there anything we can do?'

'*Nein*,' Frau Dreyfus said sombrely. 'There is nothing left for us here now. We'll go to Samuel's parents' in Stuttgart and decide what to do from there.'

Herr Dreyfus and Sarah's two brothers appeared at the door, resting their suitcases on the front steps while Sarah and Frau Dreyfus did the same. Relieved but heartbroken, I cried heavy tears.

'Sarah', Frau Dreyfus said gently, 'we must be going. Say your goodbyes.'

'I guess this is it,' Sarah said miserably as she stood in front of me.

'I … I … I don't want you to leave,' I stuttered.

'Ingrid,' she said, hugging me so tightly it hurt. 'We'll see each other again. I'm only going to Stuttgart.'

Ignoring the pain, I embraced her even harder than she had hugged me. '*Danke* for everything you have ever done for me. I never would have made it through school without you.'

'You are the best friend anyone could ask for,' she said and kissed me on each cheek. 'Take care of yourself.'

Her hands lingered on mine briefly, before she dropped them, picked up her suitcases, turned and ran to catch up with her family. When they reached a distant corner, Sarah turned to look at me, gave me one last wave – then disappeared.

CHAPTER 2

HADAMAR

1 September 1939

Mutti set down a simple meal of vegetable soup and stale black bread. My stomach begged for more, but this was all we could afford.

Convinced it had aided me in my recovery, Mutti had Herr Schuster bring the radio back downstairs and, in the background, Wagner's *Faust* played. I did not much like classical music. I preferred the jazz music of Billie Holliday and Duke Ellington, which Vati used to play me until the Gestapo arrested him and confiscated his records. Mutti's taste was different. She loved Mozart and Beethoven, insisting I listen to them to nurture my German side. I hated Wagner in particular – not because I disliked his music, but because he was Hitler's favourite.

The music stopped and the presenter excitedly announced that he had important news.

The previous night, Polish saboteurs had attacked the radio station *Sender Gleiwitz* in Upper Silesia and transmitted anti-German messages. There had been other attacks by Polish forces upon the German people of Danzig. In response to these and other 'unprovoked' attacks, *Der Führer* was about to make a speech to the Reichstag.

Hitler's voice crackled through the radio. He condemned the Polish attacks. He insisted that Danzig was a German city and that the creation of the Polish Corridor after the war had separated these true Germans from their people. These now 'ethnic' Germans of Danzig had been subjected to 'ill-treatment in the most distressing manner'. He said that he had exhausted all means of a peaceful resolution with the Polish government, and there was no choice but to send in the Luftwaffe in retaliation because Polish regular soldiers had fired on our territory. He talked of meeting bombs with bombs, poison gas with poison gas. His next words chilled me most of all. If the Poles wanted to move away from the rules of humane warfare, he said, then *we* could only be expected to do the same.

I hated him. I hated every word that came from his lips – particularly about how he would endure the hardships to come, along with every other German. What did he know of the hardships Mutti and I had to endure? After all, *he'd* created them.

Two days later, as Mutti and I sat down to lunch, the news came on the radio that Britain and France had declared war on Germany. I bombarded Mutti with questions about what this meant for us. How long would it take the British to win? How long would it be before the Nazis were defeated? How long before we would be free?

'Stop asking so many questions and eat your lunch, Ingrid,' she scolded.

CHAPTER 2

I picked up one of the two shiny green apples before me and eyed the tantalisingly fresh loaf of bread.

'Mutti, where did you get these?' I asked. Times were hard. Apples, especially of this size, were tremendously expensive, as was fresh white bread.

'There is something very important that I need to tell you.'

'What? What is it?' I asked, warily placing the apple back on the table.

'I have to sell the house.'

'What? Why?'

'We have only survived this long because your grandmother and grandfather give us money every week. Now that war has come, they have to save their money.'

She wasn't finished. Something bigger was coming. 'And we have no choice but to move in with them.'

'I don't want to move! I don't want to live with them!' I said as I stood and stamped my feet like an impetuous child.

'Ingrid, we have no choice,' Mutti said firmly as she began packing away the supper. 'Go upstairs and pack your things.'

I picked up an apple and threw it at her. Then I stomped upstairs. I began pulling stuff from my drawers, soon realising I didn't have much with which to fill my battered old suitcase: just a few dresses and a ragged old pair of black shoes. I looked at my favourite books, more worn than my shoes, and wondered if I should take them. *Nein.*

My grandparents had never accepted me. I was leaving tonight. The world would take me where it would and my books would only slow me down. I closed the latch on my suitcase and marched downstairs, determined to keep going out the door. I didn't. Deep down I knew I was too afraid. Instead, I slammed my suitcase on the floor and slumped into a chair.

'Good girl, Ingrid. Everything will be okay, you'll see.'

'That's what you always say! You sent me to school and you said it would be okay but it wasn't. Why should I believe you now?'

'Ingrid, *bitte*, this is not easy for me either. All my memories of your father are in this house.'

'Don't you dare mention him!' I screamed. 'Vati would never have let this happen. I am not going to live with *them*. They never wanted me. They never cared about me. They're just like everyone else!'

My mother threw up her hands. 'So what are you going to do, live on the streets?'

'*Ja*, I will. You'll see. Or I will go to Africa to live with my grandmother there.'

'Ingrid, you have never even *met* your grandmother in Africa! Besides, how long do you think you would last on the streets before the Gestapo, picked you up and sent you to one of those awful camps – or worse?'

I was about to argue, but a knock came at the door.

'That will be your grandfather.'

Mutti opened the door. Two men stood there, illuminated by the street lights outside. The taller of the two men was a perfect Aryan, perhaps thirty years old. The other man, dressed in the trademark black leather jackets of Gestapo agents, looked more sinister. He was small and unassuming; the beady eyes beneath his round, thick-rimmed glasses made him look half-rat, half-man.

'Frau Marchand?' the rat-man asked.

'*Ja.*'

'May we come in?'

'*Ja*,' Mutti said as she stepped back from the doorway. Without invitation they sat down. The rat-man picked up the remaining apple from the table and started shining it on his coat. He took a bite, chewing and chomping loudly, then said, 'Now where are two lovely ladies such as yourselves going on such a dark evening?'

Frozen, Mutti didn't answer; nor did I.

He took another loud bite of the apple before he put it down. He reached inside his coat and withdrew a packet of Ecksteins, which he tapped on the table and offered to Mutti.

'*Zigarreten*?'

She cautiously eyed him before walking from the door and taking a cigarette. He lit it for her and she sat opposite him, sucking on it, once her trembling hand had found her lips.

'My name is Herr Kuntz and my associate here is Herr Schreiber.'

'So what do the Gestapo want from us now?' Mutti asked as she nervously removed a piece of tobacco from her lips. 'You have already taken everything.'

'Frau Marchand, we are not from the Gestapo.' Herr Kuntz laughed as he lit his own cigarette and returned the packet to his coat pocket.

'But, given the way you are dressed, I just assumed ...' Mutti's shaking hand sent wisps of blue smoke away from her fingers. 'If you are not Gestapo then who are you – and what do you want with us?'

'We are from a new program that the Führer has established: the "T-4 program" in Berlin. Are you aware of it?'

Mutti inhaled deeply on her cigarette and shook her head.

'As you know, the Führer cares greatly about the welfare of all Germany citizens and all members of the Reich.'

I could feel the scars on my stomach burning.

'The T-4 program has been designed by the Führer and the best doctors in Germany to bring the greatest of benefits to the sick and infirm amongst our German brothers and sisters. We are, therefore, here to discuss your daughter.'

'Ingrid?' Mutti asked, taking quick puffs on her cigarette. 'What does this have to do with her? There's nothing wrong with her.'

'Frau Marchand!' he said, throwing his hands up in the air. 'There is no need to be worried. However, if my records are correct – and I am sure they are – your daughter has not been to school in some time.'

'*Ja*, that's right.'

'But Ingrid here *would* benefit from an education, would she not? We are here to discuss how we can *help* your daughter.'

'Help her?' Mutti asked cautiously. 'How can you help her?'

'Frau Marchand, *Der Führer* is a very caring, kind and considerate man who has promised to work for the benefit of all German and Austrian citizens. He has authorised the establishment of a series of brand-new paediatric clinics in both Germany and Austria so that the

National Socialist Party can ensure that we are fulfilling that promise. We are part of the Reich Committee for the Scientific Registering of Serious Hereditary and Congenital Illnesses and we have decided that Ingrid is a candidate for the *Aktion* T-4 program.'

Mutti hesitated, confused. '*Ja*, but she does not have any illnesses. The only time she has been sick was when the Gestapo made her sick.'

'I did say "hereditary illness",' he replied. 'Your daughter is black. The colour of her skin is an illness enough.'

Mutti stamped out her cigarette, trembling. 'How can the colour of someone's skin be considered an illness?'

'If you were amongst the Reich's leading scientists or doctors I would expect you to understand, but you are not. Your husband left you because he was a Communist and, were you not blinded by a wife's and mother's love, you would understand that Negroes are preponderantly predisposed to wildness and outbursts of crazed behaviour – thus constituting an illness.'

'My husband didn't leave us and you will not take my daughter anywhere,' Mutti growled.

Herr Kuntz paid her no mind. Herr Schreiber handed him a leather-bound file. Placing it on the table, Herr Kuntz started to read. 'The records here state that the reason your husband was arrested was because he attended numerous Communist Party meetings. You attended many of those meetings with him, did you not? Are you a Communist, Frau Marchand? A radical Socialist perhaps?'

'I am neither. I am a proud German.'

'If you are as proud as you say,' he snarled, 'you would never have had sexual relations with, nor married, a Negro – and problems like your daughter would not exist. Now, if you will just sign these papers authorising us to take Ingrid we will be on our way.'

'I will do no such thing!'

'Frau Marchand,' he bellowed. 'I am certain that you are familiar with the word *Rassenschande*, and therefore I am going to assume that you are aware that people who are found guilty of racial mixing are being sent to concentration camps such as Dachau.'

'I am aware,' Mutti whispered.

'It would be a shame if we had to send you to Dachau. Poor Ingrid here would become a ward of the state, and who knows what would happen to her then? In any case, your decision not to sign would all but guarantee that you never see your daughter again.'

My throat tightened. I didn't fully understand the magnitude of what he was saying, but I knew I was to be taken away. Mutti's face was twisted, etched with torment. She was torn. She did not want to lose me the way she had lost Vati – but what choice did she have?

'It's okay, Mutti,' I said, putting my hand on her shoulder. 'Sign it. You have no choice.'

Herr Kuntz pushed the papers towards Mutti, handing her a golden pen and indicating where she needed to sign.

'And I'll be able to visit her?' Mutti asked as she wrote her name.

'In time, if Ingrid behaves herself. Frau Marchand, you may not realise it now, but you have just done a wonderful thing for your daughter,' Herr Kuntz said as he picked up the papers and pen and returned them to the pocket inside his jacket.

CHAPTER 2

Mutti stood, stared deep into my eyes and wept. I cried too, promising myself that, no matter what happened, I would see her again. She hugged me; I hugged her back. I pulled back and looked into her face, trying to remember every line, every wrinkle. Herr Schreiber pried me away. I let go of her hands; I reached to her as she slumped in a chair and began to sob. Herr Kuntz's arm stayed around my waist as he escorted me outside, Herr Schreiber following close behind with my suitcase in his hand.

The air outside was frozen; the street lamps thinly veiled by the mist. Another black car awaited me, surrounded by an eerie yellow glow.

Herr Kuntz opened the rear door. I slid inside. A man in an SS uniform waited in the driver's seat. Herr Kuntz sat on one side of me, Herr Schreiber on the other. When they closed the doors, the SS man drove away from the house. Squashed between the two men, I wrinkled my nose at the horrid stink of Herr Kuntz's breath and Herr Schreiber's stale sweat. I gazed steadfastly forward, trying to catch glimpses of the street signs outside so I could remember my way home.

Ten, maybe fifteen minutes passed before the houses and street lamps disappeared. I pictured Mutti still crying at the kitchen table. I wondered where they were taking me. I tried to put an optimistic spin on things; perhaps they were taking me to the same concentration camp as Vati. I pictured myself in striped pyjamas, wondering what type of work they would make me do.

Was I strong enough to survive? Was Vati strong enough to survive?

Another hour passed. The night outside darkened, with nothing but the tiny lights of the country houses to break the blackness. I caught a glimpse of a sign for the road to Wiesbaden, then another for Limburg. Finally, we came to a sign that said 'Hadamar'. Turning off the *Autobahn*, we drove a little while longer before I started to make out the lights of the houses.

Herr Kuntz had said I was being taken away to join a program for children. If this were true, I wondered if where I was being taken was going to be just like school. I prayed it wasn't.

One Thursday, the morning bell rang and scores of girls hurried towards their classrooms. Sarah and I waited for the crowds to clear before we headed towards ours, lingering near the door and waiting for the others to be seated as the teacher had ordered us to do.

'Alright, girls, you may enter now, but stand at the front of the room,' Frau Kellner said. We did as we were told but, exposed in front of our peers and terrified of what was to come, we kept our heads down.

'Look at your classmates!' Frau Kellner shouted. She placed her stick under our chins and forced us to raise our heads.

'Our great Chancellor, Adolf Hitler,' Frau Kellner bellowed as she struggled to move her bulging body up and down the front of the room, 'has declared, amongst many other important things, what you see on the board, children.'

Following the stick, Sarah and I turned to see white writing, in Frau Kellner's perfect cursive: '*No boy or girl should leave school without complete knowledge of the necessity and meaning of blood purity. Adolf Hitler.*'

Frau Kellner waddled towards us, tapping our bottoms to shepherd us towards the left-hand side of the blackboard. Wobbling to the opposite side, she stood there in her lisle stockings; a beige tweed skirt came halfway down her shins and her twin set jacket was stretched over her arms and chest. Her grey hair was twisted into an unusually tight bun, and around her neck was her signature long chain of white pearls.

'You children are six years old now and this is the perfect time for you to begin to learn about your history and your race. This is the age that our *Führer* says you should start learning about these things.'

My heart pounded as Frau Kellner unfurled a white chart from above the blackboard. It displayed images of people: different faces, different ages, some black, some white.

'Now, the majority of you are good Aryan children,' Frau Kellner began as her pointer found its way to Sabine, a little girl in the front row with blue eyes and tight blonde curls. 'Can anyone tell me what the word Aryan means?'

Before anyone could answer, Frau Kellner whacked Sarah's bottom and mine with her stick. 'I said: face the class! Keep your heads up!'

We did. Every single girl had her right hand in the air, begging for Frau Kellner's attention. I knew Frau Kellner would choose Bridget Pallenhoffer, sitting there with her bright blue eyes glistening like two sapphires, her tightly wound golden plaits sitting perfectly on either side of her head.

'Bridget?'

'An Aryan is someone who has blue eyes and blonde hair!' Bridget replied, her face beaming with pride.

'*Ja*! *Sehr gut*, very good, Bridget! An Aryan is from the Nordic people and they trace – we trace – our proud Aryan history back a long, long way. We Aryans are God's chosen people and because of this we are superior in every way.'

I looked at Sarah, who dutifully stared ahead, above and beyond our classmates' heads. One look at my black skin told me why I stood at the front of the class, but I didn't understand why Sarah did. I knew they hated her because she was a Jew but, physically, she was more Aryan than any of them. Her eyes were bluer; her hair was blonder.

Daring to take a peek in Frau Kellner's direction, I watched her struggle under her own weight as she headed towards the gramophone on her desk. She wound it to set the record spinning and, once she had placed the needle down, our ears were soon filled with '*Das Deutschlandlied*'.

'*Deutschland, Deutschland über alles*,' a man's deep voice sang. All the girls stood behind their desks, their right hands resting over their hearts, their chins held high, their chests puffed out. When the anthem finished, Frau Kellner took her hand from her heart, removed the needle from the record, picked up a book from her desk and resumed her lecture on the virtues of the Aryan race.

'This book in my hand is a very important book,' she said as she eased her pointer under our chins. 'Do any of you know what book this is?'

Every girl's hand went up.

'*Ja*, you,' Frau Kellner said to Helga Hoffenheim sitting in the front row.

'That is *Mein Kampf* by Adolf Hitler.'

'*Ja*, Helga, very good; that is right! And to begin your lessons on racial purity in the new German Reich I am going to begin by reading some passages from the Chancellor's book: "It is a scarcely conceivable fallacy of thought to believe that a Negro ... will turn into a German because he learns German and is willing to speak the German language and perhaps even give his vote to a German political party".'

There were many words I didn't know, and neither did the other girls; some asked what 'scarcely', 'conceivable' and 'fallacy' meant. Simply put, Frau Kellner explained, it meant that a "scarcely conceivable fallacy" was a lie that was impossible to believe.

'You see Ingrid here,' Frau Kellner said as she pushed my chin up with her stick, before running it along my cheek, 'she is a Negro, as Hitler has referred to here. The word Negro is a Spanish word meaning black. And do you know why we use a Spanish word to describe people like Ingrid, class? It is because the Spanish used African people as slaves. Negroes are slaves. And why does Germany have black half-breeds like Ingrid?'

Bridget Pallenhoffer put her hand up. 'Because the French brought them at the end of the war.'

'Excellent, Bridget!'

Bridget's grin grew even wider at Frau Kellner's praise. The teacher continued reading from *Mein Kampf*: "The Jews had brought the

Negroes into the Rheinland with the clear aim of ruining the hated white race by the necessarily resulting bastardisation. It was, and is, the Jew who brought Negroes to the Rhein; brought them with the same aim and with deliberate intent to destroy the white race he hates by persistent bastardisation, to hurl it from the cultural and political heights it has attained, and to ascend them as its masters."'

A collective gasp went around the room.

'Why are you all gasping?' Frau Kellner grumbled.

Bridget, buoyed by praise, confidently spoke up. 'Frau Kellner, you said a bad word!'

'Bastardisation!' the teacher spat. 'This is not a bad word! It is the correct word, the truth of the matter! Ingrid here is *die schwarze Schande*: the black shame. She is a Rheinlander bastard!' she boomed as she pressed her thumb and forefinger into my cheek.

'You see the colour of her skin! This disgusting skin!' she exclaimed, brushing her hands together as if trying to remove the black from her fingers. 'It is meant to fool you. You see, Ingrid here is not as black as the Negroes and this is to make you think that perhaps, one day, the Negroes could become white like us – but this is something of which we must be careful, girls. Oh, *ja*, we must be very careful! For you see, the more we allow the Negro blood to be diluted with our Aryan blood,' she said as she used her stick to point to the black faces on the chart covering the blackboard, 'then the higher the chance we will lose our pure Aryan blood. And, as Hitler says, who brought this black shame to the Rheinland? It was the Jews! The Jews, just like Sarah here! We must be careful of the Jews too, girls, because they are sneaky, underhanded criminals! You can see Sarah here is a Jew because of the hook shape of her nose; you see here, girls, just like the number six!'

Frau Kellner roughly grabbed Sarah's chin, jerking her head sideways then tracing her pointer along the bridge of Sarah's nose, making an invisible six with it. 'And the size of her ears, girls: this is another way to tell a Jew!'

'*Heil Hitler*!' she cried, her voice trembling at the height of her range as she extended her right hand to forty-five degrees.

'*Heil Hitler*!' the girls repeated as they too extended their arms.

I had never felt so ashamed. *Ja*, I was 'mixed', but I had always felt as much German as I was French and African. My classmates, their faces consumed by blind hatred, glared at Sarah and me as if we were the Devil's children.

That was only the first day of many.

The car wound through the streets of Hadamar town, climbing higher and higher until we came to a large building at the top of the hill. Herr Schreiber stopped the car at the gate and waited as two uniformed guards slowly opened it. We drove past them and parked in the centre of a large gravel courtyard.

'Come on, Ingrid,' Herr Kuntz said as he opened the door and stepped from the car. 'Let's get you inside and settled.'

Herr Schreiber switched the car off and retrieved my suitcase. I sat motionless.

'It's alright,' Herr Kuntz said, leaning inside, his face was a few inches from mine. His breath was foul. 'We're not going to hurt you. We brought you here to help you,' he said with a crooked smile.

Realising I had little choice, I got out of the car, scanning my surrounds, looking for any possibility of escape. We'd come up a forked road, each arm of which was lined with skeletal pine trees. Two dilapidated wooden fences ran parallel to small cobblestoned gutters. In front of me was an enormous building. Near the main entrance were ten windows, some opened, some closed, some with lights, some without. Some were covered with blinds; some were not. The middle windows in the centre of the second-storey of the main entrance had a white balcony with two giant glass doors; I noticed that many of the windows were covered in white bars.

Slowly walking towards the entrance, I looked to my left. In the distance there was a medieval castle on top of the hill, its white-painted walls glistening brightly in the moonlight. Down below, the city lights covered the valley floor and surrounding hillsides like a swarm of fireflies.

Mutti had always told me I was extremely tall for my age. Part of my African heritage, she had said. But I felt dwarfed as we walked through a set of rectangular doors with three windows above, the bricks below them forming an archway. A bright light radiated from inside, spilling out through the windows and through the vertical panes of glass. The place did not look like a school but one giant prison cell.

I was taken to a reception area. At first the lights were blinding and all I could hear was the distant sounds of children's voices. I was surrounded by the distinct smell of disinfectant. I blinked several times until my eyes adjusted. I saw an older nurse sitting in a small room to one side. The more I looked around, the more I realised that everything here was white. I felt the scars on my stomach begin to itch and burn.

The men led me further inside. The floor changed to a slightly grey colour and the light dimmed. On the wall each side of me was a series of black electrical boxes. Since the Gestapo had taken Vati, I had often dreamed of them torturing him. I pictured his body, arms tied above his head as he hung from a hook and they electrocuted him. I began to shake. Were they about to do this to me?

The further we moved on, the more I felt I was lost in a white maze. I lost my bearings as we turned down a corridor and into a wide, open room with scores of beds – some singles, some double-bunks – filling every available space on either wall. In each bed was one older child or two younger children. Some stood beside their beds and stared at me. Others sat, knelt or lay prostrate on top of their beds.

I wondered if this was similar to the *Bund Deutscher Mädel* camps. I thought back to the days at school when I had watched the others march around the quadrangle in their black skirts and ties and white blouses. They all looked so pretty, and being forced to stand to one side as I watched them made me feel ugly and unwanted, left out of something great – something I wanted to be a part of. Here, in this new place, there was a uniform of sorts. Every child wore the same, ill-fitting white gown.

Some had their heads shaven. Some lay quiet, others moaned and groaned. Others sat on their beds with their knees pulled up to their chest, mumbling as they rocked back and forth. Some were missing arms or legs or both.

If this was a camp, I thought, it was for the most useless people in Germany. I hated myself for thinking this way. This was how *they* thought. I couldn't see how I fit in here. I just wanted to go home.

I was ushered away from the bigger room and taken to a smaller one. Standing inside was a busty woman dressed in a white uniform, dress and apron, her sandy blonde hair knotted over her head in the typical German plait. Her thick, trunk-like arms stayed folded across her bulky chest. She was even bigger than the nurses who had helped to sterilise me, and the sight of her terrified me. Standing beside her was a tall man with receding grey hair, a round belly and an elongated red nose, criss-crossed with spider veins, who stood at the end of a long, steel bed. Next to it were two liquid-filled containers with thin cords hanging from them. To the right was a square steel table with an assortment of needles, scissors and a small, white porcelain bowl.

'Ingrid, this is Doktor Alfons Klein. He is going to give you a check-up,' Herr Kuntz said.

'Undress,' the *Herr Doktor* said coldly.

I didn't move.

'UNDRESS!' the *Herr Doktor* shouted. I trembled with fear. The fat nurse stood behind me, roughly grabbed my arms then forced them upwards. She pulled my sweater over my head and tossed it on the bed. She unbuttoned my blouse, removed it and tossed it aside; she grabbed the hem of my dress and pulled it over my head and threw it onto the rest of my clothes. Standing in nothing but my underwear, I crossed my arms across my chest in a vain attempt to hide my shame but, in the whiteness of the room, I was painfully aware of my dark-coloured skin.

'Lower your arms,' the *Herr Doktor* ordered.

I didn't move. I was paralysed by fear and humiliation.

'Lower your arms!' the *Herr Doktor* shouted as he ripped my arms from my chest and forced them by my side. 'I need to check your heart and lungs to see if you are suffering from tuberculosis.'

The *Herr Doktor* put in the earpieces of his stethoscope and placed the chest-piece onto my skin. It was freezing; it felt as if he was tracing my chest with an ice cube.

'Cough,' he ordered. I obeyed. He moved the stethoscope around my chest.

'Breathe in.'

I did. He circled it again.

'Breathe out.'

He removed the stethoscope, reached for a clipboard, wrote down some notes and said, 'She's fine, no sign of tuberculosis. Here, sign.'

He handed the clipboard to Herr Kuntz, who scribbled his signature at the bottom and handed the clipboard back to the *Herr Doktor.* Herr Kuntz turned and left the room, Herr Schreiber following close behind. Once they had left and I was allowed to dress, I breathed a sigh of relief. The doctor and nurse departed, leaving me standing there – cold, afraid, and unsure of what I was supposed to do next. A girl dressed in a white shirt and trousers, with blonde stubble on her head appeared at the door.

'Come with me. I will take you to your bed,' she said flatly, refusing to look at me.

She led me back to a ward much like the one I had seen earlier. As I walked between the rows of beds, some of the children stared over their blankets, clearly terrified by me. I must have been the first black person they had ever seen. I was taken aback by their reaction. They were themselves victims of Nazi policies, but Nazi propaganda about blacks had infiltrated even this part of the German population.

'Here,' the girl said as we reached an empty bed at the far end of the ward that had my suitcase on top of it. I did not unpack, but simply slid my suitcase under my bed and lay down. I was pleased I had a view of sorts – the adjacent window doors overlooked an internal courtyard.

As I gazed out the window I could feel the weight of the other children's stares. My bed was a little distance away from the others. Even here I was an outcast. I rolled back over and stared out of the gigantic windows at the bright face of the moon; it stared coldly and blankly back at me. I pictured Mutti still sitting at the kitchen table as she cried. I pictured myself safe and warm in her arms. If I could have run home and told her I was happy to live with my grandparents, I would have; anything to be away from here. Tears leaked silently from my eyes onto my pillow.

Stop torturing yourself! I thought. *Face it: you're a prisoner here. You have no hope of freedom.*

CHAPTER 2

I tried to sleep but it was useless; I tossed and turned. I found myself looking back into the ward; the moonlight was bathing it in an eerie and unsettling glow. A bright light shone from the fat nurse's office, allowing me to see her clearly as she sat and read a magazine. Many of the other children, the excitement of a new arrival now having passed, settled in to sleep. Some rocked back and forth, while others made repeated incoherent and garbled noises, wrapped in worlds of their own. I suddenly felt enveloped by loneliness, as if the whole room was saturated with it. I rolled onto my back and stared at the ceiling.

'Wondering why you're here?' a boy's voice rang across the gap between our beds.

'Sort of,' I replied, surprised and pleased to be spoken to. 'They told me I was to be part of the *Aktion* T-4 program. The only thing is I am not completely sure what that is,' I said as I propped myself on my elbow and faced the boy in the adjacent bed. Despite the dappled moonlight and the shortness of his hair he looked particularly Aryan – the kind of young boy who should have been leading a band of Hitler Youth marching through the streets of his home town, not lying in a bed in an asylum next to me.

'It's for different kids. Don't worry, you'll get used to it.'

Clouds covered the moonlight, darkening the room just as we heard the gruff hollering of the fat nurse.

'I can hear voices! Don't make me come down there!'

The boy placed his right index finger to his mouth, smiled and whispered, 'I'll talk to you more soon. She'll be asleep soon enough.'

Minutes of silence passed.

'My name's Erich,' the boy whispered. 'I'm from Köln. What about you? Where are you from?'

Fearful of the fat nurse, I stayed silent at first but, when she said nothing, I eventually whispered back. 'My name is Ingrid. I'm from Mainz.'

'Pleased to meet you, Ingrid from Mainz.'

Down the ward the fat nurse was leaning back in her chair, her head tilted, her mouth wide open. Suddenly, she let out an almighty snore that reverberated throughout the ward like a cow's bellow. I bombarded Erich with questions.

'How long have you been here? How long will they keep us here? How long will it be before I can go home and see my Mutti?'

'Slow down, and don't talk so loud or you'll wake that fat pig nurse. I know she is squealing, she does that when she snores, but too much noise and she'll wake up and we'll get punished. Trust me, you don't want that.'

Erich took a quick look over his shoulder to ensure the fat nurse *was* still snoring.

'I've only been here for a few weeks now, but I've figured it all out. I'm smart like that,' Erich boasted.

'I still hear voices!' the fat nurse's voice boomed.

Silence ensued, except for the sound of her heavy footsteps. Erich hurriedly pulled his blankets up over his chin and pretended to be asleep. I did the same. The footsteps ceased at the end of our beds.

'You have been trouble ever since you came here, Erich! I warned you, didn't I? I told you if you spoke out of turn again I would punish you.'

Annoyed, she wrenched Erich from his bed and dragged him through the ward much like Frau Kellner did when she used to drag Sarah and me to Herr Waldheim's office.

'At least you won't be my problem for much longer,' she muttered as they disappeared around the corner.

I watched until she returned, read her magazine a little while longer, then turned off the light and disappeared down the corridor. Unable to sleep, unable to stop my thoughts, I had no choice but to let them play over and over in my mind. What did she mean by 'not her problem for much longer'? Where had she taken Erich? Was he going somewhere else? Was I to be taken somewhere else? Was I going to be taken further and further away from Mutti?

Eventually tiredness took me.

'Wake up! Wake up!' shouted a thin, older nurse as she stormed down the corridor banging a pot and a pan. 'If I have to get any of you out of bed there will be trouble!'

The others stood to attention at the end of their beds but I didn't move. Maybe, if I stayed hidden under my blanket, she would ignore me. But the thin grey blanket covering me was ripped away and I was confronted by the stick-like frame of the new nurse as she stood over me. Although diminutive in stature, this woman, I sensed, was the one who wielded power. Tossing the blanket to the ground, she reached for the clipboard hanging from the end of my bed.

'Ingrid Marchand,' she said as she read. 'My name is Chief Nurse Huber. You're the first black one we've had here so I will put your disobedience down to the fact that your mind is not as developed as the others. But if you keep me waiting again I guarantee your stay here will be a short one.'

My will to resist disappeared as I glanced at Erich's empty bed.

'Turn left!' the nurse thundered. Almost in perfect synchronicity we marched from the ward. Passing them by, I realised that the severely disabled children were not required to stand or follow. After a short walk down the corridor, we came to a wide, open hall, within which were rows of long timber tables with equally long benches on either side. Silently, the other children began sitting at seemingly pre-assigned seats. Uncertain and confused, I was the last one standing.

Hearing a noise behind me, I turned around to see Erich struggling to walk. I ran to him and helped him towards the last of the empty seats. There were bruises covering his arms and legs. Erich squeezed between the others, lowering his voice as he winced from the pain. All the others bowed their heads as two men dressed in long white coats – one of whom was the *Herr Doktor* who had examined me the previous night – entered the hall. As if they were royalty, they stood behind two of the three seats sitting on a platform that was raised above the rest of us. The last seat, it seemed, was reserved for the skinny nurse. It was, albeit more solemn, just like lunchtime at school.

'Bow your heads!' the skinny nurse ordered.

Every head went down – except mine. I held mine high in a feeble attempt at a silent protest.

'Ingrid!' she called out. 'Put your head down! If I have to come down there I will beat you to within an inch of your life!'

My head snapped downwards. My resistance had lasted but a few seconds.

'Alright, children, place your hands together,' the nurse said loudly. Then her voice softened. 'Let us thank the Lord for our wonderful *Führer*, for the wisdom he has shown to bring you all here, and for his compassion in wanting to help you all have better lives.'

She recited the Lord's Prayer.

'*Heil Hitler*!' she said loudly when she finished. She and the others stood and raised their hand.

'*Heil Hitler*!' the other children repeated with false and forced enthusiasm.

'I hate Hitler!' I said more loudly than I should have. No-one heard.

'*Heil Hitler*!' was repeated several more times before we were allowed to sit down. The children from the first two tables, bowl and spoon in hand, lined up near a row of large vats. Adults who appeared to be mentally disabled ladled out breakfast, keeping their heads down.

Table after table followed. Soon it was my table's turn. To reach the vats, we had to pass below the doctors' platform. The line slowed then stopped, and I found myself standing directly below them.

'Is that her? The new one?' the *Herr Doktor* whom I didn't know asked.

'*Ja*,' the older *Herr Doktor* responded.

I didn't like being singled out, and was greatly relieved when the line moved and I came to the last vat. It was manned by a decrepit old lady whose twisted and gnarled fingers delved a steel ladle into the vat, her arthritic hands shaking as she slopped a spoonful of the grey sludge into my bowl. The ashen slush did not look appetising, but it was food and I was starving. I held the bowl up.

'You want more?' the old lady croaked, or maybe laughed. 'There isn't any more.'

I trudged back to my table and sat down. Glancing up, I saw the first of the children already cleaning and piling their bowls on a table next to the vats. I placed my spoon into the watery mixture, stirring it as I tried to find something remotely edible in it. All I found was a few stale oats floating in the muck. But hunger got the better of me. I took my first spoonful and slurped. Never in my life had I tasted anything worse; it was like liquid cardboard. I scrunched my face up in disgust.

'Are you going to eat that?' Erich asked after he had glanced at the doctors and nurse. I was starving, my stomach ached, but I couldn't force another spoonful of that horrid concoction into my mouth. I slid my bowl towards him and watched, disgusted, as he devoured my breakfast like it was the most delicious and nutritious thing he had ever eaten.

'What happened to you?' I whispered to him.

'They beat me with broom handles.'

I examined the purple and blue bruises on his legs. They were surrounded by old and yellowed ones.

'Don't worry,' he said as he licked my spoon. 'You'll get used to it. You'll learn to eat what they give you and do what they tell you to do. Trust me.'

'Do what they tell you to do, hey? What, just like you?' I said as I gently poked one of his bruises.

'Well, maybe you won't learn,' he smiled and slurped the last of the liquid in my bowl before he took our bowls to the front. I watched him stack them with the others and resolved to starve myself. Surely if I became sick enough they would be forced to send me home.

CHAPTER 3

GNADENTOD

1 November 1939

Days melted into weeks as I settled into the routine of Hadamar.

Outside the snows began to fall and the weather turned cold, as did my heart. I missed Mutti terribly and, with each passing day, my resolve to resist weakened. Erich was right. I ate what they told me to eat. I did what they told me to do. Sometimes Erich resisted, but each time he was taken away for hours, sometimes days at a time, and I became even more scared to follow his lead.

I hated being here but, deep down, part of me thought that I would be rewarded for my good behaviour. Herr Kuntz had hinted that if I was good I would be returned to Mutti, or she'd at least be allowed to visit, but I had not seen anyone else leave or any visitors arrive. Instead, apart from meal times, our days consisted of cleaning the wards and washing the bed linen of the enfeebled patients who were constantly soiling themselves. At night, before lights out, Erich and I would sit in our beds and talk.

'When we get out of here, where do you think you'll go?' I asked him.

'What makes you so sure we're ever getting out of here?'

'One day the war will end. One day we'll be able to leave.'

'Ingrid, do you know what *Lebensunwertes Leben* means?'

'Life unworthy of living?'

'I have heard the nurses talk. They call us *Lebensunwertes Leben*. Even if the war ends we will have to leave. Germany doesn't want people like us.'

My face must have fallen, for, realising he had crushed my hopes, Erich tried to be more upbeat.

'Don't listen to me,' he said. 'I just get down because I try to resist but they keep beating me down. I guess when we get out of here and the war is over I think I might like to go to America.'

'America? Why America?'

'I have heard it called "the Land of the Free". That's the life for me – free to do what I want, go where I want, be who I want without someone telling me what to do. California. That's where I want to go. I've seen pictures in magazines. Ingrid, you should see how blue the ocean is!'

'Perhaps I'll come to America too, but only if I can take Mutti with me.'

Our daydreaming was rudely interrupted by the nurses and orderlies as they came charging down the ward. The skinny, frightening nurse – Chief Nurse Huber – was at their head, ordering us out of bed and into the dining hall. We stood, followed and sat down in the dining hall according to routine, but no sooner had we been seated than we were ordered to stand to attention. An important announcement was about to be made.

Chief Nurse Huber stood on the raised platform and told us that, because Hitler was helping so many children, Hadamar was becoming overcrowded. Some of the wards were being shut down and children were going to be sent to other institutions.

We were told to listen carefully for our names. The children on the first list were to be sent to Herborn. Those children were instructed to gather their possessions immediately and follow one of the orderlies outside. The second list were to go to Weilmünster. More lists: Kiedrich, Idstein, Nassau, Langenfeld, Andernach, Wiesloch and Weinsberg. Hundreds of names were read out and still Erich and I had not heard ours. As the numbers in the dining hall dwindled we exchanged nervous glances. Only two dozen children remained. Outside we could hear the splatter of engines bursting to life and the sound of the crunching gravel as the buses drove away.

'We have also been ordered from Berlin to transform this institution into a military hospital,' Chief Nurse Huber announced as she paced like a caged lion back and forth along the platform. 'You children, as you are older and much fitter than the others, are to stay here. You will continue to do your duties as you have always done, but with fewer children you will have to work harder. If this is unacceptable to you, I am certain I can make alternative arrangements.'

She sent us back to the ward. The seriously infirm, bedridden children remained as they were and, as Erich and I sat back on our beds, I wondered why they hadn't been moved too. Children from other wards began appearing at the entrance to ours, cautiously looking around before they began taking the empty beds.

CHAPTER 3

Months passed and no wounded soldiers or children appeared. When the first day of spring arrived we were told to freshen all the bed linen and sweep the entire first floor. A handful of soldiers arrived later that day, but they only trickled in at intervals after that. We didn't ask. We didn't care. But it was due to the ease of our victories, Chief Nurse Huber told us, that the hospital was receiving so few casualties. It was because our glorious *Führer* was making Germany even greater. It was because Germany was the height of civilisation and culture and it was Germany's destiny to rule the world. We'd heard it all before. We paid little heed to her speeches.

Weihnachten was approaching and the children couldn't help but be excited. I didn't understand why – I had never liked *Weihnachten* anyway. Perhaps I was just angry because it made me think of Mutti and how much I missed her. I knew that if there were any way she could have come to see me she would have, but it hurt that she still hadn't. The more I thought about it, the more my mind began to toy with me. Had they taken her too? Was that why she hadn't come? Or had she forgotten about me and started a new life for herself? With Vati and I gone, she had nothing more to fear, did she? She could live her life how she wanted to. Perhaps she was better off without me. Perhaps the world would be better off if I were dead.

The week before *Weihnachten* we were ordered into the dining hall. Chief Nurse Huber stood on the platform and forced us to sing carols. I mouthed the words but only until one of the orderlies realised and hit me across the back of my legs with his belt. I sang, looking at the others who did the same with a joyfulness I didn't understand.

Even when we weren't forced to sing, I couldn't escape the carols. Through the speakers scattered around various rooms they played *Radio Nazi*, as we had come to call it, which broadcast '*Stille Nacht*', '*O Tannenbaum*' and other *Weihnachten* carols over and over. Trees went up, and wrapped presents lay beneath them – but only in the soldiers' wards and staff offices. We children talked amongst ourselves, wondering whether boots would be left for us.

On the night before *Heiligabend*, the ward was filled with uproarious chatter. Children sat three, four to a bed discussing what they hoped *Der Weihnachtsmann* would bring. I didn't care. From the time the Nazis rose to power, I had only ever seemed to be an afterthought to *Der Weihnachtsmann*. I was, however, jealous when I heard the other children's stories of *Weihnachten* from their hometowns. They were allowed to talk late into the night. I went to sleep pitying the younger ones, whom I could still hear talking about what *Der Weihnachtsmann* might bring.

On *Weihnachten*, the others woke early. The first of the children rose from their beds and began checking around the ward for presents. Upon finding none they returned and sat forlornly on their beds. Some even sobbed quietly. The only 'present' we received was a second helping of gruel at dinnertime. I devoured both portions and longed for more. When bedtime came, Erich and I sat on our beds. The children's disappointment filtered through the room. Erich was unusually despondent.

'Ingrid, you don't seem as upset as the others.'

'I hate *Weihnachten*,' I replied.

CHAPTER 3

'Didn't you ever have at least one nice *Weihnachten*?'

'There was one, I guess. It was the night before Saint Nicholas' Day and I put out one of Vati's boots. I just knew that, when I woke in the morning, the boot would be filled with candy, nuts and oranges, because all year I *had* been a good girl – the best I could be, even though I had to put up with teasing at school every day. When the sun came up I ran downstairs, opened the door and peered into the boot. There was no candy, but there was a chocolate bar. At least Saint Nicholas hadn't left me a lump of coal. That powdery snow began to fall – you know, the type that leaves a thin layer on roofs and gardens, like frosting on a gingerbread house. Up and down our street, children stood at their doors, boots in hand. Some overflowed with candy. Even when times were harder, other children always had *something* more than I in their boots. I couldn't stand to see their joy, so I went back inside. I tried to hide my disappointment from my parents but I had to face the reality: even Saint Nicholas didn't think I was German enough.'

'What did you do then?'

'I asked my Mutti why I hadn't been given more. I'd been a good girl! I asked her if Saint Nicholas and *Der Weihnachtsmann* hated me because I am black.'

'That's hard. What did they say?'

'They tried to tell me that things didn't make the person and the fact that Saint Nicholas left me *something* meant I had been good. But as I watched the other children playing in the street from my window, I prayed my luck would change. At *Heiligabend* we didn't go to church like the other families. Vati said that religion was the drug of the masses and religion always led to evil in the world.'

'"Drug of the masses?"' Erich asked. 'What does that mean?'

'I'm not really sure. Vati always said that religion is just a way to distract people from seeing the real world. Mutti didn't want to go to church either. She didn't want to face the glares and sneers of the townspeople. There was no bell, *Christkind* didn't come, and there were no lights or lanterns, and no *Weihnachten* tree. There was no singing, no poetry, no presents. All we had was Mutti's simple potato and radish soup boiling on the stove. I collected the bowls and cutlery and peered into the pot as Mutti threw in a dozen fatty offcuts that looked like caterpillars. The thought of those chunky pieces of fat in my mouth made me sick...'

A knock came at the door.

'Quick, Guillaume, hide!' Mutti said. Vati ran upstairs. When he was safely hidden, Mutti opened the door. A gust of snow blew inside.

'Fräulein Rothenberg!' Mutti exclaimed. 'What on earth are you doing here?'

It was my kindergarten teacher, standing at the door, wrapped in layers of coats and scarfs, holding a bundle in her arms as if she were holding a baby.

'Can I come in?' she asked through her chattering teeth.

'Why, of course!' Mutti said. 'Where are my manners?'

CHAPTER 3

Fräulein Rothenberg hurried in and placed the bundle on the table as Mutti closed the door.

'I hope I am not intruding,' she apologised as she thawed herself by the stove. 'Many people are struggling this year and I wanted to bring a little something over for you.'

'Fräulein, you are always welcome in our home,' Mutti said, smiling. 'Guillaume, you can come down now. It is only Ingrid's teacher.'

Vati appeared at the top of the stairs, then came down and spied the bundle on the table. Fräulein Rothenberg unwrapped it, revealing two smaller packages, one wrapped in newspaper, the other in a red cloth. Ripping the newspaper open she revealed an enormous carp, as thick and plump as it was long. I had never seen a fish that big before! She then peeled back the red cloth, revealing two huge fruit and nut–filled loaves of *Stollen*.

'I know it's not much, but Ingrid has been such a shining light in my class this year, and I wanted to lighten your *Weihnachten* a little,' Fräulein Rothenberg said apologetically.

'*Gott in Himmel*!' Mutti exclaimed. '*Fräulein*, there is enough food here to feed three families!'

Fräulein Rothenberg's already reddened cheeks made it difficult to tell if she was blushing.

'I am a single woman, Frau Marchand. My family are well-to-do, my father is a lawyer and my mother is also a teacher. They send me money from time to time. I have my salary too but little to spend it on. Helping out a few families is the least I can do.'

Mutti took out four plates and we started eating. Vati didn't say much; he just listened to Mutti interrogate my teacher. Fräulein Rothenberg didn't seem to mind and I learnt a lot about her. I found out that, like Mutti, she was from Berlin. Her family had very strict, traditional values and, after completing her teacher training, she was offered a job in Mainz, which she gladly took to create an independent life for herself.

'I needed to move away and to live my life how I wanted to, not how my parents wanted me to,' she told us.

'And you have been in Mainz for three years?' Mutti pushed. 'And you are still not married?'

'For God's sake woman, leave the poor girl alone!' Vati finally interjected. 'She has done a wonderful thing for us and you are giving her the third degree!'

Fräulein Rothenberg blushed, twirling her hair in her fingers as she tried not to look at Vati.

'If she doesn't want to answer my questions, she doesn't have to!' Mutti snapped back. 'I am just interested to know about her, that's all.'

'I guess I just haven't met the right man yet,' Fräulein Rothenberg mumbled.

'You will,' he said, placing a large piece of *Stollen* in his mouth.

Mutti, Vati and Fräulein Rothenberg talked long into the night, mostly about the state of affairs in Germany, of politics and of women's rights. I felt special that I knew so many things about my teacher that the other girls didn't. Soon enough, however, I became tired and asked to be excused to go to bed.

'*Ja*, I really must be going too,' Fräulein Rothenberg said as she stood. She grabbed her coat, kissed me on the cheeks, and disappeared into the snowy evening. That night, with a full stomach, I slept more soundly than I had in months.

'You see, *Weihnachten* can be wonderful,' Erich offered as we lay back in our beds.

Recalling Mutti, Vati and my favourite teacher saddened me. I missed them all so much.

'What was *Weihnachten* like for your family?' I asked Erich. Immediately sensing his reluctance to tell me, I persisted. 'What? What is it?'

'I don't think you want to know about my *Weihnachten*.'

'*Nein*, I do. I really do.'

Erich's family *Weihnachten* was exactly how I dreamed it should be. The singing of carols, the meat dumplings, dozens and dozens of presents. It all sounded so wonderful, but his memories and words were tinged with sadness. He told me about his two sisters, Hannah and Sofia, and his parents, Paul and Helga. He reached beneath his bed and retrieved a battered cardboard box, which he rested between his legs. He opened the box, revealing a series of letters. He reached for the top one and began to read. It was from his mother. She told him how much she loved him and said she couldn't wait to see him. I didn't know whether this made me feel better or worse. Mutti hadn't sent me a letter. She hadn't sent anything at all.

I began thinking about Mutti more and more. Fewer children and fewer than expected wounded soldiers meant we had little to do. Boredom became our constant companion.

The staff seemed to relax. The better I got to know them, the more I began to realise that they weren't all evil; many of them had taken the job to support their families through the war. We quickly learnt which staff we could interact with and which ones to avoid. With the staff seeming to care less and less about what we did, we were permitted to explore more and more of Hadamar.

It was much bigger than I had first thought: a playground for bored children. Hide and seek became our favourite pastime, especially amongst the younger ones. At first we stayed mainly in and about our own ward but, eager to prove who was best, we soon searched for better and better hiding places. We found dozens more wards like ours as well as closets, cellars, cupboards and all types of nooks and crannies. But we never went near the medical rooms. We knew they were *verboten*.

The New Year came, then springtime arrived. Instead of the soldiers we were expecting, streams of mentally and physically disabled men, women and children began to fill the wards. Hide and seek became harder because the mentally feeble patients, if you asked them, would point to where someone was hiding.

'Ingrid,' Erich whispered to me as he glanced at the two children facing the wall and counting. 'We've used up all the good hiding places, but I think I've found somewhere where they'll never find us.'

Taking me by the hand, he dragged me from the ward just as we heard the counters reach one hundred.

'Hurry!' Erich said, quickening his pace. Winding our way down the halls and past the dining hall, we entered parts of Hadamar I had never seen. Part of me wished I was more like Erich: carefree and reckless; even in the midst of our tedious existence he still managed to make life exciting. But another part of me still wanted to be cautious and good so I could see Mutti.

He led me further and further along. Adrenaline pulsed through me. I wasn't convinced Erich truly knew where he was going. I wanted to turn back before we were discovered, but I also felt a rush to see what was around the next corner.

Erich turned one final corner and, as we went through a door, we stopped. We tried to comprehend what we saw before us.

The ward was full of bedridden children – worse than any Erich and I had ever seen. They were emaciated; the spectre of death hung over the room. We didn't say a word. We just exchanged puzzled looks and slowly walked down the ward.

In the fifth bed we came across a girl. Her head was twisted to one side, her right arm stiff and straight. Her left arm was bent back behind her head until her fingers touched her skull. Her blanket had fallen below her feet, revealing rigid legs pressed together at the knees. She was grotesque. Fascinated, yet equally disgusted, I could not look away. I edged towards her bedside, and the extent of her deformations became more apparent. It was hard to tell, but I guessed she was about the same age as me, or perhaps a little younger. Her head hung limply, as did the right side of her mouth. She stared blankly into the distance but her face carried an odd smile, as if nothing in the world mattered.

I waved a hand in front of her face. Nothing. Erich examined a boy three beds up who looked much the same.

'What do you think is wrong with these children?' Erich asked, bending over to examine the boy.

'I don't know, but they are disgusting. Perhaps they would be better off dead.'

'What do you think you two are doing in this ward?' Chief Nurse Huber bellowed. 'You know it is *verboten*!'

Our heads whipped around to face Chief Nurse Huber; her face redder than we had ever seen.

'Sorry, Frau Huber,' I apologised. 'We were just playing.'

'Playing?' she asked as she cast her evil eye over us.

'*Ja*, playing!' Erich retorted. 'There is nothing else to do in here!'

'Ah, I see,' Chief Nurse Huber sneered. 'So, you have nothing to do? Well, I will have to find enough work for you to keep you both occupied.'

I glared at Erich. He should have known better than to antagonise her.

'Go up to the dispensary right this minute. Bring down fresh sheets and blankets and change the bedclothes for these children. This will be your new work and I expect you to do it every day.'

She had seemed so angry but now she seemed calm. This bothered me. But I was glad to have something to occupy my time – I felt I was a little too old for hide and seek anyway – and I was glad we hadn't gotten in more trouble. I actually felt pleased that I could do something to help these unfortunate children. Before Erich could incur more of Chief Nurse Huber's wrath I snatched up his hand and led him to the dispensary, where we collected as many sheets and blankets as we could.

We went to the girl I had first seen. I lifted her up while Erich pulled the sheet from the bed. It was soiled, stained yellow and brown with her sweat and urine.

'This smells disgusting!' Erich muttered as he held the girl to him, scrunched up his face and turned his head away.

'Don't blame me!' I snapped at him. 'You're the one who had to open your big mouth!'

His lips parted as he was about to speak, but he closed them just as quickly when we heard footsteps coming from the corridor. I smoothed out the sheet and Erich gently placed the girl back down. We looked up to see Chief Nurse Huber, another nurse and the tall, scar-faced Commissioner and Head Physician at Hadamar, Dr Wahlmann, walking down the the ward towards us.

'Chief Nurse Huber, where is this girl I need to examine?' Dr Wahlmann asked as they stood beside Erich and me.

'Here, *Herr Doktor*,' Chief Nurse Huber said as she reached for the girl's clipboard and handed it to Dr Wahlmann.

'Eva, twelve, cerebral palsy. Definitely a candidate for *Gnadentod*,' Dr Wahlmann said as he perused the clipboard. He returned it to the end of the bed without looking at Eva.

Gnadentod. I had never heard the word. As we exchanged looks, it was clear Erich did not know it either. I was not brave enough to ask, but Erich had no such compunctions.

'Chief Nurse Huber, what does *Gnadentod* mean?'

Expecting her ire, I stepped back. But she moved beside Erich and put her arm around his shoulder.

'Kaufmann, look at the children here,' she said with a sweep of her arm. 'They are all *Lebensunswerte Leben*. What kind of life do you think these children could ever have? We have a sacred medical duty to ease their suffering. We are doing God's work here. That is what *Gnadentod* means.'

Erich stepped back and watched on as they moved closer to Eva's side.

'All right, dear,' Chief Nurse Huber said as another nurse appeared, and the two of them placed their hands under Eva's shoulders and picked her up. 'Time to come with us now. All your suffering will soon be over.'

Eva barely noticed what was happening, staring blankly into the distance as they manoeuvred her into a wheelchair. Erich and I pretended to change the next bed while we watched them reach the end of the ward and turn left towards the medical rooms.

'Come on,' Erich said excitedly. 'Let's see where they're taking her.'

'Erich! *Nein*!' I protested as I felt my feet fix to the floor. 'They've taken her to the medical rooms. If they find us there, they might do something to us.'

'Ingrid, they can do whatever they want to us, whenever they want. Live a little.'

He set off down the corridor. I hesitated, wondering if I should follow, until my curiosity got the better of me and I went after him. By the time I reached the ward entrance, he – and they – had disappeared. Glancing in both directions, I caught sight of Erich's leg as he skittered around the corner. I ran to catch up with him, but my feet slipped and I tumbled over.

'Sssh!' Erich whispered, catching before my body hit the floor. 'They'll hear us.'

He placed one hand over my mouth; with the other he pointed down the darkened corridor to the only room that had light coming from it. As we edged closer we could hear the humming of the electric lights. My heart pounded. I was sure I could hear each beat echoing around the corridor. Common sense begged me to run to the safety of my own ward, but Erich's hand in mine pulled me forward. I could have broken free. I could have turned back … but now I had to know what they were about to do to her.

We tiptoed on, then crouched down with our heads just below the windowsill. Slowly we lifted our heads to peer through the window. Chief Nurse Huber, the other nurse and Dr Wahlmann stood with their backs to us. We felt brave enough to stand a little taller. Inside the room there was a crucifix-shaped chair covered in white upholstery with the same black leather arm and leg straps as the bed on which they had sterilised me. Beyond the white chair was Eva in her wheelchair, facing the window. She stared at us, her face seemed to be crinkled with fear, her eyes imploring Erich and me to save her. All we could do was stare back helplessly.

The nurses picked her up from the chair, and her arms and legs crumpled together like a dead spider's. The nurses took hold of her limbs, having to unfurl her before they splayed her body to fit the contours of the crucifix bed. They stretched her limbs further in order to tighten and fasten the leather straps. Eva let out a blood-curdling cry, followed by a series of incomprehensible, garbled screams. Unperturbed, Dr Wahlmann stepped slowly and deliberately towards her.

In his right hand was a large syringe filled with a clear liquid. He placed it on the bed beside her while he grasped her left arm and tapped it several times until a vein was revealed. He reached for the syringe then tapped it too before he roughly jammed it into her arm and depressed the plunger. Eva's smile returned, ever so briefly, before her head dropped to one side. My hand flew to my mouth to stop myself from screaming. The rest of me was paralysed. Erich wrapped his arms around my waist and had to drag me away from the window before I recovered myself enough to run back to the ward with him.

CHAPTER 4

DR OPPENHEIMER

January 1940

I didn't know anything about her. I didn't know anything about her life. I didn't know her dreams or even if she had them. I knew nothing of her family or her suffering, but Eva's death shook me more than I could imagine. I couldn't shake the visions of her terrified eyes from my mind. Worst of all, I felt bad for thinking she was better off dead. She may have been disabled. She may have struggled to move. Her life might not have been full of joy like the lives of most German children – but she still deserved to live, didn't she? If I thought she was better off dead, was *I* any better than the people who used to taunt me back on the streets of Mainz?

After Eva's execution my mood became as melancholic as the darkening winter. Erich reacted differently. Often, I tried to talk to him about what we had seen and whether it was happening to the others, but he would cut me off and say it was better not to think about it – that was their fate and there was nothing we could do about it. We could only look after ourselves. He did his best to cheer me up, often stealing extra food for me whenever he could; more often than not he was caught and punished. True to his nature, he would back-chat and disobey, which resulted in frequent trips to solitary confinement for sometimes days at a time or whacks across his legs with broomsticks, or whatever else one of the orderlies could find.

'You heard Chief Nurse Huber yourself: we're not useless like the others. They're not going to take us away,' he would say confidently whenever he returned from his punishment.

Despite his optimism, sadness gripped my soul. More and more children disappeared. Every time I watched one of them being led away, my despair deepened; my mood darkened further still whenever a taken child's bed was filled by another. Life became meaningless, worthless. I became engulfed by paranoia and fear, certain that at any moment the doctors and nurses would come for me. I hated having to go into the wards to change the beds for the sickest and most disabled, knowing I was seeing their last moments on earth. Nevertheless, I took to my work with extra vigour. Chief Nurse Huber had said it herself. I was one of the least useless. I was determined to make myself invaluable so I did not receive *Gnadentod*, which we had come to learn meant a 'merciful' death.

One day, I was watching the other children running up and down my ward, when they suddenly stopped and ran towards the window. Outside, I heard a car pulling up. I hurried to the window and looked over their heads. There was a black Mercedes, identical to the one that had brought me here. I swallowed. My throat felt dry. More and more children crowded around the window, excited by the break in the monotony. A tall, well-built man dressed in a white doctor's coat emerged from the rear of the car. He strode regally towards the main entrance, his step confident and assured.

'He must be a special doctor,' one child said.

'I bet he's here to get rid of us all,' said another.

'We're all gonna be taken and killed!' a third added.

Some of the younger ones began to cry. Others returned to their beds and whimpered.

'What is going on in there?' Chief Nurse Huber hollered from the Nurse's Office.

Children scattered and dove for their beds, their eyes sneaking glances towards the door as they hid under their blankets. We heard the front entrance doors creak open and the shrill voices of the nurses as they chattered.

'*Fräuleins, Fräuleins*, please, give Dr Oppenheimer some air!' I heard the familiar voice of Dr Wahlmann say with unfamiliar joviality. His words did little to dampen the nurses' excitement, but their schoolgirl giggling gradually faded to silence. Curious, we all stared at the exit. Erich was the first to muster enough courage to leave his bed to investigate. Warily making his way towards the door, he peered either side.

'They're gone,' he said, mystified as to why they had all disappeared, but not enough to lose his senses. 'Quick! Let's make a run for it before they come back!'

But at that moment, the group of staff walked in with the new doctor at their head, and Erich sprinted down the ward and leapt onto his bed. Even from a distance I could tell he was an extremely handsome man. He had a strong, chiselled German jaw and perfectly styled blond hair. It was as if he had stepped right out of one of the Nazi propaganda posters. His cursory glances as he walked past each child comforted me, but only when he reached the window at the end of the ward, turned on his heels and walked out did I let myself truly relax.

Shortly afterwards, the dinner bell rang. We leapt from our beds and hurried to the dining hall. Handing out pieces of bread as I did each night, I spied the new doctor as he casually walked in, his hands clasped behind his back as if he were out on a Sunday stroll. Behind him were Chief Nurse Huber and Dr Wahlmann, the three of them making their way towards me. Busying myself with my work, I put my head down and tried to remain inconspicuous.

'And who do we have here?' I heard a stern, yet soft, voice ask.

'Which one?' Dr Wahlmann said.

'The Negro one. What is she doing here?'

'Dr Oppenheimer, do you really need to ask? Look at the blackness of her skin; she is as useless as the rest of them!'

'*Ja, ja*, true,' was all he said.

After handing out the last of the bread except for mine, I retrieved my bowl of soup and sat next to Erich.

'So why do you think that new doctor is here?' he asked through a mouthful of soup-dipped bread.

'I don't want to think about it,' I lied as I dipped my spoon into my soup and whirled it in circles.

'You should. I saw what happened. He seemed quite interested in you.'

'He only asked why I was here – that's all.'

'I've been here longer than you. Take it from me, it's *never* a good thing for a doctor to be asking about you.'

I had come to love Erich as if he was my own brother – a younger one at that – but I hated how he lorded things over me. Just because he had arrived at Hadamar a few weeks earlier than I, he thought he had every right to tell me what to do and how to act and think. After finishing our supper and putting our bowls and utensils in the tubs for the older patients to wash, we returned to our ward to ready ourselves for bed. Shortly after, the doctors appeared at the ward entrance. Dozens of children hid under their blankets. I half hid myself but only because I watched Erich sitting confidently against his pillow as he stared at the half-dozen nurses and doctors trailing behind the new *Herr Doktor*.

'See, I told you so,' Erich whispered through clenched teeth as we both realised the doctor's eyes were fixed on me. Waving the others to stay behind him, the doctor stopped at the end of my bed. I hid under my blanket, but I could still hear the rattle of my clipboard as he picked it up from the end of my bed.

'Ingrid,' he said.

I ignored him.

'Ingrid,' he repeated.

Realising I had no choice, I slowly pulled my blanket down and lifted my eyes as far as I dared.

'The polite thing to do is to look at someone when they are talking,' he said with a strange softness.

I did not want to give them any excuse to take me away for a merciful death so I did as I was told. Immediately, I found myself lost in his smile and the blueness of his eyes. I saw something in them I had not seen in the others: true compassion. I wondered if he was different.

'Ingrid, I would like to run a few tests on you,' he said.

So much for compassion. He *was* just like the rest of them.

'Would that be okay?'

I shrugged my shoulders. What choice did I have? I hopped off my bed and stood next to him, keeping my head down to avoid the stares of the others.

'Come on then,' he said as he put his arm around my shoulder. Oddly, his touch didn't make me shudder, but I wasn't convinced this wasn't just a ruse to get me to go quietly to the injecting rooms. He escorted me to the end of the ward. His colleagues trailed closely behind.

'I will not be needing any of you for the moment,' he said.

I didn't need to look back to know the other staff were confused. But as he led me towards the medical rooms, I dared to take a quick glance behind me to see if they had obeyed his orders. In the silence of the corridor he held the door opened and motioned for me to enter.

'You see: no-one else has come. In you go. I swear I am not going to hurt you.'

'How can I believe that? That's what the other doctors and the nurses tell the children right before they take them away and kill them.'

'Then I will have to prove to you that I am not like them,' he said as I tiptoed into the room. I sat down on the bed. He ordered me to take my top off. I felt very uncomfortable as I pulled my shirt over my head and placed it beside me. I looked around and realised he was not in the room. I was beginning to wonder if this was some kind of sick game he was playing, when he reappeared carrying a yellow folder under his arm.

He circled as he looked me up and down. I could feel his eyes tracing over my body, particularly when his gaze became fixed on my stomach.

'You can put your shirt back on,' he said as he stood in front of me.

Blushing, I reached for my blouse and re-dressed.

'My name is Dr Oppenheimer,' he said. 'I have never come across a Negro patient and I am interested to learn more about you. Will you speak with me?'

'I am not a Negro,' I said firmly. 'Negroes are American. I am German.'

'Ingrid,' he said as he reached for the folder, opened it and began reading. 'According to the state you are a Negro, a "Rheinlander bastard", as it says here.'

'*Ja, ja, die schwarze Schande*, the black shame, *die schwarze Schmach*, the black disgrace. I know what I am. I have heard it all before.'

'I have been brought here to make certain operational changes, to improve how things function here, but having a black girl here is a bonus. I am very interested in your experiences, your life, before you came to Hadamar. I am most interested in your – shall we say – genetic differences. One day, perhaps very soon, you will leave this place but, before that happens, I would like to study you more. Would that be okay with you?'

I shrugged my shoulders. 'I suppose.'

He placed the yellow folder on the desk and picked up a stethoscope, which he slid under the front of my shirt.

'Breathe in,' he said as he placed the stethoscope on my sternum. 'Now: out.'

Tracing his hand down my abdomen, he felt my scars. He lifted my blouse high enough to see them.

'What are these?'

'They are from when the Gestapo doctors cut me open.'

'Remarkable,' he said as he ran his fingers along the right-side scars. 'I knew they were doing it, but I didn't know they had moved on to Negroes as well.'

I shivered.

'You are a *Mischling*, are you not?'

'*Ja*, Mutti is German and Vati is French Senegalese.'

'Fascinating,' he said as he removed the stethoscope, turned around and made notes in his file. 'Ingrid, there is much I wish to learn about you. You can go now but know that, for as long as it takes for me to complete my research, no harm will come to you.'

Fixing my blouse, I hopped down from the table and walked from the room pondering what he'd just said. Was he telling the truth? Had he just guaranteed my safety, at least for a while? *Nein*, I'd heard the lies they'd told the children before they took them for *Gnadentod*. That's what Nazi doctors did best: lies and deception. Their promises were hollow. Still wondering about Dr Oppenheimer, I wandered back into the ward.

'So? What did he want?' Erich asked as I slumped into my bed.

'He asked about me and my life before here. He told me he wanted to study me.'

'Study you? That's weird. Glad I'm not you,' Erich offered.

'Thanks for being so supportive,' I teased. 'You really are a great friend.'

'Sorry, but if he said he wants to study you, that can't be a good thing. More and more I get the feeling we are like lab rats to them. You have the scars on your stomach to prove it. Who knows what he intends to do?'

I didn't want to believe Erich. But after all that had happened, how could I trust anything they said? 'He said that as long as he wants to do his research, no harm will come to me,' I said.

'That's all well and good, but what happens when he's finished his research?'

'How many times have you said to me we are never guaranteed tomorrow – all we can do is make the best of today?' I snapped.

Erich went to speak but changed his mind.

'Exactly,' I said as I rolled over and closed my eyes. Despite my brave words, I was terrified to think about what this new doctor's true intentions really were.

April 1940

Dr Oppenheimer called me to his office again and again. He asked me questions about Vati, Mutti, my early childhood – everything. One day, after he had conducted yet another physical examination, he asked me to sit down at the chair opposite him.

'Ingrid, are you familiar with the term "Social Darwinism"?'

'*Nein.*'

'How about the word "evolution"?'

'*Ja*, I think I heard that word at school once. It has something to do with how and why all Aryan people are better than everyone else. *Herr Doktor*, Mutti took me out of school when the taunts and teasing of my classmates became too much. She tried to teach me herself, but after they took Vati she wasn't the same.'

'They took your father? Would you mind telling me about it?'

A tall, rake-like man arrived at our house. He was wearing a black Gestapo hat with a silver skull on it. With him was a tall, solidly built Aryan man with sandy yellow hair, just like in the movies they showed us in school about the 'perfect' German.

'Hello, little girl,' the tall man said as put his hands on his knees to bring himself down to my level. 'Is your mother or father home?'

His face was inches from mine and I remember he had a mouth full of perfect, shining white teeth, but his skin was pale, wrinkled and leathery. His thinning hair was greasy, and wisps of it stuck out from beneath his cap like thin black worms. My skin crawled and my bones shivered at the sight of him.

'Who is it?' Mutti called out as she came out from the laundry drying her hands with a towel. As soon as she saw them, she ran over and placed her arms around me.

'*Guten abend*, Frau Marchand,' the man said as he doffed his hat. I saw that his hair was combed over to try to cover his bald patch. 'Pleased to make your acquaintance.'

He took Mutti's hand and bent down to kiss it. I saw her shiver at his touch.

'Is your husband home?'

Mutti shook her head. He let go of her hand and she wiped it as if it was covered in oil.

Mutti offered the men coffee, apologising that it was only *Ersatzkaffee*. As she put on the pot they walked inside and made themselves at home. When she returned and sat back down the tall man asked her if she knew what the words '*Rassenschande*' and '*Blutschande*' meant.

'Did she, or you, know what these words meant?' Dr Oppenheimer interrupted.

'Not really, but Mutti seemed to become quiet and worried when she heard them.'

'What did your Mutti do?'

'She fetched the coffee pot from the stove, returned to the table and poured.'

'What did the man say?'

'Danke, Frau Marchand, allow me to introduce myself. I am Herr Schleck and this is Herr Hartmann. Good Frau, I will ask you again, where is your husband?'

'Out. I do not know where.'

'Frau Marchand, are you aware that women who sleep with Jewish men are being paraded down the street wearing phrases such as "*Ich bin am Ort das größte Schwein und laß mich nur mit Juden ein*!"'

Mutti nodded. I had seen them too – German women who were marched around the *Domplatz* with white placards hanging around their necks bearing phrases, like Herr Schleck had said, that spoke of being a great pig and preferring to be with the Jews.

'Herr Schleck, I am not Jewish and neither is my family.'

'That much is true, but the racial purity laws extend to people of colour also. While you are married, for the moment, the law can do nothing. However, it will not be too long before you may find yourself in the same position as those women. It would be in your best interests to nullify your marriage and entrust your daughter to our keeping. Your daughter is a Rheinlander bastard but she is not as black as your husband; perhaps we can find a place in society for her.'

Before Mutti could respond, the door flew open and in marched Vati.

'I swear this country just keeps getting worse and worse!' he grumbled as he put his coat and hat on the stand near the door. 'It is run by a group of ignorant white idiots!'

He turned and noticed Herr Schleck at the table. His face filled with fear.

'Ah, Monsieur Marchand, so good to see you! My name is Herr Schleck and this is Herr Hartmann,' Schleck said as he stood and extended his hand, indicating he wished for Vati to take his seat.

'Monsieur Marchand, are you familiar with the words "*Rassenschande*" and "*Blutschande*"?'

Vati nodded.

'Then you understand why we are here.'

Vati nodded again and glanced repeatedly at the door.

'And you are familiar the government's new Nuremburg Laws?'

'*Ja*,' Vati said as he rubbed the bridge of his nose.

'Now, these laws came in on the fifteenth of September, did they not? And I can safely assume that, considering you and Frau Marchand here are married, you have had intimate relations since that time?'

Herr Schleck's silent Aryan partner bared his teeth in a sneer.

'Please, Herr Schleck, can we not discuss such things in front of my daughter? State your business here or kindly leave.'

'Of course, you and your wife here are in violation of the Law for the Protection of German Blood and German Honour.'

'The law you refer to, *Herr Schleck*, only applies to unmarried couples!' Vati snarled. 'But you must already know this. If this is all you have, I will kindly ask you to leave.'

'Monsieur Marchand,' Herr Schleck said as he stood beside Vati and put his face close to his. 'We have a whole lot more on you, I assure you. Shall we discuss your Communist leanings and your affiliation with the Communist Party?'

Vati was mute.

'Perhaps some other time,' Herr Schleck said as he nodded towards the front door. He and his companion left. Only when we heard the screeching of the car tyres did Vati allow himself to breathe again.

'All right, Ingrid, time for bed,' Mutti ordered.

I wanted to know more about what was happening – who these men were and why they had come – but I sensed now was not the time.

I was in no mood to argue. I went upstairs but only as far as the top landing.

'Guillaume, what are we going to do?' Mutti's voice quivered in a way I had never heard. 'We have to leave. Tonight,' Vati said resolutely. I could hear him pacing up and down the kitchen.

'And go where? They have made us stateless. They have made our passports invalid. There is no way the authorities will give us permission to leave.'

'We can slip across the border to France without passports,' Vati replied. 'I know a way. I know people who will help us through the forests of the Ardennes without being seen. Go upstairs and get Ingrid packed. I will gather together what money we have left and we will leave tonight.'

CHAPTER 4

My mind ran so wild with ideas of what France might be like and the realisation that we were actually leaving Germany that I didn't notice Mutti coming up the stairs.

'Ingrid, pack your things. We're leaving. Only take what is most important to you.'

I stood and went to my room. I did as I was told, staring into my cupboard trying to decide what to take. I had only placed one old dress in my suitcase when, suddenly, I heard an almighty *crash*. Dozens of bootsteps thundered up the stairwell. Another crash, and Mutti shouting. I ran to my door. A dozen or so *Allgemeine SS* in black uniforms and caps with red swastika bands around their right biceps were charging into Mutti and Vati's bedroom.

Then Herr Schleck mounted the stairs.

'What is going on? What are you doing?' Mutti screamed.

Four SS men grabbed Vati, holding him by the arms and legs as they dragged him from the bedroom and down the stairs. They forced him into a chair.

'We haven't done anything wrong!' Mutti shouted, running down the stairs after them. 'We haven't broken any laws!'

Herr Schleck strolled to the mantelpiece and picked up a photograph of me, looked at it momentarily, and then replaced it in its original position. 'Your husband is a Communist and you are guilty of race-mixing. You are both guilty of crimes against the State, therefore I have the authority to do whatever I please. Take him away.'

I looked at Vati. He'd always told me, and taught me, to fight. I knew he would not go without one. But to my surprise, he tamely let two of the SS men place their hands on his shoulders and walk him out. A shiver ran through my body and panic took hold. I swayed on the spot, dizzy with shock. Mutti held me tightly as we stood at the door and watched them escort Vati to a waiting black Mercedes. I remember the raindrops on its metallic surface, shimmering in the light of the street lamps. One of the SS men tilted Vati's head as they pushed him into the back of the car. He resisted, but only to turn his head towards Mutti and me and mouth the words, 'I love you.'

'*Nein*!' I screamed as I broke free from Mutti and rushed towards the SS men, trying to tear their arms away from Vati. It didn't work. They pushed me hard, knocking me onto the snow-covered pavement. I leapt back up and tried again. They knocked me back down. As I lay on the pavement, the coldness of the sleet seeped into my jacket. I remember the taste of my tears.

'*Liebschen*,' Vati shouted. 'Don't worry, everything is going to be alright. I am just going to have a talk with these men. I won't be long. I'll be back before you know it.'

'Promise you will come back to us, Vati!' I sobbed.

'I promise,' he shouted, and then the door slammed, the motor of the black Mercedes roared to life and the car sped off down the street. I chased it until it disappeared around the corner. I fell to my knees and wept until my eyes hurt.

It broke me inside. He was my whole world, and my world had come crashing down. My Vati was my protector, my defender – and he was gone. But I picked myself up, wiped the tears from my eyes, brushed the snow from my knees and headed back towards the house.

Mutti was waiting at the door. Even in the frosty evening air I could see her hands shaking. Her lips trembled; she wanted to cry but was forcing herself not to. I rushed into her arms.

We walked inside but she only made it as far as the living room before she collapsed to the floor. The tears burst from her eyes like streams from a dam, flowing freely down her face as she lay on the living room rug and curled herself into a ball. I sat beside her and wrapped my arms around her. She buried her head into my chest. We cried in each other's arms until our tears ran dry.

In the early hours of the morning I forced myself up off the floor, draped Mutti's arms around my shoulders and managed to help her upstairs to her bedroom. She lay in the foetal position and stared blankly at the wall. I pulled a blanket over her and kissed her on the cheek before I went to my own bed. I lay there thinking about Vati until the first rays of sunlight came through the window. I rushed to Mutti's room. She lay in the same position and, thankfully, slept soundly.

'What happened to your Mutti after that? Where did they take your Vati?' Dr Oppenheimer asked as he leant towards me with his elbows on his knees. His eyes told me he was hanging on my every word. I felt like I was beginning to trust him, but experience had taught me to be cautious.

'I don't know. I remembered that Herr Schleck had accused him of being a Communist and I had read that they were sending them to camps like Dachau.'

'*Ja*, that is true. They have sent many Communists to concentration camps and Dachau is one of the main ones. And your Mutti?'

'She did not get out of bed for a few days but, ever so slowly, she recovered herself. I looked after her as best I could.'

'Your Mutti did not have work and *you* could not work. How on Earth did you look after her?'

'I went down the street to kindly old Herr Schuster and asked for his help. He brought eggs from his chickens and vegetables from his garden for us until Mutti was back on her feet. Mutti has never been quite the same though. For weeks she sat in a chair in her room and stared out the window waiting for Vati to come home. Finally, when she accepted that he was not coming back, she started to try to live her life again.'

'You left school, but clearly you are a highly intelligent girl who seems to know a lot about the world. How come?'

'Before the Nazis, Vati was a jazz musician. Vati always brought me books on music, science, history. Many were much too hard for me when I was little but, as I got older, I started trying to read them. Sometimes Vati would read them to me. I also scrounged as many newspapers as I could find and read them cover to cover. Mutti always taught me that knowledge was important and that the best way to gain knowledge was to read.'

'Your mother sounds like a very wise woman. Tell you what, Ingrid, I will see if I can find the whereabouts of your father and, as long as you are here, I will bring in as many newspapers as I can find for you to read. How does that sound?'

'That would be fantastic, *Herr Doktor! Danke*!' His flattery and his promises were making me start to relax.

'Now, back to what we were discussing before. In your science books you must have read about Charles Darwin. He was an Englishman who sailed to a place called the Galapagos Islands on a boat called the *Beagle*. While there he noticed that different species of the same animals had minor differences. To cut a long story short, Darwin came up with the idea of the theory of evolution. That out of the most suited of a species, the strongest will survive.'

'*Ja* – what you Nazis call "the Aryan race".'

'Ingrid,' the doctor said, 'I am going to conduct more experiments on you.'

My heart pounded. 'You mean *kill me*? Give me *Gnadentod*?'

'Where did you learn that word?'

'Chief Nurse Huber told us what it means.'

'Ingrid, that is for only the most seriously ill patients. Ones who are going to die anyway. I told you: no harm will come to you as long as I am here!' he laughed. 'I have never met a black child like you. I want to learn more about your biology, your mental aptitude. I am fascinated. I wish to learn more.'

I didn't believe him. My eyes told him so. He checked his wristwatch.

'All right, Ingrid, that will be all for now,' he said. 'Time for you to do your dinner duties.'

I didn't see Dr Oppenheimer again for some time. I felt immensely relieved. I was certain that underneath his kind façade there was something more sinister to him and, despite his reassurances, I feared his true intentions.

My days returned to the regular mundane routine of sweeping the wards and changing the beds. Now that Dr Oppenheimer had asked me about her, I couldn't stop thinking of Mutti. Had she sold the house and gone to live with my grandparents? If she had, how would I find her? I had never met my grandparents. I didn't know much about them at all. All I knew was that they lived in Wiesbaden. If she'd moved I would have to search the whole city to find her. I hoped she would visit soon and save me the trouble.

For now, I was stuck in this humdrum existence, the boredom of which was only broken when the staff played broadcasts from *Reichs-Rundfunk-Gesellschaft*, or 'Radio Nazi', as we called it. Occasionally they played classical or orchestral music but mostly it was just Nazi propaganda and news reports telling us how *our* troops were winning victory after victory, and how all of this proved how wonderful *Der Führer* was. I overheard the nurses talking about it. German troops had taken Paris. This, they said, made up for all that had been done to us in the previous war. Hitler was going to control all of Europe before too long, they said. I didn't know what to think.

As a German I felt I should be as excited and optimistic as they were but, to me, the war was something distant and unreal. What I did know was that *Der Führer* was the most powerful man in the country and it was, therefore, *his* fault I was here. *He* was the one who had decided we were different. *He* was the one who had decided that people like me needed to be locked away from the rest of society. How dare they expect us to be excited about *our* victory over France, about *our* wonderful successes in capturing and defeating Denmark and Norway!

I had just finished changing an empty bed when the radio broadcast suddenly switched off, signalling dinnertime. I returned to my bed to find Erich sitting on his.

'Do you think we will ever get out of here?' Erich sighed as he sat crossed-legged and played with his toes.

'*Ja*,' I said as confidently as I could, even though I didn't believe it. 'Of course we will.'

'How can you be so sure?' he asked me. It was strange; something about him was off. Erich had always been the strong one, the defiant one, the optimistic one. The scowl on his face didn't seem right.

'Of course we will leave this place,' I said more enthusiastically. 'We might walk out on our own two feet or be carried out lying flat on our backs. One way or another, we will leave.'

I hadn't meant to make such a tasteless joke. Erich glared at me. I stared back and stuck out my tongue. He smiled, but only briefly.

More and more I worried about him. Lately he had not been the same Erich as when I first arrived. He had become surlier and was back-chatting the staff more than usual. The letters from his family had ceased. Several times, he had accused the staff of keeping them from him or destroying them. A week earlier he had worked himself into such a rage it took two orderlies to control him and they gave him a sedative to calm him down.

'Erich, why are you sitting on your pillow?' I asked as I propped up on mine.

'I was cleaning pots in the kitchen and I fell over. Nurse Willig came in and saw me. He called me a *Dummkopf*.'

'Did you say anything back?'

'*Ja*,' he said, a wry smile returning to his face. 'I said *fick dich*! *Blödes Arschloch*!'

I was stunned into silence.

'He dragged me into his office and flogged my buttocks with some electrical cable. It hurts pretty badly.'

'You're lucky he didn't kill you!' I said as I leapt from my bed. I fetched some clean towels and antiseptic from one of the nurse's trays before retrieving a bowl of water. Rushing back to his bedside I said, 'Pull your pants down.'

'Ingrid!' Erich mocked, his familiar smile returning. 'You are like a sister to me. It wouldn't be proper!'

I flicked him with the towel, pushed him onto his side and pulled the back of his trousers down. His backside was purple with bruises and criss-crossed with thin red lines, some of which seeped. I wet the towel with antiseptic and gently dabbed his sores.

'Erich, how many beatings is it going to take before you learn to behave?'

'Behave? Why? They are just going to kill me anyway. I don't know about you, but I am not going without a fight.'

'Erich, if they were going to kill you they would have done it by now,' I said, wiping the excess liquid from his bottom and putting the towel and bowl on the table between our beds.

'Ingrid,' he said as he lay back on his pillow. 'You know that is not true and I don't have some handsome doctor to protect me.'

'Erich, that's unfair. I didn't ask for him to protect me.'

'Sorry, Ingrid, it's good he's taken an interest in you. At least one of us might actually get out of here.'

'I'll talk to him. We'll both get out. I swear it!'

'I have managed to last this long,' he said as he ran his hands up and down his legs. 'But one day they *will* come for me. Ingrid, come here. I want to show you something.'

Jumping from my bed to his, I sat on the edge while he reached beneath the bed and pulled out a small canvas bag. He opened the flap. Inside were two small loaves of bread, cheese, butter and – best of all – chocolate!

'Erich! You had better take this all back before they find out it's missing!' I hissed at him as I kept a watchful eye on the ward entrance.

'Ingrid, you saw what Nurse Willig did to me. I figure I deserve all of this. Besides, they have so much they won't even notice, but if you don't want any …'

'Okay, but we should be quick,' I said as he broke a piece of chocolate away and gave it to me. If Heaven had a taste, this was it. We devoured the rest of the bar and moved on to the cheese and bread.

Then I sat up straight; it had just dawned on me that I still didn't know why Erich was in this place.

'Erich,' I said awkwardly, through a mouthful of bread and cheese.

'*Ja*.'

'I have never asked you this, but why are you here?'

'Why am I here? There's something wrong with my muscles.'

'But you're one of the hardest workers!'

'Because I have to be,' he said resolutely. 'The day I stop working hard is the day they strap me to a chair and give me *Gnadentod!*'

'You always work hard,' I protested, but fear took hold of me. 'You have nothing to worry about!'

Erich reached forward and shuffled his trouser legs up, wincing as he did. 'Look closely at my knee,' he said.

I held his right knee and examined it closely. It felt extremely thin. He tried to straighten it but it was impossible.

'It started when I was eleven. I was always weaker at school than the other kids so they picked on me.'

'I know *exactly* how you feel.'

'Some days I was in absolute agony, but I forced myself to do as the other kids did. If they ran, I ran. If they jumped, I jumped. I willed myself through it, all so they wouldn't pick on me. It's the same here, Ingrid. Every day I fight through the pain. I do what I have to just to survive.'

'What *is* wrong with you?' I asked as I gently stroked his knee.

'I don't know. All the doctors said was that there is something wrong with my muscles and they will keep wasting away until they don't work at all. I have had electric therapy in the past, but it didn't do any good.'

'If you managed to hide it for it so long, how did you come to be here?'

'The same way as you. Some Gestapo doctors came to the house one day and forced my parents to sign some papers and I was brought here.'

'Erich, have you noticed how it's only the mentally *and* physically deformed ones that they take away and inject? They have never taken ones like us yet.'

'*Yet*,' Erich said forlornly. '*Yet*, Ingrid. I'm sure they mean to kill us all. One day my body will fail. Even if we do get out of here I'll spend the rest of my life in a wheelchair. Maybe I *would* be better off if they killed me.'

'No, Erich, don't talk like that!' I protested.

'Why do you think I disobey them like I do, Ingrid? They remind me of all those kids at school who picked on me. I don't want to give them the satisfaction of beating me down any more. If I am going to die in here, then so be it.'

Nurses Ruoff and Willig, the 'Nurses of Death', as we had come to call them, strode into the ward.

'Erich Kaufmann!' Nurse Willig called out.

I wrapped my arms around Erich and he buried his head into my chest.

'Erich Kaufmann!' Nurse Willig repeated angrily. I hugged Erich tightly as if my arms were shields that would make him invisible. Erich pulled away. He raised his head and looked into my eyes. I expected him to be terrified, horrified, but he wasn't. His eyes told me that he was resigned to his fate.

When the nurses reached the bed they saw the remains of our ill-gotten treasure.

'Kaufmann, we warned you, didn't we?' Nurse Willig hissed.

'*Ja, ja*, you warned me,' Erich said, emotionless.

'You just don't learn do you, Kaufmann? If you think your backside is sore now, just wait until I am finished with you!' Nurse Ruoff snarled as he stepped forward and ripped Erich from my arms. Erich tried to walk by himself but, whether it was his wasting muscles or his pained backside, he stumbled. He glanced back at me at the ward exit. I couldn't let them take him. I had seen what Nurse Willig had already done to him. Erich wouldn't survive another beating. I leapt from his bed and ran down the ward. The two nurses stopped and turned.

'What do you want, Marchand?'

My mouth was dry, my tongue felt swollen, but I had to get the words out. I knew I had the protection of Dr Oppenheimer. I knew they would be cautious with how they treated me.

'Erich did not steal the food. I did.'

Nurse Willig did not ask for clarification nor did he question us. He merely took his hands off Erich's shoulders and placed them on mine.

'Your doctor friend can't save you now! Damn Negroes! It's bad enough Germany is filled with all these useless eaters, but we have to put up with Negroes too! I've been waiting for an excuse to deal with you, Marchand,' he said coldly.

He grabbed my arm and dragged me to the door. Straining to turn my head, I caught sight of Erich, his face etched with confusion as Nurse Willig began walking me down the corridor. I looked around for any sign of Dr Oppenheimer. He was Nurse Willig's superior; surely the nurse would not disobey his orders.

'Nurse Willig! Wait!'

Erich appeared in the corridor.

Nurses Willig and Ruoff turned me around until all three of us faced Erich.

'What is it, Kaufmann?'

'Ingrid is lying. She didn't steal the food. I did.'

Nurse Willig huffed with frustration. 'Look, I don't really care which one of you took the food but one of you is going to be punished for it. Now, which will it be?'

'Me,' Erich said before I could respond.

Nurses Willig dropped my arm and turned to snatch Erich's. I watched him walk down the corridor. Right before they reached the end he turned to look at me. He went to say something but closed his lips just as quickly. He didn't need to say a word. His eyes told me he was saying goodbye.

CHAPTER 5

SONDERBEHANDLUNG

13 January 1941

Days and days disappeared and still there was no sign of Erich. At first I assumed that Nurse Willig had administered his beating and placed Erich into solitary confinement. Every time Nurse Willig passed me by I wanted to ask where Erich was, but I could never work up the courage. I did my chores with extra vigour, partly because I didn't want to give them an excuse to punish me, but more because it took my mind off Erich's disappearance. If I ever had a pause in my day my thoughts turned to the inescapable thought that they had taken him away and injected him.

Nein! Erich was a good worker. He was not useless. Surely they would have spared him.

But I had to *know*. Mopping the floor of the most disabled children's ward, I noticed that there was an unusually large number of empty beds. Troubled, I returned to my ward and cleaned it, then headed to the adjacent courtyard to tip the dirty water down the drain. When I was done, I stood up and turned around to see Nurse

Willig standing at the entrance.

'You have been working extra hard lately, Marchand. Don't think it hasn't gone unnoticed.'

His compliment didn't comfort me.

'As I am sure you have noticed, there are a lot less children around. You'd better keep working as hard as you have been or you might just disappear too.'

I didn't think before my words came out. 'What happened to Erich?'

'One of you stole, so one of you had to suffer the consequences.'

'What do you mean?'

'Marchand, you niggers really are stupid, aren't you?' he sneered. 'That boy was never going to learn. I warned him. Again and again, I warned him, but he didn't listen. Erich was sent for *Sonderbehandlung*: special treatment,' Nurse Willig said with a sickening smile.

Despite the coldness of the day, I sat on a bench in the courtyard and stared at the barren oak tree. My body felt numb. Erich was gone. I knew it was he who had stolen the food, but we had both eaten it. I was, for the most part, as guilty as he. I should have received the same punishment. Erich and I should have died together. I knew it was Dr Oppenheimer's authority that kept me alive and that, despite his veiled threats, Nurse Willig didn't have the guts to disobey.

The cold began to bite, restoring my senses ever so slightly. Wrapping my arms around my chest, I went back inside, making sure to close the door behind me. The sky outside turned grey, and the ward darkened until night fell. Storm clouds rolled in. The ward sporadically lit up from bursts of lightning, followed by cracks of thunder so loud they shook the windows. Each lightning strike, each time the ward was illuminated, I became painfully aware of the empty beds – mostly the one next to mine.

I was sure Erich's ghost haunted me that night. I thought I saw him but I soon realised that it was nothing more than a trick of the light and shadows from the tree branches outside.

As the days went by I withdrew completely, only speaking when spoken to and trying to avoid human contact. My only company – if one could call it that – was Radio Nazi reporting on all of Germany's wonderful victories.

General Rommel was poised to take over North Africa. Japan, Italy and Germany had all signed an agreement to fight together. The world was falling to the Fascists. Erich had been right: I was never getting out of here, and to live would only prolong my suffering. I didn't have the courage, as he did, to goad them into killing me but, when I felt at my worse, I prayed to the God I had never known, that Vati had told me not to believe in, that they would come and take me away.

As if Erich's passing was a death knell, Hadamar began to change. More and more wounded soldiers arrived to convalesce, but their presence cast an even darker shroud. One after the other they came in: Germany's finest, broken in body and soul, surrounded by depression and despair. During the course of my daily duties I kept my head down, not daring to look at a single man, fearing what Chief Nurse Huber would say if I did. I didn't need to look at them to feel their dejection – it hung in every room like a fog.

But as I worked I listened and learned that, just as I had thought, Radio Nazi had been bending the truth. Germany was winning, but the war was not going as Hitler and his supporters had said.

The main upstairs wards that had once housed dozens of children were now filled with maimed and wounded soldiers. My heart ached for them. These men had believed the lies. They had rushed off to 'defend' the Fatherland, searching for glory and honour, and what had they received in return? Now they were little better off than the children Germany had tried to hide away. Callously discarded by the Reich once their purpose had been served. More men arrived, as disturbed as any of the mental patients, sitting silently on their beds or aimlessly wandering around the wards.

In the middle of winter in 1941, Chief Nurse Huber told me to prepare a second upstairs ward for the arrival of a new batch of soldiers. I had just finished folding the corners of the sheets on the last bed when I stood tall to stretch my back. The ward smelt stuffy and stale so I opened the window to circulate some fresh air. Through the white bars I looked at the sickly thin trees, the browned and barren fields beyond. The countryside surrounding Hadamar seemed to have succumbed to the same desolation as the people inside. In the distance I spied a black car speeding up the gravel road separating the fields. It came to a screeching halt near the entrance below me. The door opened. A man stepped out. It was Dr Oppenheimer.

Leaning as far as I could through the bars I watched him as he trudged along the dirt driveway that snaked its way from the front gates around to the rear of the building. He stopped at a series of newly-built fences that led down into the cellar adjacent to the bus garages. He grasped the fences and rocked them back and forth, testing them. Happy that they were secure, he walked back towards the main gates. One of the guards opened the main gate as wide as it would go, and he and Dr Oppenheimer started to walk down the driveway.

Two grey buses with blacked-out windows slowly motored up the hill towards the buildings adjacent to the main institution, their wheels slipping in the slushy ground. They drove through the gates before stopping directly in front of the fences. Dr Oppenheimer walked past the main entrance and was soon joined by Dr Wahlmann and some others. The bus engines were switched off. The doors opened. Several SS men stepped down and shook hands with Dr Oppenheimer and Dr Wahlmann as if they were long lost friends reunited after years of separation. They conversed briefly.

Then I saw children emerge from the buses. The SS men were ushering child after child – all dressed just like me – down from the buses and ordering them to line up near the fences. Then I saw the SS men herd them towards the building.

Dr Oppenheimer rested his hands on his back and began to stretch, twisting himself from side to side. As he turned around, he looked up at the top floor, directly at me. My eyes caught his. I broke away from the window, confused.

I hurried downstairs and busied myself with dinner preparations, but one thought consumed me: *why was Dr Oppenheimer so friendly with the SS*? I didn't want to see him again. I didn't want to talk to him again. As I gathered together the plates, cups and cutlery and placed them on the tables I kept one eye on the dining hall entrance, expecting him to walk through at any moment, readying myself to flee as soon as I saw him.

I heard a noise outside and rushed to the small courtyard at the back of the kitchen where the vegetables were stored. I picked up a basket of potatoes and, as I turned to go back inside, I noticed smoke pouring from the chimneys that rose from the building adjacent to the bus garages.

Two of the male mental patients entered, paying me no mind as they sat down and began peeling potatoes. I lingered in the kitchen until more people arrived. As the two potato peelers took the last of the soup vats out to the dining hall, I shielded myself behind one of them. After retrieving a bowl of soup and a small chunk of bread I sat down and ate as hurriedly as I could, looking around the whole time for any sign of Dr Oppenheimer. When finished, I rushed back to the kitchen, placed my bowl in the cleaning pots and cautiously made my way back to my bed. Only when I sat down did I realise how stupid I had been.

Where could I go that he couldn't find me?

Over the next seven days, however, I tried to keep myself hidden and out of sight. Dr Oppenheimer's interests had always been in the disabled and mental patients, so I figured he had little interest in the wounded soldiers. I made any excuse I could to work in their wards. Whenever I had a moment, I glanced out the windows to see if he was there. I didn't see him.

But, day after day, the buses with the blackened windows continued to come, unload the children then depart again. Where were all these children going? Hundreds had arrived and yet the children's wards were hardly full. If anything, they were emptier. It didn't make sense.

Early the next morning I woke with the sense that someone was standing over my bed.

'Ingrid,' a deep male voice said.

Instantly waking, I snapped myself upwards so that my back was against the bedhead. The shadow belonged to Dr Oppenheimer.

'Put on your jacket and come to my office.'

I was desperate not to follow him, but I knew I didn't have a choice. Finding my jacket, I put my arms in the sleeves as I walked as slowly as I could down the ward. Sheepishly, I made my way to his office, dawdling at the door as I tried to delay the inevitable.

'Come in, Ingrid,' I heard him say.

The yellow folder in which he kept his notes on me sat open on his desk. He didn't look at me. He just flicked through his notes as I sat down. He carefully placed his pen down, smiled at me and said, 'Ingrid, I am sorry I have not been around. I have had a lot of work to do. There were many important meetings I needed to attend and things I needed to take care of. I just want to run a few tests on you. I don't think I should need you for very long.'

He told me to stand. He checked my breathing before he pushed me against the wall and measured my height. He took out a tape measure and measured my ears, nose and my skull. He sat down to record his findings and indicated for me to sit across from him. Not knowing his intentions, but fearing the worst, I boldly asked the question that had been burning my mind for some time.

'Did your meetings have to do with all those bus loads of children and the new fences that have been built?'

'*Ja*, sort of, in a way.'

He seemed in a mood to answer honestly, so, encouraged, I pushed further.

'So, why are all the children taken into the cellar?'

'They are children from other institutions who have come here to be deloused. There are showers down in the cellars – big ones.'

'Don't they have showers at their own institutions? Why do they need to come here?'

'Some of the other places are not as big as here and do not have big enough showers to accommodate them. The war has also taken its toll on many families. Hadamar is taking orphans now too.'

I had a thousand questions but could not give them voice. I simply looked at him.

'You can go now,' he said without looking at me.

As the spring arrived, Dr Oppenheimer disappeared again or, if he hadn't, he was doing a good job of avoiding me. Either way, it pleased me not to have to see him and, with each passing day, I allowed myself to relax a little and even convince myself that maybe, someday, I would get out of here.

The doctor's prediction that more children would soon be arriving did not come to fruition. The buses arrived almost every day and yet there were an increasingly large number of vacant beds. On the one hand it made life pleasant. I had fewer beds to change, fewer bedpans to clean and fewer soiled sheets to wash, hang out and dry.

But having less to do gave me more time to think about the people I had loved and lost. When I cleaned upstairs I often gazed out the windows, watching as the fields became greener and the yellow flowers of the distant daffodils began to bloom. Then the orphaned children began to arrive. I didn't pay attention to their faces. I didn't pay attention to their names. I was never getting close to anyone else ever again. It would only be too painful when I lost them.

24 July 1941

So many children came and went, I became all but invisible. The nurses ignored me, except when they ordered me to work. I started to listen when they talked among themselves and I came to realise that, for the most part, they were just ordinary people and, for that matter, not very bright. Mostly, they did what they did because it was easy work with reasonable pay. Like me they did what they had to do to survive.

The senior staff were different. They were educated. They knew what they were doing. Well, the doctors did – and so I avoided them at all costs. Chief Nurse Huber was harder to understand. I became suspicious when, all of a sudden, her personality changed. Spring was such a beautiful time of the year, she said, and we were finally to be allowed outside to have picnics. To the rear of the main buildings were three tiers of grass and garden beds then fields where the crops grew.

The first time they took us out for a picnic we were permitted to sit on the grass in front of the rose bushes on the first tier. They may have only given us simple sandwiches, but it felt like a feast. The grass was green and felt wonderful between my fingers and toes. The warm sunshine on my back, the blossoming red roses made me feel free – at least for a moment. Chief Nurse Huber even went so far as to bring cupcakes.

I began to wonder how many of the staff were actually involved in the worst of what went on within the walls of Hadamar. I decided that, with the exception of Dr Wahlmann, Nurse Ruoff and Nurse Willig, most of them were not. Did they even know what was going on? Surely they must have. Perhaps they just chose to turn a blind eye. Perhaps it made doing their work easier.

Still, I never quite felt like I could forgive them – not after what they had done to Erich. The lower staff may have not been the most important cogs in the system but they were still cogs. Without them, the system wouldn't exist, the machine wouldn't function.

The doctors, however, were a different story. It was clear they had *asked* to be transferred here, clear that they had agendas of their own. The doctors *were* highly educated, with years of study at university behind them, and yet they assumed each child in Hadamar was a simple-minded idiot who, like garbage, required disposal. The only one who had ever shown a semblance of compassion was Dr Oppenheimer, and I had become increasingly wary of his intentions.

I hated the doctors. I hated all the staff, but what I hated most was that, the more I heard them talk, the more I began to wonder whether they were right.

Perhaps these children did deserve to live. Perhaps if we all died then the world would be a better place. Too much time to think twisted things in my head. The more I thought about things the more I turned everything into a negative. Even when it came to Mutti and Vati, I would take a cherished incident from my childhood and think and think on it until I had convinced myself that neither Mutti nor Vati wanted me and that I was the reason for all their troubles. I knew it was stupid, but I couldn't help myself. I deconstructed every memory I had and decided that my life had been a waste and it was best for all concerned if I just disappeared.

One morning as I lay in bed and watched the specks of dust dancing in the morning sunlight, Satan's minions came for me. Their coming was heralded by the sound of a dozen footsteps echoing through the ward. Three doctors and three nurses, including Chief Nurse Huber, stood in the centre of the ward. They examined the children in the first beds. Three more unfamiliar doctors came in after them and the nurses began handing them clipboards from the ends of the beds. They read them, ever so briefly, and then I heard them say: *Sonderbehandlung.* Special treatment.

They moved rapidly from bed to bed. Some children were ordered to receive special treatment, and others were let be. I could see no rhyme or reason to their decisions. The chosen children were hesitant at first, looking at the staff then each other, unsure of what to do. Seeing their reluctance to move, Chief Nurse Huber and a younger, far prettier nurse, stood in the centre of the ward. It was then that I saw the pretty nurse was holding a picnic basket in her right hand.

She reached inside and took out a sandwich. Whether it was the sight of food or the prospect of a picnic, it had the desired effect. Like tame animals, the children rose from their beds, assembled around the nurses and began peering into the basket.

'Ah, ah, children,' Chief Nurse Huber said as she slapped away one child's hand. 'You will have to wait until we go outside before you can enjoy your treats.'

Perhaps I would have believed her, were it not for the presence of the new doctors, who continued advancing down the ward, selecting children at random. By the time they reached me, at least two dozen children had risen from their beds and were crowding around the nurses. The tallest of the three doctors stood before me and retrieved my clipboard, perusing it only momentarily before he looked at me. I stared back indignantly, my eyes radiating pure hatred.

We were not going on a picnic; we were going to die. Part of me was glad of it. No more pain, no more thoughts, no more suffering. On one level, I expected Dr Oppenheimer to run down the ward and tell them to leave me be but, on another level, I suspected he could have been behind it all. I didn't know. Either way, I wanted these men to know there was nothing they could say or do that would break me. I was all but dead inside anyway. If I was going to die, I was going to die on *my* terms. My stare was so powerful it forced one of the younger doctors to avert his eyes and shift uncomfortably from foot to foot. The taller doctor was not so easily intimidated. He not only reciprocated my stare, but the side of his mouth began to curl upwards.

'*Sonderbehandlung,*' he said.

'All right, children, gather your things together,' Chief Nurse Huber said as she made for the ward exit. 'Before we go for our picnic, you're all going to take a little shower. It won't take long. There has been an outbreak of typhus and we need to make sure we delouse you all. When you go outside you will see buses. If you are good, children, those buses will take you on a picnic afterwards where I will have cupcakes for you all.'

We were rarely allowed to bathe. The itching from the lice was sometimes unbearable. The threat of typhus was ever present, and the thought of a shower and a delousing made some of the younger, feebler children clap with glee. Some of the older ones seemed pleased too. Others had their heads bowed, telling me they knew what I knew. I wondered what they were thinking. Were there thoughts of their families too? Had they decided, as I had, that their families were better off without them?

'Follow me, children,' Chief Nurse Huber said merrily. 'Get dressed, grab your things.'

The selected children ran back to their bedsides and hurriedly collected their few possessions. I looked beside my bed. There were a few newspapers, a knitted jacket Dr Oppenheimer had given me and my battered old suitcase. I didn't need any of it. I left it all behind as I watched the others line up behind Chief Nurse Huber.

'All right, children, follow me now,' Chief Nurse Huber said. Had she been playing a pipe she would have looked just like the Pied Piper.

Blindly, obediently, they followed. The younger ones even skipped as we went outside and were ordered to stop at the top of the gravel driveways. We stood, waiting, as the summer sun beat down on our backs. I felt as if I was in a furnace. Beads of sweat formed on my forehead, and I wiped them away with my forearm.

Two buses lumbered up the hilly driveway from the direction of Hadamar town. We were ordered to move forward as the buses motored past us, then stand at the entrance to the fences leading down into the cellar. The two buses pulled up beside us and I didn't need to see through the blackened windows to know what was inside. The bus doors squeaked open and the doctors began unloading children and ordering them to line up.

Were it not for the fact we were in a Nazi mental asylum, the whole scene could have just been teachers taking their students on an excursion. When the last of the children were offloaded, we were ordered to join the back of their lines. Children on stretchers were brought down from the closest bus and, while we waited, I watched two grey-uniformed men feed a long pipe through a side window. Another fixed a gas bottle to the end of the pipe while a fourth man fiddled with knobs and gauges on top of the gas bottle. I turned back to the children in front of me and tried counting them, but I couldn't see them all. At best guess there was at least one hundred.

The children on the stretchers and the children who struggled to walk by themselves were the first to be taken through a steel door. Ten, maybe fifteen minutes passed. The heat intensified and I was sweating profusely. Beyond the cellar roof, smoke rose from the chimney stacks. As if he had been waiting for this smoke signal, the tall doctor began separating the boys and girls into lines. In doing so, he came close to me, his white collar slipping down his neck, enough to reveal the double, lightning-shaped 'S' insignia.

I knew the end was near. Like Vati had taught me, I was going to be strong until the last. I knew the other children did not share my courage. I could feel the fear seeping out from their pores. Suddenly, I felt as if I had left my body, as if I was someone else watching the scene playing out before me. I wasn't confused. I wasn't scared. I knew exactly what was about to happen.

'Girls to the left, boys to the right!' the SS doctor shouted as he made his way back to the front. We marched a few feet until the first girl stood in front of the opening between the two fences, while the boys were marched around to the far side of the building.

'*Ausziehen*! Move!' Chief Nurse Huber yelled. The sweetness in her voice had been replaced with a chilling harshness. She was helping the SS men herd us through the sluice fences as if we were cattle. Once I was inside the sluice, the wire gate was shut and locked behind me.

We were led down a small flight of stairs and into the cellar, a heavy steel door clanking loudly as it shut behind me. Inside the cellar it was pitch black. I heard a loud clicking sound and the room lit up. Momentarily blinded, I fumbled my way forward as we were pushed into a room full of identical cubicles, each with a wooden hook sticking out from the centre of the back wall. Each girl stood in front of a cubicle and waited to be told what to do next.

'*Gesicht links*!' the tall SS doctor ordered. We faced left. 'Undress!'

We removed our clothes and placed them on the cubicle benches. The other girls crouched over, covering themselves as best they could with their hands and arms. I stood tall. My virtue didn't seem to matter anymore.

'Face forward and follow the nurse!' the tall SS doctor ordered.

Chief Nurse Huber stood in a doorway, stepping out of the way as she indicated that we were to walk through it. The other girls scurried along, several almost tripping over as they tried in vain to conceal themselves. I marched past with my head held high.

'*Halt*!' said an older man, who wore a *Kriminalpolizei* uniform.

The line of girls immediately stopped. The *Kripo* man knotted his hands behind his back as he ambled towards me.

'Mmm,' he said as he looked me up and down. 'Seems a shame to waste this black one,' he said to no-one in particular before he placed his hand in the square of my back and pushed me into the next room. The other girls were gathered in the centre, standing above a drain in the middle of a white-tiled floor. Standing guard in a circle around them were several doctors and nurses, including the SS doctors and Chief Nurse Huber. On the far right side of the room, two clerks with thick-rimmed glasses sat at two desks, yellow folders placed in front of them, pens poised in their right hands.

Chief Nurse Huber and the tall doctor grabbed girls at random and steered them towards the desks. The clerks asked a series of questions and recorded each girl's responses. When the clerks were done a doctor standing behind each desk checked the girls over with their stethoscopes. I was the last one.

'Name, place and date of birth,' the clerk asked.

'Ingrid Marchand, 6 March 1924, Mainz.'

'Have you ever had any diseases such as tuberculosis, typhus or any fevers of any kind?'

'*Nein*,' I lied. I had a fever once but only because of what they did to me.

'Over there,' he said coldly, pointing at one of the doctors with his pencil.

The doctor gave me a cursory examination before he pointed in the direction of the other girls, who were shuffling back towards the cubicles. By the time I entered they had all lined up at their original cubicle awaiting instructions. Chief Nurse Huber told us to split our clothes and personal items into separate piles. She and another nurse labelled everybody's possessions before stamping each girl's back with a number which matched a piece of paper that they put on top of each girl's items.

'Once you have been disinfected in the showers,' Chief Nurse Huber hollered. 'You will come back out here and collect the belongings that match the numbers on your backs.'

With that we were ordered back into the white-tiled room. The clerks were gone, replaced with two of the pretty young nurses. One stood with a measuring stick in her hand; the other stood next to a set of scales. The first girls stepped forward, were measured and weighed, then were instructed to head through a door to the right. After we were weighed and measured, we were moved down a corridor into a completely white room. It was empty except for a single man standing at an enormous tripod upon which was a camera with a huge flash bulb.

One by one, the girls were lined up against the far wall for a photograph. I covered my breasts, aghast. I couldn't believe they would photograph us in this state. The girls were crying and whimpering and trying to hide their nakedness. Then they were sent into an adjacent room, where they stayed for a few minutes before they came back out again.

When it came to my turn, I entered the tiny room and found only a doctor seated at a desk with a nurse standing beside him. It didn't make sense why there was yet *another* doctor. They asked me more of the same questions about my health. Did I know if I had ever had tuberculosis or any other major illness? Had I suffered from typhus? Did I ever have fevers when I was young? I told them I was perfectly healthy. The doctor instructed me to open my mouth. I resisted but he roughly grasped my jaws and forced them to open. Bowing his head close to me he checked my teeth as if I was a horse at a sale yard. Satisfied, he snapped my mouth closed and made two markings on my right biceps. I returned to the other girls who were huddled together in one group.

'*Raus*! Out!' Chief Nurse Huber ordered as she pushed me then the others towards a door opposite the one through which we had entered. The first two girls disappeared from my sight. Moments later they came rushing back out, knocking into Chief Nurse Huber and several other girls in the process. They ran through towards the cubicles then disappeared. Two uniformed SS men came running after them and vanished through the same door. Seconds later we heard four loud bangs.

'Move!' one of the SS men ordered as he waved his unholstered gun in the direction of the door. Driven at gunpoint, we shuffled along in tiny steps towards a large shower block. Standing next to the entrance was Nurse Willig, his face wearing the same sadistic smile he'd had on the day he came to take Erich. He handed out pencils and postcards. Confused, the girls flicked the postcards over. I looked at the one he gave me. There was a picture of Hadamar town, the fairy-tale castle, the white painted houses, the rolling green hills. When I turned it over the other side was blank, except for a Hadamar postmark.

I looked up at Nurse Willig.

'Write to your parents,' he ordered, an instruction that was clearly meant for all of us. 'Tell them you are here and safe and say something about what a good time you are having.'

One girl wrote furiously, as if composing a masterpiece would save her. I handed mine back to him.

'There's nothing on it,' he said, looking at me quizzically. I glared back at him.

'Okay,' he said as he returned the card to the bottom of the pile. 'Suit yourself.'

He collected the postcards and pencils. Satisfied, he nodded to the SS men, who waved their guns in the direction of the shower. They forced us into two lines. A wave of fear rippled through us. I could see the girls shaking as trickles of golden liquid pooled on the floor beneath them.

I watched them closely. I may have felt nothing. I may have accepted my fate, but the way they shook made me feel for them.

I traced my eyes over my chocolate brown skin. I knew why I was here. It was the same with the heavily disabled children they had brought in on the stretchers. I hated myself for thinking it, but it didn't seem to matter now; those children might be better off dead. If God – if He existed – was turning a blind eye to what was happening in Hadamar, surely He could not turn those children away from the gates of Heaven itself. These girls in front of me, though, were *not* disabled. They didn't deserve to be here. They didn't deserve to die.

'Forward!' a deep voice bellowed.

I recognised it as Dr Klein's: the doctor who had examined me when I'd first arrived. Had I had any illusions of survival, knowing he was here meant they were now gone. I had only spoken to him on a few occasions since our first meeting, but I knew *he* was the one most responsible for the disappearing children and mental patients. *He* was the one who ordered, and signed off on, people's deaths.

'Are you ready, *Herr Doktor*?' the tall SS doctor asked Dr Klein.

He gave an almost imperceptible nod.

'*Raus*, into the showers,' the tall SS doctor ordered.

Two enormous steel doors, each of which had a circular window in the centre, clanged shut behind us. I turned around at the loud banging of a metal bar as it was dropped into the lock. The other girls clung to each other for comfort but I stood alone, circling around as I examined my surroundings. Above the door was a line of black electrical wires. Next to them was a white cylindrical pipe leading directly to a window with two doors, almost square in shape except for a slight rise on the top. Beyond them were two steel poles that extended from wall to wall like parallel bars.

The other girls were now huddled tightly together, their scrawny bodies entwined like sickly trees. The end of the pipe I had seen the men outside feeding through the frosted, cross-hatched window lay on the floor beneath them. It had a series of holes along it. The walls were covered in white tiles. There was a water pipe running along the join between the ceiling and the furthest white-tiled wall until it turned at right-angles to form an L-shape. At the base of the L-shape was a black shower head. There was a pipe running across the centre of the roof, connecting to a network of pipes. Along each pipe were two smaller shower nozzles.

I looked down at the floor. It was black-and-white checked, like a huge chessboard. A buzzing, tapping noise started, which sounded like the bus engines starting again. The lights were switched off. The girls panicked and screamed. I stumbled away from them, towards the door through which we had come. I stared through the windows. I wanted the last thing they saw to be the hatred in my eyes. The doctors, the SS men and the *Kripo* man had their faces pressed up against the glass, peering through as if we were nothing more than animals in a zoo.

Another loud click. Then another. My thoughts turned to Mutti, Vati, Sarah, Fräulein Rothenberg. I wondered what Heaven might be like as I tried to take one last deep breath. It was impossible. The air was too thin. The other girls' screams turned to gargles as they gasped for air. Some collapsed to the floor, their mouths wide open, their chests heaving from the effort of trying to force air into their lungs. The sound of another generator starting echoed through the room. More girls collapsed to the floor.

It took all my strength to force the last of the air into my lungs. My knees wobbled. My head whirled. I kept my eyes fixed on the windows and, through the last flickers of my eyelids, I thought I saw Dr Oppenheimer's face in the window, red, twisted and contorted as he shouted. Then I collapsed. The world went black. For a moment I thought I was dead. The excruciating pain radiating through my lungs told me I wasn't.

'*Warte ab! Warte ab*! Wait! Wait!' I thought I heard someone shouting. Starved of oxygen, my mind was playing tricks on me. Suddenly, the locks creaked and the doors grated open. Moments passed and it felt slightly easier to breath. I heard footsteps. Opening my eyes, ever so slightly, I saw a blurry figure.

I tried to scream but I couldn't get enough air in my lungs. I tried to lift my arms but, weakened as I was, they flopped limply back onto the tiles. My eyelids flickered. My vision alternated between light and dark. I thought I saw Dr Oppenheimer standing beside me, holding a handkerchief over his mouth, standing dejectedly, his shoulders slumped as he looked at me then around the room. I sucked in as much air as I could and whispered, '*Herr Doktor*.'

'Ingrid!' he cried as he fell to his knees. I felt his hands wrap around my body and neck as he lifted me up, held me like a limp ragdoll in his arms, and ran from the shower block. I heard the steel doors close and the lock shut behind us.

'*Herr Doktor*,' I heard Dr Klein say. 'You have your papers guaranteeing this girl's life but, if you will be moving along, we have business to conclude here.'

'*Ja, ja*,' Dr Oppenheimer snapped.

'*Herr Doktor*', another man laughed, 'if you are saving this girl for what I think you are saving her for, you'd better be careful. The penalties are very severe for *Rassenschande* these days!'

The sound of laughter faded away. I could taste the fresh air as I rapidly breathed in and out and the oxygen streamed back into my lungs.

'The others. We have to save the others,' I whispered.

'I'm sorry, Ingrid, I only have permission to save you,' Dr Oppenheimer whispered back.

'The others! The others!' I gurgled.

'Ingrid,' he whispered again. 'It's too late. I have to get you into the fresh air. I have to check you over.'

I caught glimpses of the cubicles as we passed by. My vision became clearer and I saw the sluice fences. The harshness of the light outside burnt my eyes. All I could make out was two silhouettes walking towards us.

'She is with me! Here, I have the papers,' I heard Dr Oppenheimer say. 'You see, signed by Dr Brandt himself.'

I had never heard of a Dr Brandt but, as I had just discovered, there were more doctors involved with Hadamar than I had realised. Whoever Dr Brandt was, the mention of his name was enough to allow us free passage back inside the main building. Dr Oppenheimer took me to my bed and lay me down. He dressed me in a white robe and then lifted me up again.

'The air is too stale in here,' he said. 'I need to get you outside. You need fresh air.'

I didn't want to move. I wanted to sleep – forever.

'Just … give me … five minutes … to rest,' I stammered.

'You can sleep when I say you can sleep,' he said as he picked me up again and took me from the ward. 'Right now, you need to be outside.'

Carrying me through the halls and corridors he headed to the back gardens where Chief Nurse Huber took us for our picnics. My sight gradually returned. I watched the even rows of irises and daffodils pass me by. They had never been so beautiful. The reds, yellows and purples seemed brighter and more colourful than anything I had ever seen. He carried me towards the gigantic pine trees whose pointy tips reached like fingers into the blue sky above. I heard the buzzing of the bees, the chirping of the sparrows, magnified a hundred-fold.

'Here – sit here, Ingrid,' Dr Oppenheimer said as he placed me down on a dark green bench hidden away under pines at the rear of the second level of gardens.

'You are one lucky girl,' he sighed as he slumped down next to me, his adrenaline wearing off, the effort of carrying me now taking its toll.

'*Ja, ja, danke* for saving me, I guess,' I responded nonchalantly as I gingerly bent down and picked up a dandelion from near my feet and began twirling it in my fingers.

'Ingrid, you were just gassed with carbon monoxide! If I had arrived a few minutes later you'd be dead!'

'Did you ever think that maybe I wanted to die? Did you ever think that maybe I would be better off that way?'

'Ingrid, how can you say that?' he said.

'What do you mean?' I turned on him, furious. 'This is what you doctors do here: you kill people! You dispose of us like garbage! What life do I have here? None. You won't let me go home to my Mutti. I don't even know if she is alive. Even if the war ever ends what life will I have when that happens? I loved my Vati and your people took him away from me! I loved my Mutti and you took me away from her! I loved Erich and you killed him!'

'Stop, Ingrid!' he growled. '*I* didn't do any of those things. There is much about what is happening here that you do not understand.'

'I understand your job, your reason to be here: to kill children.'

He sucked in a sharp breath before sighing heavily. 'Ingrid, I have never directly killed a child. Like everyone else, I do what I have to do to survive. The reason I have been away so long is because I have been trying to guarantee your safety. I came to find you to tell you that I had but, when you were nowhere to be found, I asked some of the soldiers if they had seen you. None of them had. Fortunately for you, one of the male patients in the kitchen said he had seen a group of children on their way to a picnic.'

'How did you know we were in the showers?'

He paused and turned his head away from me. 'I ... I looked out to the gardens here, there was no-one, and I thought a mistake might have been made and you were taken away with the other children.'

'A mistake! A *mistake*! Of course killing people is a mistake! Hundreds of boys and girls are dead. Don't you get that? They are dead and *I* am alive! You don't understand what it's like to live here day in, day out. You can come and go as you please. You don't have to watch children arriving one day and dying the next!'

He put his elbows on his knees and stared at the ground. I had lost control of my emotions and everything I had pent up for so long came flooding out. 'Sure, you saved me once but what happens the next time when you're not here? What happens when they decide to take me to the crucifix bed and inject me the way they did Erich? What happens when they send me back to the showers or put me in one of the black-windowed buses and take me somewhere else? People in here, kids in here, they're like this dandelion,' I cried as I blew the moon-shaped clumps of seeds and scattered them to the wind. 'We're nameless! We don't matter! They kill us – and nobody cares!'

'*I* care – about you, anyway,' he said as he ran his fingers through his hair. 'But, in a way, I *am* responsible for those girls and boys dying. That was why I was sent here, to oversee the construction of those gas chambers.'

My mind was still muddled but I knew the magnitude of what he had just said.

'*What? You* designed them? You *murderer*!' I bawled as I tried to stand up and run away from him. It was no use; my legs were still too weak. Like a dying flower, I wilted back onto the bench.

'Ingrid, I only designed them,' he pleaded. 'I have never ordered any children to be injected nor sent into the showers. Let me explain a few things. There is not going to be a next time. These papers I used to save your life are signed by Dr Karl Brandt himself – the head of the T-4 program. Your life is safe – I promise! I don't expect you to understand, but I have to do the work I do here. It's only because of what I've done that I was able to guarantee your safety. You are, as you said, like the seeds of the dandelion – but your seed will fly away and, some day, it will land, grow and become a beautiful flower.'

'Your work! Your work! You mean that all those other girls had to die so I could live?'

'I try not to think of it that way. Ingrid, the world has gone mad and a God-almighty mess has been created. When it's all over, I want to be able to say that something good came out of it all.'

'By keeping me alive in a place that's taking away my soul, piece by piece?'

Realising I was not going to come around to his way of thinking, he let out a resigned sigh as he pushed off his knees and stood up. 'Come, I think you've had enough air. You need to rest now.'

Softening my voice and sweetening my tone, I asked, 'Can't we wait just a little longer?'

'*Ja*,' he smiled. 'But only for a few minutes. The other doctors and nurses won't like it that I've saved you. They can't kill you, but I don't want to give them an excuse to make your life a misery.'

'My life is already a misery,' I said as I took in a fresh, deep breath, arched my head upwards and watched the white, fluffy clouds rolling across the sky. I took more deep breaths before I tried to stand. Dr Oppenheimer reached out to help me but I brushed him off.

'*Nein*, I want to do it,' I said.

Several times I stumbled and almost fell as we walked back inside. I didn't mind. I wanted to make this fleeting feeling of freedom last as long as I could. Overwhelmed by all that had transpired, when I reached my bed I collapsed onto it.

'I have to get back to work,' Dr Oppenheimer said as he pulled my blanket up over me, tucking me in as if he were my father. I wanted sleep to take me over, to rest for all eternity, but my troubled mind would not let me. I drew my knees to my chest and watched the *Herr Doktor* walk away until he disappeared from view.

I was awash with guilt. I was alive, but what about the lives of hundreds – perhaps thousands – of others. My chest felt constricted, as if a great weight had been placed on it. I struggled to get air. I started to breathe too rapidly. I forced myself to sit up and leant against my pillow in an attempt to open up my lungs.

Breathing more freely now, I looked around the ward. Apart from me, it was empty. Why had they even bothered selecting people if they were just going to kill them all anyway? I knew the answer to my question before I had even asked it: it was all a sadistic game to them.

A lone owl hooted from the oak tree outside. It echoed eerily through the vacant ward.

I had never felt so lonely.

I lay down and tried to sleep, but each time I closed my eyes all I could see was visions of the other girls' lifeless bodies and staring eyes.

I couldn't think of anything else but the black and white floor of the showers, the emaciated girls huddled together before they fell to the floor, their thin, helpless bodies struggling to breathe.

Exhaustion finally took hold and I fell into an uneasy sleep only to wake in the middle of the night coughing. When it subsided I was unable to get back to sleep so I sat with my back against my pillow and stared around the ward. The dull humming of the lights was my only company and I suddenly realised I *was* glad to be alive. I had begged for death, prayed for the Grim Reaper to come and take me away from this hell but when I'd stared Death in the face, Death had told me that now was not my time. There was much to live for – or so I hoped. Someday, I *was* going to get out of here and I would try to make the most of my life. I knew now that the best way to show my defiance, to get justice for all the children who had died, was to stay alive. They had tried to kill me and failed. Now, I was determined to *live*.

I realised I had been naïve. I had not seen the truth of things when the truth was right in front of me. I needed to know why Dr Oppenheimer had saved me. Why had he chosen *me* to be the one to live? What were his intentions? What exactly did he want to do with me? What had I done to earn my life when all the others had been left to die?

I needed to find him. I needed answers. I slid out of bed and tip-toed down the ward, unsure if my legs were steady enough to walk and unsure of where the staff might be. My legs felt okay but the whole sanatorium seemed unusually quiet, haunted by the phantoms and ghosts of murdered children. At the end of the ward I warily checked the male and female nurses' offices. Chief Nurse Huber's office was empty. Nurse Ruoff's office was empty. Perhaps they were off somewhere, celebrating their dastardly work. Momentarily, I contemplated escape, but my legs were too weak. I wouldn't get far.

As soon as I set foot in the corridor, one of the male orderlies suddenly came marching from the direction of the foyer, stopping halfway between the front desk and the main exit. I waited for him to see me, to order me back to bed, but he continued on to the front desk, sat down and began reading a newspaper. I headed into the depths of the right wing, towards Dr Oppenheimer's office. In the stairwell that led up to the men's wards, I could hear soft moaning.

I continued down the corridor where lights spilled out from some of the doctors' offices. I peeked inside each one as I crept past. There were doctors – ones I didn't know – seated at desks, scribbling away with stacks of paperwork either side of them.

Hidden in the semi-darkness, I walked as quickly as I could towards Dr Oppenheimer's office. He sat engrossed in his paperwork, like the others. A large stack of papers sat on the left-hand side of his desk. On the right was a similar pile, except it was a fraction of the size. He retrieved a piece of paper from the left pile, scribbled on it, and placed it on the right-hand pile. I crept into the room and began reading over his shoulder. With a start, I realised what he was signing. The papers were death certificates.

'Ingrid!' Dr Oppenheimer cried as he jumped in the air and put his hand on his heart. 'You startled me!'

He dashed out into the corridor, checking that his outburst hadn't aroused any unwanted attention. Satisfied it hadn't, he returned and sat back down.

'Ingrid, what on earth are you doing here? You know these offices are *verboten*.'

'I...couldn't sleep...I started coughing again,' I stammered, struggling to keep my voice steady. 'I wanted you to check me over. What…what…are these?' I asked as I picked up a certificate and began reading it.

'It is to go in *Das Sterbebuch*: the Death Book.'

'There is a Death Book?'

'*Ja*, and *ein Krankenbuch*, the Book of Patients.'

Disgusted, yet strangely intrigued, I read the death certificate:

Klaus Hoffen.

Day of death: 15 July 1941.

Time of death: 18.30 Uhr.

Cause of death: Pneumonia.

Name of physician: Dr Hans Oppenheimer.

Place of death: Hadamar Psychiatric Hospital.

'I knew Klaus!' I protested. 'I spoke to him just the other day. He did not have pneumonia.'

'Ingrid, keep your voice down,' Dr Oppenheimer grumbled. I ignored him, instead picking up another certificate:

Sofia Ana Lieberenz.

Day of death: 16 July 1941.

Time of death: 20.30 Uhr.

Cause of death: Pneumonia.

Name of physician: Dr Hans Oppenheimer.

Place of death: Hadamar Psychiatric Hospital.

Reading more of the certificates, I recognised many of the names, but many more I didn't. Tuberculosis, appendicitis – the causes of death went on.

'These are all lies!' I blurted out as I slammed a certificate on the table. 'The doctors and nurses murdered them and you helped them!'

'Ingrid, please, keep your voice down. If you get me in trouble, and I am transferred, I doubt that I will be able to protect you, Dr Brandt's signature or not.'

Despite my outrage, I knew if I stayed as angry as I was, he wouldn't give me any of the answers I so desperately desired.

'Sorry,' I said bitterly. I noticed a pile of letters on the desk; I picked one from the top and read:

Dear Frau Hoffen, we regret to inform you that our patient died suddenly and unexpectedly of acute pneumonia on 15 July 1941. While it is regrettable that your son died you must regard his death as a form of deliverance.

I tried to picture the parents' reactions when they received these letters. Were they even shocked? Had they forgotten about their children, like I thought Mutti had forgotten about me? Perhaps they never came to visit nor sent any letters. Perhaps they agreed that their child's death was a form of deliverance.

Once I had asked Chief Nurse Huber how all of this had started. At first she told me to shut up and mind my own business. Then she said she couldn't tell me because she had a medical responsibility not to do so. Clearly this piece of gossip was too juicy to keep to herself, however, for a few days later she took me to one side and told me. After all, I wasn't going anywhere, so who was I going to tell?

She told me that there was a couple from a village called Pommsenn, near Leipzig. They were simple farm folk, she had said: the most ardent of Nazis. They had written to *Der Führer* himself to ask if he would grant a 'mercy killing' to their son, a blind and mentally disabled boy with no legs and only one arm. 'The Monster', his father called him. Hitler had sent one of his personal physicians, the same Dr Brandt whose signature had saved me, to investigate.

Dr Brandt had labelled the boy an 'idiot' and this was enough to sign his death warrant. Hitler agreed that the boy – Gerhard, she thought his name was – should be killed. The doctors in Leipzig, though they knew it was illegal, were told that Hitler would have it thrown out of court should it ever go that far. So Gerhard Kretschmar died of 'heart weakness' and was buried in a Lutheran churchyard. These Nazi parents had not only condoned and allowed the killing of their own child but actively asked *Der Führer* himself for permission to do. This spoke volumes about the minds of some Germans.

'That is the letter we send to the parents of the deceased,' Dr Oppenheimer said.

'But this is a lie! You don't even refer to Klaus by name. Don't the families ask more questions? Do they even get the bodies back?'

In the back of my mind I knew that, if the parents considered *Gnadentod* a form of deliverance, then there would be no questions.

'We send them the ashes.'

I paused for a minute to let this sink in. 'If you and the people of Germany, think that killing us is a form of deliverance, why did you save *me*?'

'Ingrid, I have a lot of work to do. I will discuss this with you later.'

'*Nein*, we will discuss it now!' I said, deliberately raising my voice to force him to answer. But his reaction was not what I had expected. He reached into the top right pocket of his white coat and removed a piece of paper.

'Ingrid, if you do not quieten down I will tear this to shreds and you will burn with the next lot.'

The harshness and cruelty in his voice frightened me. What was this man truly capable of? Despite my determination to act like a woman, I reverted to a little girl; the tears streamed down my face and I ran back to my bed. Cuddling my pillow, I cried and cried, and coughed and coughed. I thought about the children who had been in these beds yesterday. I tried to picture their faces but I couldn't. They were nothing more than a collection of ashes in jars now. Whether it was the guilt of still being alive or the after-effects of the gas, I felt sickened to my stomach. Suddenly, I heard footsteps in the ward. Dr Oppenheimer's lanky frame appeared, striding towards me. I buried my head in my pillow and prayed he would go away.

'Ingrid,' he said as he sat on the side of my bed, his back pressing against my midriff as he put his hand on my shoulder. 'Are you asleep?'

'Go away! Leave me alone!' I said childishly.

'Why don't we go and sit under the oak tree in the courtyard. We will have some privacy there.'

Still unsure of his intentions, I didn't want to be alone with him. But what did it matter? I had resolved to do whatever it took to survive. I needed him as my ally, no matter what the cost. The springs of my bed creaked as he stood up. He hadn't ordered me to follow and, for a minute, I pondered staying put. However, there were still many questions I wanted answered so I got up and followed him. He ambled out into the courtyard, keeping his back to me as he stood in front of the oak tree and stared at the night sky. Even though I stood directly behind him he continued to stare upwards, waiting until I had sat down on the bench before he joined me. Night had settled in but the full moon illuminated the courtyard almost as if it were daytime. For several minutes we sat in silence. I tried to think of every reason why he might have saved me and only one thing came to mind. I remembered what they had said when he took me past them: *Rassenschande*. He had saved me because he considered me to be the prettiest one to save. He wanted a plaything while he was here.

'Did you save me because you find me attractive?

'What!' he exclaimed, shocked by my insinuations. 'What are you talking about?'

'I am the only young woman here, apart from the nurses, who is not disabled. Not that that seems to bother some of the others. I know what some of the male nurses – and even some of the doctors – do.'

'I am horrified that you would even think such a thing. I am a respected doctor with a wife and children. The thought has never crossed my mind,' he said. He sighed, rested his elbows on his knees and dropped his head. 'Ingrid, I was given two choices.'

'What do you mean?' I asked.

'I was given two choices. One: be sent to the Russian Front as a lead surgeon. Two: to use my connections with Dr Brandt to have me sent here. They ordered me to set up the showers. They told me that if I did not I would be sent to the east. I have three daughters, Ingrid, and my wife is sick and unable to work. I have to do something to feed them. I am no good to them dead.'

'But in order to save *your* family you are destroying others! You are killing children!' I shouted as I stood and paced the length of the courtyard. Was it selfish, what he had done? Was it right to contribute to acts of unspeakable evil to preserve your own family? I tried to imagine Vati in the same situation. Would he sacrifice others to save me? I wanted to think that he would not, but … I knew how much he loved me. Perhaps he would. I tried to hate the *Herr Doktor* for what he had said and done, but I couldn't.

'I have never directly participated in the killing of a child, Ingrid,' he said forlornly. 'I designed the gassing mechanisms and I do the paperwork. You *must* understand.'

Understand what? I thought as I paced and tried to convince myself to hate him. He was sacrificing the lives of thousands of children to save his own. Upon reaching the opposite wall I turned around and walked slowly back towards him. When I was close enough I whispered, 'It's a process, *Herr Doktor*. You didn't push them into the shower but you are still part of the process.'

'Ingrid, I saved you from a certain death,' he coldly reminded me.

'*Ja*,' I yelled. 'And you still haven't told me why!'

My voice bounced off the walls, the echo causing upstairs lights to come on.

'*Why*? Why did you save me?' I repeated more quietly.

'Do you really not understand?' he asked as reached up and put his hand on my cheek.

'You can do what you want to me. You and I both know I have no choice if you want to touch me.'

'Touch you?' he said as he snatched his hand away. '*Nein*, Ingrid, you have me all wrong. I saved you because you are *exactly* like my youngest daughter. *Ja*, I am here. *Ja*, I have to do things I do not like and I do not agree with, but I am here. How can I go back to see my youngest daughter, any of my daughters for that matter, if *all* I do is assist in the killing of people each day? At least, if I save you, if I save *one child*, I can go home to my family and have enough of my shame erased to at least look them in the eyes.'

His eyes implored me to believe him. In the moonlight I could see them welling with tears. He was begging for my approval, perhaps even my forgiveness. I was still reconciling my feelings about him and I was in no mood to forgive. 'So, saving me was not about me at all, but yourself.'

'You are very wise, Ingrid. But do my reasons for saving you matter? Isn't your *life* the thing that matters?'

'Until yesterday I didn't care whether I lived or died,' I said as I sat back down beside him. 'But after surviving the showers I now realise I want to live. But if I had to die so thousands could live, I would gladly do so.'

'Ingrid, if you die it will accomplish nothing.'

'And if I survive, what life will I have, especially if we *win* the war? Of all the girls you could have saved, you saved *me*. *Herr Doktor*, your decision may prove to be a waste.'

'It will be no waste. Germany won't win the war, and when it ends I'll need someone to tell the Americans and the Russians what went on here. I need someone to tell them that I didn't kill anyone. It may be selfish but, when the time comes, I'll need someone to save me from the hangman's noose,' he said. Then he raised himself from the bench and walked back inside. I sat there staring up at the stars. I wished I could believe him that the war would end, but I doubted that I would ever leave Hadamar or be around long enough to tell anyone anything.

CHAPTER 6

A SICK CELEBRATION

August 1941

In the following weeks I only saw Dr Oppenheimer twice: once when the physicians ordered that all of the remaining children have physical examinations and once, in passing, at dinnertime. Throughout the summer my health had improved but as the weather turned colder, my coughing worsened. I could still do my daily chores, but I often found myself short of breath; I was always careful, however, not to let the staff notice me struggling lest I be branded *Lebensunswerte Leben*. Dr Oppenheimer's absences were disconcerting because, despite his guarantees, my ill health made me live every moment in fear. I was constantly looking over my shoulder.

Each day, as I swept and changed the beds of the upstairs wards, I watched the grey buses coming and going. Hundreds upon hundreds of children were unloaded and sent into the showers. My heart hurt as I watched them standing there, confused, before they were led away like lambs to the slaughter. Yet there was always a small piece of my heart that was glad it wasn't me. I hated myself for feeling like this.

Not all the new arrivals went to the showers; sometimes there were too many to kill in one go. The wards filled with more children, many of whom were more physically deformed than the children who had first been here.

Chief Nurse Huber told me in no uncertain terms that neither she nor any of the senior staff wanted anything to do with these children. The junior nurses and I were told that we must feed, bathe and change these 'useless' children. Existence for these children was a daily routine of suffering. I could hear their gurgled cries of pain like a sickening symphony as I swept and cleaned. When I changed their bedding or turned them over they cried out as if I was stabbing them with knives.

I found it difficult to sleep; I was haunted by my dreams. Every night I relived what had happened. The heavy clatter of the steel doors and the lock as they closed. The naked bodies of the girls huddled together. The clicks as the gassing mechanism kicked into life. The humming of the engines outside. The smaller ones the first to cough. The older ones embracing the younger ones in a vain attempt to protect them. Then the dead bodies, limp and lifeless on the black-and-white floor.

Sometimes I thought I heard their screams. Children running this way and that. Sometimes I thought I could hear the crunching of their nails as they clawed at the floor. I dreamed of children clasping at their throats as the last of their breath left them, their faces contorted as their lips turned blue and their eyes bulged from their sockets. I dreamed of the room piled with corpses. The doctors and nurses entering to check that they were truly dead. I pictured them kneeling beside the bodies and putting their fingers to their throats as they searched for a pulse.

I had seen the chimneys, the stacks belching out acrid black smoke for hours on end. Some days I thought I saw the faces of the dead children floating away in the plumes of smoke. Only in the worst of my dreams did I imagine how they disposed of the bodies. I dreamed that after the gassings the male mental patients would enter the showers and load the bodies onto trolleys. They would take them into the crematorium and push the bodies into the oven. The children's corpses would burst into flames, the stench of burning fat filling the air. No matter how hard I tried to forget, the spectre of death followed me everywhere.

One day, when I had a few moments' rest after breakfast, I retrieved an old copy of *Das Reich* from under my bed and read through it once more. I knew Vati would not be in there, but part of me always thought I had missed something and that if I looked hard enough, I would find him. But I found only articles that I had seen before. It may have been nothing more than Nazi propaganda, but I felt the need to keep some contact with the outside world – to have some idea of what was going on outside Hadamar – for I feared that if I didn't, the last thread of my sanity would disappear.

Footsteps came down the ward, but I did not dare look up.

'Hello, Ingrid.'

Dr Oppenheimer stood in front of my bed, then he moved to Erich's old bed and placed a package wrapped in brown paper tied with twine on it.

'Hello, *Herr Doktor*,' I said, emotionless.

'Ingrid, I'm sorry I haven't been here,' he said in a fatherly tone as he sat by the package. 'But I was ordered by the highest ranking of Party members to perform some very important work. They are not the type of people I can say no to.'

I wasn't sure how I felt about him. He had come to be my protector but, equally, I knew he was an integral part of the system and I hated him for it.

'Where have you been?' I asked. I may have been unsure of my feelings about him, but he did hold my life in his hands and there was some comfort in having him around.

'Those same people to whom I cannot say no also decree that I cannot tell you where I have been. Look, I brought you a stack of newspapers,' he said as he reached for the bundle. He started to hand them to me then pulled them back. 'Ingrid, I want you to promise me one thing.'

'*Ja*, what is it?' I asked as I eyed the bundle, more interested in having something new to read than what he had to say.

'The Nazis, all of them, but particularly the highest-ranking ones – Hitler, Hess, Himmler, Goering – all of them are insane,' he whispered. 'The whole country has gone completely crazy. There is no telling where this absurdity will end.'

'But you're a Nazi. Are you telling me you're insane too?' I said flippantly.

'You don't understand, Ingrid; the world beyond these walls is not what you remember,' he said as he handed me the bundle. I tore the cover off it and looked at the date on the top right corner of the top newspaper. March 1941. I had been in Hadamar for three years! I had left home as an adolescent girl and now I was almost a fully-grown woman. Days, months, years had lost all meaning here. I had missed two birthdays and I had not even realised.

'They should be the ones in Hadamar,' I said. 'Hitler, Hess, Goering, they should all be sent to the showers.'

Dr Oppenheimer laughed, a little too boisterously. 'That is what makes the world nonsensical, Ingrid. A Reich run by insane people is murdering thousands upon thousands of children for being insane. Germany will not win this war, I promise you that, and there will be repercussions. The Russians, the Americans, will look to point fingers. Never mind what our great Führer says. Rest assured we will lose and when that time comes I want you to swear that you will tell them how I saved you.'

'Okay,' I said.

'Ingrid, *promise* me that when the time comes you will tell them that I saved you!'

'*Ja, Herr Doktor*, I promise I will,' I said as I crossed my heart.

'*Danke*,' he said as he stood, kissed me on the forehead and walked away.

I returned to the newspaper on the top of the pile. According to *Das Reich*, the German armies were rampaging through Europe and defeating anyone and everyone. The Nazis all but controlled the entirety of Western Europe and parts of Eastern Europe too. Despite what Dr Oppenheimer had just said, I couldn't see how we could possibly lose.

It was a stifling hot summer's day. Chief Nurse Huber came and ordered me to sweep the courtyards because, she said, my black skin meant that I was the least likely to suffer from the heat. It was hot in Africa, she told me, so this should be like a spring day to me. I reminded her that I had never been to Africa so I wouldn't know. It was in my genetics, she said, and so was talking back, something I needed to learn not to do. As I swept the last of the leaves that had blown into the courtyard beside my bed, the heat finally started to get to me. I rubbed the sweat from my brow and took a deep breath. The air smelled sickly. I looked up – all I could see was thick, black plumes of smoke. The sky was almost completely darkened. Ash began to rain down, blanketing the trees and benches in the courtyard like a winter's snow. The scent of death blew through Hadamar and I pulled my blouse over my nose and went inside, shutting the doors and windows behind me. Even still, it took a great deal of self-control to not throw up.

I sat on my bed and stared out the windows at the melancholic sky. I wondered how many places like Hadamar were scattered throughout Germany. I was certain of several more but, given Dr Oppenheimer's lengthy absences, there had to be dozens, maybe hundreds. I wondered where the Nazis would stop. My life had made two things clear. First: they hated anyone who was different and, second: they were prepared to do whatever it took, however immoral, to 'cleanse' the country. If they and the people of Germany were prepared to allow and deliver *Gnadentod* to the country's own children, there was no telling how far they would go.

I had only survived this long through fortune and fluke. The colour of my skin should have condemned me to death long ago. It was then, as I watched the black smoke twirling into the atmosphere before it disappeared, that I finally admitted to myself that Vati was dead. I wanted to cry. I tried to, but there were no tears. My hope of a joyous family reunion had always kept me going, but I knew now that this would never be. I knew I was never leaving Hadamar. One way or another they would find a way to kill me.

I suddenly felt desperate for company – any company. The ward was unnervingly quiet and almost empty, but it sounded as if someone was laughing at me. It was the dead children, happy as they rested in peace, mocking the fact that I still lived. This was it. All I had seen, all that had been done to me, had made me lose my mind. The ward went silent again, except for the sound of the chirping crickets outside. Then the laughter returned, more boisterous than before. I rose from my bed, braved the stench outside, and went back out into the courtyard. The laughter was gone.

Back inside I checked every bed, every crammed-in bunk, certain there was a mental patient hiding away somewhere who was lost in their own world, laughing at something I would never know or understand. The closer I came to the ward entrance, the louder the laughter became. I crept towards Chief Nurse Huber's office.

It and all the others were empty. Spurred on by my desire to prove to myself that I wasn't going crazy, I continued on. The sound of laughter became louder and louder, mixed in with exuberant cheers and shouting.

As if pulled along by some unseen force, I floated into the bowels of Hadamar. Past the offices, past the medical rooms, past the dining hall and kitchen I moved unseen until I came to a dead end, where a huge wall barred my way. Confused, I looked from side to side and ran my hands along the stones. They were ice cold. There was no mistaking the laughter and the voices now, but where were they coming from? I was about to turn around and continue my search elsewhere when I noticed a crack of light emanating from the bottom corner at the join of the two walls. Slowly moving my hand towards the light, I found a gap between the walls which was, surprisingly, large enough for me to fit through. Putting my foot out as if I was testing water, I found a solid base for my foot.

Step by step, I made my way down a spiral staircase. The light intensified, until I came to a small room with electric lights hanging from the ceiling. Stacked against the wall were crates of wine and beer. In between these were potato sacks and bags of bread. Suddenly, silence fell. I contemplated rushing back up the stairs, back to the safety of the ward, but the laughter soon resumed and I needed to know its source. I crept towards the far wall, placed my back up against it and edged towards the opening. Straining my neck, I peered around the wall.

I had only seen him twice before. Herr Schmidt. The man who

outranked Dr Klein. He was in charge of administration and, therefore, in charge of Hadamar. He was a very important man, Nurse Huber said – always away here and there on official Party business. I was glad of it. I had heard horrible stories about him from Erich. Erich said that Herr Schmidt was a pretend Nazi, always strutting around the place, fully dressed in his SS uniforms as if he was one of the highest ranking of them, threatening to shoot people on a whim as if he was Heinrich Himmler himself. He stood in the middle of at least a dozen staff, a glass of champagne in his hand, a wry smile on his face.

Behind him stood Dr Klein. A lit cigarette hung from his mouth, and he held a bottle in his right hand and a glass in his left. Next to him and slightly in front was an unfamiliar man, dressed in a black SS uniform, his arm wrapped around one of the younger nurses as he whispered in her ear. The sight of him, Herr Schmidt and Dr Klein all together made me shudder. I doubted there had been three more evil men ever standing together. The man I knew as the gravedigger, Herr Blum, hugged one of the older nurses; considering his state of drunkenness, he might have been using her to keep himself standing. Beyond them, a man was playing an accordion.

Herr Schmidt suddenly raised a hand and the music stopped. 'Friends! It is time!' Herr Schmidt announced.

Time? Time for what?

Herr Schmidt waved his hands in the direction of a door on the opposite side from where I hid in the darkness. He waited until they had all entered before he followed. When he had gone, I crept forward ever so cautiously. Beside the door was a tall cupboard which, when I pushed myself up against it, allowed me to see in but – I hoped – not be seen. Besides, they seemed too intoxicated, too enraptured in whatever they were celebrating to notice me.

I watched as they gathered around a stretcher in the centre of the room. On it lay the body of a dead man, perhaps in his late twenties, his skull unusually large, his forehead bulging as if someone had sewn a football into his head. One man dressed in black robes much like a priest's stood on the far side before leaning over the body. Herr Schmidt stood between me and the stretcher and, as he put his hands up to ask for their silence he moved sideways and obscured my view of the dead man.

'Charge your glasses!' he ordered. They each held up a champagne flute. The bang of a popping cork scared me half to death. I almost turned to run away but I was morbidly fascinated by the big-headed man and I had to see what they were about to do to him. Herr Blum finished filling their glasses before filling his own and taking his place in the circle that had formed around the dead man.

'To Hadamar!' Herr Schmidt said.

'To Hadamar!' they all repeated before they drank.

Struck numb by my fascination, I felt like I was in the audience of a ghoulish opera. It was then that I saw the ghastliest thing I had ever seen in my life; the moment from Hadamar that would haunt my dreams forever. The moment I realised that the people standing before me were not humans but monsters.

The gravedigger stood beside a large washtub. On the left of the washtub was a table covered in dozens of skulls, many of which still had remnants of human skin and hair hanging from them. Each member of the party retrieved a skull from the table, drinking as they waited patiently to take their turn. One by one, they took their skull to Herr Blum, who held it over the sink and cleaned it off with brushes before polishing it with rags. When he was satisfied, he handed the skull back and its bearer returned to the circle gathered around the big-headed man. When all the skulls were cleaned, Herr Schmidt reached underneath the stretcher and withdrew several bottles of beer. He opened them and handed them out.

Then each member of the party poured beer into the empty skulls.

'Friends!' Herr Schmidt slurred. 'Raise your glasses, for today is a momentous day! Today we have much to celebrate. This afternoon you all gazed into the skies. You all saw the black smoke drifting away and disappearing into the wind. That smoke, my friends, is the birth of a new Germany – a new Fatherland! That smoke is the mistakes, the wrongs among our people, disappearing forever. The more smoke we see, the greater the Third Reich becomes! Today marks the day when we reached our ten thousandth death! To our ten thousandth victim!'

'To our ten thousandth victim!' they all repeated as they held the skulls up and drank.

They refilled the skulls and sipped from them as they watched the man dressed as a priest give a muffled funeral oration. Then Herr Blum pushed the body off the stretcher and onto a semi-circular trolley that sat on rails like a small train. The gravedigger pushed the trolley towards a square-shaped enclosure. Inside the enclosure was a roaring fire.

Too shocked, horrified, disgusted and appalled by what was unfolding in front of me, I had not noticed the ovens, but now that I did, they chilled me to the bone; they were exactly as I had imagined in my dreams! My knees weakened. My body trembled and I knocked over a broom that leant up against the cupboard. The wooden handle clattered on the floor, the sound echoing loudly through the draughty cellar.

The party fell silent, each member scanning around for the source of the noise. I held my breath, waiting to be discovered and thrown, alive, into the oven.

'What was that?' the SS officer asked.

'It was nothing,' Herr Schmidt slurred. 'This cellar is hundreds of years old; it creaks all the time.'

Satisfied, they resumed their celebration, the alcohol making them grow ever rowdier. I had dodged detection, but if I stayed any longer my luck would run out. My legs agreed and I scurried back up the stairwell, through the corridors and back to my bed. I thought I heard the accordion begin to play but my mind was so muddled I couldn't be sure. I pulled the covers up over my head and wondered if I had imagined it all. Surely I had dreamed it. Human beings did not do that to one another, did they? To kill – to murder – was one thing, but to take sadistic pleasure in it was another. *Nein*, I had completely lost my mind. The whole scene was just a figment of my imagination.

Then the accordion music became louder and louder until it

was almost deafening, as if it were right outside the window. I tried to shut it out, but it was no use; the music reverberated around the ward. I had to see, even if just to convince myself that I wasn't going crazy. I went to the windows and looked in either direction. Nothing. I paused, about to return to my bed, before turning to take another look.

There they were: the celebration party, marching, staggering, up and down the gravel driveway. Their left hands held bottles while their right hands were raised in the Nazi salute. I watched for several minutes until they moved on and disappeared from view. I crawled back into bed then lay and listened to them until exhaustion finally took me.

That night convinced me I was on borrowed time, Dr Oppenheimer's promises or not. They had said their ten thousandth victim! *Ten thousandth*! Naïvely, I had convinced myself that I had some importance here – that, in some small way, I *mattered*. I had blindly let myself believe that I had a place in Hadamar – that my life had at least a fraction of meaning.

But I was wrong: my life was void. My existence was forfeited. I was only one of thousands and, one day, even if I was the last, they would come to kill me.

Perhaps it nothing more than Herr Schmidt's drunken boasting. Maybe the number was not that high. I had not seen ten thousand people come through Hadamar; even with the buses arriving night and day, there hadn't even been close to that number. *Ten thousand.* How would it even be possible to kill that many people?

But they were Germans and, if there was one thing I knew about Germans – apart from their predisposition to hate people like me – it was that they were efficient. Hadamar was a killing factory. There was no telling when they would stop. If the war endured, they had the desire and the means to dispose of us all.

Realising I was of little value brought me a strange sense of relief. The world and the events transpiring here were far bigger than me. There was nothing I could do but accept my fate – accept that whatever was going to happen was going to happen. My destiny was beyond my control. Once I came to this realisation I undertook my work with renewed vigour – not because I feared death or punishment, but because at least serving the others food would give them strength to fight. Whenever I could, I snuck extra servings to those who I thought needed it most.

One morning, as I started rolling the vats into the dining hall, Dr Oppenheimer appeared. I hadn't seen him since the beginning of the month and his presence was strangely disconcerting.

'Ingrid, leave your work for a moment and follow me.'

Manoeuvring the vat into position, I wiped the sweat from my forehead with my sleeve and followed him. He walked with a strange gait, his arm folded over as if he were trying to hide something. When we reached the children's ward, I saw that several new arrivals were settling in; they didn't bat an eyelid when they saw Dr Oppenheimer. They looked at him almost as if they knew him. Chief Nurse Huber and the others were nowhere to be found.

Dr Oppenheimer continued through the ward and out into the courtyard, taking fleeting looks behind him before he sat down on the bench and patted the space next to him. I sat, my eyes fixed on his face, intrigued by what he hid under his left armpit. He handed me a newspaper.

'I thought I'd better bring you this one,' he beamed.

He had brought me dozens of newspapers before; what was so special about this one? Why all the secrecy? I unfolded it and looked at the front cover: *Das Reich*. It looked the same as any other edition, carrying a front-page story about how well our troops were doing on the Eastern Front. *Why should I care about how well the Nazis were doing?* I thought.

'There is a story in here I think might interest you,' Doctor Oppenheimer said as he impatiently reached over me and turned the pages. He found what he wanted and tapped it wildly. I glared at him impatiently.

'If you would let me read …'

It was a story about some place called Absberg in Franconia. I looked up at him, confused.

'Who cares about Absberg? I don't even know where Absberg is.'

'Keep reading,' he chuckled.

Hundreds and hundreds of Catholics, even some Nazi Party members, had staged a protest after the removal of a large number of children from the Ottilien Home. I looked up at him and smiled.

'*Ja*,' he said. 'It has begun.'

'Does this mean the end of the war is coming?'

He laughed. I scowled.

'*Nein*, Ingrid, it is not the end of the war, but it could be the end of your incarceration – and the same for other people like you. At least, it must surely mean that the killing will stop.'

My heart fluttered like a butterfly. Could the end really be this close? I thought of Mutti. I pictured her euphoric face in the moment when I was finally reunited with her if she wanted me back. Lost in my thoughts, I barely listened to Dr Oppenheimer as he told me that the feelings of the German people had begun to change as more and more of the truth came out. People's suspicions had turned into knowledge and they were rising up in opposition. People were openly standing up to the Nazis. Hitler and his henchmen would soon be gone. Soon I could return home!

Later, as I sat on my bed and read that same newspaper, my hopes rose higher. Two of the younger doctors paid no mind to me as they walked past and stopped at the courtyard doors to smoke. Pretending to read, I raised the newspaper so that I could peer over it and watch them as I listened.

'You know', the younger and taller of the two doctors laughed as stuttering streams of smoke left his mouth, 'we have given so many children deliverance, relieved so many of them of their suffering, we are starting to run out of excuses!'

'What do you mean?' the other doctor asked as he dragged on his own cigarette.

'You know how we have been told to write so many died of

tuberculosis, then so many died of appendicitis and so on?'

'*Ja*.'

'Well, people from the same towns have been receiving death certificates on the same day. I also heard of one instance when we sent the parents a death certificate which stated the cause of death as appendicitis.'

'*Ja*, so what of it?'

'Well!' the younger doctor laughed as he inhaled and exhaled. 'It turns out that the child had already had their appendix out! As you can imagine, the parents were asking some serious questions.'

'Ha!' the other doctor laughed as he took a final drag on his cigarette, threw it to the ground and stamped it out. 'Who are they going to complain to? We have orders from the *Führer* himself!'

'I don't know,' the younger doctor said. 'I have heard that, last year, even some higher-ranking Nazi party members complained to the Reich Chancellery.'

'Complained about what? That we are saving them from a life of pain, relieving them from their suffering?'

'I know,' said the younger doctor as he extinguished his cigarette. The two of them walked inside. 'It's crazy. I read in the papers a few weeks back that the townspeople in Absberg were even openly protesting.'

My cheeks went as red as roses, flushed with hope. Even Nazi party members were beginning to question what was being done.

Surely the end must be coming.

CHAPTER 7

NEW ARRIVALS

20 September 1941

The weather became colder; the last of the flowers bloomed before the autumn came. There must have been some serious summer offensives because more and more soldiers began to arrive. I rarely spoke to them. Not because I couldn't, but because I was afraid of them – especially the more Aryan-looking ones. I waited for them to taunt me about my colour like the girls had done at school. 'Monkey', they would call me. 'Nigger', 'jungle ape', 'banana eater': the list went on.

Some of the soldiers looked at me with disdain but none of them said a word. I couldn't quite figure out why. That was, until I met Old Wilhelm. Old Wilhelm was a colonel and, as far as I could tell, the highest ranking of the men. He had a long white beard like Kris Kringle, and under the worn old Wehrmacht cap that he always wore there were wisps of grey hair that hung down like the branches of a willow tree. His left leg was missing and several fingers on each of his hands. Despite his vagabond-like appearance, he commanded great respect from the men around him.

I first spoke to him when Chief Nurse Huber had ordered me to prepare some new beds in the soldiers' ward with some fresh sheets. I reluctantly made my way upstairs, resolved to do my job as quickly as I could. As I folded the last corner on the last bed, Old Wilhelm came slowly moving forward, his crutches clicking on the floor. He stood by me and stared out the window.

'They're beautiful, aren't they?'

I tried to ignore him, to pretend I thought he was talking to someone else, but I was somehow drawn to him.

'What are?' I asked as I stared down at the gardens below.

'The dahlias,' he said. 'Perfect in form and shape, every petal completely symmetrical.'

Examining the flower beds, I couldn't be sure which ones were the dahlias.

'The pink and purple ones there. A wonderful combination of colours, just like you, young lady.'

At first, I assumed he had insulted me. '*Danke*,' I said when I realised he hadn't.

'I love to look at the flowers,' he went on. 'They remind me when I am sad about all the evil that is in this world – that there are beautiful things that are worth preserving. Bah!' he said as he turned from the window. 'I am sure you have better things to do than listen to an old man like me!'

'Not really,' I said, as I helped him to his bed.

We talked for hours. He told me he had been in the first war too when, just as in this one, he had been tricked into thinking it was noble and righteous to fight for the Fatherland. He chided himself for falling for their lies twice.

'Who are *they*?' I asked.

'The men in charge – the ones who convince us that we need to fight for the honour and glory of Germany. We don't fight for honour and glory; we fight so they can have more while we get poorer. I fought for the Kaiser and that was just so he could have more colonies in his Empire. This Hitler fellow is just the same. I can't believe I re-enlisted, fell for his lies. Then again, what else is an old soldier like me good for?'

Warming to him, I said, 'Sir, you'd better not let anyone around here hear you talking like that or they will kill you too.'

'Let them,' he said as he wiggled his leg. 'That would be a relief from all my pain and suffering.'

It was strange to hear him talk like that. I had seen the fear in the eyes of the children who had been taken away and given *Gnadentod* and here was a man who would happily receive it. Old Wilhelm and I talked so long I lost track of time. He did most of the talking. Only when the sun began to set and the curtain of darkness descended outside did I realise I was needed to perform my dinner duties. I told him so, wished him well and promised I would return to talk to him as soon as I could.

With the vats in place, I ladled out the soup, paying close attention to those who I thought needed bigger servings. It was only when I filled my own bowl and tried to find somewhere to sit that I realised that there were dozens and dozens of new children. Scanning the room without making eye contact, I spied a gap three tables over. After sliding myself in between two girls, I slurped down my soup as quickly as I could.

'Wow! You must really like that stuff!'

I kept my head down, but peered out the corner of my eye at the girl who was sitting on my left. Her hair was so blonde it could have been spun on a golden loom. I didn't need to take a long look at her to realise she was Bridget Pallenhoffer's *Doppelgänger*. At first I couldn't figure out why she was here. Then I reminded myself that Hadamar was taking orphans now. I didn't say anything. I just slurped down my soup as fast as I could and hurried away to take my bowl to the kitchen. Seeing Bridget Pallenhoffer again – or at least a girl who looked exactly like her – made me think back to school. As I washed the first of the plates, a sweet voice played over and over in my head. That of my old teacher, Fräulein Rothenberg.

~~~

'Girls', her whispered hush came through the semi-darkness, 'come sit here, by me.'

Sarah and I looked left to see Fräulein Rothenberg's silhouette beckoning us. Several other 'undesirables' had already filled the nearby seats but Fräulein Rothenberg had saved a seat on each side of her. As we pushed by and took our seats, the auditorium filled with a faint light and the film titles began to roll.

The black and white numbers flicked across the screen, then the title: *Das Erbe: The Inheritance.* The film began with the usual
~~~

pictures of Hitler and thousands of people saluting him. Then there were images of fawns. The narrator talked about how nature was perfect and how nature always rids itself of imperfections. Pictures of mentally disabled people flickered across the screen. The narrator explained just how many Reichsmarks Germany had to spend on these 'useless' people. Dozens of people of different races, some with quite dirty faces and skin, flashed across the screen. These were followed by deformed children with heads the size of footballs.

It went on to show animals fighting: beetles, roosters and dogs. The narrator discussed 'natural selection': the process by which nature keeps only the strongest alive. It then moved onto the obligatory shots of healthy Germans doing athletic activities. I didn't need the lights to come on to know that, even if the girls were not looking at me, they were thinking about me. I wasn't like the children in the film – not even close – but that wouldn't matter to my class 'mates'. A girl behind me pushed me in the back, then another, and another. I fell forward in my chair. I reached out for Fräulein Rothenberg's hand. She held mine tightly as she turned around and told the girls to stop.

The credits rolled and the lights came on. I felt the full weight of their hateful gazes. Herr Waldheim stood in front of the projector screen and told us it was time for recess. Sarah and I waited, our heads down to avoid the sneers of the other girls and teachers as they walked by.

'Girls, I think it best you come to my room,' Fräulein Rothenberg said as she stood and formed a human barrier between us and them.

We waited patiently until the last of them had left before we filed out behind her and followed her to her room. We spent our break talking to her about the film and how we thought it might affect us. She reminded us that things like this caused excitement for a few days and then were forgotten just as quickly. I loved her for her optimism. Still, when the bell rang, and Sarah and I had to return to our separate classrooms, I was fearful of what was to come. My terror intensified when Fräulein Pletcher went to her desk, picked up the new, Nazi approved mathematics textbook and held it proudly in her right hand before she walked to the blackboard.

'Children, our mathematics questions today will be based around the film you have just watched. Ingrid, come and stand at the front of the class.'

I did as I was told, moving to the right-hand side of the blackboard where she indicated for me to stand. While my classmates took out their mathematics books, Fräulein Pletcher wrote the first sum on the board:

It costs, on average, four Reichsmarks a day to keep a cripple or a mentally ill person in hospital. There are currently 300 000 mentally ill, lunatics and so on in Germany's hospitals. How much would the German government save if they got rid of all these people?

The other girls worked studiously in their books before Fräulein Pletcher asked for the answer.

Bridget Pallenhoffer was, of course, the first to answer.

'One million, two hundred thousand Reichsmarks, Fräulein.'

'One million, two hundred thousand Reichsmarks *per day*!'

Fräulein Pletcher repeated as she pointed at me with her right hand. 'That is what Ingrid and people like her cost the Reich *each* and *every* day! Now, if someone like Ingrid costs the Reich four Reichsmarks per day, how much does she cost the Reich per year?'

They dutifully did their sums again before Anna Müller put her hand up.

'*Ja*, Anna?'

'One thousand, four hundred and sixty Reichsmarks.'

'*Sehr gut*, Anna!' Fräulein Pletcher praised as she rubbed the blackboard clean. She began to write again as she spoke to the class. 'If a mentally handicapped student can cost up to 1800 Reichsmarks per year, an average pupil costs 320, and a brilliant pupil costs only one 125, what is the solution to this problem?'

I could see that the girls were confused that Fräulein Pletcher had not asked for a numerical answer. She finished writing and turned to face the class.

'Anyone?'

The girls shrugged their shoulders.

'The answer, girls, is that we need to get rid of these mentally handicapped children because a society can only survive if its citizens are genetically sound!'

I wasn't sure they understood, but I knew what she was implying.

She continued writing more questions: *The construction of a lunatic asylum costs 6 000 000 marks. How many houses, at 15 000 marks each, could have been built for that amount?*

The others furiously tried to figure out the answer, but I already knew it was 400. While I waited, my frustrations boiled away inside me like a pressure cooker. I was ready to explode, to shout out the mistakes I heard in their calculations. I *was* sitting in the same classroom as the rest of them. I was, I knew, smarter than the rest of them. So, according to the Nazi's theory, I cost, at a maximum, 125 Reichsmarks a day. I wanted to grab Fräulein Pletcher's chalk, write the sum on the board, and prove that I cost the least of all of them … but what would be the point?

When the others finished their work, Fräulein Pletcher decided it was time for some hands-on mathematics/history. She divided the girls into six groups of four. Then she reached inside a box beside her desk, retrieved six tape measures and handed one to each of the groups before she wrote the instructions on the board. They were to measure their own heads, noses, ears and chins, and record their findings in their books. I stood there watching, wondering what was happening. When they were all finished, my teacher stood beside me, measured my head, nose, ears and chin, and wrote the results on the blackboard before she began telling the other girls how their results compared with mine.

'You see, children,' she said as she alternated her pointer stick between the board and my chin, nose and ears. 'Ingrid here has a bigger skull, chin and ears than the rest of you. This is because she is a Negro and she is much closer to the physical make-up of a monkey. You, my good Aryan girls, have much smaller skulls, chins and ears because you *are* Aryan and are, therefore, more advanced and more intelligent.'

With that, she pulled out several charts, laying them out on the floor at the front of the room as she explained what exactly made a good Aryan. Ordered not to move, I watched as the others checked the colour of their eyes and the texture and length of their hair against the Nazi definitions of Aryanism, before standing next to me to compare themselves.

Our last lesson for the day was to write down our biological family trees. I started to return to my desk, but I was ordered to stay where I was. There was no point me doing a family tree, Fräulein Pletcher told me, as my ancestors were all monkeys who lived in trees.

Instead, I tried to trace my heritage in my head. I knew, because Vati had told me on many occasions, that my grandmother was from Senegal; she was a Dahomey Amazon. Vati said that I had my grandmother's strength inside me. On Mutti's side, I knew – though I had never met my grandparents – we had a long German lineage. I looked around the room and wondered whether, if I looked back far enough, I might find that I had more claim to Aryan heritage than they did.

The final bell rang, but I had to wait until all the others had left before I was allowed to return to my desk to collect my bag. When I did leave I found Sarah outside waiting for me.

'Did you have to stand at the front of the class too?' I asked her.

'*Ja*,' she said as we walked towards Fräulein Rosenberg's room. 'And another Jewish girl and a simple girl had to stand at the front while they did their sums; the first one was something about some aircraft and bombing a town full of Jews. I didn't listen much after that.'

'My class did one about how the Reich could save money by getting rid of disabled people,' I said as we reached Fräulein Rosenberg's room and knocked politely.

There was no answer. We opened the door. Her room was empty.

'What do we do now?' Sarah asked nervously. Fräulein Rothenberg always walked us as far as the school gates, if not all the way home. We waited and waited but still she did not arrive. We went to the windows and looked out across the playground.

'There doesn't seem to be anybody around. We should make a run for it,' I suggested.

Sarah smiled and nodded as she took hold of my hand. Together we ran faster than we ever had before, down the hallways and out across the front quadrangle. Despite the air being filled with the chill of autumn, beads of sweat formed on our brows and trickled down the sides of our faces. We closed in on the gates; if we could only get through we would be safe.

'Where do two you think you are going?'

The voice was unmistakable.

'Run!' Sarah shouted hopelessly. Half a dozen girls, all dressed in the black skirts and ties and white shirts of the *Jungmädel*, now blocked the gate. Another half-dozen girls, dressed the same, appeared from behind nearby trees and buildings. Sarah gripped my hand tightly as, from behind the group of girls guarding the gate, Marta appeared. She was the self-appointed school bully and daughter of Herr Richter, the local *Oberst* of the *Ordnungspolizei*. I looked at Sarah. I could feel her trembling. I willed her to be brave, but her ruby-red bottom lip started to quiver as she began to bite it. I turned my attention to Marta, who looked deceptively respectable in her crease-free clothes. The other girls had their chests puffed out. As Marta moved to the front, she stamped her foot and flared her nostrils like a bull.

'Fight, Sarah! Fight with all you have!' I whispered.

'*Ja*, Sarah,' Marta mocked. 'Fight! It's ever so much more fun when you try to fight back!'

Sarah burst into tears, howling like a hungry baby. It made our tormentors stop dead; some of them covered their ears, unable to bear the shrillness of her cries. Even Marta stopped marching towards us. Sarah's wailing stopped abruptly.

'Let her go,' one girl said. 'She's just a Jew, she'll get what's coming to her one day anyway.'

The bullies discussed their next move. While they were distracted, I spied an opening in their ranks. Nudging Sarah with my elbow, I flicked my head in the direction of the gap. Before I could move, Sarah had snatched up her bag and run. I grabbed mine and followed. Sarah made it through, but I was not so lucky. They encircled me. Several stepped forward and spat in my face, their saliva dripping down my hair, cheeks and eye lashes. I wiped my face with my sleeve.

'Retard!' one girl teased.

'*Die schwarze Schande*!' another said. 'You're what's wrong with Germany.'

'*Ja*,' another girl joined in. 'If we got rid of you we'd all be rich. We'd all have more food and nice houses to live in!'

A blow to my face jerked my head sideways. Another, harder blow struck me on the opposite cheek, roughly forcing my head back in the other direction. Both my cheeks throbbed wildly as they began to swell. My vision blurred but, oddly, I felt no pain. Instead anger bubbled up inside me, as if my stomach was a lake of lava. I no longer cared what happened. I was fed up and tired of their harassment.

If I was going down, I was not going down without a fight. Lashing out at whatever face appeared in front of me I alternated my fists, connecting again and again. I knocked two girls to the ground, but it was no use – there were too many of them. They swarmed around me, pushed me over and punched and kicked me as hard as they could. I had given it my best shot, but my resolve weakened with every blow. I curled myself into a ball, clenched my fists and put my forearms over my face.

'Hey! Stop that!' I heard a woman's voice call out. 'What do you girls think you are doing?'

Through my blurred vision, I saw a pair of feet in high-heeled shoes running across the quadrangle.

'Ingrid, Ingrid! Are you okay?'

It was Fräulein Rothenberg.

It had been a long time since I had thought of her. I happily pictured her living her new life in Long Island, married with a new husband. I thought of all the little American children she would protect and inspire as she had done for me. I pictured her in a house with a white-picket fence, a swing hanging from a willow tree in the front yard, and daughters who looked just like her running around the tree. I missed her greatly and longed to see her again. Doubting I ever would, I ran back to my bed, buried my head into my pillow and cried for the first time in a long time.

'Are you okay?'

I lifted my head from my pillow to see Bridget Pallenhoffer's *Doppelgänger* sitting on Erich's bed. Her face was soft and caring. I forced a smile at her.

'Everything will be alright,' she said as she stood up and put one hand on my shoulder and offered me the other. 'My name is Mia.'

'Ingrid,' I said as I sat and shook her hand.

At first, I hated that she had sat on Erich's bed. Whenever we had new arrivals I told them the bed was occupied and so no-one had ever taken it. I knew it was stupid, but part of me thought that, if I kept his bed for him, I would someday see him walking back into the ward. He would lie down on it, laughing about where he had been, and everything would be back to how it was. I looked around the ward and realised that while I had been completing my duties, they had brought in more beds. As summer progressed, the wards had steadily filled, but this was something else. More bunk beds, and even triple beds, had been shoved into any spare space. Some of the bunks even had two or three children to a bed. Children were crammed into every crevice like suitcases stacked on a train luggage compartment. Mia hadn't chosen Erich's bed herself; it had been given to her. I couldn't hate her for it, but I wanted to; the memories of what the girls used to do to me at school still burned into my mind.

'What is this place?' she asked.

'What do you mean?'

'I mean, what is this place? We were brought here on a bus this afternoon but they did not tell us where we were going.'

Perhaps she was simple. Her hair, body, eyes: they were all perfect but, perhaps, her mind wasn't all it could be.

'It is called Hadamar. It's for special children.'

'So it is the same as Brandenburg. That is where I came from.'

I had never heard of Brandenburg and I wondered if I really wanted to talk to her any more. If she had been transferred here there must be only one reason: she was destined for the gas chambers.

'Do they kill children here too?' she asked me.

'What?'

'Do they kill children here too? They did at Brandenburg.'

Her frankness and apparent lack of compassion made me sit up.

'*Ja*, they do,' was all I could think to say.

'Well, maybe we'll live long enough to see the end of the war, but then again, maybe not.'

'You don't seem to care very much either way.'

'Why should I? These children are not my friends; my friends are all at home in Hamburg. All I can do is try to save my own skin. Besides, I heard the nurses on the way here saying something about how *Der Führer* himself had ordered the killings to be stopped while he reconsiders things. So, it doesn't seem like we need to worry about them killing us any more.'

'But the chimneys here still billow smoke day and night. That can't be true.'

'Well, that is what I heard them say.'

Perhaps it was true, given what I had read about Absberg. Perhaps there would be no more burning. Before I had a chance to ask Mia more about Brandenburg and her life before the war, the lights were switched off and we were informed it was bedtime.

When morning came, I was woken by Chief Nurse Huber as she stood over my bed.

'Ingrid, get up. I have a new job for you.'

I rolled out of bed and lazily stood to attention.

'You are no longer going to work in the kitchen. We need to give jobs to the other imbecilic idiots we have here. You're the most physically capable idiot we still have. I have to find jobs for a new batch of retarded children coming in tomorrow, and their useless bodies won't handle anything else but kitchen work. Besides, you're the only female here with full use of your arms and legs. Go out to the garden and find Herr Mentz. You're black. You should be used to working in the fields anyway. It's a shame we don't grow cotton out there – then you'd feel right at home.'

I did not understand her strange reference until many years later, but I was excited by the prospect of increased freedom. I even contemplated the idea of escaping but, as she so often did, she pre-empted my thoughts.

'You may be working in the garden but don't you even dare think of trying to escape. If you do, Herr Schmidt will have you shot.'

I had forgotten about Herr Schmidt and, after seeing their grisly celebration, I was more afraid of him than ever.

'Besides, even if you did manage to get away from the grounds, how far do you think you'd get – looking like *that*?'

'Looking like what, Chief Nurse Huber?' I said, instantly regretting my words.

'As black as the midnight sky, child!' she snapped as she slapped me across the face. 'You would be turned in to the Gestapo the first instant someone spotted you.'

She was right. My head came back down from the clouds. Her words were a stark reminder that, even if I did manage to survive and get out of Hadamar, I would still have to return to a society that hated me. The war could end but prejudice would remain.

'Who are you?' she suddenly questioned.

'Ingrid,' I said, confused.

'Not you, you black idiot,' she snapped back. '*You*.'

Following her outstretched finger, I saw she was pointing at Mia.

'My name is Mia,' she said quickly as she leapt from her bed and stood to attention next to me. 'What do you need me to do, *Frau* Nurse?'

'Who are you and what are you doing here?'

'My name is Mia Zimmermann, *Frau* Nurse. I was transferred here from Brandenburg yesterday.'

'Hmm,' Chief Nurse Huber said as she looked Mia over. 'There seems to be some mistake. I can't see anything wrong with you, child.'

Mia shrugged her shoulders.

'I will have to check on this. In the meantime, you can help Ingrid out in the garden. Off you go then,' Chief Nurse Huber said. 'I have to ready the place for the new arrivals.'

New arrivals, changes of jobs, being allowed outside – it was all a little overwhelming. Mia looked at me and smiled.

'After you,' she said as she pointed an open hand towards the ward entrance. 'I don't know where I'm going.'

Threading my way through the corridors towards the back entrance, I kept looking over my shoulder, waiting for one of the staff to chastise me and question where I was going. When we reached the back door, I stared out the window, took a deep breath, opened the door and stepped outside. I looked around. To my right there was the end of the driveway that led into wooden sheds where the buses were parked. I shivered as I remembered the last time I had been so close to them. In front of me were the expansive grounds at the rear of the main buildings. The trees, their branches still filled with leaves of red, orange and yellow, towered above me. There was no-one else around.

'What do we do now?' Mia asked. 'Make a run for it?'

'I don't know what the staff were like at Brandenburg, but the staff here have eyes everywhere. I guarantee one of them is watching us right now. If we did try to make a run for it, we wouldn't get far. Well, *you* might, but I certainly wouldn't.'

Escaping Hadamar would have to wait. For now, I was just happy to feel the sunshine on my skin. For the moment, that was freedom enough. I needed to find Herr Mentz, and the only place I could think he might be was a small annexe to the back of the right wing of the main building, which I had only ever seen from the windows above. When Mia and I came to the door, I knocked.

'*Eintreten*!' a deep voice resonated. Cautiously, I pushed the door aside and stepped in. The walls looked like a medieval torture chamber: clippers, scythes, cutters, chisels, saws, screwdrivers and a hundred more garden implements hung from the roof and walls.

'Who are you?'

'My name…is…Ingrid,' I stuttered.

'What are you doing here, Ingrid?' asked the bellowing voice belonging to the silhouette of an extremely tall, slender man who stood behind the hanging tools.

'Chief Nurse Huber ordered me, I mean us, to come out and assist you.'

'I don't need any assistants,' he said bluntly.

I shrugged my shoulders and put my hands up, 'I don't know what to tell you. Go and check with her, but that's what she told me to do.'

'All right, I suppose I can find something for you two to do,' he grumbled as he stepped into the light. His height made him terrifying; his face remained hidden, which instilled me with fear. He moved past me, his face remaining obscured as he ducked under the door frame and stepped outside. Mia and I followed, one of us standing each side of him. I looked him up and down. He wore black boots that went about halfway up his brown corduroy trousers. His white shirt and black waistcoat made him look like a farmer or a working gentleman. What struck me most was his protruding ears, which stuck out almost perpendicularly from his head. Above his ears, his hair was parted to the right, glistening in the summer sun from excessive amounts of oil.

'Come with me,' he said.

We made our way along the gravel path leading to the back fields, passing by the bench where I had sat with Dr Oppenheimer. We walked up a set of wooden stairs leading to the next level of the garden, further up the hill. The pathway was bordered by different-sized trees and shrubs; the thicker the bushes became, the more I felt like I was walking in a forest. Perhaps escape *would* be possible. As I pondered the possibilities, we walked up two more levels until we reached the top of the hill where there were several fields, bordered by trees on three sides. Herr Mentz immediately pointed to the fallow fields, barren except for a few old corn husks.

'I need these fields ploughed,' he said as he picked up two nearby hoes and handed one to me and one to Mia. 'Dig the rows like you see in that field up there.'

With that, he headed back down the path and stairs. Once he had disappeared from view, I paused and looked around. The main buildings were a few hundred feet away. This was the furthest I had been from them in years. I looked at Mia, who stood leaning on her hoe.

'We could make it, you know!' she said as she pointed in the direction of the forest.

'*Nein*, we can't be sure if Chief Nurse Huber, Herr Mentz, or worse, even Herr Schmidt are watching us.'

'So what if they are? By the time they realise anything we'll be into the forest and long gone.'

'*Nein*, it is like Chief Nurse Huber said, how far would I get with my skin colour being as it is?'

Mia laughed, 'What, you think you're the only black girl in Germany?'

I knew there were others. I had seen some in Mainz, but the way Mia spoke made it sound like there were more than I had originally thought.

'What do you mean?'

'There were quite a few black girls and boys in Brandenburg. There was one boy, Heinrich, very attractive. We had a thing for a while, me and him. He was from Frankfurt. Where did you say you are from again?'

'Mainz.'

'That's on the Rhein too, isn't it?'

'*Ja*. It is.'

'The other children I met were from towns and cities on the Rhein too. What did they say people used to call them?'

'Rheinlander bastards?'

'*Ja*, that's it.'

'You said there were quite a few. What happened to them?'

Mia's look was enough to remind me of the stupidity of my question.

'Anyway,' I went on, 'the staff here seem to *always* know what we are up to. Chief Nurse Huber especially. I wouldn't be surprised if she gave me this job to give me a chance to escape so she'd have an excuse to kill me.'

'Well, the killings are supposed to have stopped,' Mia said as she grasped her hoe by the handle and began driving it into the dirt. Then she stopped just as suddenly. 'Come to think of it, why haven't you been killed yet?'

'I could ask you the same question,' I responded as I started digging in the dirt beside her.

'There was a doctor there,' she said as she began to dig. 'He took a liking to me. Let's just say, as long as I kept doing favours for him, I survived.'

'Favours?'

She gave me that same look – as if she refused to waste her breath on answering such a stupid question – before she said, 'So?'

'There's a doctor here who guaranteed my safety.'

'Ah, I see.'

'*Nein*, it's not what you think it is.'

'Sure it isn't! I am not here to judge. We all have to do what we have to do to survive. Perhaps we can escape another day when you feel more up to it.'

Mia and I talked and talked as we worked. I learnt her schooling was the opposite to mine – until she had her first seizure and was diagnosed with epilepsy. Then her so-called friends turned against her, her teachers ignored her, and the teasing and taunts started.

'It could have been worse,' she said as the sun slipped behind the distant horizon, the blackness of Hadamar Castle silhouetted against the orange and purple sky.

'How could it have been worse?' I asked as we made our way back towards the shed.

She stopped me at the end of the top field, looked around several times then leant close to me and whispered in my ear. 'I'm going to tell you a secret, but you have to promise you will not tell anyone.'

'*Ja*, I promise.'

'I can trust you. You swear you won't tell anyone?'

'*Ja*, I swear.'

'I'm a Jew.'

My mouth hung wide open. I was about to say something but was interrupted by Chief Nurse Huber hollering from the kitchen.

'You two get yourselves in here now! Some of these new arrivals are truly useless and the others need help in the kitchen!'

We hurried into the dining hall, where one of the nurses stopped us and told us to help serve the soup. Once we were done, Mia and I ate in silence. The staff decided the new children were able to wash dishes and dismissed us. On the way back to our beds I had a thousand questions for Mia. Most of all, how she had managed to escape the Nazis and – more specifically – the Gestapo for so long. As we sat on our beds, I wanted to ask her about everything, but I didn't want to risk being heard by one of the other children or, even worse, one of the staff. I went to sleep that night thinking of the last time I had seen Sarah. If Mia had managed to evade detection for so long, maybe the Dreyfuses had too. Maybe I would see my friend again.

The next morning, Mia and I were up early, before dawn. We made our way out to the fields. I felt excited. I knew that as soon as we were clear of the buildings, I could ask her whatever I wanted. We turned the corner towards the tool shed. The door was open. Inside I could see the intermittent blaze of Herr Mentz's pipe in the darkness.

'Ingrid,' he said as we entered. 'I am to be transferred to the East first thing tomorrow morning. I have been ordered to do my part for the Fatherland.'

'What? What do you mean?' I asked. Herr Mentz's life did not concern me; what did was my desperation not to return to kitchen duty.

'The T-4 program is officially over. I'm not needed here anymore. More wounded soldiers will come and, I would imagine, one of them will be given my job. But for now, you are in charge of the gardens and the fields.'

He took one last puff on his pipe, tapped it on his chair until the spent tobacco fell to the ground, and left. I looked at Mia. She looked back, smiled and shrugged her shoulders.

'So, what now?'

'Um, we work, I guess.'

We retrieved our tools, slung them over our shoulders and made our way up to the fields. As we walked, every part of my body urged me to ask her. When we reached the top field, I couldn't hold it in any longer.

'Why did you tell me you were a Jew yesterday?'

'I figured I could trust you. I *can* trust you, right?'

'*Ja*, of course you can trust me. I have more reasons to hate the Nazis than most people.'

'That's why I told you,' she said as she grabbed her hoe, lifted it high above her head then slammed it down into the soil and dragged it back towards herself.

'Why is it such a big deal, anyway?' she asked. 'There must be other Jews here.'

'*Ja*, maybe, some … but if there are, I haven't seen or met them.'

'You're wondering how they haven't found out yet, aren't you?' she asked as I began digging beside her.

I stopped what I was doing and leant on the handle, looking at her, nodding.

'Look at me,' she said as she made circles around her face with her hand. 'Were it not for my religion, I'd be in a *Jungmädel* camp – not here. In fact, before I had my first seizure that was exactly where I was headed.'

'But, they must have known you were a Jew. How can you hide it?'

'Ingrid, clearly you don't know much about Jews.'

'I thought I did,' I protested. 'Before I came here, my best friend was a Jew.'

'Then why couldn't she hide it?'

'Because the Gestapo and the Polizei knew her father was a Jew.'

'I don't know my father, but I think he's a German not a Jew. My grandparents died when I was very young. For all of my life, it has only been me and my mother. Mother never told anyone we were Jewish either.'

'I still don't understand it. How have you hidden it for so long?'

'Ingrid, when the Gestapo or the Polizei suspect a boy to be a Jew do you know how they check to see if he is lying?'

I shook my head.

'They pull his pants down.'

I looked at her, confused.

'Surely, you must know that all Jewish men have to be circumcised.'

I didn't.

'Well, that's how they tell. Clearly, it's easier for a girl to hide.'

'And you never told anyone?'

'After I had my first seizure, I didn't think it made a difference, so I didn't say anything. The doctors and everyone else were only interested in my disability, not my religion. When the Nazis came and started treating the Jews how they did, I was already an outcast and so no-one thought to ask me or question my mother. I certainly wasn't going to say anything. I knew one way or another they were going to take me. I figured what they would do to disabled people would be better than what they would do to a Jew. Guess they proved me wrong, didn't they?'

'Then why did you tell me?'

'Because I've kept it a secret for so long and I wanted someone to know. Besides, it doesn't seem to matter any more. They wanted to kill me because I wasn't "normal" and they'll want to kill me if they know I'm a Jew, so either way I'm doomed.'

'Don't worry, you can trust me,' I said as we resumed our digging. 'Besides, who am I going to tell anyway?'

We spent the remainder of that day and the next swapping stories, mostly about the cruelty of the treatment we had received at the hands of our classmates. We paused for breaks, going into the kitchen and retrieving bread and butter and sitting out in the fields with the sun on our backs as if we were two best friends out for a picnic. On the second afternoon, as we rested beneath an elm tree, I went to stand but my shirt got caught on a branch.

'What are those?' Mia asked, pointing at my bare abdomen.

'What are what?' I replied as I fixed my shirt.

'Those scars on your belly.'

I didn't know why I felt embarrassed and self-conscious about them. Perhaps it was because Mia was so flawless.

'Oh, those – they're nothing.'

I tried to scamper away from her, picking up a spade and digging, hoping she would let it go. Instead, she hopped up and followed me, reaching for my shirt as I tried to brush her hand away.

'Tell me, what are they?'

'*Nein*, just leave it.'

'Ingrid, tell me. I told you a secret, didn't I?'

I breathed deeply before I sighed. 'The Gestapo did it to me,' I said as I let her lift my shirt and stare at them.

'What do you mean, "the Gestapo did it"? *What* did they do?'

'I didn't know at first; all I knew was that they cut me open and did some kind of operation – sterilisation, they said. I asked one of the nurses here about it once; she told me it meant I could never have children.'

'Oh, that's terrible!' Mia offered as she ran her fingers over the course scars.

'Maybe it's for the best,' I said as I resumed digging. 'With all I've suffered because of my colour, I don't know if I'd want to bring a black child into this world.'

'Nonsense,' she said as she dug alongside me. 'I think you would make a great mother.'

We – mostly she – talked about what our future husbands would be like and how many children we wanted, even though I would never be able to have my own Mia wanted three and hoped to live in a big house near a river. She wanted two girls and a boy and had even picked out names for them: Heidi, Frida and Gunther. The longer she went on, the more I realised that if she hadn't been an epileptic Jew she could have been a perfect Aryan mother; a *Lebensborn* mother, perhaps even earning the *Mutterehrenkreuz* – the Cross of Honour – for bearing and raising a large and wholesome Aryan family.

When sunset came, we went inside. No sooner had Mia and I lay down on our beds to get a few moment's rest, than it was dinner time and we had to rise. The wards and corridors were filled with the sound of dozens of footsteps and distinctive thudding, as if someone was limping. I was sure I could hear the scraping sound of wheelchairs and crutches.

'Ingrid! Get your worthless backside down here now!' Chief Nurse Huber called out.

I leapt out of bed and ran to the main reception area.

'*Ja*, Frau Huber?'

'Take your black hide upstairs and make sure all the beds in the first two rooms of the men's ward have new sheets and blankets.'

'Of course, Frau Huber. Does this mean I am not to do my gardening and field duties any more?'

She stood up from behind her desk, marched towards me and backhanded my left cheek.

'Don't ask questions! One day I will find a way to kill you and make it look like an accident!' she hissed.

I put my hand to my cheek, said nothing, and hurried off to the laundry to gather the sheets and blankets. I rushed upstairs and quickly made the beds, finishing the last of them when the first of the men began to appear at the top of the stairwell.

What I saw next flew in the face of everything Radio Nazi and *Das Reich* had said: Germany's finest, each of them in their grey *Wehrmacht* uniforms, the eagle and swastika still proudly worn on their right breast and hats, bent over and broken, struggling to walk. Dozens more young Aryan men followed; men who had rushed to war to 'defend' the Fatherland leant on crutches as they inched forward. Others were carried by their comrades or male nurses until they could be placed into a bed or a wheelchair. I stood to one side and tried to remain inconspicuous as a stream of men stumbled, staggered or were carried into the ward.

The scene made a mockery of the idea of the proud and noble German soldier. I watched some of the men unpacking their belongings until I heard heavy footsteps on the stairs behind me. I turned to see two orderlies carrying a legless man. A third orderly wheeled over a chair onto which the man was placed. I watched as he wheeled himself past me. He had the blondest hair I'd even seen, parted across the top of his head. He rolled past me and glanced in my direction, momentarily revealing his piercing blue eyes. He was the epitome of the perfect Aryan – the epitome of everything I hated and everything that hated me – yet he had a magnetism that was so powerful I couldn't take my eyes off him. Even without legs, he was captivating.

'Ingrid, what are you doing standing around all these brave men!' Chief Nurse Huber shouted as she appeared at the top of the stairs. 'You're a Negro and Negroes belong in the fields, so get yourself out there now.'

'But Chief Nurse Huber, it's late and you just told me …'

The rest of my words were cut short by her raised right hand. Chief Nurse Huber had derided me hundreds of times before; so often it had lost all meaning. However, the fact she had put me down in front of the blond man in the wheelchair hurt more than it should have. I meant to say my next words in my head, but I muttered them instead. 'Just because no man has looked at *you* in a thousand years.'

The nearest soldiers chuckled. I couldn't take it back. There was no apology that would suffice. Chief Nurse Huber raised her hand in fury but she only glared at me as she shoved past and headed downstairs. I bowed my head, allowed myself a smile, before I followed. I made straight for my ward, creeping past her office, waiting for her to come raging from it with a belt or an electrical chord in her hand. She didn't appear. I rushed to my bed.

'What happened?' Mia asked as soon as I leapt onto my bed. 'What did you say to Chief Nurse Huber?'

'What do you mean?'

'She just went charging down the corridor – she was furious! She was boiling away like one of those big old stinky vats.'

'I told her she was just jealous because no man had looked at her in a thousand years.'

'*Mein Gott*! You didn't!' Mia laughed, stunned. I nodded.

'So, a new bunch of soldiers came in. Any handsome ones?'

'I don't know. I wasn't paying attention.'

'There were too many going past. I couldn't see very well, but I did see a handsome blond one. Mia —' I broke off. 'I don't think we should be concerning ourselves with handsome boys right now, do you?'

'Why not?' she asked as she turned to face me, crossed her legs, put her elbows on her knees and her clenched fists beneath her chin.

'Survival is more important.'

'And that's exactly why we should be doing even more than just *talking* about boys. Tomorrow we could be dead. I say we have a little fun.'

'A little fun?' I asked, shocked. 'What do you mean?'

'*Gott in Himmel*, you really are innocent, aren't you?' she said. 'What, did your mother keep you locked away from the world or something?'

'*Nein*,' I gasped. 'Of course not! She was – *is* – a wonderful woman.'

'Sorry, Ingrid, I didn't mean to offend you,' she said. 'In some ways you seem to know so much about the world and in others you are clueless.'

'I've never thought much about boys. I went to an all-girls school. There were dances that the nuns organised but I only went a couple of times before the teasing of the others became too much. Besides, the boys in my town never took even the slightest look at me.'

'Why not? Look at you! You're stunning?'

'What?' I said, blushing.

'Okay, I understand, with the way Germany has been for the last decade – and I don't imagine there are too many chances to look in a mirror here but, Ingrid, you are a very, very beautiful girl. Way more than I.'

'*Nein*, that's not true. You're by far the prettiest girl here.'

'Okay, we'll call it a draw. We are both the prettiest,' she said. 'And that's why we should use what we have and have some fun with the boys upstairs.'

I wasn't convinced. 'Wait,' I protested, looking for excuses. 'Where would we...*do* it? Look around the ward! People are jammed in here like sardines.'

'I was going to ask *you* about that. You've been here longer than anyone else; surely you must know some places where a boy and a girl could find some ... privacy.'

I ran through all the cellars, wards and rooms in my mind. Each place that I pictured involved me and the young man in the wheelchair.

'Ingrid! Come here, now!' Chief Nurse Huber yelled from the corridor.

Excited by our talk, I had forgotten about her and what I had said.

I skulked down the ward and stood waiting at her office door. She sat behind her desk, neat as always, two tidy piles of paperwork on either side. She slowly placed her pen to one side, folded her arms and leant back on her chair. Icily, she stared at me. It sent a shiver through my spine.

'Ingrid, you black Rheinlander bastard,' she snarled. 'If you *ever* speak to me like that again I will strap you down to a table and inject you myself. Do you understand?'

I wanted to remind her that *Der Führer* himself had banned the practice, but as if reading my thoughts, she said, 'I know it has been discontinued by *Der Führer*, but I would make a special exception to the rules, just for you – and damn the consequences. Besides, *Der Führer* is not going to make much of a fuss about a little black whore like yourself. And if you think you'll be able to run off to your little protector, I'll make sure I do it when he's off on one of his trips. Do you hear me?'

I didn't want to say a word.

'Well, do you hear me?

'*Ja*, Frau Huber.'

'Very good, now, starting tomorrow you and your little harlot of a friend will no longer be working out in the gardens and in the fields. There are men upstairs who can still work. The last thing that I want is dozens of men sitting around idle. You, wretched girl, are to return to the kitchen. Soon we will have hundreds of more mouths to feed.'

'*Ja, ja.*'

'*Ja*, what?'

'*Jawohl*, Chief Nurse Huber.'

She picked up her pen and resumed her paperwork, which was my signal to leave. I slowly walked back to my bed. Chief Nurse Huber's threats and the fact I had lost my job working outside should have occupied my thoughts, but they didn't. All I could think about was the young soldier in the wheelchair. Mia still sat on her bed, watching me closely until I sat down.

'What happened? I thought you were dead – literally.'

'She told me if I ever spoke to her like that again, she would kill me.'

'Remember, the T-4 program is over. Their threats don't mean anything now.'

'You don't know Chief Nurse Huber. If she decides she wants to kill me, she'll find a way.'

'Lights out!' a male orderly called down the ward. The lights went off and we lay down on our beds.

'By the way,' I whispered through the semi-darkness. 'We're back on kitchen duty as of tomorrow.'

'*Gut*,' Mia replied. 'More chance to talk to the boys.'

My dreams were filled with visions of the blond boy in the wheelchair. When I awoke at dawn, I leapt from my bed, eager and excited by the prospect of serving the men their breakfast. Barely had the last vat of porridge been placed down before the first of the soldiers came – limping, rolling and hobbling in. I ladled the porridge into the bowls and handed them out, checking out soldier after soldier as they moved past me. Mia flirted and smiled at any soldier she thought even remotely handsome, but my thoughts dwelled only on him. As the last of the men arrived, I resigned myself to the fact that he wasn't coming.

Just as I was about to serve myself my own breakfast, there he was, rolling himself towards me. I tried to catch his eye, but his head stayed down. My heart pattered wildly as he came closer and stopped directly in front of me. I handed him his bowl. He looked up at me. I wanted to flirt, to smile, to giggle like I had seen Mia do, but all I saw in his beautiful blue eyes were pain and sorrow. He rested his bowl in his lap, put his head back down and rolled away.

I wanted to sit next to him, talk to him, ask him what had happened, ask him why he was here. But how could I? He'd barely even acknowledged my existence. Besides, what would an Aryan war veteran want with a silly little black girl like me?

In the few moments I had to eat my breakfast before the men began returning their bowls, I glanced often in his direction, hoping to catch his eye. I willed him to look, but he kept his head down as he ate, not even engaging in conversation with any of his comrades. The men finished their breakfast and I wolfed mine down so that I could stack their bowls and take them to the kitchen. As I washed the first of the bowls, I stared down into the sink and said to myself: *stop being so stupid! What do you want with some Aryan boy anyway? He is white, you are black, and the two do not mix!* I stared at my black hands in the white, soapy foam and knew he would never want me. We were from two different worlds. I needed to brush my childish crush aside. Butterflies in the stomach, nervous glances, chasing boys: these were all things that good Aryan girls in the *Jungmädel* got to do – not some Rheinlander bastard, *eine schwarze Schande* who was stuck in Hadamar.

When Mia and I returned to our beds after breakfast I ignored her.

'What's wrong?' she asked as she came and sat on my bed.

I turned away, but she put her hand on my shoulders, turned me around and forced me to look at her.

'What's going on, Ingrid? You ran into the kitchen this morning and now you won't even talk to me.'

'Why did you do it?' I hissed.

'Do what?'

'Get my hopes up like that.'

'What are you talking about?'

'You made me think that I could have something with a boy – a man – even if it's in a place like this and only for a short while.'

'Of course I did! What's wrong with that?'

'He didn't even look at me, Mia,' I complained. 'He doesn't even know I exist. I don't know how to put myself forward like you do.'

'Of course you do! You're just quieter than me and you haven't had the practice yet. Boys are strange things. Give it time. He'll notice you.'

'So what if he does? He'll never go for a girl like me.'

'Why not?' Mia asked.

I held up my arm and shoved it into her face.

'What?' she said as she pushed it away.

'What part of my being black do you not understand? The only boys I'll ever get are other Rheinlander bastards like me and, who knows, maybe the Reich has done its job and I *am* the only one left. Maybe I'll have to go to Africa, or maybe America, to find a boy like me.'

'Stop being so melodramatic, Ingrid. So that boy didn't look at you. He's only been here for a day. Give him time! Or go and talk to him yourself; don't just wait for him to come to you.'

'How?'

'Make excuses to go to the ward; when you get close to him, *talk* to him – like you do to me.'

I did as Mia suggested. I made excuses to go to the men's ward whenever I could. I offered to do extra cleaning duties or to help turn the bedridden men over to prevent bedsores. Every time I passed the young man's bed I looked at him for as long as I dared. But his head seemed permanently fixed downwards, his eyes constantly staring at where his legs had once been. One day, as I bent over to help an orderly push the wheelchair of an invalid soldier, a brown-haired man in his early twenties whose face was covered in a thousand scars, he said, 'Mmm, you can put that in front of me anytime you like.'

I instinctively pulled the edges of my shirt collar together tightly and hurried away from him. I overheard another soldier chastise him. '*Mein Freund*, I know it has been a while since you have seen a woman but you'd better keep your eyes off that black bitch!'

Their stares and comments made my skin crawl. What concerned me more was that if they all thought I was a 'black bitch', there was no way the young blond boy was ever going to look at me. They made comments about Mia too, but she took it in her stride, bending down so low when she served their porridge that they had no choice but to stare at her cleavage. When she was clearing their bowls, she arched herself over in front of them until they grabbed her around the waist and pulled her onto their laps. She'd pretend to try to escape as she wriggled around on top of them.

Mutti had taught me how a good German girl should behave, and part of me was disgusted by what she did; another part envied her carefree attitude. She was right: our futures were uncertain. We should enjoy ourselves while we could.

Days and weeks passed and the comments grew ever more frequent and lewd. Mia revelled in it, and the more she did, the more the men thought it was okay to act as they did. Some of the men would openly make sexual suggestions. I wished they would stop. I tried to block it all out, to ignore their attentions, but it was no use. All my life I had been made to feel as if I was nothing. I just wanted them to leave me alone.

I thought about asking Chief Nurse Huber to take me off the ward, but I could see she delighted in watching me suffer. On more than a few occasions she had been standing right next to me when the men insulted me. I knew she'd heard what they had said, seen what they did – and not once did she intervene. In fact, she seemed to laugh just a little louder each time.

One evening, as I cleaned the tables after dinner, I let my guard down and found myself standing in front of a group of soldiers, right beside the scar-faced man. Realising my mistake, I tried to turn and move away but he grabbed me, wrapped his arms around my waist and forced me to sit on his lap. I struggled and squirmed but he was too strong. His friends spurred him on as I felt his hands moving over my body and descending to places I did not want them to be.

'Take your hands off her,' came a firm, steady voice from the far side of the dining room. My heart pounded; it was the blond boy in the wheelchair.

'Mind your business, boy,' the repulsive scar-faced man snapped back.

'Franz, don't you know who that is?' one of his comrades warned.

'*Nein*, he looks like a little boy who has come straight out of the Hitler Youth and in his first time in battle got his legs blown off!'

'Franz, that is Johan Kapfler,' the comrade whispered.

The scar-faced man released me. I rushed away, stopping at the nearest empty tables. The boy – Johan – wheeled himself towards my attacker. When he reached the head of the table he looked Franz directly in the eye and said, 'You touch her again, I'll kill you.'

Franz looked around and, realising he was losing face with his comrades, retorted, 'You'll have to catch me first! Oh, wait! You'd have to be able to run to do that!'

Franz laughed loudly as he stood up and strutted out of the dining hall. His subdued comrades followed, eyeing Johan warily as they walked past him. I worked up my courage and moved as close to him as I dared.

'*Danke*,' I said timidly.

He didn't say a word. He didn't even look at me; just placed his hands on the wheels of his chair and rolled away. My whole body felt electrified as I watched him wheel himself into the corridor. Who *was* this boy? Perhaps his parents were high-ranking Nazi Party members. Perhaps his father was a general. Whatever it was, it made the other soldiers scared of him.

'Ingrid!' Chief Nurse Huber's hoarse voice interrupted. 'Get that kitchen cleaned up, now!'

'*Ja*, Chief Nurse Huber.'

Excited by Johan and what he had done for me, I braved the soldiers' ward again the next day. After reaching the top of the stairs I began to sweep, waiting for the lecherous comments, but no-one said a word. Buoyed, I swept myself closer and closer to him until I was a few feet from his bed. I lingered, hesitating, trying to work up the courage to talk to him again, but I couldn't. I just didn't know what to say. I silently begged him to look up and say the first words, but he didn't. His eyes stayed transfixed on the two stumps that were his legs.

I came the next day and tried again. The same result. On the third day his bed was empty. I scanned the ward. He was nowhere to be seen. They must have sent him home – or worse, decided he was *Lebensunswerte Leben!* Maybe they had taken him away to be killed. I felt sick with dread.

Then he appeared, wheeling himself from the direction of the showers. The thought of water cascading down over his perfect muscles made me giddy. I pretended to sweep myself away from his bed, but out of the corner of my eye I watched as he wheeled himself closer. He backed his chair beside his bed, put his hands on the armrests and tried to fling himself onto his mattress, only to miss and fall to the floor in a heap. I looked around quickly, hoping no-one else had seen.

'So, you're gonna kill me, huh?' the scar-faced Franz, several beds up, laughed. 'I'd like to see you try! You can't even get yourself into bed!'

'Franz, remember who he is,' the soldier in the next bed reminded him.

Franz didn't say another word. Johan sat on the floor, his hands gripping the steel bars on the side of his bed as he tried to lift himself from the ground. I desperately wanted to pick him up, to help him into his bed, but I was afraid to touch him. Johan, still grasping the bars, grunted and groaned as he strained to lift himself.

Dejectedly, his body slumped. He looked around helplessly until his eyes found mine. I held his stare briefly until he dropped his head in resignation. My desire to help him overwhelmed my fears. I knelt down beside him and wrapped my arms around his torso. I tried to lift him but he was too heavy. All I could do was prop him up against the bed. He closed his eyes, put his chin to his chest and sighed. My pity for him fuelled my determination. I was going to get him into his bed, no matter what it took. I bent down and positioned my arms under his armpits. Mustering all of my strength, I tried to lift him. He didn't budge – not even an inch.

'Help me get you back in your chair,' I said.

He nodded. The chair was lower than the bed, and our combined efforts worked; with my help, he flopped into his chair. My hands lingered on his. He looked into my eyes again. It was only slight, but it was the first time I had seen him smile.

'Come on, together we'll get you back into bed.'

He leant over and placed his hands on the steel rails along the side of his bed. I wrapped my arms around his midriff. My hands traced over his taut chest and abdomen. My heart beat wildly. I thought my legs were going to buckle beneath me.

'Ready?' I said as I composed myself. 'On the count of three. *One, two, three.*'

I held him until he put his hands down flat, steadied himself and shifted along until he was resting comfortably against the bed head. I leant over him, reaching for his pillow before I fluffed it and placed it behind his back. My face was so close to his I could feel him breathing on my neck. I broke away and stepped away from the bed, eyes down.

'*Danke,*' he murmured as he tilted his head back and closed his eyes. I looked up at him, taken aback. I stood there for several minutes before I reached for my broom and set about completing my chores. I had only swept a few steps away when he said, 'My name is Johan.'

'*Ja*, I know,' I replied. 'My name is Ingrid.'

'*Ja*, I know.'

'How do you know?' I asked, surprised, as I pretended to sweep back towards his bed.

'I asked around,' he said, shifting himself to a more comfortable position, his eyes remaining shut. There was so much I wanted to ask. I longed to know everything about him, but I held back. Instead, I started with the question.

'How old are you?'

'I am nineteen.'

'Nineteen! But the other men fear you as if you are fifty.'

'*Ja*, I guess,' he said dismissively. 'How old are you, Ingrid?'

'I am seventeen. Nobody fears me. Why do the men fear you the way they do?'

'I don't know,' he said bluntly. 'Ingrid … a pretty name for a pretty girl. It's a pleasure to meet you.'

Chief Nurse Huber yelled from downstairs, 'Ingrid! Get yourself down to the kitchen – *now*! If you're one minute late, I'll beat you to within an inch of your life.'

'I have to go,' I said as I smiled coyly and dashed downstairs.

My thoughts were consumed by the young *Wehrmacht* officer as I robotically served the men their lunches. I knew I was enamoured – but, equally, I knew I *couldn't* be. What was I even thinking? We were from two different worlds, brought together by extreme circumstances. Maybe we could have something in the time we had together in Hadamar – but what then? What life would we have together beyond these walls? In the real world, a man like him would never consider a girl like me. Besides, he was not a permanent resident here like I was. As soon as he had recovered they would send him home – and that would be it. There was no future for us.

CHAPTER 8

A LIFE NOT WORTH LIVING

October 1941

I couldn't do it. I couldn't keep away.

Each moment away from him was torture.

I did everything I could to be near Johan. Being the Gestapo of Hadamar as she was, Chief Nurse Huber seemed to sense my affection for him. Every time I tried to speak to him, one of her spies was watching. If one nurse left, another arrived before I could say anything. I knew I had to be patient. I knew they couldn't watch me all the time.

As each day went by and I kept an eye out for my opportunity, I noticed that there were more and more empty beds. I knew that men were sent home as soon as they were well. But I was puzzled, for I also knew that not so many of them were well enough to leave. They were disappearing at an awfully rapid rate. I needed to know why. I had to talk to Johan.

I watched the nurses over the next few days. When the night shift handed over to the day shift there were a few minutes when there were no nurses, so I resolved to take this opportunity. In the early hours of the morning, I crept upstairs and stood silently at the end of this bed.

I whispered, 'Hello.'

He didn't hear me at first. I repeated myself, just a little louder.

'Ingrid?' he said as he exited the dream world, rubbing his eyes as he sat up.

'*Ja*, it's me. Um … how are you?' I asked awkwardly.

'As good as can be expected for a man with no legs. It's too early, Ingrid, what do you want?'

I wanted to leave Hadamar and Germany right now, with him, and have the picturesque life that Fräulein Rothenberg had, but I couldn't very well tell him that. I glanced towards the stairs. I knew I was short of time. Chief Nurse Huber or one of the others might appear at any moment.

'Have you noticed how quickly the men are disappearing from this ward?'

'Maybe. I don't know. I haven't been paying attention,' he said as rubbed more sleep from his eyes and took a quick look around. 'I hadn't really noticed. They must have been sent home.'

There were hundreds, thousands, millions of things I wanted to say, and yet nothing came out. I lost my nerve and hurried away. When I glanced back at him I saw him staring at his legs.

I spent the next few days deciding what to say and when to say it. However, on the third night, my decision was made for me. One of the nurses ordered me into Johan's ward to remove and change the sheets of a man who had died during the night from meningitis. It was my job, they said, because it was contagious – and *I* was expendable.

As I folded the last of the corners of the fresh sheets, the harbingers of death, Nurses Ruoff and Willig, appeared at the bedside of the oldest patient in the ward. His name was Carl. I had never spoken to him and all I knew was that he was a veteran of the first war, like Colonel Wilhelm. The men called him 'grandfather' and he commanded a lot of respect, despite his diminutive stature. His long white beard and tied back long hair made him look like one of the Seven Dwarfs. Perhaps he had been a taller man in his day, but time and two wars had left him frail and limping. His right arm was missing as was part of his left hand. Even the simplest things caused him pain.

While Nurses Ruoff and Willig stood silently by his bedside, two of the younger and prettier nurses arrived. The other men watched the two nurses, dressed in white aprons and hats, with interest. They stood beside Carl and helped him from his bed. One nurse placed a hand on each of his shoulders as they led him down the ward, still proudly dressed in his shabby and worn uniform.

'If you can handle two wars, you can handle two women, old timer!' one of the men lounging in his bed called out.

'Look at old Carl!' cried another who sat in a wheelchair by one of the windows. 'He's got the best two nurses to play with!'

The two nurses walked Carl from the ward. Nurses Ruoff and Willig followed closely behind.

We never saw Carl again.

With the nurses occupied, I seized my chance. I ran to Johan's bedside. This time there was no clumsiness, no delaying. I simply came straight out and asked him. 'Johan, do you know where they took Carl?'

'He's being moved to an old man's home in Düsseldorf, to be nearer to his family.'

It sounded like one of the excuses they used when they gassed the children.

'It sounds like a lie,' I whispered. 'They used to tell lies like that when they took the children away to kill them.'

'Kill them?'

Johan's incredulous response told me the men didn't really know the truth of what had gone on at Hadamar.

'I'll tell you about that some other time. Right now, we have to find out where they have taken Carl.'

'Ingrid, they're not going to take away their own soldiers and kill them. That doesn't make sense.'

Before I could say anything further, I heard noises downstairs.

'I'll come back in the morning. We can talk more about it then.'

I awoke early but I only made it as far as the end of the ward before I saw Chief Nurse Huber walking down the corridor. Why was she awake at this time of morning? I wasn't prepared to take the chance so I hurried back to bed.

Later that day, new truckloads of men arrived – but still, the beds kept emptying. I desperately wanted to discuss it with Johan, but it seemed that every time I went near the stairwell, Chief Nurse Huber was standing there.

One night, I caught a break. The stairwell was unguarded. I rushed up to talk to Johan but I had barely taken a few steps when I realised he was asleep. As I walked back towards the stairwell I realised the closest bed to Johan's was empty. It belonged to Reinhart, a man with whom Mia had become friendly.

I whispered to the man in the adjacent bed. 'Where's Reinhart?'

'They told us he was being sent home. That his fits had stopped and he was being discharged.'

Dread took hold of me. I'd heard too many stories like that before. Hearing more noises from downstairs, I knew my time was up. I crept downstairs but as I crawled into bed I wondered: why hadn't Reinhart said anything? Surely he would have told Mia if he was going away.

I passed Mia's bed and wondered whether I should wake her. Maybe it could wait until morning. I lay in bed and tried to sleep, but I couldn't shake the image of them killing Carl. I couldn't close my eyes without picturing him strapped to the crucifix bed as they jabbed the needle in his arm – and now that I had seen Reinhart's empty bed I wondered about them doing the same to him too.

I had to talk to someone about it.

'Mia,' I whispered through the darkness. She slept soundly, only murmuring as I called her name.

'Mia,' I said as loudly as I dared. She grunted and groaned.

I hopped from my bed, put my hands on her shoulders and shook her. 'Mia!'

'What? What do you want?' she grumbled. 'I was having a beautiful dream about Reinhart.'

'Something's not right. There's something they're not telling us.'

'There are thousands of things they don't tell us.'

'*Ja*, like the reason they sent Reinhart away.'

The mention of his name woke her. Of all the men Mia had flirted with, Reinhart was the one with whom she had been most private. At first we had thought there was nothing wrong with him, but later we had learned he was prone to fits that would make him blank out. Sometimes he would be awake but stare blankly at the walls. Sometimes he had physical fits and sometimes not. Maybe that was why the two of them got along so well.

'What do you mean: they sent him away? I was with him yesterday.

'We have to find out what's going on,' I whispered. 'But it's risky. We could get beaten or put into solitary confinement for sneaking around at night.'

'As if that's going to stop me! Besides, if something has happened to Reinhart, I want to know.'

We crept slowly through the ward and past the staff offices. Chief Nurse Huber was nowhere to be seen; nor were any of the others. It was strange that they were all absent. Maybe they already knew our plans and were waiting in hiding for us. It didn't matter. I had to know.

'Come on,' I urged Mia as I took her by the hand and ran as fast as I could towards the medical rooms where they'd killed Eva years before. The same lights emanated from the same windows. Mia and I crept towards the first one. Inside, there was a body strapped to the crucifix bed. We pressed our faces up to the glass. We saw the face of the dead man.

Reinhart.

'*Mein Gott*,' Mia shrieked. '*Mein Gott*!'

'Shhh!' I hissed as I put one hand over hand her mouth and used the other to pull her further down the corridor. She wouldn't budge. Instead, she stared in horror at Reinhart's corpse. My hand still over her mouth, I could feel her tears trickling down her cheeks. Suddenly, she broke free and ran back towards the ward. As the sound of her sobbing died away, I thought about following her. It was the safest option … but I was overwhelmed by an irresistible compulsion to continue. I moved towards the next window and peered inside.

Chief Nurse Huber, Dr Wahlmann and two others stood over a young soldier who was strapped to a crucifix bed.

At first I couldn't make out his face, but when Dr Wahlmann moved aside I saw it clearly. His name was Heinrich. Since his arrival he had only ever sat on his bed, rocking back and forth, gargling incoherent sentences. Were it not for his *Wehrmacht* uniform, he would have been considered one of the mentally disabled patients.

Chief Nurse Huber handed Dr Wahlmann a syringe filled with a yellow liquid and, as it pierced the skin on the inside of Heinrich's left elbow, he suddenly regained his sanity.

'Please! Please!' he begged as he gazed up at them. Even from where I stood I could see the terror in his eyes. 'Please don't kill me!'

His cries faded away as I ran down the corridor. The moonlight that normally lit the corridors had disappeared and I almost ran past the stairwell – *almost*. I ran up it, not caring about the sound my footsteps made as they pounded down on each step. I ran down the ward. Johan was in his bed, snoring loudly.

'Johan,' I whispered.

He didn't move.

'Johan,' I urged as I kept one eye on the stairwell.

Rolling over he sleepily said, 'What? What do you want?'

'I saw them,' I said.

'Ingrid?'

'*Ja*! Johan, I was right. I saw them.'

'Saw who?' he muttered. 'Saw what? What are you talking about?'

'The doctors and the nurses. I saw them. Reinhart was dead – and they killed Heinrich!'

'Don't be silly, Ingrid. You must have dreamed it. Go back to bed.'

I grabbed him by the shoulders and shook him but he brushed me aside. It was no use. I could not get his attention. I made my way quietly back downstairs. I found Mia crying into her pillow. I sat beside her and stroked her hair.

'How *could* they?' she sobbed, her voice muffled by her pillow.

'They are evil – pure evil. There's nothing more to it. They kill Germany's children and now they are killing war veterans. We are all *Lebensunswerte Leben* to them.'

It was all I could think of to say.

'But those men fought for the Fatherland; how could they kill them?' Mia wept. 'I didn't even like Reinhart *that* much, but he didn't deserve to die. He did his bit for Germany.'

'Reinhart, Heinrich: neither of them could work,' I explained bitterly, 'so, like I said, they're *Lebensunswerte Leben*.'

'Lives unworthy of living?'

'*Ja*,' I said.

'But they were *soldiers*. They deserved better.'

'*Ja*, they did,' I said as I lay beside her and stroked her hair until the morning came.

December 1941

I tried to sneak in to see Johan as often as I could. I tried to convince him of the truth but he would not believe me. Whenever I brought it up he told me I was being silly. Winter progressed and one morning as I sat and watched the thickening snow gather on the windowsill, I decided to go upstairs and try one last time to make Johan see sense. I reached the stairs only to find Chief Nurse Huber blocking my way.

'Where are you off to now?' she said as she furrowed her brow.

I had no real excuse. I did not have rostered duties in the men's wards but I tried to bluff. 'I came up to clean the floors.'

'I gave you no such order,' she said, looking at me suspiciously.

I averted my eyes and bowed my head.

'Look at me,' she hissed as she grasped my chin and forced me to look into her eyes. 'I see how you look at that boy. Don't think I haven't.'

'Which boy, Frau Huber?' I asked, trying my best to pretend I didn't know what she was talking about.

'Don't play dumb with me, you little black bitch. You, you black whore, are becoming a very bright girl. And you'd be smart to learn to be more honest with me. Which boy? The boy missing his legs.'

'There are many boys missing their legs, Chief Nurse Huber. Which one do you mean?'

'You know exactly which boy I mean. I will be watching you.'

'*Ja*, Frau Huber.'

She stood there with her hands on her hips, barring the stairwell. I slunk back to my bed where I sat and contemplated ways to make my visits to Johan even more clandestine. My thoughts were interrupted by the sound of Johan's squeaking wheels as he wheeled himself down the ward. What was he doing here? I looked past him towards Chief Nurse Huber's office. The lights were on. I expected her to come marching down the ward at any moment.

'Hello, Ingrid,' he said shyly as he stopped his chair at the end of my bed. My eyes flicked from his face to Chief Nurse Huber's office and then to Mia, who sat on her bed, a Cheshire grin on her face as she nodded. He wheeled his chair to my bedside and reached out for my hand. I shivered. Indescribable feelings, feelings I had never felt before, pulsed through me. My feelings swung between anxiety and euphoria. I felt nauseated. My arms and legs tingled.

We heard a loud bang. I turned to see Mia's body thrashing around wildly.

'What's happening?' Johan asked.

'I think she's having a seizure!'

'Nurse! Nurse!' Johan shouted.

Nurses came running down the corridor, Chief Nurse Huber amongst them.

'Quick, get some Phenobarbital,' she ordered. 'Lieutenant Kapfler, hold her steady.'

One of the younger nurses ran down the ward, returning with a small clear bottle and a syringe and handing it to Chief Nurse Huber. The young nurses helped Johan hold Mia's bucking body down to let Chief Nurse Huber get a good grasp of her left arm. She stuck the syringe in Mia's arm and depressed the plunger. Mia went limp. I was sure they had killed her.

'She'll be okay,' Chief Nurse Huber said as she handed the syringe back to the nurse. 'She just needs to rest for a while.'

Johan waited for Chief Nurse Huber to chastise him, to ask him what he was doing in our ward. I waited for her tirade about how a little black whore like me needed to keep my hands off our brave soldiers, but she didn't. She just looked both of us over before she and the other nurses departed. Johan breathed a sigh of relief.

I don't know why I did it. Maybe I longed for a feeling of safety and protection. I hopped off my bed and into his lap. He put his arm around my waist and we both stared at Mia, who slept soundly, as if nothing at all had happened. I couldn't help but wonder: if the situation was reversed, would they have done anything to help me? I doubted it.

Suddenly, she seemed more lucid and looked around the ward, blinking. It took her a while to remember where she was but it was clear she was still dazed. When she saw Johan and me, she ducked her head shyly.

'I … I … I'm … so … sorry,' she finally stammered. 'I … I wish … you had not seen me … like that.'

'Like what?' Johan said unconvincingly.

'The seizure, the drooling, the spasms,' Mia mumbled.

Johan leant forward, took her hand with his free hand and bent forward to kiss and squeeze it. 'You don't need to apologise. We're all here because there is something "wrong" with us. I've seen worse in battle. Besides, you can't control it, can you?'

'*Nein*,' she said, blushing.

I flipped myself around to face him. I realised I'd forgotten to ask why he was down here.

'What are you doing here? Why did you come and see me?'

He looked down the ward and then back at me. Satisfied no-one else was around, he whispered, 'Because I think you might be right about what is happening with some of the soldiers.'

'I've been telling you that for months, but you wouldn't believe me. Why have you changed your mind?'

'After you said it was Heinrich they'd killed, I kept asking the doctors and nurses where he was. At first they told me they'd found a piece of shrapnel in his shoulder that had become infected and he was in another ward. But he didn't come back, and I kept on asking. They told me they'd shipped him back to his home village of Hoffenheim. But we all knew Heinrich wasn't quite right in the head, and there's no way they'd send a man like that home to his family. One day they came and took all of his possessions except one cardboard box. Yesterday, Colonel Wilhelm and I decided to have a look. Inside were bits of paper with writing all over them. Most of what he wrote was incoherent rubbish but on one piece of paper there was an address and a phone number. We bribed one of the nurses to let us use a staff phone. We rang the number. It was his mother's. She said she hasn't seen or heard from Heinrich since he had left to fight.'

'You see!' I cried. 'I told you! They kill anyone who they decide is *Lebensunwertes Leben*!'

'Ingrid, I believe you – but what we are going to do about it?'

With a start, I realised I was going to be late for breakfast duties. Chief Nurse Huber might have ignored Johan's presence in my ward – and I was still curious as to why – but if I was late for my duties there would be hell to pay, especially now I had to do the work of two.

'Meet me out in the courtyard after breakfast,' I said as I jumped off Johan's lap and rushed to the kitchen. Johan didn't come in for breakfast. Eager to get back to him, I did a second-rate job of the cleaning. I ran the risk of Chief Nurse Huber's ire, but it didn't matter to me. Sitting on Johan's lap had been intoxicating. I wanted to be near him again.

Back in the ward, I glanced at Mia. She slept soundly. Through the windows I could see Johan sitting in the courtyard playing with some black rosary beads that sat in his lap. I stood at the doorway and watched him. Although he still seemed melancholy and lost in his thoughts, there was something different about him – something happier.

'Ingrid,' he said when he noticed me. I sat down on the bench beside him. 'Where are you from?'

'Didn't I tell you? I am from Mainz. What about you?'

'Düsseldorf.'

He was silent for a moment, and then he asked, letting the rosary beads fall in his lap, 'What are the people of Mainz like?' Then he took my hand and held it in his.

'What do you mean?' I asked, distracted by the touch of his hand.

'Are they Nazis? Are they obsessed with the Fatherland and *Der Führer*?'

'More than you can imagine.'

'And how did you cope? I can only guess at the names they must have called you.'

'I don't know. *Ja*, it hurts, but after a while you learn to ignore it. You just learn to live with it.'

'And when the townspeople stare at you?'

'You ignore that too. You look the other way or you just kept staring straight on ahead. Why?'

'No reason.'

I didn't realise I was doing it. I didn't mean to do it, but I was staring at his legs; the shadows from the buildings made it look as if they had regrown.

'You're wondering what happened to me, aren't you?' he said as he picked up the rosary beads and twirled them.

'*Nein, nein*,' I said as I looked away.

'It's okay,' he said. 'You can look. I don't like other people looking, but *you* can.'

As hard as I tried to keep them focused on something else – his face, for instance – my eyes found their way back to his stumps.

'I am – was – a lieutenant in the *Wehrmacht*,' he continued as he slapped his thighs. 'I was wounded in the Battle of Kiev.'

'I read about that in the papers that Dr Oppenheimer brought me,' I told him.

He gave me a brief forlorn look. 'It was a tremendous victory for us. We encircled them and captured thousands and thousands of them. I was leading my men in the final assault on the city centre when the Russians launched a fierce and final counter-offensive. They came from everywhere, like ants rushing from a nest; there were just so many. I fired and fired, maybe three or four magazines' worth. Dozens upon dozens of Russians fell dead but it didn't make a difference; they just kept on coming.

'My men and I were going to be forced into a retreat but something came over me. I don't know how to explain it – but I thought I was invincible. I grabbed one of my fallen comrade's machine guns and charged forward. I shot in and around the buildings to my left. Man after man came from every conceivable hiding place. I killed every one of them. Every one! I reached the next rows of buildings and reached for my grenades. I pushed my back up as far as I could against the wall and threw the first one through a broken window. It exploded. There was a loud bang and dust and glass from the explosion went everywhere. I didn't wait for it to settle. I used it as cover as I ran to the next window, then the next.

'The whole time the Russians kept firing at me. They fired from windows, from doorways – everywhere! There were piles of rubble scattered around the square. I ran from one to the next, throwing grenades and firing my weapon wherever I saw movement. Just as I reached the middle of the square I ran out of ammunition. They opened up on me with everything they had.

'That was when I thought God had abandoned me. I was sure I was going to die. But, all of a sudden, the firing stopped.'

He paused. His voice was heavy with pain as he went on. 'Next to me, wedged under a boulder, was what was left of a German captain. His machine gun was still lying beside him. I picked it up and ran for the nearest building. I kicked the door open and fired and killed two Russians. I picked up their guns, moved onto the next building and then the next. When I came out from the last building, scores of Russians emerged from their hiding places with their hands knotted behind their heads. My men streamed in through the entrance to the square.

'My adrenaline began to subside and I keeled over. My men took the Russians prisoner and marched them back to our lines. I gave myself a few more minutes to regain my breath. I was the last one to leave the square. Then a Russian came from an alleyway and hurled a grenade. I saw it turn end over end, like it was in slow motion. It hit the ground and rolled towards me. Ingrid, there was nowhere to run, no escape. The next thing I knew I woke up in an army hospital.'

'Wait,' I said excitedly. 'I read about this in *Das Reich*. You're *that* lieutenant? You're a war hero!'

'Some have called me that,' he said as he showed me two Iron Crosses that were pinned under his collar. He seemed neither proud nor excited by them. 'You know, being a "hero" is not quite like people think it is. For a few months I was paraded around to inspire the men. I was treated like a celebrity. I had everything I could ever want – except for my legs. I even met *Der Führer* once. But then the next hero comes along and they parade him around and forget about you.'

It all made sense now. Why the other men ceded to his orders, why they were fearful of upsetting him, why he had such an air of authority despite his youth. He put his head down, staring at a ring on his right hand as he rubbed it with the fingers from his left hand. I wasn't sure what to do. I didn't know what to say. I reached for his right hand. He looked up at me, his eyes glazing over as he fought back the tears.

I kissed him, letting my lips linger long on his. Time stood still. Nothing else in the world mattered. I forgot where I was as I buzzed with euphoria. My first kiss! I had just had my first kiss! I turned back to him, wanting to kiss him again as I looked into his eyes. I remembered what Vati had told me about the eyes being the window to the soul. In Johan's I saw he felt the same way about me – but there was something more. I knew he had only told me a fraction of his story. I wanted to hear it, but now was not the time.

'You know,' I said as I put my hand on what remained of his right leg. 'Having a disability is not the end of your life. You can still do most of the things you did before.'

He stared down where his legs had once been.

'Tell me more about your childhood in Düsseldorf,' I said as I sat on his lap and put my arms around his neck.

'I joined the *Deutsches Jungvolk* at ten, then the Hitler Youth when I was thirteen. Clearly, I was the perfect Aryan,' he said bitterly as he brushed his blond hair back with his hand. 'I've always been … well … I was always really fit and strong. Any athletic competition I entered, I won easily. I suppose I was popular. I behaved the way I was expected to, I suppose.

'When the war came there wasn't any doubt about my future. My whole life had been building up to it. I would enlist and serve the Fatherland. At first it all seemed like one big adventure, another place for me to prove how strong I was – but, deep down, I knew I went because I wanted to leave the life that had been set out for me. The war was an escape, a place to find a new me, to find out who I really was.'

Tears trickled down his cheeks. I wiped them away with my hand but when the tears became a stream there was nothing I could do to stop them.

'What's going to happen to me when I go back home, Ingrid? Imagine what people will say when they see me like this. Imagine what they'll think. Everyone will stare at me. The whole town will pity me. People won't even look at me, they'll just turn their heads away in disgust. I'm just a disabled freak! I'm not fit to call myself German anymore!'

Burying his head into my neck, he sobbed and sobbed, his tears soaking my shirt. Finally, he looked up at me through reddened eyes.

'I know how you feel,' I said.

'Sorry,' he sniffed. 'I'm being selfish. *You're* different too. You've put up with people thinking you're not a true German your whole life.'

'*Danke* … I think. Johan, despite everything, I still made some good friends; I still had a family who loved me. I still loved people and was loved by them.'

I was trying to console him but it made me realise that, in many ways, I *had* been fortunate.

'Tell me more about your family,' he said as he nuzzled his chin into my shoulder. I stroked his hair and was about to answer when I heard Chief Nurse Huber's shrill shouting.

'*Was ist das*? What is going on here?'

I didn't move. I couldn't remember a time when I had been this happy and I wasn't about to let her spoil it. She stood, glaring at me, with her hands on her hips like a little grey teapot. For the first time, I wasn't afraid of her – she seemed more comical than threatening.

'*Entschuldigen* – excuse me, Matron!' Johan said, embarrassed, as picked me up and threw me off him. I landed on my feet and turned to face Chief Nurse Huber as she set off on one of her rants.

'Lieutenant Kapfler! I had my suspicions that there was something going on between you and this girl when I had to come down here to help that idiot, Mia! But then I thought to myself, *nein*, you must have been passing by and you rushed in to help. Now I find you here with her! I am disgusted! How could you – a decorated war hero – come down here and consort with this girl, this *schwarze Schande*! You were part of the Hitler Youth, the *Wehrmacht*! Don't let this little black Jezebel bewitch you with her temptress ways. You can never be too careful around coloured women, Lieutenant Kapfler, they are like the Sirens themselves. Before you know it, she will have led you to your demise!'

Maybe it was because I had heard them so often. Maybe it was the euphoria of the kiss, but Chief Nurse Huber's insults were barbless now. The only thing that pained me was Johan's obvious embarrassment. I couldn't blame him, though, could I? He was the product of years of brainwashing; they all were. It was going to take him time to ignore their rules, unlearn their ideas and live life the way he wanted. For now, he wheeled himself away, head bowed like a scolded child.

'And *you*!' Chief Nurse Huber barked once Johan disappeared from the ward. 'You keep your little black whore hands off those brave boys who fought for the Fatherland! Now, get yourself into the dining hall and get lunch ready! If I even see you taking a sideways glance at that boy there'll be hell to pay!'

She turned on her heels and charged back through the ward, grumbling something about how she wished she could kill me and be rid of me for good. I stuck my tongue out and waited until she was well out of sight before I headed to the kitchen. As I brought the last soup vat out, I spied Chief Nurse Huber sitting at the front table, intently watching my every move. Out of the corner of my eye

I searched for Johan but did not see him. Lunch finished, but only after I had packed everything away did she finally leave.

Back in the ward I retrieved my stash of newspapers and laid them out neatly on my bed in chronological order. I hoped I'd kept the copy of *Das Reich* that carried the story about Johan. I carefully flicked through each of them. Then I saw it, on the front page: a picture of him proudly wearing his Iron Crosses. The article confirmed what he had just told me. The picture showed him smiling but, on closer inspection, I thought his smile looked forced. Hearing footsteps in the hallway, I quickly stacked my newspapers together and put them back under my bed. Chief Nurse Huber came and stood at the end of my bed.

'I have more work for you,' she snapped. I followed her. She gave me a mop and told me to clean the floors in the front foyer. They were already clean, but I finished as quickly as I could and went and stood at her office door to tell her I was done. She told me to follow her. For the rest of the day she kept me busy. 'Ingrid, clean this. Ingrid, wash that. Ingrid, change this. Ingrid, change that.'

It was late into the night before I finished. I made my way back to my bed, peering up to the men's ward to see if all the lights were out. I contemplated making a dash upstairs to see Johan, but I was just too exhausted. Besides, he'd be asleep by now. It would have to wait until tomorrow. I thought I would fall asleep as soon as my head hit the pillow, but thoughts of him kept me awake. I turned on my side to look out the window. It *was* late. The moon was almost past the edges of the buildings. It was well after midnight.

I replayed everything that had happened, everything he'd said. I pictured every outline of his face, every inch of his muscular body. I knew I had to find a way to see him. The thought of not being near him was unbearable. Forget Chief Nurse Huber; I had to follow her orders, *ja*, but I didn't think she had the courage to kill me – though she *might* have the power to have me transferred somewhere else. *Nein*, it was worth the risk. I knew I *wasn't* scared of her any more. I had to see him.

'He's quite something that Johan, isn't he?' Mia whispered. I rolled over. She was lying on her side, staring at me, that same huge grin on her face.

'*Ja*, I suppose he is.'

'Well, what are you waiting for? Go up and see him.'

'It's late. He'll be asleep by now.'

'He really is handsome, you know, and that body – well, aside from him having no legs ...'

'*Ja*, maybe.'

'If I was you, I'd be running up there.'

'*Nein*, it can wait until morning. I don't want to disturb him.'

'I tell you one thing: if you don't chase that boy and make him yours, then you have rocks in your head. If you don't go after him, I will.'

'Just leave it,' I told her as I rolled away from her and pretended to sleep. I didn't like how she was talking about him, nor did I like her declaring her intentions. Maybe she was just trying to make me do what I needed to; either way, it made me furious.

Eventually I fell asleep. I dreamed of Johan, but in my dream it was not me sitting on his lap; it was Mia. I was not held tightly in his arms; *she* was. Several times I awoke with a start, and each time I started to fall asleep again, I found it hard to shake one thought: they were both Aryan. Perhaps they *should* be together. Barely had the first light filtered through the windows than I sprang out of bed. Breakfast would provide my best and quickest opportunity to see him and I wanted to make sure I was there if he arrived early. I hastened to the end of the ward, stopped, turned around, and went back to the bed next to mine.

It was empty. Mia was gone.

I wanted to search for her, but she could be anywhere and I knew I couldn't be late for breakfast. In the kitchen, I waited as the mental patients brought out the vats of porridge. Men started to file in and, as I ladled out the porridge, I watched for Johan. The dining hall was almost filled. He hadn't appeared – and neither had Mia.

My imagination ran wild. I tried to remain calm, to focus on my work, but I couldn't. All I could do was picture them engaged in some secret tryst in the depths of Hadamar. I pictured them kissing, her hands all over his body and his over hers. Just as I became enraged with jealousy a direr thought entered my mind.

What if they were both missing because, during the night while I slept, Chief Nurse Huber had ordered their deaths? The thought sickened me to my stomach. When the last man had been served I quickly cleaned out the vats and ran to the men's ward. Johan's bed was empty.

I wheeled in circles as I held my abdomen, my stomach burning as if it was on fire.

'They took him to have his wounds re-dressed and to check how his legs were healing,' Dietrich, the older man from the next bed, said as he smiled and looked up from the book he was reading. 'He'll be back soon.'

I tried to slow my breathing, to calm my nerves. I knew I needed to be somewhere else. During the breakfast preparations one of the male orderlies had told me that we needed more vegetables for dinner and that when I had the chance, I was to go and find as many fresh vegetables as I could from the stores or in the gardens. I hurried back to the kitchen to retrieve a basket and made my way outside.

The air was icy. I pulled the collar of my flimsy jacket up over my neck in a vain attempt to shield myself from the cold. As quickly as I could I went up to the fields, found a hoe that had been left lying around, picked it up and used it to rummage through the frost-covered dirt. It took a little digging in several different places but, eventually, I found some carrots and potatoes. They were old but they would do the job. With my basket half full, I decided to return the hoe to the garden shed. When I reached the shed I put the basket beside the entrance, opened the door, and walked inside, returning the hoe to its place on the wall.

'I think that garden may just be as beautiful as you,' I heard a man's voice say. I smiled and turned around.

Then my stomach twisted in knots. My heart pounded. My hands went clammy, my mouth went dry. The stout figure of Franz stood blocking the entrance. I glanced either side of him, wondering whether I could get past and make for the safety of the buildings.

I stepped forward. When I stepped out of the darkness and the light hit my face he apologised.

'Sorry,' he said. 'I thought you were Mia.'

'No problem,' I said as I tried to step past him. I knew he was lying. 'Mistakes can be made.'

'It's that Mia, you see,' he said as he stroked his chin and paced back and forth across the doorway. 'Always coming into our ward with her blouse halfway down her chest and her skirt way up above her knees. It's enough to drive a man crazy. I see how she flirts with the others. I've seen her sneaking kisses from some of them. Not once has she ever even looked at me – not once! But why would she? Look at me, all disfigured and disgusting!'

He moved and left a gap wide enough for me to fit through. I tried to run past him but his outstretched arm stopped me dead. He wrapped one of his gigantic arms around my pencil-thin waist and ran the fingers of his other hand down the side of my cheeks.

'Look at me!' he demanded as his hand covered my face, squeezing my cheeks together as he forced my eyes to stare into his. 'The war did this! I can't help how I look! These scars on my face will never go away. I'm going look like this for the rest of my life. Do you think a woman is ever going look at me again the way I see you look at that cripple boy? *Nein*!'

Given no choice, I examined his face. Yes, he was ugly – but the battle scars were nothing compared with the ugliness inside him.

'Franz, I am sorry about what happened to you. I really am,' I mumbled through my compressed cheeks.

'What do you know about it?' he said ferociously. 'You've lived your whole life being a nothing – a nobody. I was *someone* once.'

His grip tightened, forcing me to cry.

'Franz, please!' I begged. 'Please leave me alone!'

'I came here to get what I wanted and I'm not leaving without it. You may not be a good Aryan girl like Mia but you're going to have to do.'

He threw me to the ground. I tried to scream but he was on top of me. My mouth was smothered by his thick forearm hair. I tried to move, to squirm, to shift my way free, but he was just too big and powerful. The foulness of his body odour consumed me, the stale stench of alcohol and tobacco worsened by his heavy breathing. I began to suffocate as his body weight pressed down on me. All I could do was suck in short, sharp breaths.

'You're actually quite beautiful for a little black whore,' he whispered into my ear as his grip tightened around my wrists and he forced my arms above my head. I turned my face away from him, trying to escape his disgusting breath. He whispered in my other ear, 'Why are you fighting me? Your kind love Aryan men. I've seen how you look at that so-called war hero.'

Fastening my wrists in place with his left hand, his right hand slid down my body. I went numb. I stopped fighting. I tried to think of Johan, his legs returned to him. We ran, the two of us, in a lush, green meadow filled with buttercups. The Alps towered high into the sky, their snow-capped peaks reaching towards the Heavens.

Franz groaned loudly before lifting himself off me. I breathed deeply, my lungs filling like balloons. The concrete floor felt freezing on my back. I wanted to run, to cry until my eyes hurt – but I dared not move.

Franz zipped up his trousers. I heard his footsteps as he walked away. I waited until I thought he was gone before I lifted myself up and walked gingerly back out of the shed towards the main building. I reached the rear door. I saw my clothes were ruffled. Hurriedly trying to flatten them, I realised I had left the basket behind. A cool wind blew, dousing the fires burning in my cheeks.

I retrieved the basket from outside the shed then stumbled inside and placed it in the pantry. I wanted to see Johan. *Nein* – I didn't want to see anybody. Confused, not knowing what I should do next, I couldn't think of anything else but to go back and sit on my bed. I pulled my knees up to my chest and stared blankly out the windows.

This was my life, my destiny, to be abused and used.

'Are you okay?' I heard a voice. Without looking, I knew it was Mia.

'Go away!' I snapped back.

'Ingrid, what's the matter?'

I felt a feminine hand on me. I flicked my shoulder to remove it. 'I said, go away!'

'Ingrid, tell me what happened? What did you see? What did they do?'

'They didn't do anything! It was all your fault! If you didn't act the way you do around them, none of this would have happened!'

'What are you talking about?' Mia asked as she came around and stood between me and the windows.

'Nothing! Never mind!'

'Ingrid?'

As if he sensed what had happened, Johan appeared, wheeling himself along the ward. I burst into tears.

'What is it?' he said as he settled his chair beside my bed. He reached for my hand. I grasped it tightly and wept.

Johan stroked my hair and said softly, 'Tell me what happened.'

'Franz …' I sobbed. Johan lifted his head and stared at me. I didn't have to finish. He understood. Disbelief flooded his face. I watched him wondering what to do next.

He didn't look at me. He didn't look at Mia. He didn't say a word. He simply turned his chair and wheeled himself towards the stairwell. I followed, but kept a safe distance behind, not wanting to arouse Chief Nurse Huber's suspicions.

'Orderly! Orderly!' he called out as he reached the base of the stairs. 'I want to go upstairs!'

No orderlies appeared, but Dietrich and another patient came rushing down the stairs, grabbed hold of him under the remnants of his legs and carried him up. The shorter man whom I didn't know returned to collect Johan's chair. Mia and I followed. Johan was back in his chair, slowly and purposefully wheeling himself up the ward. Franz lay leaning on his pillow, a satisfied smirk across his face as he smoked a cigarette. The sight of him made me want to vomit.

'What do you want, cripple?' he chortled. Johan's knuckles whitened as his grip tightened on the wheels. I was sure he was about to explode, but he merely wheeled himself further down the ward.

'*Ja*, that's what I thought!' Franz laughed as he lay back and inhaled deeply on his cigarette, blowing the smoke towards the ceiling. Johan stopped at Old Wilhelm's bedside. Leaning forward, he whispered into Old Wilhelm's ear. The colonel looked at Franz, then at me, and back to Franz again. His face reddened and his normally unflappable exterior was clearly ruffled. He nodded as Johan spoke, patting him on the shoulder, before he stood up and whispered something to the man in the next bed. Old Wilhelm stretched his left hand out towards me and motioned for me to come to him. I walked down the ward, my eyes firmly fixed ahead. I fell into Old Wilhelm's outstretched arms.

'Don't worry, you poor girl,' he said as he hugged me and kissed my cheek. 'Life has a way of balancing the ledger and, in this case, *we* are the ledger.'

He released me from his embrace and gently pushed me aside.

'Hans,' he called another man over and murmured softly but urgently to him. 'Tell the other boys what has happened. Tell them that we won't tolerate what Franz has done. Have some of the men create a diversion to keep the nurses and orderlies away.'

Hans grabbed the back of Johan's chair and gave me a quick smile as he passed by.

'Stay here, Ingrid,' Johan told me.

Old Wilhelm stood in front of me, as if to shield me from what was about to happen. But I could see past him. I saw Hans and Johan move from bed to bed.

Franz sensed something was amiss. He sat bolt upright and furled his brow as he tried to make sense of what was happening. One by one, the men rose from their beds – even those who struggled to walk. Suddenly, the able-bodied men broke into a run and circled Franz's bed. He tried to escape but all he could do was struggle like a fly caught in a spider's web. Two men, named Dietrich and Hans, grabbed him by the arms and dragged him down the ward until they stood in front of Old Wilhelm and me.

Johan wheeled himself closer.

'You don't have to watch this,' he said quietly.

Did I want to? I had seen enough abuse, pain and torture to last me a thousand life times. I wasn't sure I wanted to see any more.

Nein. Franz had taken advantage of me, stolen whatever remained of my innocence. He needed to suffer. He needed to pay. I wanted revenge for *everything* that had been done to me. No-one had ever paid for the atrocities they'd inflicted on me. Franz may have only been at the bottom of a very tall ladder but he was, just the same, on the ladder.

I nodded firmly. Dietrich and Hans forced Franz to his knees, holding his arms out as if he were Jesus on the cross. Franz's bottom lip quivered like Sarah's had done on the day we were confronted by the school bullies. I had no sympathy – only hatred. Half a dozen men who were guarding the stairs took one last look for any sign of the nurses, doctors or orderlies. The closest of them nodded.

Blow after blow rained down on Franz. He was helpless to resist. He was a human punching bag. He lost consciousness and fell to the ground. They kicked him in the ribs and stomped on his head. Their retribution was so brutal it was almost sickening. I was afraid; I wanted him to suffer but I didn't want him to die. One of the men guarding the stairwell cried out, 'Quick! They're coming!'

Men scattered in every direction. Franz lay prostrate, a bruised, bloodied and beaten pulp.

'*Was ist das*? What's going on here?' one of the orderlies cried when he saw Franz. Two more appeared at the top of the stairs, the three of them rushing to Franz's side to check him over. He came to, writhing and groaning in agony. The orderlies looked around the ward. The soldiers pretended to read, looked out the windows or lay on their beds as if nothing had happened.

Knowing they would never discover the truth – and not caring – the orderlies picked Franz up and carried him downstairs. They didn't notice me or Mia. We crept to the top of the stairs, cautiously peering down as the orderlies put Franz into a chair like Johan's.

Franz never did get out of that chair. Eventually he disappeared. Perhaps he had become *Lebensunwertes Leben*.

CHAPTER 9

FALSE HOPE

January 1942

Franz had taken from me any remaining spark. I retreated inside myself, doing my daily chores as required and speaking only when spoken to. Mia and Johan tried to talk to me, but I ignored them and they eventually gave up. Spring approached and I decided I just wasn't going to work anymore. What was the point? My life had lost all meaning. I just wanted to die.

One morning, I just didn't get out of bed. When I failed to appear for my breakfast duties, Chief Nurse Huber came hunting for me.

'Ingrid, get your worthless behind out of that bed, now!'

'*Nein*.'

'Ingrid, if you do not get up right now, I will have one of the orderlies come in here and drag your black hide from this ward.'

'Okay.'

She grunted in exasperation.

'It's okay, Chief Nurse Huber,' Mia interjected. 'I can cover for Ingrid.'

Chief Nurse Huber ignored Mia, stepped towards my bed, leant down and growled, 'Ingrid! If you do not get up and do your chores, I will have someone come and inject you here and now!'

I sat up in my bed, looked her squarely in her eyes, and said, 'Do it.'

'Oh!' she huffed, stamping her right foot on the ground like a two-year-old. 'You can be sure Herr Schmidt will hear about this!'

Gut, I thought as I waited for Herr Schmidt to march down the ward and give me a patriotic speech before he put a bullet in me.

He never came.

Mia looked at me strangely before she ran off to do our chores. I had not seen Dr Oppenheimer recently, but I still had occasional access to newspapers through some of the newly-arrived soldiers who brought papers with them. When they left the newspapers behind in the dining rooms or tossed them in the rubbish bin, I collected them and added them to my stash. I read through the most recently-dated papers, hoping to find something – anything – to suggest the war might be coming to an end. There was nothing. Not only had our armies advanced well into Russia, but they were also entrenched in North Africa and it looked like they would soon take Cairo. The Japanese had attacked Pearl Harbor in early December of the previous year, and they were now in control of most of Asia. The world would soon be divided between the Axis powers.

When this happened, the killings of undesirables like me would resume. The evil forces would prevail; my life was forfeit anyway. Why couldn't they just take it now?

On several occasions after I'd stopped speaking to him, Johan appeared at the ward entrance, but he never ventured inside. He would just pause, look at me, drop his head and leave. I wanted to tell him I still cared for him, that I wanted to be with him. But how could I explain that my black skin felt like a coat of dirt that would forever stain me, both inside and out? He deserved better than that. He deserved better than me. Besides, I was never going to live a long and happy life; there was no point imagining that life with him.

Winter in Hadamar ambled along with nothing much to separate one day from another. More men arrived and some disappeared. More children came – and some of them disappeared too. The staff hadn't resumed the mass killings, or so I thought. I knew that the children, the soldiers and some of the mental patients had died from natural causes. Dozens of children had been quarantined due to an outbreak of typhus. Nevertheless, Hadamar became decidedly overcrowded. The staff kept their distance from us, not seeming to care what we did. Perhaps it was their revulsion; perhaps it was the fear of catching diseases … or perhaps their orders had changed. I didn't know and didn't care. In any case, it was clear their authority remained absolute.

Mia had more seizures, more violent than the first. They began to scare the smaller children, so the doctors had her moved to a ward where the patients were too far gone to care. I still saw her every now and then. Part of me was happy she was gone so I could be left to my own devices, but her absence made me lonely.

CHAPTER 9

Springtime arrived in full force and, like the outside world, Hadamar suddenly sprung back to life for me. Perhaps it was the blooming of the flowers or the return of the warmth of the sun. I began to feel better about myself. It was time to mend the bridges I had burned. It was time to talk to Johan again. I was bored and so I decided to do my chores again. I did not even think to look around for Chief Nurse Huber before I made my way upstairs.

Johan sat in his chair. Mia was on his lap with his arms wrapped around her waist. Her face obscured his; they were kissing.

I let out a cry. Breaking from their embrace, they turned and looked at me. I ran downstairs and dove onto my bed. I buried my head in my pillow and wept. Before long, I heard the squeaking of a wheelchair getting closer.

'Ingrid,' Johan said as he stopped his chair near my bed.

'Go away! I don't want to speak to you ever again!'

'Ingrid, *bitte*, there is nothing going on between me and Mia. What you just saw wasn't what you think it was.'

I tossed over angrily and glared at him. 'I don't ever want to speak to you again.'

I saw the dejection and disappointment in his face but I didn't care. How could he do that to me? True: I had not spoken to him for months – but I thought he knew that I just needed time to deal with what had happened to me. Why didn't he wait? Why did I ever think he even cared about me? I was stupid to have thought that he was any different to the others.

And … Mia.

How *could* she? I knew she was a flirt – but how could she go after Johan? I thought she was my friend. Why hadn't I seen it? Why hadn't I realised?

I bounded from my bed and marched down the ward straight into Chief Nurse Huber's office. She leant over her desk, engrossed in whatever it was she was doing.

I pretended to cough. She looked up. 'What do you want, Ingrid? I'm busy.'

'Chief Nurse Huber, there's something I need to tell you. Something very important.'

'Well, out with it, you black idiot. I have a lot of work to do.'

'Chief Nurse Huber, do we have any Jews here at Hadamar?'

She pushed her paperwork to one side, motioned for me to sit in the seat across from her, leant back in her chair and folded her arms.

'Why do you ask?' she said suspiciously.

'I was just wondering – that's all.'

'*Nein*, Ingrid, we do not have any Jews here. Before this war ends there won't be any Jews at all. Now, have you come here to tell me something important, or have you just come here to waste my time, because if you have …!'

'Chief Nurse Huber,' I said, keeping my voice soft and steady, 'we do have one Jew here.'

'What? What are you talking about?'

'Mia,' I paused. 'She's a Jew.'

Chief Nurse Huber narrowed her eyes at me. 'This better not be some silly game you are playing.'

'I'm not playing games, Chief Nurse Huber. Mia told me herself. She's a Jew.'

'And why are you only telling me this now? Why are you telling me at all? I thought you two were thick as thieves.'

I started to answer, but she cut in.

'Wait,' she sneered. 'I know why. It's because she's been hanging around Lieutenant Kapfler, isn't it? You want her out of the way so you can have him all to yourself.'

I didn't say anything, but her self-satisfied smirk told me that she knew she was right.

'Maybe I had you pegged wrong, Marchand. You could never be a true German, what with the colour of your skin and all, but perhaps some blacks may have a role in the new Reich. You may be filth but you are not as bad as a stinking Jew.'

I didn't care about her backhanded compliment. I didn't care about a new Reich. I just wanted Mia gone. Chief Nurse Huber stood up, which was my cue to do the same.

'You have done the right thing by telling me, Marchand,' she said as she escorted me to the door. 'I think life in Hadamar may just get a little easier for you.'

I inched slowly back to the ward. I turned to watch Chief Nurse Huber walk quickly then break into a run down the corridor. She'd barely reached the end before she started calling out, 'Herr Schmidt! Herr Schmidt! Come quickly! There's something I need to tell you!'

I lingered at the ward door to watch. Herr Schmidt marched

around the corner dressed in his customary black SS uniform, his boots shiny, goose-stepping as if he were marching in front of Hitler himself.

'Herr Schmidt, I have just discovered that there is a Jew hiding among the mental patients.'

'What! A Jew, you say?'

'*Ja*,' she hissed, pausing for emphasis before leaning in to say, 'That epileptic girl.'

'One moment,' he barked as he disappeared into one of the offices. My heart pounded as I waited for his return. He emerged with a murderous scowl on his face. 'Irmgard, we must send this Jewish whore where she belongs, and I want you to do a full review of *every* patient here. If there is one Jew in the mental and disabled wards, we may have more. But I am pleased with you for discovering this Jewish swine hiding in our midst. I am going to tell General Müller about this. He will be extremely pleased.'

Chief Nurse Huber was clearly chuffed. It was the first time I had seen her smile; not just the half-smirk that she often gave, but a genuine smile. I was told to go back to my ward. Half an hour passed and I I heard a loud creaking noise coming from the main corridor. I got up from my bed and crept closer to the entrance. One of the male orderlies opened the front doors, and in marched two Gestapo men dressed in long, black trench coats. The sight of them made me shiver. What had I done? The men stopped in front of Herr Schmidt, who nodded to his right. They rushed into Mia's ward.

I held my breath and waited. It must have taken seconds, but it seemed like hours. Then the black-clad men reappeared, holding Mia between them.

'Wait! Please! It's a mistake!' she wailed as she wildly kicked her legs. Her eyes caught mine as she passed me. I will never forget her look of sheer terror as the Gestapo men bundled her out the doors. Herr Schmidt and Chief Nurse Huber stood and watched.

'Where are they taking her?' Chief Nurse Huber asked.

'Ravensbrück.'

March 1942

As the year progressed wearily, my feelings oscillated between guilt, remorse and vindictive satisfaction.

At times I felt bad for what I did – but she had brought it on herself, or so I told myself. Now that she was out of the picture, I knew it was time to talk to Johan again but, try as I might, I could not pluck up the courage. *Nein*, I had tried to keep track of the days and I was sure my eighteenth birthday had come and gone without a word or a single candle. All that marked my passage into adulthood was my ability to act like one. I had spent the last four years as a scared teenage girl cowering to them, fearful and alone; now it was time to stand up for myself and to be who I wanted to be.

Then one day, out of nowhere, Dr Oppenheimer appeared. He arrived first thing in the morning, accompanied by another younger doctor whom I had never seen before. He and his companion walked down the ward, the younger doctor holding a clipboard. At first, I thought they were picking children at random, but I soon realised, as they stopped to consult with each other repeatedly, that there was a method to their selections. The other children began to wake and eye them warily. The ones who understood what was happening began to shake and cry.

Dr Oppenheimer stopped beside the bed of a boy who was a few years younger than me but much taller. He asked him to stand up while the other doctor measured him. Then he asked him to take five steps forward, turn around, and come back. The boy's gait was a little odd, but otherwise he seemed normal. Dr Oppenheimer checked the tall boy over with his stethoscope and told the other doctor to record details as he dictated them. Then they moved onto the next child, and the next.

Finally, they came to me.

Dr Oppenheimer took the clipboard from his young colleague and dismissed him with a wave of his hand. Then he turned to me. 'Ingrid,' he said quietly. 'I'm sorry I've been away for so long. But the Reich has been keeping me extremely busy. How are you?'

'I'm okay,' I said dryly.

'You don't seem yourself. Has something happened?'

I shrugged.

'Well, I have some news that just might cheer you up.'

'Where have you been?' I interrupted.

'I was ordered to oversee some building at a new camp for Jews just outside Krakow in Poland: a place called Auschwitz. The order came from Reichsführer Himmler himself. I had to go. Ingrid,' he whispered as he began examining me, 'I shouldn't tell you this, but … I was called to a very important meeting at a place called Wannsee, and that meeting was the reason I was sent to Poland. Things outside the walls of Hadamar have taken a turn for the worse. Come what may, this war will change Germany and all Germans in ways we can't imagine. The part I've played in it ….'

'So why have you come back? Why are you testing me again? Are you going to go back on your word? Are you going to send me to the showers?'

'*Nein*, Ingrid,' he hissed. 'I promised you I would spare your life, and as long as I'm alive I will. After the decisions made by the Reich at that conference, some of the other doctors and nurses decided to get together to re-examine and, hopefully, reclassify some of the T-4 patients so we could get them sent to other institutions – or even home.'

He asked me to breathe in and breathe out as he put the stethoscope to my chest.

'I think', he said as he picked up a clipboard and began scribbling some notes, 'I may just be able to get you out of here. It may take a few weeks, but it looks promising.'

He patted my head as if I was a child and then disappeared from Hadamar as quickly as he'd arrived. I spent the following days watching for his arrival. At times the thought of going home filled me with excitement. All that had been done to me, all I had seen – none of it mattered. I was going home.

But the days passed and he did not come. I began to wonder if he'd been lying. *Nein*, he had always told me the truth, hadn't he?

He had always kept his word. Perhaps he had not been able to secure my release after all. And in between all my thoughts of Mutti, and of going home, guilt for what I had done to Mia began to creep in. After betraying her as I did, did I even deserve to go home? Did I even deserve to see my mother again?

Three weeks later, early in the morning, Dr Oppenheimer and the other doctor appeared. They strode down the ward towards me. In his right hand, Dr Oppenheimer was waving a piece of paper.

'Ingrid! I have wonderful news!' he said as he reached my bedside and sat on the steel-framed chair beside me. He handed the piece of paper to me. It was covered in minute typing and dozens of signatures as well as the black eagle stamps of the Reich. It didn't make any sense so I handed it back.

'It's your release form!' Dr Oppenheimer smiled as he leant back on the chair – almost tipping it over – and folded his arms.

I'd heard what he said, but I couldn't believe it.

'I promise it's true!' he laughed. 'You're free!'

I stared at him in disbelief. I tried to gather my thoughts as they raced through my mind. I was free. I was actually *free*. Soon I would return to Mutti and start to rebuild my life. Everything that had transpired here would be forgotten. Adjusting would be hard, I supposed, but I didn't care; anywhere was better than here.

Then dozens of boots thundered down the corridors. Herr Schmidt appeared, his black SS uniform crisp and creaseless, the red Nazi band proudly wrapped around his biceps. He goose-stepped down the ward, followed by Chief Nurse Huber, who bounced around behind him like a puppy. Behind her were two Gestapo *Gefreiters*.

'Is this her?' Herr Schmidt asked as he stopped at my bed. I glanced at Dr Oppenheimer. He didn't return my gaze; his head was bowed as he stared at the floor.

'*Ja*, that's her,' Chief Nurse Huber replied from behind Herr Schmidt's right shoulder. Herr Schmidt jerked his head in Dr Oppenheimer's direction. The Gestapo *Gefreiters* grabbed him by the shoulders and ripped him from his seat.

'*Herr Doktor*,' Herr Schmidt said as the other men dragged Dr Oppenheimer to his feet. 'It has come to my attention that you have been conducting unauthorised "re-evaluations" of some of our patients here.'

Dr Oppenheimer glared at Chief Nurse Huber. She avoided his eye. *Coward,* I thought bitterly.

'Other institutions have dealt with the doctors involved in this little conspiracy and you are the last. You may have managed to slip children out of here without my authorisation, but that stops *now*.'

Herr Schmidt nodded again. 'Examine her,' he ordered. A third 'doctor' appeared from behind the Gestapo men and performed a 'medical' inspection on me. In fact, he did nothing more than look at me for a few seconds and nod. My fate and Dr Oppenheimer's were sealed.

'Apart from the colour of this girl's skin, she clearly has other medical defects and disabilities. She must remain here,' Herr Schmidt said as he reached for my freedom pass and tore it to shreds.

Tears rolled down my cheeks as I watched the hundreds of fragments flutter and float to the floor. The two men holding Dr Oppenheimer marched him down the ward and took him away.

I never saw him again.

May 1942

Dr Oppenheimer's arrest devastated me. Every man I had known as a protector had been taken from me. I had no-one. After the way I had treated Johan, I doubted even he would want me any more. I knew he was still in Hadamar. I saw him most meal times. I knew he thought about me because I sometimes caught him stealing glances in my direction as he ate. What he thought of me, I wasn't sure. I hadn't spoken to him since I had betrayed Mia.

I hated working in the kitchen and dining hall. I didn't want to be around people any more. I just wanted to be left alone, to retreat into my own world and be left in peace. Anybody who had ever come into contact with me had been taken away or had their lives destroyed because they knew me. It was best for everyone if I spent the rest of my life alone. I longed to be reassigned to work in the fields, although this reminded me of Franz.

Summer approached. Radio Nazi broadcast that Japan now controlled all of Asia, the United States was losing the Battle of the Atlantic, and our glorious hero General Irwin Rommel was about to defeat the British in North Africa. In the east, our troops were advancing towards Stalingrad. Germany and her allies were on the brink of decisive victories. The war was close to being won, they said.

I'd learnt long ago that Nazi propaganda always had elements truth served with a helping of lies. The Hadamar staff, however, did not share my unspoken scepticism. They believed everything they heard and felt impervious to any Allied retributions for their crimes.

I was certain the killings had resumed. The sickest of the sick soldiers, children and mental patients disappeared. The staff fed us the usual stories about people being transferred, sent home or dying from natural causes – but *I* knew the truth. Despite this, Hadamar was still becoming more cramped and crowded. Moving through the ward had become a daily ritual involving stepping over bodies, bed linen and clothing, as if I was walking through a minefield. Chief Nurse Huber told me one morning that I must now ration supplies. Our brave men were winning so many victories and advancing so quickly, she said, that food supplies were starting to run short, especially on the Russian Front. All Germans, even civilians, had to send whatever extra they had. Because I had done a wonderful thing for the Fatherland with my betrayal of Mia, she said, I was allowed to have more – but the other children's rations were to be cut to next to nothing. My extra food was hard to swallow, but I did it anyway.

After serving breakfast one morning, I returned to my ward. I walked slowly past each bed, closely examining the children. On some beds were three or four smaller children, sitting huddled together. On others were two or three lying side by side. All seemed sadder than usual, clinging to each other as if clinging to life itself.

Days passed and all but a few of the children now lay down, their energy spent as if they'd had the life sucked out of them. I checked the bedridden ones for sores, turning them over if I suspected one. I fixed the pillows for the children who had the strength to sit up. Whatever afflictions they had, there was one thing they all had in common. Their faces were becoming gaunter every day. I knew what was happening: the children were starving. I decided I would eat less and give them what I could spare.

A few weeks later, I found myself stopping at the bed of one young boy, Walter, a polio sufferer who looked worse than the others. I leant in close to him, my face hovering over his. His eyes were closed. I thought he was dead. I looked down his body and realised he was still alive. His breathing was shallow but his chest still rose and fell. I gently tapped him on the shoulder. His eyes flickered. I drew his blanket halfway down his chest, revealing skin hanging from his ribs like curtains. His eyes opened wide at my touch. It became painfully apparent how much they had sunken into his skull.

'Ingrid,' he whispered through laboured breaths. I pulled the blanket down to his waist. His stomach was swollen and distended.

'Oh, Walter,' I said.

'I am hungry … thirsty. Could you … bring me something? Please, please,' he pleaded.

I nodded and hurried to the kitchen. Some of the other inmates were in the pantry area – there was no way I could steal anything. I went out into the dining hall and scanned the floor. I found a few round end pieces of bread that some of the men had left behind, and stuffed them into my pockets. Back in the kitchen, I filled a jug of water and hurried back to the ward. Walter had fallen asleep. I woke him, reached inside my pocket and tried to hand him a piece of bread. He was too weak to lift his hands, so I gently placed the bread into his mouth. I waited for him to chew, but he did not even have the strength to do that. I gripped his jaw and helped him.

I didn't see the other children who were sitting on their beds waiting for the right moment. As soon as I bent down over Walter they seized their opportunity. Two of them jumped from their beds, thrust their hands into my pockets and stole the bread before I knew what was happening. As they sat back down, they held their prize in both hands, nibbling away like rats, eyeing off anyone who dared to come too close.

No sooner had my hand released Walter's jaw to allow him to swallow, than one young girl grasped hold of it.

'Please, Ingrid,' she begged with sad eyes. 'Please get us some more food! We're so hungry!'

I raced back to the kitchen but I didn't find anything. I searched and searched. I was about to give up when I discovered half a loaf of bread that had fallen behind one of the central heating ducts. It was decidedly mouldy and I was surprised the rats hadn't claimed it. I had barely taken a step inside their ward when the children swamped me, stole the bread and ripped it to pieces, swallowing whole the large chunks they shoved in their mouths.

Over the next few days, the pantries were restocked. A supply truck must have arrived. I stole as much bread as I could – and anything else I could get my hands on. I tried to feed only the sickest ones, but they were all so weak that it was difficult to decide who needed it most. The more food I brought, the more the children begged. I never had enough; not even close. At night I was often woken by their hungry sobs. For weeks and weeks, I tried to keep them all alive. It was no use. Some were just too far gone. Dozens upon dozens died.

One day, Chief Nurse Huber summoned me to her office.

'Ingrid, I know I said you could have a little more food than the others as a reward for bringing that Jewish girl to our attention, but I also told you to cut back on the rations for the others. You have been careful with the food, haven't you?'

'*Ja*, Chief Nurse Huber, I have been giving them exactly how much you told me to.'

'Are you sure?'

'*Ja*, Chief Nurse Huber, like you said, we have to cut back for the boys at the front. They need it more.'

'Hmm,' she said, unconvinced. 'More children in Ward 3 died during the night. I need you to go and prepare beds for new arrivals.'

I'd barely smoothed the sheets on the first bed when Dr Wahlmann and Chief Nurse Huber entered.

'I just don't understand it,' Dr Wahlmann said as he made his way up and down the ward, running his eye over the children in their beds. 'They should be losing more weight than this. More of them should be dying.'

My throat constricted as I tried not to say anything; he wasn't even pretending to hide his purpose from the children – or from me.

Walking a step behind, Chief Nurse Huber checked the chart on each bed after Dr Wahlmann passed by.

'We have reduced their rations to next to nothing,' she offered. 'I don't know what to tell you, *Herr Doktor*.'

'These children don't look like they're starving to me!' Dr Wahlmann said angrily. 'I told you they are nothing more than rats! Little rats, sneaking into the kitchen and stealing food.'

My heart hovered in my mouth. In my desperation to help these poor children, I had just signed my own death warrant. I willed Dr Wahlmann to look anywhere else but at me. I had reduced my rations, but I had been eating more than the others; my body was not nearly as withered as theirs. I was certain that when Dr Wahlmann discovered my healthy state, my identity as the food thief was sure to be revealed. He slowly turned and faced me, his black eyes staring straight into my soul. I tried to stare nonchalantly at the ceiling, but my eyes found their way back to him. He was striding towards me. I swallowed hard.

He stopped right next to me, looking me up and down.

'Who is this *schwarze Schande*?'

'Her name is Ingrid Marchand, *Herr Doktor*,' Chief Nurse Huber said as she hurried to stand beside him. I wasn't sure if I should be happy that he did not remember me or my name.

He examined me more closely. 'Why does this girl look healthier than the rest of them?'

'She is the one who discovered the Jew hiding in our midst. I have her working in the kitchen. As a reward I have been allowing her more food than the others.'

'Hmm,' he said as he took four slow paces towards the windows and stared outside. 'While discovering a Jew is something that should be rewarded, the fact that we have not killed her yet is reward enough. Cut her food rations like the rest.'

He spun on his heel, turning back to face Chief Nurse Huber. 'Put some of the wounded soldiers on watch in the kitchen. Make sure these children do not get any food. We have to ration the food for the people of Germany – not these *Erbkrank*; these *Lebensunwertes Leben*. And tell the soldiers that if any more food goes missing it will come out of their rations.'

Dr Wahlmann marched out of the ward. Chief Nurse Huber skipped quickly behind him as she struggled to catch up. 'I just don't understand this, *Herr Doktor*. I really don't.'

I finally allowed myself to breathe again. I ran back to my bed, sitting with my knees drawn into my chest and my arms wrapped around my legs as I wondered what to do.

I knew why I had been helping these children. I finally admitted it to myself: I had to make up for what I did to Mia. I would save as many children as I could. I had ruined her life, but surely saving dozens of lives would balance things out? Besides, if their intention was to be rid of us all, then I could at least do one good thing before my time came. Who knew what the future held? Perhaps the Allies would win. Perhaps I could keep the children alive long enough until that day.

CHAPTER 9

I had barely managed to steal enough as it was. How was I going to get even more food to these children?

There was only one way. But given how I had been treating him, would he even look at me, let alone talk to me and figure out a way to save them? I had to put my feelings behind me. There was a greater good now and he was the only one who could – who *would*, I felt sure – help me. I hurried up the stairs and found Johan sleeping.

I gently prodded him awake.

'Ingrid?' he said sleepily. His tired eyes registered surprise to see me.

'*Ja*, it's me.'

He rubbed the sleep from his eyes as he sat up. 'What do you want?'

'They're starving the children,' I whispered as I sat on the edge of his bed and looked around to make sure no-one else was listening. 'They want them all dead.'

He immediately woke up and put his powerful hand across my mouth. I flinched; it was the first time he had touched me since that awful day.

'Not here, not now,' he hissed. 'Go back downstairs. I'll meet you in the courtyard.'

I nodded. He removed his hand and I ran back downstairs, went outside, sat on the bench in the courtyard and waited. An eternity passed. I kept looking back into the ward but he didn't appear. He was not coming down. He would not help me and I doubted if he would ever speak to me again. Minutes passed and still there was no sight of him.

Then I saw movement at the end of the ward. I stood to get a better view. It was Nurse Willig. He walked down the ward, his head moving from side to side as he checked each bed.

I ran to the one corner of the courtyard that was hidden from his view, breathing as softly and as quietly as I could. Nurse Willig appeared at the doors, taking a brief look around the courtyard before he disappeared. I waited a few minutes more before sliding my back along the wall and carefully peering through the doors. I saw Nurse Willig's back as he disappeared from the ward. Suddenly Johan appeared, carefully wheeling himself forward as he threaded his way through the mattresses and children on the floor. His wheels clattered as they went over the small step leading to the courtyard. He looked around for me.

'Ingrid?'

'I'm here,' I whispered as I stepped out of the corner.

I checked to see that Nurse Willig had not returned before I sat on the bench. Johan wheeled himself beside me.

'What do you mean about them starving the children?' he said without preamble.

'I heard Chief Nurse Huber and Dr Wahlmann talking about it. They're deliberately starving the children.'

'And what exactly would you like me to do about it?' he asked guardedly.

'What do you mean? I want you and the others to stop it.'

'Why do you think any of us will help you?'

'Because killing children is wrong!' My heart ached. Did he truly not care or was it just because he angry with me? 'The men can pressure the doctors and nurses to stop. Or they can share their rations.'

'Ingrid,' he laughed bitterly. 'Some of these men are true Nazis! They *believe* every lie they've been fed. They *agree* with everything they've been told. Not only won't they help, they *approve* of what's being done.'

'But how can they still think killing is okay when the staff here have even killed their comrades?' Tears of exasperation pricked my eyes.

'These children are not their comrades. They're disabled, deaf, dumb and blind. The men don't care about them! Ingrained beliefs are hard to dislodge. You mightn't want to hear this, but I used to be the same. Meeting you helped changed me. The men have grown to like *you*. Some of the older ones – like Colonel Wilhelm – even talk about the bravery of the black soldiers they fought against in the first war. But they *don't* feel that way about the disabled children. As long as their bowls are full, they *don't care*.'

I couldn't believe what I was hearing. I had been certain he would help me. He was the last hope I had for saving the children and he was shutting me down.

'This isn't about the children, is it? It's about you and me.'

'I didn't think there was a you and me,' he said coldly as he turned his chair away from me and rolled towards the oak tree. 'Before today, you haven't spoken to me in a long time. At first, I was giving you time alone after all that had happened … but then when you didn't come and talk to me, I knew things were different.'

'I saw you with Mia!' I shouted, more loudly than I should have.

'You didn't see what you thought you saw, Ingrid.'

'She was sitting on your lap. You were kissing!'

'When you wouldn't talk to me, Mia did. I asked her how I could help you. She told me we would work it out together, that we could make you like me again. She came to see me more and more. I tried to talk only about *you*, but she lost interest in the subject after a while. She started flirting with me, but I wouldn't have it.'

'I know what I saw.'

'*Nein*, you don't! That was the first time she actually touched me.'

'But you had your arms around her!'

'She sat on my lap! She begged me to be with her and forget you. I had my arms around her because I was trying to push her off me.'

I didn't know if I believed him. The anguish in his voice sounded genuine, but perhaps he was just a good liar.

'Ingrid, I can't make you believe me, but I swear there was never anything between Mia and me.'

'It doesn't matter,' I said dismissively. 'Saving the children is all that matters now.'

'You're the reason they sent her away, aren't you?'

'*Nein*,' I said, heart pounding, ducking my head. Johan may have been a good liar, but *I* wasn't.

'You knew she was a Jew, didn't you?'

'*Ja*, I did,' I said as I turned to face him.

'Do you know where they sent her?'

'Ravensbrück.'

'Ravensbrück!' His face was stricken with horror. 'Ingrid, do you know what Ravensbrück is?'

'*Nein*.'

'It's a work camp for women.'

'So, it's the same as here. So what?'

'When I was in Russia there was a group of SS men that were called the *Einsatzgruppen*. They were recruited from the Gestapo and the *Kripo*. Their job was to go around and hunt Jews. Any they found, they killed. Mass shootings, gassing vans, throwing them off bridges, any way they could find to kill them, they did. But there were too many Jews. So they put them in 'work camps' like Ravensbrück. Ingrid, the Reich is trying to kill as many Jews as it can. Mia won't survive.'

I put my hand up. I didn't need him to continue.

'I thought she was …' my words caught in my throat as I began to cry, confronted by the reality of what I had done. 'I didn't know …'

'What's done is done,' he said as he rolled himself towards me and took me by the hand. Of course I *had* known – if not the details, then at least that I had sent my friend to a terrible fate. How could he forgive me? The warmth of his hand told me how: none of us was innocent in this dreadful war.

'When did they give the order that the soldiers are to control the food?' he interrupted my thoughts.

'Downstairs, just now.'

'They can't keep soldiers in the kitchen twenty-four hours a day. When you are serving the men's meals, take little pieces – only little pieces – and sneak them into your pocket. Take enough each day to keep the children going, but not enough to arouse any suspicions. You may just be able to keep some of them alive. You have access to their wards when you do your cleaning – give them the food then.'

Awash with guilt, knowing now I had sentenced Mia to death, I was desperate to save more children. I had seen so much death and cruelty at Hadamar; now a determination to ease some suffering filled me. Leaving Johan behind, I ran towards the kitchen, ready to start stockpiling supplies before the soldiers began guarding them. I sprinted through the dining hall but came to an abrupt halt when I reached the kitchen door. At least half a dozen men were positioned at points around the dining room and in the kitchen. They eyed me suspiciously.

'What are you doing here?' the man closest to the kitchen door asked.

'I thought I was late for my serving duties.'

'You don't need to be here for another hour yet.'

'Oh, I lost track of time. I'll come back.'

Thankfully, my presence in the kitchen was not out of the ordinary, and the men didn't seem to give me a second thought. I returned to the courtyard to find Johan was gone. At least he had spoken with me. I sat on my bed and thought about what I had done to Mia. I should have asked him. I was an adult now; how could I have acted so childishly? *Nein*, in the big picture – I tried to tell myself – my actions didn't matter. She was a Jew. She would have been discovered eventually – only pure luck had allowed her to survive this far. Now that they had resumed killing children, albeit in a different way, her epilepsy made her a useless eater. They would have found an excuse to kill her here, sooner or later.

Still, her death was on my hands. I had to make amends.

When lunchtime came I returned to the kitchen. This time the soldiers paid me no mind. I entered, expecting one of the men to be guarding the main food cupboards. There was no-one. Bags filled with loaves of bread sat on the benches. Glancing behind me, and still seeing no-one, I broke a loaf into pieces and jammed them as deeply down into my pockets as they would go. Only a few men had arrived for lunch and no-one had yet arrived for guard duty. I could slip back to my bed, hide the bread, and return before anyone was any wiser. I walked towards the door, but one of the soldiers stepped forward.

'Where are you going?' he asked, looking me over.

'I forgot something. I'll be back in a minute.'

Fortunately, this soldier was not astute enough to realise that I had few possessions and, therefore, no real need to return to my bed. I tried not to attract attention as I retrieved the newspapers from under my bed, took one from the middle, opened it, placed the bread inside and wrapped the paper around it, hoping that this would be enough to keep the rats away.

I hurried back to the kitchen. Scores of men had arrived for their lunch. I briefly contemplated stealing more food but I feared being discovered. If I was killed, I would be no good to the children. I stood in front of the vats and started serving the soup.

I couldn't stop thinking about Mia and what I had done to her. I tried to convince myself that she was still alive. She was a survivor; she had overcome so much to get to the point where she was hidden in Hadamar. Surely she would find a way. She would charm the guards and more. She would do whatever she had to do. I wished I could take back what I had done – but I couldn't. I tried to convince myself that if I hadn't betrayed her, they would have found out anyway, but it was small consolation.

Lunch finished and I began cleaning and packing things away, putting as many leftover bread crusts in my pockets as I could find. The soldiers remained on guard as the patients from the mental wards finished the cleaning and sweeping. Not daring to look at them as I went past, I returned to my bed and unwrapped the newspapers to find that the bread I had stolen earlier was still there. I added the extras I had managed to gather. With little to do until dinnertime, and not wanting to be left alone with my thoughts, I decided to talk to Johan, to try one more time to see if he could convince the men. He was leaning back on his bed, staring at the ceiling. When he realised I was standing beside him, he sat up and seemed genuinely pleased to see me.

'Did you manage to get much?' he whispered as he leant close to me.

'A little. I'll sneak in tonight and give it to the children. There'll be less staff and soldiers around then.'

'I spoke to some of the men. They won't help.'

This upset me – though I was pleased that Johan had at least tried – but I shouldn't have expected anything else. The children and Mia had reminded me of the fragility of life and the ease with which death came to us. Life was short and there were things I needed to say to Johan before it was too late. I would have preferred to say them somewhere more private, but privacy was not a luxury one had in Hadamar. I looked around at the adjacent beds. They were mostly empty, and the men who were close enough to hear were either sleeping or daydreaming.

'Johan,' I said as I took hold of his hand. 'I'm sorry … for how I treated you.'

'Forget about it. It's all in the past now. It's okay, really it is,' he said with a sad smile.

'*Nein*, it is not,' I said. 'I stopped talking to you. I ignored you. It wasn't fair.'

I closed my eyes and took a long breath before I began. 'There was Franz, of course … but then … I was jealous, this much is true, but it's more than that. I pushed you away because … how could there be a future for us?'

He patted the bed beside him. I sat with my back pressed up against him.

'Ingrid, I've seen the worst that war has to offer. I've seen hatred in a man's eyes as he kills another. In battle those things make sense, if you understand me.'

'I'm not sure I do.'

'When you find yourself in battle, things are clear. It's killed or be killed. That's easy to understand. But in this place? Nothing makes sense. Everything is shrouded in fear and mystery. It's what makes people in here act the way they do. In a way, living here *is* like being in battle. Your instincts kick in and you do what you must to survive. It's every man for himself. Look at Germany. We're one of the most sophisticated and cultured societies in the world – and we still act like animals. You pushed me away because your survival instincts kicked in. You were only doing what you thought you needed to in order to survive. I don't hold that against you.'

Perhaps pushing him away was self-preservation, but doing what I did to Mia was not. I felt guilty, but I pushed the feeling aside as I became lost in the calm wisdom of his speech and the blueness of his eyes. I was overcome by a desire to touch him. I leant in towards him. Our mouths came closer and closer. We kissed.

Startled by a noise from downstairs, I quickly broke away.

'I have to go. It's getting near to dinnertime.'

I floated on air as I made my way to the dining hall. Forgetting myself, instead of putting the bread into the hessian sacks to take them out to the tables, I started putting loaves in my pockets.

'What do you think you're doing?' a male voice demanded to know.

'Nothing!' I said as I turned around, trying to hide my bulging pockets.

'You'd better put those back where they belong before the nurses see you,' Old Wilhelm said, a grin spreading across his face as he winked.

I allowed myself to breathe again.

'Some of the boys do want to help,' he murmured, 'but they're worried that if they're caught, their rations will be cut too. That doesn't mean we can't keep you out of trouble now, does it?'

Putting all but one of the loaves back into the bags, I bent down to kiss Old Wilhelm on the cheek before heading out to the dining hall to complete my duties. While I was serving, Johan entered. I smiled coyly at him whenever he caught my eye. When the time came to start cleaning up, I made sure I stopped close to Johan, brushing my hair behind my ears before I let my hand hang freely and touch his shoulder.

Chief Nurse Huber stepped between us.

'Don't think I don't know what is going on, Marchand,' she said as she assumed her teapot stance. She had seen my pockets. I was done for.

'I don't know what you are talking about, Chief Nurse Huber.'

'I may have given you some privileges for what you did, but that does not extend to allowing any *Rassenschande* between you two! Just know I am keeping a close eye on you!'

She stomped towards her seat. I sighed with relief. She hadn't seen the bread in my pockets after all. I watched her sit down before I resumed cleaning the tables, trying not to take a glimpse in Johan's direction, and paranoid about the bread in my pockets. Even so, when dinner ended I lingered in the kitchen, trying to find the courage to steal more bread. I had to. Each piece of bread I didn't take was one more child I condemned to death. I jammed as many end crusts as I could find into my pockets and under my shirt, careful not to make the bulges too apparent, then trotted back to the ward, keeping an eye out for Chief Nurse Huber. Safe back at my bed, I stowed the bread in the newspapers.

Now I had to wait. I couldn't venture into the ward until the nurses and orderlies were asleep, which could be hours from now. I thought about going to see Johan to pass the time, but Chief Nurse Huber's threats had made me cautious. Even if she stopped short of having me killed, she could still put me in solitary confinement. That was the last thing I needed. Only God knew how many children would die without me to feed them. I reached under my bed and pulled out one of the newspapers to re-read, keeping one eye on the windows. When the moon finally dipped below the walls, I stood up, retrieved the bread, and crept towards the children's ward. There were no nurses, no doctors, and no orderlies to be seen. I reached the doorway.

It was as if they smelt me long before they saw me. Some of the children were already sitting up in their beds; some had even managed to get out of bed and were staggering towards me.

'Quick!' I whispered. 'Get back in your beds! We don't want to make any noises that will make the nurses come.'

The fear of the nurses overpowered their hunger and they did as they were told. I moved rapidly from bed to bed, distributing the food as fairly as I could. It was difficult in the diminishing moonlight to tell who was the sickest. When all of the bread was gone – even the crumbs – I snuck back to bed.

January 1943

Night after night I tried to feed them. Sometimes I managed to; sometimes a nurse or orderly was around and the children had to go hungry. Chief Nurse Huber became increasingly suspicious and upped her surveillance of me. I knew she couldn't stay awake all night, so once she was asleep I went to the children's wards. If I couldn't get to other wards, I fed the children in mine. During the day, however, she watched me like a hawk, which made it hard to see Johan. It was almost as if she were jealous of our love. It wasn't just that Johan and I were different colours and from different worlds; she wanted to keep us apart because she was envious of our happiness. She was going to do everything in her power to keep us apart.

The weather changed and, no matter what I did, the youngest and the sickest succumbed to the cold. The older and 'healthier' children became thinner and thinner too as they wasted away to nothing. They walked around Hadamar like living skeletons until they became too weak to move and they lay down on their beds, sometimes even on the floors, and waited for Death to come and take them. I tried to care for them in their beds, but I couldn't get to them all quickly enough. Bedsores began to grow like fungus on their sickly grey skin.

My own strength was beginning to waver too. Chief Nurse Huber finally ordered my rations cut even further, telling me there was barely enough for the staff so I was not to have any more extras. I stole food, but every mouthful tasted like pure guilt. Every morsel I ate was taking away another child's chance to survive. On the rare occasions when Chief Nurse Huber was not around and I could speak to Johan, he commented on how thin I had become. He begged me to keep the food that I stole for myself – to keep up my strength – but I told him I couldn't bear to see the children so helpless. I had already sent one girl to her death. I was not going to let any more go without a fight.

CHAPTER 10

THE GRAVEYARD

March 1943

I reached my second year of adulthood. I had spent the first year wasting away. I had wanted to be strong, to be grown up, but the lack of food made it difficult. Now I knew that if more food did not arrive or the war did not end soon, I would probably not reach twenty.

One night as I went about my dinner duties I heard the men whispering among themselves. Despite what Radio Nazi had been saying, the Battle of Stalingrad had been a failure, and the Sixth Army had been surrounded and surrendered. It was a disaster. Hundreds of thousands of soldiers had been taken prisoner and those who had escaped were badly wounded. There would soon be an influx of soldiers coming to Hadamar. The defeat and *Der Führer's* handling of the battle had made many of the top generals begin to question him and his authority. Many of the men in Hadamar did too. The fact that the men – even though they only dared whisper it – were openly criticising Hitler renewed my hope that the war would soon be at an end.

Day after day, more crippled and maimed men arrived. They stacked them in the soldiers' wards and, when they became too full, they crowded the surviving children into the other wards to make space. Hadamar was so overcrowded I thought it would burst at the seams. Seeing so many wounded soldiers filled me with mixed emotions. It was clear we were beginning to lose the war. The end, and an Allied victory, seemed inevitable – but the demand for free beds had skyrocketed and I could only see one way for them to make more room. Each day the orderlies removed dead children from my ward and replaced them with children from another. So many were dying that the staff hovered around like vultures, ready to pick the carcass of the next victim clean.

I had terrible nightmares. I couldn't shake the images of dead children, their pale bodies placed on the steel trolleys, forced into the crematorium ovens until they burst into flames. One day they were alive, the next they were nothing more than a pile of ashes. When I woke from my tortured dreams, the survivors were still crying and moaning with hunger. The worst ones were the mentally disabled children, unable to fathom what was happening to them. The hungrier they became, the louder they wailed.

And I could do nothing about it.

More and more men arrived, but the supply trucks brought less and less food. Even the soldiers found the courage to complain. My rations were reduced to next to nothing. I became weaker and weaker. My mind grew hazy. Despite my wavering strength and sanity there was no let-up. Fewer children were physically capable of working but the amount of work to be done continued to increase. I had to work harder than I had ever before. I had to tread carefully because I no longer had Dr Oppenheimer's protection; Chief Nurse Huber would only let me live while I remained useful. The more time I spent in the wards, the more I thought that, perhaps, it would be better to let these poor children die quickly; feeding them was only delaying the inevitable. I had been so determined to try and keep them alive. Now they lay on their beds, nothing more than piles of bones, and I knew it had all been a waste of time. I hadn't brought salvation, I'd only prolonged their living hell. I gave up trying to save them.

Hunger became a constant companion, but it also forced me to take more chances to steal the food *I* needed. In times gone by, I hadn't cared if I lived or died; indeed, I had often wished for Death to take me. Now I clung desperately to life.

More soldiers were sent home, or perhaps they were injected and killed. Either way, any soldiers who could be removed had to make way for the ever-increasing numbers of wounded men. There was a brief lull in new arrivals at the end of winter; there were even some empty beds. It was a blessing. Less soldiers meant more food and less work. When no-one was looking, I shoved as much food in my mouth as would fit. I stole food and hid it anywhere I could: under my bed, under my pillow, inside the newspapers. Sometimes the rats found the food and I would go hungry until I was able to steal more.

As the war deteriorated for the Nazis, so did Hadamar itself. Paint peeled from the walls and plaster fell away in huge chunks.

The timber slats began to rot and break away. Behind my bed, I discovered a loose slat, perfect to conceal extra food in.

Under the increasing workload and with ever-decreasing amounts of food, my body began to falter. At the end of the day, I felt utterly exhausted and the few hours' sleep I managed to get were my only relief. Somehow, I continued to rise early, gather together my strength and work. I knew that if I showed any signs of weakness, my days would be numbered. Some days I wandered around the hospital in a daze, unsure of what I was doing and where I was going.

One day, muddled with fatigue, I left the ward and turned left. I missed the dining hall and continued walking down increasingly darkened corridors. I found myself near the medical rooms. Knowing I shouldn't have been there, a momentary burst of adrenaline allowed me to recover my senses. I was about halfway down the corridor and I knew I had to leave before my presence was discovered; however, something in the nearest window caught my eye. A dead child was laid out on a gurney.

Dr Wahlmann hovered over the child, dressed in a long white gown, a white hat and white gloves up to his elbows. He picked up a scalpel, which glinted silver in the flickering light. I was taken back to the day they sterilised me as I watched him make several careful incisions. He placed the scalpel to one side before reaching both his hands inside the corpse. He pulled out a large, reddish-brown, triangular-shaped organ and placed it on a steel tray next to him. He then reached back inside and removed two red, bean-shaped organs. I shook my head to clear my mind. Was I imagining this scene?

The doctor began to turn around as he removed his gloves. I ran back to my ward, stopped and stood between the rows of steel beds, panting, as I tried to compose myself. My chest was tight, my ribs crushing my lungs. Madness had reached new levels inside these walls. It had to stop. The food rations had diminished enough to affect the men. I knew the soldiers were disgruntled. Hadamar was filled not only with the weak, desperate and dying but also the anger of men who had fought for their country and were being treated like prisoners. It was time. The men had to stage a rebellion. The men had to take control of Hadamar.

I hadn't had the strength to even try to see Johan. Except for the odd conversation on the rare occasions I had to go to the men's wards, I had barely seen him. But if anyone was going to lead the men in a coup, it was him. My adrenaline had subsided, my strength was fading. Each step up to the men's ward was an arduous task. At the top, my eyes went straight to Johan's bed.

It was empty.

The whole ward was empty, except for one man: Old Wilhelm. The ward was dim, except for a small lantern that burned and flickered beside Old Wilhelm's bedside, for the staff were always trying to save power and switching the lights off. In the dappled light he was silhouetted as he sat smoking his pipe, the wisps of smoke rising and shining briefly before they disappeared into the darkness.

'Are you okay, Ingrid?'

'Where is Johan?' I fretted, my grand plans for a revolution forgotten.

'They transferred him last night,' Old Wilhelm said as he sucked on his pipe, an eerie redness lighting the room.

'Transferred?' I gasped. 'Where?'

'Back to a soldier's home in Düsseldorf and then home to his family, I believe.'

I was afraid to ask, but I had to know. 'They didn't kill him, did they?'

'*Nein*, they came and collected him last night. He was supposed to go today and he said he was planning on seeing you before he left. I guess they ordered him out before he got the chance.'

'*Danke*, Herr Colonel,' I said forlornly as I stumbled back downstairs. I lay on my bed wondering about Johan. Had his predictions come true? Did the people of Düsseldorf see him as a freak or was he still being treated like the hero he was? Was he happy to be back with his family? I had never seen pictures of his mother, his father, his sister. In fact, he had barely spoken about them. Nevertheless, I imagined them in my mind, all three of them embracing Johan as he returned home. I imagined him happy, being treated how he deserved to be treated.

I remembered I still had the copy of *Das Reich* with him on the front cover. I took it out and stared at the picture of him. Part of me felt angry that he hadn't said goodbye. Maybe he had, as Old Wilhelm had said, tried his best to do so. I should have made more of an effort to see him. I should have spent more time with him. Now he was gone and I doubted that I would ever see him again. I only had myself to blame. Regretting that I had never had the chance to tell him how I truly felt, I resolved to try to find him – if I managed to survive the war. If I survived Hadamar, I would tell him all that was in my heart.

July 1944

Summer came. If Hadamar was not already hell on earth, the hot nights made it so now. Sleep became almost impossible and I spent many nights lying awake, tossing and turning. Early one morning, in the coolest part of the night, I had just drifted off to sleep when I was woken by shouts coming from the front entrance. This was nothing out of the ordinary, but there was something in the tone of the shouting that piqued my interest – an interest that grew to dread as the powerful electric lights were switched on, beaming like lighthouse beacons through the ward.

Six SS soldiers marched past and stopped in the corridor, shouting orders. I leapt from my bed and ran to the doorway to see what was happening. A handful of ragged-looking people appeared and stopped a few feet short of the soldiers. Dozens more crowded in behind them, bustling and shuffling forward at the tips of SS rifles. The soldiers barked more orders. I tried to listen, to hear what was going on but, despite the volume of their shouting, I couldn't make sense of their words. I was sure they were speaking a different language but I couldn't be certain which one. Maybe Russian? Maybe Polish?

'*Raus*!' one soldier finally yelled in German. 'Men line up to the left, women to the right, children in the middle!'

Lines of men, women and children trundled by, filling the ward with the echoes of their footsteps. The men wore dark-coloured corduroy trousers, tattered black or brown jackets and floppy caps. The women were wrapped in filthy shawls and dark-coloured headscarfs. The children were dressed like their parents; and, like their parents, they walked with their heads bowed.

I backed away and fled to my bed as the SS soldiers ordered some of the children into my ward. The first of them was a young boy, maybe six or seven years old. Dozens of downtrodden and terrified children followed. A young woman, whom I guessed might have been about fourteen, hurried down the ward, looking anxiously from side to side. Her clothes were dirty, her blonde hair tangled and dishevelled, but her face was beautiful and innocent. I was captivated by her. Despite her ragged physical appearance, she emanated warmth. She came to the bed next to me, smiled awkwardly then placed her small bundle down and waited for further orders.

When each newcomer had been assigned an empty bed, the SS officers disappeared. Unsure what to do, the new arrivals stood motionless. When no orders were forthcoming, one by one, they rigidly sat on their beds. They began to relax and lie down. I watched the new girl sit on her bed, prop up her pillow and lean on it as she faced me. I wasn't sure where to look. I tried to stare at the ceiling but, sensing her eyes on me, I looked at her again. She gazed wide-eyed at me. Despite the warmth emanating from her, her eyes held a haunted look as she curiously studied me.

CHAPTER 10

'Hello, my name is Ingrid,' I found myself saying, wondering if she even spoke German.

'Hello,' she said cautiously. 'My name is Anka.'

'Where have you come from?'

'We were in a work camp at a place called Ravensbrück.'

'Ravensbrück?'

A thousand questions raced through my mind, all of them centred on Mia.

'*Ja*, Ravensbrück. When the Nazis came to my town, they forced many of the men and women into work camps. The men and the women were separated into different ones. The women were sent to Ravensbrück and so that's where I was sent. Where is this place?' she asked as she looked at the walls, the barred windows and the ceiling.

'You're in Hadamar.'

'Is it a work camp? What kind of place is this?'

How could I explain Hadamar? I wondered as she nervously twisted a rope on the frayed dark-brown bag that sat between her legs.

'It's for mental patients and people with disabilities. It's also where wounded German soldiers come to recover.'

'For mental patients,' she repeated, confused. 'We are not children with disabilities. We are just workers. I wonder why we're here,' she mused, more to herself than to me.

'I don't know,' I lied. I knew exactly why they were here. There was only ever one reason civilians were brought to Hadamar.

'Tell me more about Ravensbrück. Were there any Jews there?'

Anka wrinkled her face as she looked at me, confused. 'Of course there were. That's what Ravensbrück is: a work camp.'

Stubbornly, I tried to convince myself that Mia was still alive. 'Did you meet any Jews? Did you know any of them?'

'Most of the women there were Polish like me, but I did work alongside some Jews. We made soldiers socks,' she smiled weakly, 'but we made them too thin, so the soldiers' feet would hurt. We also made little things like bracelets for ourselves.'

'Did you ever meet a blonde girl with blue eyes?'

'*Ja*, many of them. Sometimes they brought Norwegian women into the camp. They had blonde hair and blue eyes.'

'Did you ever meet a German girl like that?' My voice was getting desperate. 'Her name was Mia.'

'*Nein*, I don't think so.'

'She was very pretty. She sometimes had epileptic seizures.'

'What?'

'Fits. Uncontrollable shaking. Her body would have thrashed around.'

'Hmm, there was one girl who did something like that.'

'*Ja*?'

'She started frothing at the mouth and her body moved this way and that. We thought she must have been possessed by a demon, so a few of the women said prayers and tried to exorcise it. An old woman said she was cursed, so most people avoided her.'

'Do you know what happened to her?'

'They sent her to Auschwitz.'

I knew I had heard that name before but I couldn't remember where. Then it came to me: Dr Oppenheimer's work. The reason he had been away for so long.

'What is Auschwitz?' I asked with dread.

'It's a death camp,' she said as she wrinkled her face again. 'It's where they send the Jews to kill them.'

My stomach knotted. I wanted to throw up. I had convinced myself for so long that I *hadn't* killed Mia – that I *hadn't* condemned her to a horrible death – but Anka had provided the definitive proof. *Nein*! I tried to tell myself, there was every chance she would have died here too. She was a troublemaker. The staff would have injected her sooner or later, or forced her to starve. Did I really believe that – or was I just trying to fool myself?

Either way, I did not want to talk to Anka any more. I rolled over and turned my back to her. I already knew too much about her. I didn't want to know any more; not when I knew what fate awaited her. In a few hours or, at most, a few days, she would be killed. Never mind that there seemed to be something special about her. Fate had made her Polish and Fate had brought her to Hadamar. There was nothing I could do to change that.

Minutes of silence passed before she said, 'I was in a *Zwangsarbeitslager*.'

I desperately tried to ignore her, but my inquisitive nature begged me to flip myself over and listen. She told me how the Germans had invaded her home town of Gdansk and how they had placed hundreds upon hundreds of her townspeople on trains and brought them to

Germany. I looked her over, noticing a patch sewn onto the top right-hand corner of her jacket. But instead of the yellow star of the Jews, hers was a small yellow diamond with purple stitching on the edges and a purple 'P' in the centre.

'P for Polish,' she said, grabbing a handful of her jacket as if she wanted to tear the badge away. 'We all have to wear one. If we don't we get beaten, starved, put in solitary confinement or worse.'

She told me that they had worked outside every day, regardless of the weather. She told me that their rations barely kept them alive. She told me people died every day from starvation and typhus. She told me about the female guards – one in particular they called 'the Hyena' – and about some of the terrible things they did. I realised that I had been in Hadamar for so long that I had no real idea what was happening beyond these walls. I knew the Nazis' crimes spread far beyond Hadamar, but what Anka told me was shocking. Only now, as I spoke with this beautiful yet scruffy girl, did I realise that there were worse places than Hadamar.

Anka seemed to forget about my presence as she talked. Speaking almost to herself, she said, 'It will be okay. *Ja*, everything will be fine. We have come this far. So many people have died but we have come this far. We will get through this too. You see this,' she said as she reached into her bag and retrieved a small black passport, which she handed to me. It had white borders with the black Reich eagle and the words *Deutsches Reich* on the front; across the top was written *Arbeitsbuch Für Ausländer*: a foreign worker's pass. I handed it back. She slipped it inside her jacket. It was clearly valuable to her; perhaps there had been occasions when it had saved her life. The way she patted it after it was inside her coat suggested her unwavering faith that it would do so again.

'Life in the camps wasn't so bad,' she said as she lay back in her bed, but I could tell by the sadness in her voice that she struggled to believe the stories she was telling herself. 'Yes, it was hard working all the time. Children had to work on the smallest things, and if we did not work hard enough we would be beaten. But if you did work they left you alone. There was never enough food and people starved all the time, but if you knew where to look and who to talk to you could find enough. The worst part was watching people slowly die.'

I knew exactly what she meant.

'I had my ways of sneaking food or bargaining for it,' she continued, becoming animated as she tossed herself over to face me again. If by some miracle she survived, I knew she would come in handy.

'Do they feed you here? It looks better than the camp at Ravensbrück.'

I didn't want to shatter her hopes, so I just nodded. Her tongue now loosened, it seemed she couldn't stop. She continued telling me about life in the camp. I tried to listen but I struggled to stay awake. My eyelids closed. My head dropped.

'I think we're safe now… Why else would they have brought us here?' was the last thing I heard her say as I drifted off to sleep.

'*Raus! Raus!*' a male's voice bellowed from the corridors. I looked out the window: the moon was half-dipped below the far courtyard wall. Inside the ward, every child sat up in their beds. Doctors came marching through, the male nurses behind them tapping the ends of the beds with batons. Behind them was Chief Nurse Huber. My heart sank. It was happening again.

'You, you, you, you, you …' Chief Nurse Huber ordered as she pointed to children with her bony finger. The selected victims stood beside our beds. I was one of them.

'*Nein*, Ingrid,' Chief Nurse Huber said as she realised her mistake. 'Not you. I need you to work. Sit back down.'

Relief washed over me, but it soon ran cold. Anka had been selected.

'Follow me!' Chief Nurse Huber ordered.

The twenty or so selected youths formed two lines in the centre of the ward and followed the staff out.

I knew I wouldn't see Anka again.

A few days later the gravedigger, Herr Blum, entered the ward, his slight frame and sunken eyes reminding me of the Grim Reaper. He only appeared when death was around. He was a scavenger, a harbinger of death, coming to the wards for one reason only: to remove the bodies of the dead children. He paced up and down the lines of beds like a jackal, counting the empty ones as he went. Normally, he made only one pass; today he made a second – but only to stand at the end of my bed.

'You,' he said. I ignored him.

'You,' he insisted. 'Come with me.'

'What?' I said as I looked up at him. He was older than I had realised. His gaunt features made him look almost as sickly as some of the patients. I doubted he was strong enough to do anything to me physically, but he *was* one of the staff. That made him dangerous.

'I was told that the only reason you are still alive is that, because you're black, you have a strong black back; that *your* kind were like oxen, and that makes you useful. Even a farmer shares his food with his beasts of burden. I need someone with a strong back for some important work. If you're not up to it, I'll tell Chief Nurse Huber, and your rations will be cut to zero … or you might find yourself the victim of an unfortunate accident.'

What could I do? I followed him out into the corridor where a small group of the mental patients were assembled. They made for a wretched sight as they stared off into the distance, some with hooked hands held up to their chests, others repeatedly tapping their own heads. Others had hooked feet and struggled to stand up, let alone steady themselves. Nevertheless, I sensed that these were still the most physically capable of the remaining patients. I joined the back of the queue. Herr Blum ordered us to move forward, and I had to shorten my shuffle to keep my place at the back of the line as we threaded our way through the corridors.

'Faster! *Mach schnell!*' he said callously, knowing full well the men walking behind him were not capable of going any faster. We came to the rear of the asylum, to parts of Hadamar where I had never been. Herr Blum stopped us in front of an enormous steel door. He spun a circular handle to unlock it, heaved the heavy door open and motioned for us to enter.

We found ourselves in a large room. I immediately felt cold, as if we'd walked into an icy cavern. The men in front of me shuffled forward. I followed, examining the grey-painted walls that looked like foreboding storm clouds. Scattered around the room were several faded silver gurneys, each with bodies lying on them. Sickened, I examined their ashen faces as I walked past.

Herr Blum moved to the far wall and retrieved a thick, black ledger from a desk. It looked like one of the medieval manuscripts I had seen in the Mainzer Dom when Mutti used to take me there as a child.

Perhaps it's the Death Book that Dr Oppenheimer referred to, I thought to myself as Herr Blum picked it up and tucked it under his arm.

'Okay, follow me,' he ordered as he strode to the far end of the room and placed the ledger to one side before kneeling down and grabbing hold of a brass ring that was in the centre of a square on the floor. He pulled the ring upwards with both hands, opening a wooden door in the floor, its hinges creaking.

'Down here,' he said indifferently as he picked up the ledger and descended into a cellar. I was apprehensive, remembering the last time I had been in one of Hadamar's cellars. My foot found the first step. I felt flushed with fear and trepidation. The darkness was like a blanket, and as I breathed in an awful stench filled my nostrils. As I walked carefully down the steps, the strengthening foulness of the odour weakened my knees.

Then a bright light replaced the darkness, forcing me to squint and blink until my eyes adjusted. I tripped on the final step and had to put my hands out to steady myself. The walls were made from rounded stones that were wet to the touch. I stepped out into the cellar. It was lit by small electric lights that sat equidistant along the walls, the wiring running between them like tiny train tracks. It reminded me of the showers. The walls, that might once have been white, now had a beige tinge. The paint was cracked and crumbling, and green and black mould and moss had taken hold where the paint had completely come away. To the right I spied lines of wooden crates along the nearest wall. Lined along the far wall beyond them were rows and rows of corpses, each one stacked at least six bodies high. Their arms hung limply and tangled together.

'Take these bodies out back to the graveyard,' Herr Blum said, emotionless as he pointed to the closest pile. Resisting the urge to vomit, I pinched my nose to ward off the stench. Some of the mental patients retched as they picked up the first body from the top of the stack. It looked to be a middle-aged man, but it was hard to tell; his body was in such a state of decomposition that his features were barely recognisable. One inmate placed his hands under the dead man's armpits while the other grasped his feet. Attempting to gain a better grip, they tossed and twisted his body. His snapping bones made a horrible cracking sound that echoed around the cellar.

I moved to let them pass. Two more inmates retrieved the next body. Then two more and two more. All of the bodies in the first stack were like the old man: twisted and deformed. Rooted to the spot in horror, I hadn't realised that only one man and myself remained.

'You,' Herr Blum snapped at me. 'Hurry up! We don't have all day!'

I looked at the last mental patient, an elderly man whose head was shaven. He stared vacantly at the piles of bodies, his head moving from side to side with a slight tremor. His skin was the colour of the walls, as if all the blood had been drained from his body.

'Come on, we have dozens of bodies to bury! If you two don't hurry up, I'll make sure the next graves we dig are yours!' Herr Blum threatened impatiently. The mental patient inched his way towards the stack of bodies. Herr Blum tapped his foot as I stood waiting beside the pile.

The top body belonged to a woman, perhaps in her mid-to-late twenties, still wearing a maroon head scarf. Her face was pallid, but nowhere near as sunken as the others. I was riveted by it. There was still colour in her lips and, were it not for the fact I was in a mortuary cellar and she lay on top of a pile of dead bodies, I could have easily mistaken her for someone sleeping.

I bent down to take a closer look. Her eyes flicked open and closed. I leapt back in fright, sucking in a breath as I tried to convince myself that I was imagining things. I stepped back towards her and examined her face again. Her eyes *were* closed – almost peacefully so. Her mouth wore half a smile and there was a definite rosiness to her lips. My hand stretched out to touch her face. I wondered who she was. Where had she come from? What had her life been like before? What were her hopes and dreams? Did she have a husband? Did her mother miss her? Did she have children? Did her children miss their mother like I missed mine?

I looked at the base of the next pile. There was a girl, maybe nine or ten years old: a smaller version of the lady I'd been ordered to carry. Stacked on top of her was another girl, maybe five or six. Then another on top of her, not more than three years old. Their faces were similar; the only thing to distinguish them was the different colours of their head scarves. Then it dawned on me. The war. Nazi ideology. This was it right here. A whole family wiped out because of some men's ideas of who was and who was not the 'superior' race.

'This is your last warning!' Herr Blum thundered. 'I am a busy man and we don't have time for this delay!'

The mental patient took hold of the woman's shoulders and pulled her from the pile. Her bones sounded as if they had snapped as she crashed to the floor. Unperturbed, he grabbed her by the arms and started dragging her. I took hold of the women's legs and, as we manoeuvred her towards the stairs, it took everything I had not to drop her. My biceps and wrists burned and, by the time we reached the mortuary door, I was sure I couldn't carry her any further.

'*Halt*!' Herr Blum commanded. I gritted my teeth, trying not to drop the woman whose legs I held. Herr Blum opened the rear door. 'Follow me.'

Outside, the other carrying parties were waiting. On Herr Blum's orders we followed him down a well-worn track that snaked its way through the thick grass on either side. I flicked the women's legs in the air to try to gain better leverage. They moved of their own accord; I was certain of it. I tried to put it from my mind as I walked at the rear of the grim column, a thin line of the living carrying the dead to their final resting place. We approached the base of the track. It sloped downwards sharply. The dirt beneath my feet was wet and muddy. I struggled to stay upright. Others were not as lucky, dropping their deathly bundles, taking up Herr Blum's precious time as they bent to retrieve them – much to his annoyance.

The trail ended and we came to an open gate with a high concrete fence running either side of it, the top of the white walls glinting like diamonds, even on this overcast day. At first I thought the glistening rim was decorative, but I soon realised it was made of jagged pieces of glass. Through the gate I was confronted by rows and rows of mounds of dirt, each with a simple white cross, stretching as far as I could see. Herr Blum halted beside a freshly dug grave before he ordered us to put the bodies down. Next to the nearest pile of soil were several shovels. Herr Blum ordered us to pick them up while he indicated where he wanted us to dig with his foot. The mental patient and I placed the woman down near a pile of crosses, retrieved a shovel and hurriedly began to dig. We dug quickly, not from pride or joy in our work, but because we wanted the grisly task done and finished as quickly as possible. Soon enough, a half-dozen or so graves had been dug.

'Put them all in this grave here,' Herr Blum ordered as he pointed to the grave beside him. The first two men in the carrying party picked up the body of the old man and threw it in, followed by the next and the next. The elderly man and I picked up the woman we had carried and moved towards the grave. The bodies had fallen haphazardly, their arms and legs already melded together. We lifted the woman, swung her away from the grave and, just as we went to toss her in, I heard her groan. Horrified, I loosened my grip. She fell to the ground.

I've gone crazy! I thought.

Shaking, every nerve in my body tingling, I bent down and wrapped my fingers around her ankles. At my touch, she groaned again – loudly. It was unmistakable.

'She's alive!' I screamed as I tore my hands from her ankles. The elderly mental patient took no notice of my screams as he attempted to drag her to the grave by himself.

'*Stop*!' I cried. 'Don't put her in! She's *alive*!'

I whirled around in circles. I checked every man's face, begging them to help me, waiting for *someone* to do *something*. They all stood silent, unmoving; all except Herr Blum, who angrily marched over, growling, 'What the hell is going on here?'

'She's alive!' I screamed as I pointed to her. 'I felt her move!'

Herr Blum knelt down beside the woman's motionless body, briefly looked her over then stood up again. 'So? Put her in anyway.'

I refused to touch her. But the elderly mental patient and Herr Blum lifted her up, swung her back and forth and tossed her in. She sailed through the air, landing on the other bodies with a thud. I heard her groan as Herr Blum ordered the others to shovel soil into the grave.

'*Nein*!' I screamed in vain. There was nothing I could do. I slumped on the pile of dirt next to the grave, buried my head in my hands and cried.

'Get up and work, or *you'll* go in the next grave,' Herr Blum threatened as he patted the last of the soil down with his foot. Shakily,

I stood up. I lingered at the graveside for a few moments before following the grim workers inside. It was as if these people had never existed; as if their lives had counted for nothing. When I looked up, the burying party was halfway back up the hill. I ran to catch up with them just as a cold wind blew through me, making my soul shudder as we trudged back along the path.

We stopped and assembled at the cellar entrance.

'Go down into the cellar and get the rest,' Herr Blum ordered.

The others descended, single file, into the cellar. I stood frozen to the spot.

'I don't have time for this,' Herr Blum said with disturbing calmness. 'Either you get yourself downstairs and help the others finish or I *will* inform Dr Klein and Dr Wahlmann of your disobedience. When you're six feet under, you'll have all the time in the world to dawdle.'

My survival instincts kicked in. I hurried downstairs. We retrieved new bodies, took them to the graveyard and buried them in a single mass grave, repeating the process again and again. I went numb. The work took hours. The elderly man and I had the task of picking up the last body. Any small parts of my heart that remained mine shattered into a thousand pieces.

The last body belonged to Anka.

I went dead inside. I had lost everyone I loved, anyone I ever cared about. Hadamar, the Gestapo, the Nazis and the Germans who believed in them had taken anything that ever mattered to me. Anka's murder affected me more deeply than anything else had. I had barely known her, but her death was, for me, the last straw. I had held on for so long, mustered everything I had to stay alive but, with her death, the last of my physical and mental reserves were gone.

The year wore on towards *Weihnachten*. I all but stopped eating. Perhaps because they expected me to die, the staff stopped ordering me to work. In fact, there seemed to be fewer and fewer of them around. I spent my days lying in bed, drifting in and out of consciousness. When I was awake, I had trouble distinguishing between hallucinations and reality. Some days, I thought I heard distant explosions, but I was sure I was just dreaming about the things I wanted to hear. The Allies had been bombing the areas surrounding Hadamar as far back as 1942, but the flashes from their bombs only ever seemed like far-off bonfires.

The first time I had seen the exploding bombs, dancing like fireflies in the night sky, I prayed to a God I barely knew that the Allied bombers would reach Hadamar, send down their hellfire, shatter the walls and set us all free. Now I prayed for their bombs again. I prayed they would land several direct hits and obliterate Hadamar and everyone in it. This was such a place of evil it needed to be wiped off the face of the Earth.

My prayers went unanswered. Night after night we could hear the wailing of the air raid sirens and see through the windows the searchlights tracing the night sky like giants waving long swords. Nearby towns burned and still Hadamar remained untouched. In my dreams I saw hundreds of bombs, falling from the bellies of the planes, slowly sailing through the air like a thousand feathers.

They blasted the buildings, and the world became awash with reds, yellows and oranges, like the courtyard outside my window in the autumn time.

In my dreams I imagined one of those beautiful bombs striking the main building. Chief Nurse Huber, Dr Klein, Dr Wahlmann, Herr Blum: all of them burned. The bomb breached Hadamar's walls as if an earthquake had hit. I stood in the centre of the huge hole, willing myself to flee, but I was always too afraid to step out into the open. Finally, one of the surviving nurses, still dressed in her crisp white uniform, would beckon me back inside and I would tamely obey.

Sometimes I found myself standing in an expansive green field surrounded by a thickly wooded forest, its leaves dark and heavy. Above me I could hear the slow rumbling of the planes' engines. The flak from the anti-aircraft guns crackled like fireworks. I whirled in slow circles, staring at the sky, searching for them. The rumbling would become louder until I saw the first plane, the sun reflecting off its silver underbelly. Other times I found myself walking at the bottom of a deep blue ocean, the silver bellies of the B-24s like a school of fish swimming above me. More and more of them appeared, six to ten planes in tight, square formations. My dreams gave me hope that the war would soon end. Then I would wake and remember I was still in Hadamar.

CHAPTER 11

LIBERATION AND REVELATIONS

16 February 1945

One day in the new year, as I lay in bed drifting in and out of consciousness, I heard the rumbling of the Allied bombers. The sound was far away but unmistakable. Forcing myself from my bed, I hobbled towards the ward entrance. There were no staff around. It was as if they too had heard the bombs and hurried down to the cellars to take shelter. I stumbled through the corridors to the back gardens. I walked until I reached the bottom level of the gardens, turning in slow circles, scanning the bright blue sky above. The rumbling became louder. I squinted. I could see them. Tiny bombs, looking no bigger than birds, began to fall.

Soft explosions boomed in the distance, intensifying in both volume and frequency as scores of B-24s flew overhead. Moving like an elderly woman, I managed to get up the stairs and to the top levels of the fields, just in time to see Hadamar town as the first of the bombs fell. Huge splinters of timber flew in every direction. Houses exploded. Shards of glass from the shattered windows rained down onto the streets. And then, as quickly as they came, the American planes were gone.

But they came back the next day, and the next. Others came in the night too, the whole of the town lighting up as if it was *Weihnachten*. Night after night, day after day the bombs rained down – and still they kept missing Hadamar.

The Radio Nazi propaganda broadcasts stopped. Occasionally, some of the staff would come to the glass doors near my bed or stand in the courtyard as they watched the bombings. Thinking I and the others were at death's door, they spoke freely, sharing the stories they would tell to defend themselves when the Americans asked them to explain all that had transpired here. I wondered why they didn't just run away. They had participated in the killing of children; they were cowards after all. But their discussions told me why: there was nowhere to run to. They could go east – but the Russians were there, and they knew the Russians were more brutal and less merciful than the Americans. It was better to be captured by the Americans, who would surely be more lenient; after all, the staff convinced themselves, they had only been following orders.

Over the next few days the sky filled with silver specks. The anti-aircraft fire stopped. The Americans controlled the skies. The areas around Hadamar were bombed again and again, but the bombs largely missed the town and completely missed us. Rumours began to spread that the Americans were close. Liberation was at hand.

One morning I awoke, my ears tortured by the sounds of wailing children. I thought I was having a nightmare about the showers again.

But my lungs stung from the biting cold air. I struggled to prop myself up onto one elbow, watching the mist of my breath in the early morning light, shivering as if I had a fever. I heard a tapping sound; wrapping the thin grey blanket around me, I slowly sat up and glanced around the ward. I realised it was the other children's chattering teeth. Painfully, I swung my legs around and stood up, pulling my blanket around me. Unable to stop shivering, I walked down the ward, pain radiating through the soles of my feet as they touched the floor. Chief Nurse Huber and her staff were nowhere to be seen. To my right, the massive wooden doors through which I had entered so many years ago were closed tight. I shuffled into the furnace room; the timber and coal had gone.

'Marchand! What do you think you're doing in here?'

She was still here.

'I came to put some timber into the furnace, Chief Nurse Huber. All the children are freezing,' I said.

'What for? Those children were useless when they came here and they are even more useless now. What little timber remains will be used for cooking the bare rations we have left for the staff.'

Turning around to face her, I stood up to my full height. I realised I was much taller than her. I stared down and looked squarely into her eyes.

'I hate you!' I spat. 'You know the Americans will be here soon, and when they find you, they will kill you! Even if they don't, your day of judgement will come. One day, Chief Nurse Huber, you will be dining with the Devil!'

She raised a hand to slap me across the cheek, but I caught her forearm and pushed her away from me, glaring.

'Haven't you learned yet, Marchand? The world doesn't want you, or people like you. Why haven't you just done the world a favour and died? Do you think the Americans will arrive and everything in your world will be happy again? *Nein*, the Americans hate black people as much as we do. Those Americans will come through that door and they'll commend people like me for doing their work for them. As for you: when the Americans are done with you, you'll wish you had died in the showers.'

She may not have been able to strike physical blows any more, but her words cut me deep. After she stormed out of the furnace room, I slinked back to my bed, shivering and shaking not just from the cold but from the thought that she might be right. *Nein*! Chief Nurse Huber's world was one big web of lies and deceit. On the other hand, her words always *had* elements of truth. After all, these were men who had done nothing but fight for years. What would they do to a young woman? What would they do, if they thought they could take whatever they wanted? But my stubbornness got the better of me, and I resolved to stay alive until the Americans arrived – even if just to spite her.

Chief Nurse Huber charged into the ward, four of the male nurses trailing behind her.

'This one, this one. This one too,' she said as she picked the sickest and the weakest children. I should have stood up to her. I should have told her to back down and leave them alone. We were so close to liberation! These poor children had survived this long; it wasn't fair that they should be selected for death at the last moment. However, if the Americans were as she said they were, perhaps the children were better off dead. The thought of trying to save them evaporated from my mind as one of the orderlies picked up a child close to me, the lifeless body hanging in his arms. It didn't matter what I did; these children would never have made it through the night, let alone until the Americans arrived.

Days passed and still there was no sign of the Americans. I began to wonder if the rumours of liberation had been exaggerated. While there had been an unwritten rule that we were to be starved, it now became official policy. We were told, in no uncertain terms, that German mothers, children and soldiers were starving and there was no food for the *Lebensunswerte Leben*. We were told we were of no value to the Reich, and that keeping us alive served only to deprive worthy Germans.

Whenever a chance presented itself, I stole the occasional potato or turnip, wolfing it down as quickly as my shrinking stomach allowed me. I did my best to feed the others too. When strength allowed, I snuck out into the gardens and gathered together grass and nettles and tore strips of bark off the trees, stuffing it all together inside my pillowcase. When the kitchen was unguarded I made soups out of the grass and nettles. I mashed the bark into a paste and mixed it into the soups. I fed as much as I could to as many children who could still eat. Some of them had become so starved that they tore open their mattresses and pillows and began to eat the straw inside.

More children died and the staff grew apathetic. More freedom allowed me more time to forage in the fields in the warmer weather. The thought of escape crossed my mind but I knew my body was too weak. All I had the strength for was to scrounge a few old potatoes and hide them in my pockets. I snuck into the kitchen, found a pot and began to boil them. They were dirty, half-rotten, but never in my life had I smelt anything better. I cut them into pieces and took them to the ward in two bowls. Most of the children were too sick to move, lying spread-eagled on half-eaten mattresses.

Who should I feed? I wondered.

As I stood there with a bowl in each hand, I looked down at my shirt hanging loosely from my shoulders. My ribs jutted out like the black keys on a piano. I knew I had to eat a whole potato if I was to survive. It was selfish, but someone needed to survive this place. Someone needed to testify to all they had done.

Nein, I thought; there is strength in me yet. I can make it.

I made one of the hardest decisions of my life. I had to choose who to feed. If they could sit up, I decided, they had enough strength to endure a few more days. If they died, they died. I stopped near a young boy sitting up; if I did not feed this boy and others like him, I was condemning them to a certain death. I placed the bowl next to his pillow, carefully placed my hand behind his head and lifted a morsel of potato to his mouth. His eyes stared vacantly as I gently slid the potato into his mouth and moved his jaw up and down to help him chew. He could barely swallow, but his eyes turned to look at me, pleading for more. I had no more to give him. I moved on to the next child, a girl of four or five, lying on her side. I sat down by her bed, unable to take my eyes off her distended stomach. I hesitated. If I fed her would it only make her sicker? I put the bowl and spoon on her bedside table and rolled her over onto her back.

She stared blankly at the ceiling – she was already dead.

I could not mourn her. I could not cry for her. I simply retrieved the bowl and moved on to the next child. In the adjacent bed was an adolescent boy of twelve or thirteen, his body so withered he looked like a pile of skin dumped on the bed. He too stared blankly into the distance. I placed my hand on his forehead. At the feel of my touch he burst into life, sucking in gulps of air as his body jerked forward. He then lay back down as if nothing had happened. His head did not move but his eyes slowly turned towards me, then to the bowl in my hand. His eyes implored me to feed him but I knew I couldn't. Death hovered all around him. Feeding him would only be a waste.

I moved to the next bed, fed a small piece of potato to a young girl, then went on to the next bed and then the next. From the second bowl I managed to feed more. When it was all gone I stood empty handed, staring at dozens more children who gazed back at me. Their eyes beseeched me to feed them. I went back to my ward, lay down and waited to die. I hoped death would come quickly. I could die happy now. I had at least done one last worthwhile thing on this Earth.

29 March 1945

I didn't die, and my feelings of elation did not last.

As I was unable to source any more food, most of the children I had tried to save died anyway. I was barely able to get out of bed and my body wasted away. I slipped in and out of delirium, the spectre of death all around me. The wards filled with the stench of decaying bodies. No-one came to collect the dead any more. There was no wood to fire the crematoriums and no-one left with the strength to dig graves or take the deceased down to the cellar. I wanted to cry one last time but there were no tears left.

My thoughts turned to Mutti and Vati. I hoped they were dead, so that I could soon join them in Heaven. We would be reunited and I would be happy again. I looked out the windows at the first of the green leaves and the buds of the acorns forming on the oak branches as I prepared to take my last breath. I closed my eyes. Hundreds, thousands, of pictures ran through my mind. The faces of dead children, the faces of dead soldiers, the faces of dead Russians and Poles in mass graves. I opened my eyes and looked back at the acorns and the tiny green husks that were beginning to grow around them.

Where there is death, there is life, I thought to myself as I closed my eyes and prepared to sleep forever.

Suddenly, shouting and the clanging of steel filled the ward. The SS and the Gestapo had arrived to liquidate Hadamar. It was one last insult: even my death would be on their terms, not mine. I turned myself over slowly to stare down the ward, expecting to see black and grey uniforms and indiscriminate shooting.

Two men appeared: one in a tattered suit and tie, the other in a dull green uniform. They walked between the rows of beds, the man in the suit conversing with the soldier as he pointed to the children. When the soldier noticed me, he focussed on me curiously. The men hurried to my bed, talking between themselves and pointing at me.

'*Wie geht es Ihnen*?' asked the soldier in flawless German.

I didn't answer.

'How are you?' he repeated as he leant his rifle against the wall, leant down and gently took my hand. 'My name is Private Jaeger – George Jaeger. I'm a translator in the United States Fifth Army.'

'*Sie sind Amerikanisch*?' I whispered.

'*Ja*, I am American,' he returned.

'I told you there was a Negro girl here. This girl's name is Ingrid,' the man in the suit said. I hadn't seen him before; were I in a fitter state, it may have bothered me that he knew my name.

'Pleased to meet you, Ingrid,' Private Jaeger said before he let go of my hand and scanned the ward.

'I didn't believe you,' he said to the shabbily suited man. His eyes widened as he looked around. 'I have seen many horrors in this war, but nothing comes close to this.'

'Come,' said the suited man in accented German. 'There is much I need to show you before any of the staff realise you are here.'

Private Jaeger's face turned a greyish white. 'There's more?'

'*Oui*, Monsieur Jaeger, much more.'

Private Jaeger took off his helmet, ran his hand through his hair and shook his head before he followed. I felt as if some supernatural force had shot from the sky like a bolt of lightning, taken control of my body, replenished a little of my strength and willed me to follow them. I was weak, I felt dizzy, but even if it killed me, I was going to make sure the Americans knew everything about Hadamar. I stood shakily and took a few steps before I crumpled to the floor. Private Jaeger stopped, ran back down the ward and cradled me in his arms before he helped me back to my feet.

'Here, let me help you,' he said as he put his arm under mine and helped me walk down the ward.

'We don't have time for this,' the suited man protested.

'This girl might know things you do not.'

'Like I have told you, *Monsieur*, I was captured as a spy and in order to escape death I pretended to be insane so they put me here. I have seen all this girl has.'

Private Jaeger was the first American I had ever met, and any notions Chief Nurse Huber may have implanted about them and their intentions were quickly ebbing away. The suited man headed towards the main entrance. With Private Jaeger's help, I followed him as quickly as I could, all the while looking around and expecting Chief Nurse Huber to come stomping down the corridor and ask what was going on. We made it to the entrance; the wooden doors were wide open. I was apprehensive about going outside; perhaps this was yet another ruse to get me into the showers. What did it matter? I was bordering on death anyway. The suited man made directly for the shower block gas chambers and crematorium.

The chimneys were bellowing smoke. I pitied Private Jaeger for what he was about to see.

We entered the cubicles. Clothes lay in neat piles. We came to the room where I had been measured and weighed. Bodies riddled with bullet holes lay on the floor. We came to the showers. Naked bodies lay scattered everywhere. Private Jaeger let me go. I put my hand against the wall to steady myself as he coughed heavily, carefully stepping over and around the dead. He kept walking. Clearly, this man had seen death before.

They moved on to the crematorium. I followed behind as best I could. When I entered the room, the warmth from the fires hit me in the face as if someone had opened a window on a hot summer's day.

'*My God!*' Private Jaeger said as he retrieved his handkerchief from his jacket and placed it over his mouth. Whatever death he had seen in combat could not prepare him for what lay in front of him. Remnants of bodies still burned in the fires, the fat draining away causing tiny, brief pops of flames. In front of the oven there were two trolleys, a body on top of each. Beside them, there were bodies stacked half a dozen high.

'Do you remember that I told you how the townspeople complained about the stench? This is why,' the suited man said as Private Jaeger examined the remnants of ash that lay in semi-circles at the base of the ovens.

'And you say the townspeople know about this place?' Private Jaeger said as he turned to look at the suited man.

'*Oui*, Monsieur Jaeger.'

'And yet they did nothing to stop it?'

It was the first hint of anger I had heard in his voice.

'Nazi Germany is a complicated place, *Monsieur*. One day I will try to explain it to you, but for now we must leave. If the staff discover an American here they will try to flee. Some have already gone into hiding.'

Private Jaeger gave a slight nod before he put his arm back on mine and helped me outside. As we walked, I got the distinct feeling it was me who was holding him up and not the other way around. When we were outside once more, he removed the handkerchief from his mouth, breathing in and out heavily as he savoured the fresh air. Recovering himself, he escorted me as far as the main entrance before he let me go.

'I can't believe what I've seen,' he said to the suited man.

'Believe it, *Monsieur*. Believe it. Now go and report what you have seen to your superiors. We will wait here until you come.'

Private Jaeger forced a smile at me before he turned and set off at a sprint down the gravel driveway, through the gates and down the road.

'Who are you?' I said to the suited man as we walked back inside. 'And why have I never seen you before?'

He wouldn't tell me his name. He just said that he was a French agent who had been captured, and to escape execution by the Gestapo he had pretended to be an insane French labourer and was put into Hadamar. Being French, he had been in a wing of the building I'd never seen. Over time he had earned the staff's trust and was permitted to go on errands into Hadamar town. A few days earlier he had been on one such errand and had seen Private Jaeger and some other Americans as they made their way through the streets of Hadamar. He had told him about the 'House of Shudders', as the townspeople called it. Private Jaeger had not believed him.

He could see the institute on the hill when the Frenchman pointed it out, but all he was really interested in was whether the Germans had any fortifications up there. The Frenchman assured him that they did not. He insisted Private Jaeger should come to Hadamar alone, so not to arouse too much attention.

'The Americans have taken the town, but it is a lawless place,' the Frenchman told me. 'You are safer here. When Monsieur Jaeger returns with more Americans, someone who knows about this place needs to tell them all that has happened here. Until the Americans return, tell no-one else that they are here. Do you understand?'

I nodded before he disappeared inside as if he had more pressing business to attend to. I never saw him again.

I stood between the main entrance doors, staring down the driveway. Private Jaeger had long since disappeared and I wondered if I should follow him. *Nein*, I had barely been able to walk to the crematorium without his assistance; how far would I get? Using the walls to prop myself up, I made it to my bed. I lay down and wondered how long it would be before more Americans arrived. A few hours? A day? A week? I didn't know how long I had left. I prayed they would come soon as I drifted in and out of consciousness. I was starting to think that the whole episode was nothing more than a figment of my imagination when, suddenly, I heard voices coming from the main entrance.

Wearily, I and some of the others rose from our beds; we started walking towards the front doors as if drawn to it by some magic spell. Three tall, thin figures were silhouetted in the doorway, weapons at the ready. Weakness took hold of me and I collapsed to the ground. One of the figures came and knelt beside me, speaking in English as he grasped me by the hand and tried to lift me to my feet. Realising I did not understand, he repeated himself in broken German. 'Are you okay?'

I looked up into the face of a middle-aged man with thick, brown hair and bright, brown eyes that gleamed through his rimmed glasses. He beckoned to someone. Private Jaeger appeared. The American spoke to Jaeger, who translated as they helped me to my feet.

'My name is Captain Alton H. Jung, from the United States First Army, Second Division,' the man in the glasses said through Private Jaeger. More men arrived. I don't know why I did it – perhaps to make sure he was real – but I wrapped my arms around the captain and hugged him as tightly as I would have if he was Vati. He returned my embrace reluctantly. After giving me a brief hug, he let me go and began walking between the rows of beds.

'He wants to know what kind of place this is,' Private Jaeger said as Captain Jung surveyed the dead and dying children lying in their beds. 'He says they were told it was an extermination camp, but it seems to be an ordinary hospital.'

'It's both,' I said as the captain took a closer inspection of the children in the nearest beds – the ones who were still alive but too weak and disorientated to realise their liberators had arrived. Captain Jung's comrades followed closely behind him, placing their arms over their mouths as they entered the ward. It was a futile gesture. The stench of rotting flesh overpowered them. A few of them put their hands up against the walls and loudly expelled the contents of their stomachs.

'What do you mean, "both"?' Captain Jung asked through Private Jaeger as he coughed and covered his nose with his hands to shield against the smell. 'Who are these people?'

'We are the *Lebensunwertes Leben* children: lives unworthy of living,' I said to Private Jaeger as I took hold of Captain Jung's free hand and led him further down the ward. 'We are Germany's unwanted children. We are the useless. The ones who contribute nothing to the Reich. The ones to be exterminated. All of us here are mentally disabled, deaf, … or black. We're the few who have survived this far; they've murdered thousands more.'

As Private Jaeger relayed what I had said, Captain Jung's demeanour turned from shock to fury. He started barking orders in English. His men disappeared momentarily, before returning with dark green packets and green drinking bottles. Captain Jung took his from his belt, unscrewed the lid and handed it to me. I drank as many small sips as I could handle before my stomach began to hurt and I gave it back to him. His forced it into my hands.

'Come now, you need to drink some more,' Private Jaeger said as Captain Jung softly put his hand on my shoulder.

I shook my head. '*Nein*, I can't. I have tried to give these children water and it's not good for them.'

Private Jaeger nodded and translated. Captain Jung gave more orders in English. His men went to each patient, titled their heads back and gave them small sips of water. Captain Jung reached into his pocket, withdrew a green packet and opened it. Inside was a chocolate bar. I stared at it intently. I began to salivate. Captain Jung handed it to me but, as he did, I looked at a young girl in a nearby bed. I couldn't take it. How could I eat something so delicious when someone else was starving? I walked over, lifted her head, broke a piece of chocolate off and gave it to her. She could barely move her mouth but as the chocolate melted she managed to swallow it.

'We have plenty more of that,' Private Jaeger said as he handed me another bar. 'You are just as weak as any of these children. Please, eat something.'

I took the second bar, unwrapped it and took a small bite. It was, without exception, the most wonderful thing I had ever tasted. I desperately wanted to take another bite, but I knew if I ate too much too fast my stomach would hurt. But there was no pain yet, so I took another bite, and another.

'The captain would like to know your name,' Private Jaeger asked me.

'Ingrid Marchand,' I said through a mouthful of chocolate.

'Ingrid,' Captain Jung kindly repeated.

'The captain would like someone to show him around. The Frenchman told us to meet him here but he doesn't seem to be around. Do you think you could show us what you showed me before? Are you strong enough to do that for us?'

I nodded. Private Jaeger told Captain Jung, who also nodded. We had barely taken a step, however, before I heard shouting in German coming from down the corridors. Captain Jung and Private Jaeger hurried towards the main reception area. I followed close behind.

'What is this? What is all this noise?' Dr Wahlmann cried as he stormed out of Dr Klein's office. He was taller and more overweight than I remembered. Odd, considering the supposed food shortages we'd had. Behind him came the bald head of Nurse Willig. They both turned pale when they saw the Americans.

'Who … who … are … you?' Dr Wahlmann stammered.

'This is Captain Alton H. Jung, of the United States Army First Army, Second Division,' Private Jaeger said. 'And by that authority, we are taking control of this institution and we are placing you under arrest.'

Two of Captain Jung's men unslung their rifles from their shoulders and marched Dr Wahlmann and Nurse Willig back into Dr Klein's office.

'How many more staff are there, Ingrid?' Private Jaeger asked me.

'I don't know,' I said. 'I think some may have left, but before you came there were dozens.'

Private Jaeger relayed this to Captain Jung, who ordered his men to search the buildings. The first group set off down the corridors while a second group climbed the stairs. Captain Jung followed, indicating with a wave of his hand that he wished me to accompany him. My bones still ached as I walked, but the chocolate had reinvigorated me enough to allow me to almost keep pace with them. I took them to another of the children's wards, then a men's ward, then a women's.

In the women's ward, when they realised the Americans had come, three elderly patients rose from their beds, walked towards the soldiers, kissed them on the cheeks and embraced them. Some of the soldiers wept. Other weaker women tried to get up but collapsed to the floor. Captain Jung's men fell to their knees as they cradled the women in their arms.

I watched one young soldier – blond, tall and good-looking, barely a few years older than me – standing in the centre of the ward as he looked around, his face a picture of utter dismay. A young girl of maybe fifteen rose from her bed and staggered towards him. She put her bony cheeks to his chest and wrapped her scrawny arms around his neck. She smiled, gasped her last breath and collapsed into his arms. He held her dead body in his arms as if he were dancing with a partner who was too short, staring blankly at her as the tears poured down his face. His legs buckled. He fell to the ground. The dead girl fell into his lap. He sat and rocked her gently as if she were his only sister. It made my heart ache.

I walked over and placed my hand on his head. He looked up at me. His eyes were red and watery but there was more. His eyes questioned me, wanting an answer for what he was seeing. I leant down and kissed him on the cheek. He looked back down at the dead girl, his lips quivering as he tried to stem the flow of tears. He stood, picked the girl up and carried her back towards her bed. Gently, he lay her down and placed her head on the pillow. He pulled her blanket up over her and tucked her in tightly before he walked from the ward, his expression blank and distant.

The Americans were clearly appalled and sickened, but I had to show them more. They had to see all of it before the staff realised they were here and destroyed more of the evidence of their crimes. I walked back to Captain Jung and tugged on his jacket, urging him to follow me. I led him and his men downstairs and out to the shower block and crematorium. It was the same as it had been when Private Jaeger had entered, except that the fires had gone out. All that remained in the ovens were a skull and ribs jutting upwards like burnt sticks. Captain Jung stepped in for a closer examination as three of his men, overcome by what they had seen, ran from the room.

'I told him this needed to be seen to be believed,' Private Jaeger commented as we stood at the entrance and let the men pass us by. 'How can anyone treat their own children this way? War is hell, but I don't think even the Devil himself could dream up such abominations.'

Hadamar had more horrors that would have to wait. It was clear the Americans had seen enough. Captain Jung marched from the building and returned to the main foyer. Private Jaeger and I followed. Captain Jung's men had completed their search and had rounded up every nurse, doctor and orderly they could find. It was odd seeing people who had controlled me for so long, who had instilled so much fear, who had held my life in the palm of their hands for more than half a decade, huddled into one of the offices shaking with fear and uncertainty. I took great pleasure in their suffering.

One of Captain Jung's men suddenly came running through the front entrance. His breathing was laboured but his arms flailed wildly as he spoke to Captain Jung. Private Jaeger turned to me and said, 'He says he found something at the back.'

The graveyard.

Captain Jung set off, but I grabbed his jacket. He stopped, turned and looked at me. I looked at Private Jaeger, 'Tell him I need to show him something before he sees the graveyard.'

Private Jaeger did as I asked. I led Captain Jung and his men to the mortuary cellar door. I pointed at it. Captain Jung heaved it open and glanced back at me. I nodded towards the doorway. Captain Jung retrieved a torch from his jacket and switched it on. He paused at the top of the stairs, peering into the darkness, before he started moving his torch from side to side. The beams illuminated the moist bricks of the walls and he took his first cautious steps downwards. He had only taken one step when he was stopped by the sound of a blood-curdling scream. He paused and looked to me as if to say, 'What was that?'

I shrugged. Screams in Hadamar were nothing new, but it put Captain Jung and his men – who were already jumpy – further on edge. Taking a deep breath, he composed himself before pushing on. The torch lit the passageway as we descended. The screams became shriller and louder. We reached the base of the stairs. Captain Jung moved the torch in a sweeping pattern, only stopping it when it shone on a man huddled in the corner. When the light hit him, he screamed, recoiled and shielded his face with his arms. Captain Jung moved the light to one side. The man went silent. When Captain Jung shone the torchlight back onto him he let out an ear-splitting scream. Captain

Jung ordered two of his men to take the man upstairs. They inched warily towards him.

As soon as their hands touched his body, he went deathly quiet. The two Americans looked up to their superior officer, clearly bemused by the man's erratic behaviour.

'They don't mind if you scream. In fact, they get a sick kind of enjoyment out of it, but if you resist in here, they beat you or kill you. That's why he stopped,' I told Private Jaeger. Two of his men retrieved their own torches, turned them on and hurried back upstairs. Captain Jung stepped past the woman, his torchlight scanning the doorframe before he moved into the next room. It was there they found what I wanted them to see: the dead inmates stacked against the walls. Captain Jung dipped the torch and covered his eyes with his hand.

He said something to Private Jaegar, who turned and spoke to me. 'Do you think you could take us to the graveyard now?' he asked.

I nodded, walking one step behind Captain Jung as we ascended to the ground floor. At the top of the cellar, I turned right, opened the door and led them along the path, past the white wall with glass on top and into the cemetery. Captain Jung and his men stood, aghast, as they cast their eyes over the football field-sized expanse of graves. Nearby was a fresh, open grave. Captain Jung inched closer and stared down while I stood beside him and did the same. There were at least twenty bodies, maybe more, carelessly tossed in and jumbled together. Closing his eyes, Captain Jung rubbed the bridge of his nose with his thumb and forefinger before he turned to me and spoke in English. Realising I did not understand, he turned to Private Jaeger.

'Who are these people? Are these German patients?'

'*Nein*. Well, maybe some are,' I replied. 'Mostly they are Russians and Poles. Men, women and children.'

'Russians and Poles! What are they doing here?' Private Jaeger exclaimed. 'Are you sure?'

'*Ja*,' I said assuredly.

'How do you know?' Private Jaeger asked.

'Because I helped bury them.'

Captain Jung ran his hands up and down his face and forehead as Private Jaeger translated. Then he started walking back up the trail. Instead of going back inside, he walked around the outside of the buildings towards the bus garages. I followed, a shudder running down my back as I spied the two buses parked inside, their windows still blackened out. Captain Jung stopped beside them, turned as if to say something to me, but instead continued on towards the entrance to the crematorium. He did not go inside; he just stood there looking the chimneys up and down as he said something to Private Jaeger.

'The captain would like to know how those people in the graves were killed,' Private Jaeger said to me.

'Lethal injections,' I replied dully. 'That was their preferred method. But they gassed us, starved us – whatever they could do.'

'They gassed you?' Private Jaeger asked incredulously.

'*Ja*, they gassed us,' I said as I walked over and pointed at the hoses and gas bottles that were still beside the windows. 'See?'

Captain Jung marched back to the shower block. Private Jaeger and I followed. We found Captain Jung standing beside the shower block, looking around as if he was searching for something.

'What's down there?' Private Jaeger asked, pointing to a small staircase that led down another corridor.

'I don't know,' I replied. 'The last time I was here they tried to kill me; I only survived because a doctor saved me.'

I sensed that Private Jaeger wanted to know more about what I had just said, but Captain Jung had already set off down the corridor. We followed him, eventually coming to a mortuary room where dead bodies still lay on the tables. Captain Jung studied them closely before he moved on to the next room further down the corridor. In the centre was a slanted rectangular concrete slab raised up on bricks. At the base of the slab was a drainage hole ringed by dark red blood stains. Below was a dried puddle of blood. Captain Jung examined it briefly. Then he marched resolutely back outside.

On his signal – a spin of his right index finger in a circular motion – his men lined up behind him. With determined steps, Captain Jung and his men headed straight for Dr Klein's office, where others still guarded the staff. Agitated, Captain Jung paced back and forth in front of the staff. The other Americans circled like sharks behind him, their young faces flushed with anger and hatred. The staff bowed their heads. They knew the Americans had seen all of their hideous handiwork. Visibly nervous, they huddled closer together, not daring to make eye contact.

Captain Jung stopped pacing and signalled for his radio man to stand beside him with his equipment. Captain Jung picked up the receiver and placed it to his ear. I didn't understand what he said, but several of the staff became visibly nervous as they tried to position themselves as far away from the Americans as possible. When his call was finished, Captain Jung pulled a chair to one side, sat down on it, reached inside his jacket and retrieved a packet of cigarettes. After tapping the packet on his leg, he withdrew a cigarette and put it in his mouth. He lit the cigarette with a silver lighter, then smoked slowly, staring down the staff as he rubbed his fingers on his lips.

With each passing minute the staff grew more apprehensive. They edged away from Jung. I revelled in the sight of it. Now they were experiencing some of the fear they had inflicted on me for years.

An hour later, a new group of Americans came, some of them wearing white coats over their green uniforms. Captain Jung leapt up from his chair and saluted before he spoke rapidly and pointed towards the staff. Curiosity overcame their fears; the staff looked up at the new arrivals. Suddenly, Captain Jung pointed at Dr Wahlmann. Without Private Jaeger's help he shouted, '*Kommen Sie hier*!'

Dr Wahlmann stumbled forward and stood in front of Captain Jung and the new American officers. He refused to look them in the eye.

'Look at Captain Jung when he talks to you,' Private Jaeger commanded.

Despite the order, Dr Wahlmann lifted his head only slightly.

'Repeat your name and your role. You are the one in charge here, yes?' Private Jaeger asked.

Dr Wahlmann stole a glance at me before he said, 'My name is Rudolf Hans. I am just a simple orderly. I do not know anything. Dr Klein is in charge, but he fled before you arrived.'

Liar! My chest burned with hatred.

'When I first arrived, you told me your name was Dr Wahlmann and that you were in charge,' Private Jaeger translated as Captain Jung stroked his chin.

'I got scared. I told you what I thought would protect me.'

'Ingrid, who is this man?' Private Jaeger asked me.

I knew Dr Wahlmann's power and authority had vanished, but still I hesitated.

'Ingrid, who is this man?' Private Jaeger said more softly.

'His name is Dr Wahlmann, Dr Adolf Wahlmann. He is the doctor in charge here.'

Private Jaeger translated.

'*Danke*, Ingrid,' Captain Jung said as turned back to Dr Wahlmann.

'I will ask you again,' Captain Jung said through Private Jaeger. 'What is your name and position here?'

Realising his subterfuge was at an end, Dr Wahlmann admitted who he was.

'Who is the head nurse here?' Captain Jung asked through Private Jaeger, turning away from Dr Wahlmann in disgust. I glared at Chief Nurse Huber, expecting her to step forward, but doubting she would. Instead she dipped her head and tried to hide behind one of the others.

'She is,' I said as I stepped forward and pointed her out.

'*Kommen Sie mit uns*,' Captain Jung ordered.

Private Jaeger informed me that Captain Jung wished me to accompany the American doctors, himself, Dr Wahlmann and Chief Nurse Huber back to the cellars. The second time we descended into the underground caverns of Hadamar there were no surprises. The bodies lay as we had left them, stacked near the walls or scattered on the floor. The American doctors placed their arms to their mouths to shield themselves from the smell, but even with their faces covered there was no hiding the shock in their eyes.

A tall, slender American doctor who wore a green woollen hat and had a long nose with a tidy moustache beneath it stepped forward. I examined his features closely. I recalled the racial classification classes with Fräulein Pletcher and thought that this man, if Nazi stereotyping was to be believed, had many of the attributes they assigned to Jewish people, especially the 'hooked' nose. I wondered if the American doctor was indeed Jewish. Even though we stood in a cellar full of dead bodies, the Americans witnessing horrors that would be difficult for the Devil himself to dream up, it took everything I had not to laugh. After all their big talk, a *Jew* was about to be the one to bring down Dr Wahlmann and Chief Nurse Huber! He affixed his stethoscope to his ears and went to one of the bodies on the far wall, a man in his late twenties.

'This is Major Herman Bolker, Chief Pathologist of the War Crimes International Tribunal,' Private Jaeger told me. When he heard this, Dr Wahlmann, who was trying to stand inconspicuously near the stairs, leapt forward and announced, 'These people all died of tuberculosis!'

The slender doctor paid no mind to the protesting Nazi as he squatted down and placed the circular end of the stethoscope on the dead man's chest. As he stood up, he turned toward Captain Jung and shook his head. They spoke some more in English before the Major turned to Dr Wahlmann and said in fluent German, 'I see no signs of tuberculosis. If I had to guess, these people were poisoned.'

'These people were not poisoned! These people died from tuberculosis!' Chief Nurse Huber argued. Captain Jung did not need a translation to understand her protestations, but his scowl was enough to silence her. The doctors finished their examinations, and it was clear from the looks they gave Chief Nurse Huber and Dr Wahlmann that they did not believe that any of these people had died from tuberculosis. When they'd completed their work, Captain Jung ordered everyone upstairs and out to the graveyard.

'Who is in charge of the grave digging?' Captain Jung asked through Private Jaeger. Neither Dr Wahlmann nor Chief Nurse Huber answered.

'Herr Blum,' I answered.

'Is he inside with the others?' Private Jaeger asked.

'I think so,' I said.

'Would you be kind enough to go with my men, identify him and bring him back here please?' Captain Jung asked through Private Jaeger. I hurried back inside with Private Jaeger and returned with Herr Blum. He looked withered and withdrawn as he slunk towards the nearest grave. Captain Jung picked up a shovel, forced it into Herr Blum's hand and pointed towards the grave with his foot. Herr

Blum jammed the shovel into the ground and drove it in deeper with his foot. While he dug, I watched the American doctors looking up and down the cemetery, awed by its magnitude. When Herr Blum's shovel broke enough soil to reach the first of the bodies, the disgusting odours of the dead poured out. The smell was indescribable.

The doctors edged closer to the graves, covering their noses and mouths.

Meanwhile Captain Jung and one of his subordinates, who held a notepad in his hand, began walking the lengths of the graves, counting as they went.

Captain Jung and his note-taker returned and spoke to the doctors.

'One hundred,' Private Jaeger said for my benefit.

I guessed that, if each grave had ten to twenty people in it, there were possibly two hundred people buried here, plus the stacked bodies in the cellar. The final total could have been as high as five hundred. While Captain Jung ordered Herr Blum to exhume more bodies, I turned around and looked at the smoke stacks that towered above the crematorium, then at the graves again. I realised that these people's lives were not forgotten. Their bodies were the final proof the Americans needed. In death, these people would punish the living.

'How many people are there in each of these graves?' Private Jaeger asked Herr Blum.

'Some have one, some two, others have maybe a dozen or more,' he replied bluntly.

Major Bolker asked Herr Blum, 'Who are these people? And why do some of the bodies have wooden discs attached to them and some do not?'

'The ones with the wooden discs are Germans, the ones without are Russian and Poles. Sick ones. They all had tuberculosis, so we did the only humane thing. We euthanised them.'

Private Jaeger translated to Captain Jung, and it was taken down in the notebook.

'And what are these graves here? Why are they open?' Private Jaeger continued.

'We haven't filled those ones yet,' Herr Blum responded.

'What?'

'We always keep three graves ahead.'

'What are those graves over there?' Major Bolker asked as he pointed to a dozen or so graves in a neat line just before a small hill. Fledgling pine trees arranged in tidy rows sat to the left of the graves, and on top of them there were what looked like rose bushes.

'They are children's graves.'

I stood and looked at them, knowing one of those graves belonged to Anka.

I was relieved when I was ordered to wait back inside while Captain Jung took the new doctors on a tour of the showers and the crematorium. When they finally came back inside the main building, his calm demeanour had gone. He shouted orders in English and his men began separating the staff and taking them away to different offices. The longer he spoke, the angrier he became. When all but a few of the staff had been removed, he turned to Private Jaeger, who turned to me.

'Ingrid,' Private Jaeger said. 'Captain Jung says he has to take our doctors back to headquarters to make a full report and to ask our bosses how to proceed with all of this. Don't worry. We'll be back. For now, some of our men will stay here. Thanks for all you have done for us.'

I smiled. I wondered what was going to happen next – now that we had, at last, been liberated.

CHAPTER 12

EXAMINATIONS AND INTERROGATIONS

7 April 1945

Captain Jung and Private Jaeger came and went over the next week. The American soldiers stationed guards to watch over not only the captured prisoners but also the inmates who, now we were liberated, were desperate to leave. In the beginning, few had the physical strength even to consider it, but that soon changed.

On the second day after the Americans came a huge green truck arrived and pulled up outside the entrance. We watched through the barred windows as one of the Americans lifted the canvas flap at the rear of the vehicle and tossed it onto the truck's roof. Half a dozen Americans leapt down from the back tray while one soldier remained inside, hunched over, and began passing down brown hessian sacks. We all watched on, intrigued, as they brought them inside. I noticed that each sack was marked with black writing. Some had 'US Army Bakeries' on them; others had 'US Army Potatoes'.

I wiped the saliva from the sides of my mouth. More people gathered at the windows, our lips smacking in unison as we watched the Americans walk past in single file and head for the kitchen. When the truck was fully unloaded they ordered all of us to assemble in the dining halls. Scores upon scores of survivors stood there – many more than I thought would have made it through their incarceration. There was only one thought on each of our minds: food.

Two Americans stood guard at the kitchen while the rest of them disappeared back outside and brought in more sacks. Our eyes opened wide. This was more food than we'd seen in years.

Private Jaeger moved to the raised platform where the Hadamar staff normally ate and addressed us.

'There's plenty of food for everyone. There's no need to push or panic. Remember, most of you have been starved for a long time; your stomachs can't handle large amounts of food yet. Don't eat too much too soon. I know you're all hungry, but we'll only be handing out small portions.'

The people's faces told me they cared little about portion size; they just wanted food. Private Jaeger asked for volunteers to peel potatoes and a dozen hands shot to the sky, mostly the elderly patients. Two Americans brought out a dozen bowls and potato peelers and sat them in the middle of one of the tables. The elderly inmates sat around the table and began peeling, chatting as they went. I stood back and watched, as did the others, eagerly anticipating the meal that was to come. The whole scene could have been one big, family *Weihnachten*.

CHAPTER 12

When the potatoes were peeled they were sent back to the kitchen where the Americans boiled them. The Americans supervised as we were handed bowls and spoons and, along with our potatoes, small loaves of bread. When we sat down to eat, some scoffed their food while others savoured it. I was one of the latter, letting each morsel of hot potato sit on my tastebuds before I let it slide down my throat. I could feel vitality returning to my body as the warmth of the potato filled my stomach. When we had finished, many of the inmates begged for more, but the Americans sternly refused. They said they would supervise our food intake until we were healthy enough to eat more.

The next evening, I was summoned to Chief Nurse Huber's office. Captain Jung and Major Bolker sat waiting for me. A third man was there, who had the same oak leaf insignia on his uniform as Major Bolker. He was introduced to me as Major Fulton C. Vowell. I eyed him warily as I sat down. Although he was clearly the same rank as Major Bolker, I sensed this man wielded more authority than he was letting on. Captain Jung invited me to sit across from him. Major Vowell said, in good German, that he wanted me to accompany them on the rounds of the patients and check on the general health of people. I agreed, of course. With each new patient they examined, they recorded details, but there was one word they kept repeating. One word in English that I did know: tuberculosis.

We visited the wards in the right wing, then continued on to those in the left wing, where I'd never been. When they were satisfied we returned to the main offices near the front entrance. Captain Jung's men stood to attention. He gave orders in English and his men raised their weapons and herded the staff into separate offices again. I watched the Americans closely, particularly their right index fingers, poised millimetres from their triggers.

I became fixated on one rather attractive man. His black hair was neatly clipped; his eyes chestnut brown. He was powerfully built – his tight uniform accentuated his bulging muscles – but his coarse, rough hands shook as if they belonged to an elderly man. His face was contorted and stiff, his eyes radiating pure disgust towards the staff. Several times he closed his eyes and breathed deeply, seeming to will himself to refrain from shooting them. His restraint was made even more remarkable when, as they moved them along, some of the male staff started telling the Americans in English and in German that they were proud of what they had done. They were proud to be Nazis.

With the staff gone, Private Jaeger asked me to tell the inmates to assemble out on the front driveway because the Americans wished to count everyone; they wanted to know the exact number of survivors. I did as he asked. As we waited for the lines of people to file outside, he started telling me that the Russians had found huge extermination camps at places like Auschwitz and Majdanek in Poland, and that the Americans had found a similar one at Ohrdruf. Shocked by what they had found, the American generals were having a difficult time finding enough medical staff to document everything. He admitted that they were unsure as how to proceed. They were astonished at the scale of their discoveries. This was why it had taken so long for

Captain Jung and Major Bolker to return, and this was why they needed an exact count: so they could ensure they placed the right resources in the right places.

As people exited the building they were assembled in a large circle. The inmates looked at one another, puzzled and confused. I was amazed at the number of survivors. There must have been a few hundred, not including those who still could not leave their beds. It filled me with hope. The Nazis had been organised, exceptionally good at their work – and still, some of us had survived.

When the last of the inmates had been brought out, Captain Jung and his subordinates moved us into ramshackle lines and began counting.

'*Dreihundert*,' Private Jaeger said.

The Captain waved his arms around to direct us into more orderly lines. All the inmates began shuffling forward. That was when the ear-piercing howling, shrieking and screaming began.

'Ingrid, Captain Jung needs you up front, now!' Private Jaeger shouted as he hurried me to the head of the lines. Only when I was clear of the people did I understand the reasons for their screams. There were three desks with a uniformed American soldier seated at each one. Behind them were three American doctors dressed in white coats identical to those worn by the Hadamar doctors. When I moved closer I realised Major Bolker was standing behind the middle table. He looked at me quizzically and threw his arms up in the air to indicate he did not understand their behaviour. I stood in front of him and looked out over the assembled crowd. The people who were closest held their hands over their ears as they rocked back and forth, their screeching almost rhythmical.

'What's wrong with them?' Private Jaeger asked.

'They're scared,' I replied. 'It's the white coats. You stand them in front of a whole bunch of medical people that look *exactly* like the brutes who have been tormenting us for years. They think you're going to examine them to choose who to kill.'

Private Jaeger translated for Captain Jung.

'Kill them?' Private Jaeger said, exasperated. 'We don't want to do anything of the sort! We just fed all of these people, why would they think we want to kill them?'

'Because this is how the staff here used to trick us! They would promise us a picnic or something nice, then when we fell for their lies it was off to the gas chambers. You need to get those doctors to take their white coats off.'

Major Bolker ordered the doctors to remove the offending coats before he said to me, bewildered, 'But I've just examined all these people.'

'*Ja*,' I replied. 'And the fact you kept saying "tuberculosis" makes them think that your examinations were to see which ones you are going to kill.'

He sighed in exasperation. 'Can you tell these people that we are here to *help* them? We simply want to check on their state of health so we know how to help them.'

I was scared – more than I had been in a long time. I had never spoken to a crowd before. I stared out at them. These people had been starved, beaten, tortured. They were teetering on the precipice of death. Now they needed medical examinations so that they would survive and possibly, hopefully, live long, healthy lives. I had to overcome my fears.

'Everyone!' I meekly shouted. It had no impact. I took a nervous look in Major Bolker's direction, he smiled and nodded.

'Everyone!' I shouted loudly. The closest ones stopped screaming and looked at me. 'These American doctors behind me are not like the ones who have tormented us all these years! They are different. They are here to help us! You have to trust me!'

The screaming stopped. I had their undivided attention.

'They are not here to kill you. This is not to decide who will live and who will die. They want us all to live. You need to trust them!'

They had all gone silent, but still they didn't move. I moved towards Major Bolker and lifted my blouse, shivering at the coldness of his stethoscope as he placed it on my chest.

'Apart from a little malnutrition, you seem fine,' Major Bolker said. 'You're one of the lucky ones.'

Given everything that had happened in my life up until this point I did not feel lucky, but when I thought about all of those who had died, particularly in the months before the Americans arrived, I realised he was right. I *was* one of the lucky ones. So were the others who stood before me. Despite my actions, however, I sensed they were still hesitant.

I walked towards the closest inmate: an older man, frail with silvery hair. Gently placing my hand underneath his elbow I escorted him towards Major Bolker. The feeble old man smiled as I passed him to Major Bolker who, after examining him, wrote notes in a book before he led the old man behind the rows of desks. Encouraged by what they saw, the others cautiously edged forward. One by one they allowed themselves to be examined and took their position behind the desks to wait for further instructions. Major Bolker left the work to the other doctors as he walked over to me.

'Ingrid,' Major Bolker said. 'We also brought as many patients out here as we could because we want to interview the staff away from the patients. Can you come with me while we interrogate the staff about procedures here? They've lied before, and we're certain they'll do it again. If someone is standing nearby who knows the truth, or they think knows the truth, they might be more honest with us. Do you think you can do that?'

I nodded. The long-held fear I had of them was starting to subside. Now, I wanted to get it all over and done with and go home to Mutti – if she was still alive and there was a home to go to. The two Majors, Captain Jung, Private Jaeger and I headed inside. Right before we entered through the main doors, I looked up to see two soldiers affixing an American flag to the balcony. Seeing it filled my heart with a joy I had forgotten was possible. My spirit soared. That flag was it. Things were now official. The Americans had taken ownership of Hadamar.

I had only placed one foot inside when it hit me like a winter's gale. The uncertainty of the staff permeated the rooms like a mist, sticking to the walls as if it were paint. Major Bolker and Captain Jung went to the first office and ordered Dr Wahlmann and Nurse Willig into

Chief Nurse Huber's office. They lined the two men up against the wall. At first I thought they were going to execute them. Instead of a gun, however, one of Major Bolker's men arrived with a camera. The two men stood in a pose of sorts: Dr Wahlmann standing on the left, towering over the shorter Nurse Willig. Dr Wahlmann wore a thick pin-striped jacket, white shirt and tie. He knotted his fingers and held them in front of his waist. Nurse Willig wore a similar white shirt, black vest and brown suit jacket. Neither man looked at the camera, but still had to blink when the flashbulb momentarily blinded them.

It occurred to me that I had never seen either man dressed in civilian clothes. This could mean only one thing: they must have had an inkling the Americans were on their way and were preparing to flee. *Cowards!* After all their spouting about the virtue of their mission – when *their* judgement day had finally arrived, they were trying to slink away and hide. If their 'work' was so righteous, why attempt to hide? But they had miscalculated. Now they had been caught, and were looking ruffled and shaken. Stripped of their authority, stripped of all their Nazi trappings, they looked forlorn – almost pathetic. Even in their pitiful state, I couldn't entirely shake my nerves, after years of subjugation at their hands. I lingered at the office door as a man with sergeant's stripes arrived.

The Herr Majors sat on the left-hand side of the desk and instructed Dr Wahlmann to sit opposite. Dr Wahlmann fiddled with his hands in his lap. Major Bolker reached down beside him and produced two brown bottles, each one with three labels on them, which he placed on the table. One bottle had handwriting that said, 'Morphine hydrochloride, half a gram, creosote five drops and distilled water to make 200 cc'. The other was similar but, instead of morphine, the writing said 'scopolamine'. Major Bolker then produced a small, white cardboard box with dozens of tubes inside, each of which was marked, 'Morphine hydrochlorate, 2/100 of a gram'.

Dr Wahlmann stared at the items on the table intently as Major Vowell started the interrogation.

'Chief Nurse Huber unlocked the cabinet in the ward containing these items you see on the table before you. Do you know what these are?'

I thought the revelation that his main accomplice was assisting them would make Dr Wahlmann more nervous, but instead he relaxed and stopped fiddling with his hands as he leant forward and examined the bottles and tubes.

'Have you seen these before?' Major Bolker asked. Dr Wahlmann leant back in his chair and looked at the Herr Major.

'It is morphine and scopolamine. We administer it to the terminally ill patients; the morphine helps to ease their suffering.'

'Suffering from what?' Major Bolker pushed.

'Tuberculosis, mainly.'

'Yes, you keep telling us that these patients died from tuberculosis, but I have found no evidence, as yet, that any of these patients were suffering from tuberculosis. I have found no X-ray or pneumothorax machines.'

'We checked the skin and checked a patient's lung function. I assure you all the patients that died here did so from diseases.'

CHAPTER 12

Major Vowell took over the interrogation, partly – I suspected – because he was the senior man, and partly because Major Bolker was becoming frustrated with Dr Wahlmann's denials. No matter how hard they pushed him, Dr Wahlmann would not acknowledge any of the evil he had perpetrated. He insisted his job was merely administrative, and that any deaths at the hands of the staff were to relieve terminally ill patients of their suffering.

His denials made be boil with rage, but I held my tongue.

Realising they would not get more out of Dr Wahlmann, they began interrogating Nurse Willig. His story was the same: only the patients who were terminally ill had received injections. Whenever either of the Herr Majors believed him to be lying, they looked to me. At first, I was too nervous to respond. When they lied, I only shook my head slightly, not even sure if the Herr Majors had noticed. But the longer I listened to lies, the more I grew in confidence. As the interrogation continued, they played the same line: they either had not participated in the killings or, on the few occasions they had, the orders had come from above – meaning they had no choice. If they had not followed orders, they would have been sent to a concentration camp.

The interview with Dr Wahlmann and Nurse Willig finished and they brought in Herr Blum. His face was dazed. He was clearly confused about what was going on. Major Bolker indicated that he should take a seat. Herr Blum sat down and fiddled with his hands, looking anywhere but at his interrogators.

'Let's begin by confirming your name,' Major Vowell began.

'Phillip Blum.'

'And you are the head gravedigger here?'

'I've already told you this,' Herr Blum grumbled as he lifted his head ever so slightly and shot Major Vowell a disapproving look.

'Answer the question. You are the head gravedigger here, *ja* or *nein*?'

'*Ja*.'

Major Vowell gave his spiel about being part of the War Crimes Investigation Tribunal and, under that authority, had arrested Herr Blum. Major Vowell then asked Herr Blum how many people had been murdered here. Herr Blum's body language became hostile, his shoulders and head held high as he puffed his chest out.

'These people were not "murdered"!' he protested. 'They were euthanised. We were acting humanely. It was for their own good.'

'How many people died here?' Major Vowell rephrased.

'You would have to check the records. I can't be sure of the exact figure,' Herr Blum stalled. 'I do remember one thing,' he said as he scratched the stubble on his chin.

'*Ja*?' Major Vowell pushed.

'I remember the night that Herr Schmidt and the others celebrated their ten thousandth victim.'

'Herr Schmidt?'

'*Ja*, Herr Schmidt. He's in charge of all of Hadamar.'

I assumed the Americans already knew of Herr Schmidt, so I had never thought to tell them about him. A ripple of excitement ran through the room as they looked at each other. Major Vowell asked him to tell them everything he knew about Herr Schmidt. Importantly, where was he?

Much to the Americans' disappointment, Herr Blum was not overly helpful. All he knew was that Herr Schmidt had fled a few days before the Americans' arrival and he did not know where he had gone.

'Returning to this … *celebration*, how many deaths did you say the celebration was for?'

'The ten thousandth. To celebrate it, they had what can only be called a drinking orgy,' Herr Blum continued.

'Sorry, did you say the ten *thousandth* death?' Major Vowell confirmed.

'*Ja*, the ten thousandth death,' Herr Blum said, emotionless.

Both the Herr Majors, clearly disbelieving, paused and turned to look at me.

'Ingrid, is what this man saying true?' Major Vowell asked me.

'Every single word. I saw the celebration myself.'

Herr Blum raised his head, creasing his face in bewilderment.

'*Ja*,' I said bitterly. 'I was there. I saw what you did.'

'Herr Blum, please continue. Tell me more about this celebration,' Major Vowell said.

'We were in the right wing. Herr Schmidt had asked all of us to assemble together as there was something he wanted us to celebrate.'

'Did you have an idea of what was to be celebrated?'

'*Ja*, knowing Herr Schmidt, we knew it would be something like this. But you must understand, we are not in a position here to refuse an order from the SS. To do so would only be to sign our own death warrant.'

'Are you saying that all of the staff here are working against their will?'

'*Nein.*'

'Everyone here is a volunteer?' Major Vowell clarified.

'*Ja.*'

'How could you not have a choice to refuse an order if you are all volunteers here? You were not forced to work here against your will, so surely there were some things that you could refuse to do.'

'Herr Vowell, I do not expect you to understand this as an American, but try if you will: if we refused an order then it would be *us* who would be sent to a concentration camp. Herr Schmidt ordered us all to the celebration so we had to go. There were crates of beer. We assembled around them. We were all given a skull.'

'I'm sorry,' Major Vowell said, not trying to hide his exasperation, 'you were given a *what*?'

'A skull.'

Both the Herr Majors shook their heads and tried to comprehend what Herr Blum was saying.

'We were given a skull, which we had to clean out before we drank from it,' Herr Blum continued.

The revelation that the skulls retained skin and hair that had to be cleaned out made the Herr Majors and their companions bow their heads in disgust. I heard a noise behind me and turned around to see a young, brown-haired American fingering the trigger of his machine gun, his face so enraged I expected him to open fire at any moment.

Herr Blum continued, seemingly oblivious to the man with the gun. 'We cleaned out the skull with brushes and rag then we were each given a bottle of beer and told to pour the beer into the skulls. Schmidt said, "To our ten thousandth victim!" We all held the skulls up in the air and repeated the words before we drank. Herr Schmidt talked about the importance of our work to the Reich. People got drunk and we began to enjoy ourselves…then Herr Schmidt stopped and ordered us all down into the cellar. He led the way and we followed him down there. He stopped at the crematoria. In front of the oven was a stretcher. There was a naked male corpse, that had a big head. Herr Schmidt made us assemble around the stretcher. He made a speech about the good work we'd done and told us we should all be proud of our part in it, that it was for the Fatherland and that our service was appreciated. He made us raise our skulls again, all refilled with beer, and we toasted the burning of the ten thousandth victim.'

Horror and disgust became like the oxygen in the room – everyone breathed it in. There was no escaping it. Herr Blum became painfully aware of the glare and stares directed at him, and he shifted in his seat as he averted his eyes to the floor.

'Okay,' said Major Vowell. 'That will be all for now.'

I watched two of the soldiers take Herr Blum by the arms and lead him back to his temporary prison in one of the offices. Major Vowell gathered his wits and said to Major Bolker, 'We'll need to exhume some of the bodies from the graveyard; test the validity of their claims that patients died of tuberculosis.'

'I'm not sure if this helps', I offered, addressing Major Vowell, 'but I met some of the Russians and the Poles before they took them away and killed them. I don't know much about tuberculosis, but I'm fairly certain those people didn't have it when they died.'

'You said that you were forced to help in the digging of some of the graves. Do you remember the graves you dug for the people you met?'

I pictured Anka on the day she arrived.

'*Ja*, I think so.'

'Do you think you could show us which graves?'

I wasn't convinced I could; there were so many graves. I remembered the smell when Captain Jung first had Herr Blum open one of the graves. Could I endure that again? *Nein* – but I had to. Those bodies were evidence. I had to do whatever it took to ensure my tormentors saw justice. I nodded. Major Vowell spoke to Major Bolker in English and they walked from the office. I followed them towards the front entrance.

Major Bolker retrieved his white coat and a leather parcel from a Jeep before he set off past the gas chambers, the bus garages and towards the graveyard. As we walked down the trail and past the white walls I sniffed the air, expecting the smell of death. Instead it smelled sweet, the crisp fragrance of roses wafting in the evening spring air.

We came to the graveyard. The grave that Herr Blum had opened had been refilled. Major Bolker stopped at the nearest corner and put his hands on his hips as he surveyed the cemetery. He kicked the dirt of the nearest grave and turned to look at me.

'Which one?' Major Vowell asked.

CHAPTER 12

I paced up and down the rows and tried to remember which one was Anka's. I walked down five or six graves then pointed with my foot. Three German civilians I hadn't noticed stepped forward from the white wall. Each of them wore gas masks that had ribbed tubing coming from the face and led down to a beige-coloured bag that they wore next to their hips. Two of them began digging while the third retrieved planks of wood and stood beside them. The stench seeped out from the grave. I longed for a gas mask of my own.

'Is that the grave?' Major Vowell asked.

I looked down into it. The bodies were well preserved, the skin still intact. There were tags on their toes, but the writing was obscured.

'I can't be sure. I think so.'

The two diggers started pulling the bodies up, separating them from each other and callously tossing them aside. Major Vowell ordered them to line up the six disentangled bodies in a row. Major Bolker stood over them and began tearing bits of their clothing away. Behind him was a man I had not seen before – an American wearing a brown leather jacket with a woollen collar. As Major Bolker shifted the bodies around, the American took photographs. Major Bolker paused to reach into his pocket and retrieve his pipe, which he lit before he resumed working. The American cameraman snapped picture after picture while Major Bolker looked on, dressed in his white doctor's coat with a brown leather apron wrapped around his waist and midriff.

Another man stepped forward. Although I had never seen him, I would later learn that he had been an inmate of Hadamar too; his name was Friedrich Dickmann and he had been forced to be Herr Blum's assistant.

'These are German,' Herr Dickmann commented. 'You see, they have wooden tags on their toes.'

Major Bolker immediately stopped his investigation.

'What are you doing?' I asked.

He turned to face me and puffed on his pipe. 'Ingrid, my mission here does not extend to Germans killed by Germans. My superiors are only interested in the Russians and the Poles that were murdered here.'

My face must have given away my feelings. What difference did their nationality make? Who cared if they were German, Russian or Polish? They were all murdered. I could not understand why Hadamar's German inmates did not seem to matter in the same way. It shook my confidence in Major Bolker, his men and his investigations. Right in front of him was the worst of the Hadamar crimes, people from one nation killing their *own* – but it didn't seem to matter to him. It made me feel that the Hadamar dead did not matter at all; their deaths would mean nothing. Major Bolker went to say something but stopped short before he began looking for another grave to open.

Herr Dickmann stepped forward and pointed to a grave. I looked at the white cross above it. No names, only a number: 470.

'This one definitely has Russians and Poles in it.'

Two of the gravediggers with the gas masks opened grave number 470, while the third man began to shore up the first grave with the planks of wood. I remember thinking, *If they're leaving it open then surely they will come back to investigate the deaths of the German patients too*. The evidence of Hadamar's greatest crimes lay there in front of them – surely they could not let it pass.

When they reached the bodies in the second grave, the diggers began lifting them to the surface. In total they disinterred three men and three women, all of them naked adults. The men in the masks laid the bodies out in a neat row. Major Bolker reached for the leather parcel, which he placed on the ground beside the first body before unfurling it. Inside was an array of medical instruments. He retrieved a scalpel, which he drove in just below the sternum of the first man they had exhumed. The scalpel, as Major Bolker worked it down the man's abdomen, made an awful crunching sound. When he had reached the pelvic region he carefully wiped the blade on his apron before he peeled back the flaps of skin to create a cavity in the man's stomach. With his scalpel he held the yellow layer of the man's fat in his hand and measured it against the scalpel.

'This man is approximately one hundred and ninety pounds,' he said to Major Vowell, who started taking notes. 'This panniculus is approximately an inch and a quarter thick.'

With the scalpel blade he began to poke around, moving up to the man's lungs, lifting one up from the rib cage before he made a careful incision in it. After bending his head down to examine it more closely he said to Vowell, 'This man has had pneumonia for approximately a week or so, but there is nothing here to suggest it was tubercular.'

He reached inside his coat for his torch and began shining it into the man's still open eyes.

'Pupils in the eyes are able to be seen but are small.'

He moved onto the second body and cut it open in the same manner.

'One hundred and sixty pounds, the layer of fat is about three-eighths of an inch thick,' he dictated to Major Vowell. 'There is evidence of left upper caseous pneumonia with tuberculosis without cavitation. No spread to the other lobes nor gross regional node involvement. There are bilateral pleural adhesions.'

On he went, cutting and examining the bodies and dictating his findings to Major Vowell. When he had finished, he stood up, wiped the remnants of the humans he had carved up onto his coat, turned to Major Vowell and said, 'Four of these bodies had tuberculosis, one had non-tubercular pneumonia, and there is one with no evidence of bodily disease.'

'Is there evidence of morphine poisoning?' Major Vowell asked as he stepped forward and took a brief examination of the bodies, while the man in the fighter-pilot jacket kept taking photographs.

'No, any morphine would have disappeared by now.'

'Is morphine usually given to treat tuberculosis?'

'No, you don't normally give morphine for diseases of the lungs; it slows down the rate of respiration too much.'

'So, these people were murdered?'

'I will have to send parts of their brains, stomach contents and livers to the First Medical General Laboratory,' Major Bolker said as he squatted down beside the first corpse and began removing the aforementioned parts of the bodies. 'But it is my diagnosis that one of these people was definitely killed without reason, and the others did not have serious enough cases of tuberculosis to warrant a death sentence.'

After watching these proceedings in dumbstruck horror, a nauseous burning started in my stomach. The acid singed my throat and I began to retch. Major Bolker stopped his work, stood to his full height, placed his hands on his hips and looked at me.

'Ingrid, are you okay?'

I placed my hand across my mouth and shook my head. Two of his men followed me as I ran to the kitchen to wash my face and mouth. When I finally felt cleansed again I knew, in that moment, that I never wanted to see death again.

CHAPTER 13

HOMECOMING

April 1945

Any hopes we had of a quick departure from Hadamar evaporated when Major Bolker informed us that, until we were considered medically fit, none of us could go anywhere. We ate in the dining hall. Bread, water and potatoes at first, but soon hot soups with actual meat. With every week and every meal, I felt myself returning to normal. I could see it in many of the others too, but some were not so lucky. I was saddened by their deaths; they had come so close to their freedom.

I had come to realise that there was little rhyme or reason to life. Who lived? Who died? It was all a matter of chance. Life was about balance. People died, then people were born to replace them. Evil existed, but there was good in the world too. Sadness was – I *had* to believe – followed by joy. So it came to pass in Hadamar.

On the evening of 30 April 1945, just before nine o'clock, the Americans switched on the radio. It was a news report, retransmitted from Radio Hamburg. They played Wagner's *Twilight of the Gods*, followed by Bruckner's *Seventh Symphony*. At first I thought the

Americans had put it on in order to comfort us, but as the funeral music began to play, soon followed by the rolling of drums, I knew something momentous had occurred.

'Adolf Hitler, our *Führer*, is dead. He was killed this afternoon in a command post at the Reich Chancellery in Berlin,' the radio announcer said.

We all looked at each other stunned. The Americans looked shocked too. Not believing what we were hearing, we stared at the speakers as the announcer went on to say that Hitler had nominated Admiral Doenitz as the new *Führer*.

Doenitz's voice came on: 'German men and women, soldiers of the German *Wehrmacht*: Our *Führer*, Adolf Hitler, has fallen. The German people bow in deepest mourning and veneration. Hitler fell for Germany. My first task is to save the German people from destruction by Bolshevism. If only for this task, the struggle will continue. Hitler fought to his last breath for Germany against Bolshevism. *Der Führer* has appointed me as his successor. Conscious of this responsibility, I am taking over the leadership of the German people in this grave hour of destiny. My first task is to save the German people from annihilation by the advancing Bolshevist enemy.'

He went on about the dangers of Bolshevism but, by this time, we had stopped listening or caring. Despite Doenitz's sorrowful tones, the wards in Hadamar became scenes of celebration. Those who could, danced, twirling each other arm in arm at the realisation that Hitler was finally gone. When *Deutschland Über Alles* and the *Horst Wessel* anthem played, still we danced.

The Americans partied harder than we did, drinking whatever they could find from the Hadamar cellars. Despite the frivolity, Hitler's death signalled that the war was truly finished, and now we just wanted to leave this place. We wanted to return home and attempt to rebuild whatever we could of our shattered lives. I decided to ask Major Bolker about it. Most of the Americans had settled into the dining hall to drink, and I found him in the far corner sharing a bottle of Cognac with his comrades. I sat down beside him and the American offered me a drink. I accepted. It burned as it went down my throat but it warmed my body and made me happy inside. I took another sip before I handed the bottle back to Major Bolker. As the alcohol took hold, my confidence grew. Over the din, I asked him if the war was over.

He told me that the war was ending, but Germany was in tatters. He told me about the extent and magnitude of the Allied bombing campaign; places such as Berlin, Dresden and Hamburg had been flattened. To cripple the Nazi war machine, the Allies had bombed the railways and *Autobahns,* making transport limited. He told me about the enormity of concentration camps such as Auschwitz, Buchenwald and Bergen-Belsen. I had heard the staff refer to these places and remembered that Dr Oppenheimer had worked at Auschwitz, but never had I imagined that *millions* of people had died in them.

On a more positive note, there were survivors – but the Allies had to process all of these people and try to find food, water and shelter for them. He told me that the Jews in those camps were worse off than the people here. I found it hard to believe that there were worse places than Hadamar but I realised that, despite our suffering, we were not the Americans' highest priority at this moment. Major Bolker also told me that all over Germany, the Americans and British were rounding up suspected war criminals and, when the time came, the Hadamar staff would be treated as such. I thought back to Dr Oppenheimer and remembered how he had told me that this was the reason he had saved me.

'Herr Bolker, I wonder if you could do me a favour.'

'Of course, Ingrid!' he said drunkenly. 'Anything.'

'There was another doctor that used to work here,' I said, raising my voice over the increasingly boisterous Americans. 'He was taken away by the Gestapo when they found out that he tried to help me escape. I was wondering you might be able to find out what happened to him. If he is even still alive.'

'Ingrid, you've been a great help to us. I'll do what I can. What was this doctor's name?'

'*Herr Doktor* Max Oppenheimer.'

'Was he involved in any of the killings?' Major Bolker asked.

'*Nein* ... maybe ... at least, I don't think so.'

'I'll look into it for you, but I can't promise anything. Anyone in Germany who thinks they have something to hide has tried to blend in and disappear.'

I nodded my understanding before I asked the other question that burned on my lips.

'When will we be able to go home?'

Major Bolker looked at me with sadness in his eyes before he rubbed his brow.

'Ingrid,' he said as he put his hand on mine. 'You and all the people here are very important to us; we need your help to prove all that has been done. We need to interview all the inmates to build a strong case against the doctors and nurses. If we were to let you all go now, all the people here would disappear back to where they came from and we'd never find them again.'

I nodded, but my desire to celebrate disappeared. After excusing myself from the table, I went and lay on my bed, listening as the Americans partied long into the night. I thought about everything Major Bolker had just told me. I thought about Mutti. Now that I knew the extent of the Allied bombing I was immensely worried for her safety. Was she even still alive? The alcohol had made me weary. I drifted into a deep sleep, wondering if the reason Mutti had never come to see me was because she was dead.

Over the next few weeks Captain Jung and Majors Bolker and Vowell came and went, and a garrison of their men stayed. Other American doctors carefully supervised our return to good health. As my body became stronger, so too did my mind. I would be a witness for the Americans. I would overcome my fears and tell all that I knew, so that Chief Nurse Huber and the others got the punishment they deserved. When the trials were over, I would search for Mutti.

Sometimes I sat in on interviews with the staff and with the inmates; other times I was left to my own devices. With little to do, I offered to help the people the Americans had assigned to cook and clean, or

I made myself useful by giving what medical assistance I could to the infirm inmates.

One morning, Major Bolker came to me. He said that even though he and Major Vowell had already interviewed Chief Nurse Huber, they had uncovered some new evidence and they wanted to interview her again, this time with me present. Under his arm he held a black leather-bound book. Seeing me looking at the book, he retrieved it from under his arm and patted the front cover.

'That's the Death Book, isn't it?' I said.

'There are Death Books,' Major Bolker said as he nodded. 'In each of them they have recorded *everyone* they killed and the *supposed* cause of death, along with 'profession unknown', 'nationality unknown'. This is the piece of evidence we were searching for.'

I followed Major Bolker to Chief Nurse Huber's office. She sat inside, still dressed in the white uniform and hat and grey woollen jacket that she always wore. She looked at me. The commanding fierceness of her eyes had disappeared. The look of authority she had once possessed had evaporated, replaced with uncertainty and fear. But when she looked at me, her disdain and hatred were obvious. She eventually looked away and stared vacantly out the adjacent window as the men who had been present at the Dr Wahlmann and Nurse Willig interviews arrived. They sat and placed their folders and notepads on the desk.

I allowed myself a smile. Chief Nurse Huber, despite any attempts she may have made to diminish her role in Hadamar, had clearly been identified as the leading nurse. There would be no escape for her.

Major Bolker and Major Vowell lit cigarettes, speaking in English as they did. I revelled in watching Chief Nurse Huber squirm. Unable to sit still, she folded and unfolded her legs as she shifted in her seat, almost jumping out of it when Major Bolker finally addressed her.

'We have spoken to you several times before but, in light of some new evidence, we need to go over a few things again. Can you please tell these gentlemen about your role at Hadamar?' Major Bolker asked.

'I am the Chief Nurse. I am in charge of looking after the welfare of the patients,' she said as she clasped her hands together, then placed them on the table in front of her and leant forward as if to give emphasis and weight to her words. Behind me the same American who had photographed the graves was taking pictures. Chief Nurse Huber kept her gaze on Major Bolker and the others.

'You must understand', she said vehemently, 'we were doing the right thing.'

'The right thing!' Major Bolker exploded. 'You murdered *children*!'

'We didn't murder them!' she protested as she folded her arms and leant back in her chair. 'We did the right thing by them. What sort of a life would these children have had? We were being merciful. The Reich told us that we were. These children were a drain on the Reich's resources.'

I had heard it all before: all the excuses, all the ideologies. But it was obvious that she truly, deeply believed in what she said. Major Bolker rubbed his face before lighting another cigarette and leaning back in his chair.

'You're trying to tell us that you were doing the Reich's work, and yet this girl stands here before us,' he said as he pointed to me, the reason for my presence now apparent. 'Now, as best I can tell there is nothing wrong with her. I don't see how murdering girls like her would serve the Reich in any way.'

It was true. There was nothing wrong with me or the many of the thousands they had actually killed. As I watched her searching for reasons that we deserved to die, I thought back to her little speech about how much the Americans hated black people too. It may have been true – I didn't know – but so far they'd given me no indication that they hated me. In fact, quite the opposite. She really was deluded.

I had never really thought about who she truly was. I knew that she was from the countryside, ignorant of the wider world, and, as I looked at her, it occurred to me that people like her – poor and uneducated – were the perfect servants of Nazi tyranny. All she knew was whatever she had been persuaded to blindly believe. I found myself beginning to pity her for her ignorance … but then I reminded myself of the children she had killed.

'Ingrid was brought here for medical reasons. I can assure you. Besides, are you going to sit there and tell me that you Americans treat your Negroes well? I don't think so!'

'Maybe we don't treat African-Americans as well as we should, but we don't put them in institutions and systematically murder them the way you've done. Neither have we murdered thousands of our own people, like you've done.'

'You must understand,' Chief Nurse Huber offered as her voice wavered. 'We were all just obeying orders.'

'But you and the others here killed thousands upon thousands of children!' Major Bolker bellowed with sudden hostility. 'We have the records to prove it!'

'I never killed any of them! I swear to God in Heaven that I never killed a single one!'

Major Vowell interrupted, and for a few minutes they spoke in English. Then Major Bolker stood up and took me outside.

'Ingrid, did you actually see Chief Nurse Huber kill anyone?'

'*Nein*,' I replied. 'I only saw what I told you.'

'So Chief Nurse Huber took part in the selection of who was to be killed as well as helping in the falsification of the death certificates.'

'*Ja*.'

'I don't know how to tell you this … but without evidence that she actually *participated* in the killings it will be very hard to gain a conviction. Perhaps as an accessory to murder – but not for murder itself.'

I looked over Major Bolker's shoulder into Chief Nurse Huber's face as she shot me a conceited smile. I felt sick, numb, weak. After all she had done – after all the crimes she had committed – she was going to get away with nothing more than a slap on the wrist. I wanted to vomit. The walls of Hadamar felt like they were closing in on me. My mind became foggy and I had to put my hand on the doorjamb to stop myself from falling. I tried to keep my knees from buckling. Seeing my dismay, Major Bolker ordered one of his soldiers to take

Chief Nurse Huber away. As they escorted her out, her face passed a few inches from mine, and she smiled more smugly than I had ever seen her do.

'Ingrid, are you okay?' Major Bolker asked, placing a hand on my shoulder.

'*Ja*, I will be fine, I just need a moment,' I said. The further Chief Nurse Huber was moved away from me, the better I felt.

'Don't worry, Ingrid,' he reassured as he called one of his men over. 'We'll find a way to make her pay for her crimes. I promise you she will not get away with this. You may have not seen her kill someone, but there are other inmates. *Someone* will have seen something.'

I nodded and the soldier escorted me back to my bed. I lay down, desperately wanting to believe the truth of Major Bolker's words, but I couldn't. She might have been a simple country woman but it seemed she was smart enough to ensure the truth of her crimes could never be uncovered. For all she had done, for all the pain and suffering she had inflicted, she was going to go unpunished.

8 May 1945

My sleep was fitful and interrupted. I awoke early the next morning and sat out in the courtyard to collect my thoughts. I cast my mind back over every day, every hour, every minute of my years in Hadamar; I tried to remember anything that might be useful to the Americans. I had to make sure they prosecuted Chief Nurse Huber. She *had* to be held accountable. I *must* have seen her killing someone; there had to be *one*. She *had* been at the injections. She *had* led us to the showers.

She *had* taken the soldiers away. But, for the life of me, I couldn't actually remember seeing her kill anyone.

Like the seasons, the world was changing. I thought about the time when this was all done, when I would be free. I thought about America. I now knew that more black people lived there than I had thought. Major Bolker had called them African-Americans. I liked the sound of that. Neither Germany nor her people had ever treated me well; it was time to move to somewhere where I would be treated how I deserved to be. If Mutti *was* alive I would consider staying in Germany; if she was gone, I was moving to America.

I would find Fräulein Rothenberg. I would sit on her porch drinking lemonade as I told her about everything I had seen and done. She would comfort me like she used to, and tell me everything was going to be okay. Perhaps I could buy a house down the road from hers, or at least nearby. Maybe I could even help Fräulein Rothenberg in her school; see children learning, playing and laughing. Enjoying their lives. Children living the way they should. Maybe I would become a teacher and give black American children the childhood I never had.

My daydreaming was interrupted by the sound of an American soldier yelling. I rushed out to the main reception area to see a young soldier skipping and jumping for joy as he hugged his comrades. Then they were all embracing and dancing around circles. I watched them intently, intrigued by what was making them so happy. I needed to know, so I walked to the edge of the circle and grabbed hold of the closest man's sleeve and asked.

'*Nicht sprechen Deutsch*,' he said, as did the second man and the third.

Suddenly Major Bolker appeared, smiling as he watched his men dance.

'What's happening?' I asked him.

'It's over!'

'What's over? What do you mean?'

'The war, Ingrid! The war is officially over! Germany has surrendered!'

The war was over!

I couldn't believe it! Major Bolker took me by the hands and flung me in circles. He gave me to another soldier, who gave me to another. Dozens of inmates began to shuffle out from their wards to see what was causing the commotion. Breaking free from the embrace of one the young Americans I went to the first group of inmates, then the next and the next, shouting, 'The war is over! The war is over!' Those who could, danced amongst themselves or with the Americans; those who couldn't sat in their wheelchairs or leant on their crutches and smiled or cried.

The Americans celebrated long into the night – again. This time I drank with them. In the early hours of the evening, the wine had made me drowsy and I decided it was time for bed. I lay down. It felt as if the whole room was spinning, but I retained enough sense to realise that the Americans were not going to keep us here much longer. Now that the war was done, they would want to return home too. Maybe it was the alcohol clouding my brain, but I went to sleep thinking about what 'home' actually meant for me now. Did I even *have* a home – or a family, for that matter?

Despite the constant cloud of death hanging over my head, Hadamar had been my home, of sorts, for six years. I had been here since I was fourteen; now I was twenty. I knew the rules. I knew the routines. I had only ever had two goals here: once upon a time that was to die – but now it was to live. The outside world would be unrecognisable to me. I was frightened of having to face it, possibly all alone.

I thought about Johan – was he even still alive? It didn't matter. I was never going to find him, never going to see him again. I'd reconciled myself to the fact that he was one soldier among hundreds of thousands. Even if I asked the Americans to find him, I doubted they could. I began to wonder why he had never contacted me. Perhaps he just didn't want me. Perhaps I was nothing more than a distant memory to him. Perhaps he was dead. Maybe he assumed, with good reason, that I was dead.

The next day, albeit with hangovers, the Americans went about their business as usual. Three days later, however, Major Bolker and the other officers ordered the inmates to assemble out on the driveway. Once they had us all together, a soldier brought out a wooden box for Major Bolker to stand on. He did not have to ask for silence. He made a short, succinct speech. He said that now the war was over, the men guarding Hadamar were needed elsewhere to act as a police force and to do what they could to help to rebuild Germany. As of today they would start sending the first of us home. People stood and stared at one another, unable to grasp the weight of his words. Only after he dismissed us and we started to file back inside did we start to talk. I thought the others would be elated, but they were as unsure and nervous as I was.

Later that afternoon, huge green trucks arrived to collect us. The elderly were the first ones to leave, carefully loaded onto the trucks before they were driven away. Each time a new truck arrived we would crowd around the windows and look to the Americans, hoping it was our turn to leave. The next morning came and more trucks arrived. Dozens and dozens of inmates were taken back to their families or to institutions where they would receive proper care. The afternoon was the same, as was the following morning. The number of inmates continued to dwindle – and I still remained. I tried to tell myself it was because I was younger and healthier than the others, but I became convinced that the reason I had not been sent home was that there was nowhere to send me. Mutti had died. I was alone in the world.

On the afternoon of the third day, I sat on my bed and looked around the ward. It was empty. Fewer inmates meant I had less to occupy my time. Then I remembered the newspapers. I retrieved them from under my bed and sat out in the courtyard flicking through them, wondering if I wanted to keep them or if I should throw them away. They were only painful reminders of things I wasn't sure I wanted to remember. I stumbled across the article about Johan. There he was: a hero, half-smiling at the camera. I stared and stared. I longed to see him again but I knew, deep down in my heart, I never would.

I closed the paper and threw it back on top of the pile, just as Major Bolker stepped from inside the ward and said chirpily, 'Ingrid! I have some great news! You've been approved to leave! You can go home!'

My face clearly didn't reflect the jubilation he'd been expecting. He sat down beside me.

'What's wrong? I thought you'd be happy.'

'I don't have a home. I don't have a family. Where will I go? What will I do?'

'Ah, but that's where you're wrong,' he said as he put a gentle hand on my shoulder. 'I figured that, because your background and surname are French, there wouldn't be too many people in Mainz with the last name Marchand. I contacted a friend of mine who's stationed near your home and requested he ask around. It cost me a carton of cigarettes, but that's okay. Eighty per cent of the city has been bombed …'

'How is that good news?' I interrupted. 'That means thousands of people are dead. My mother could be one of them.'

'The city has been under American control since the *Wehrmacht* units guarding the town surrendered without a fight at the end of March. It's taken my friend some time but he managed to locate a woman by the name of Angelika Marchand. That's the name of your mother isn't it?'

'*Ja*?' I sprang to my feet.

'Ingrid, I found your mother! She's alive and well. I have a Jeep waiting out the front ready to take you to her!'

CHAPTER 13

Elated, excited, ecstatic, delighted. None of these words seemed apt, as waves of emotions washed through my body. I didn't know what to do. I embraced Major Bolker.

'*Danke! Danke! Danke!*' I shouted over and over as I kissed both his cheeks.

'You're welcome!' he said, blushing. 'Hurry; gather your things together. It's time to go.'

'What things?' I said as I took one final, fleeting glance at the newspapers. 'I don't have any things.'

'Is there nothing else you wish to take?' Major Bolker asked as we walked back inside.

'*Nein*. Anything from here would only remind me of all the terrible things that happened. As soon as I walk out that door I want to forget Hadamar forever.'

'Ingrid, you've been through a lot. It may not be that easy to forget all of this,' he said as we walked past the bed I had called mine for so many years.

I walked towards the exit. I took my last glimpses of the peeling white paint on the walls, the crumbling plaster on the ceiling, the bent and broken beds and steel chairs. We came to the entrance. I did not look back as I walked outside to the Jeep waiting for me. Major Bolker opened the passenger side door, waited for me to climb in, then closed it again.

'See you soon, Ingrid,' Major Bolker smiled.

'Aren't you coming?' I said ruefully.

'*Nein*, I have too much work to finish here. You'll be safe. I promise.

Hopefully I'll see you again when this all goes to trial.'

The Jeep pulled away. The gravel crunched beneath the wheels as the vehicle bounced down the driveway. I held tightly to the rails on the side of the door. When we were about halfway down the driveway, past the first rows of pines, I looked back to see Major Bolker waving goodbye. The Jeep reached the end of the driveway and suddenly jerked right as it turned the corner. I looked back again; Major Bolker had disappeared from view.

We zigzagged across the hillside, the greenness of the grass making the yellow daffodils scattered haphazardly across them stand out like a thousand little suns. They looked exactly like the meadows I had escaped to in my dreams – and here they were, only a few hundred feet from Hadamar. We reached the base of the hill and continued on towards the town centre. The streets and houses of Hadamar town flashed by. For years, I had lived so close to this place and yet I had never actually seen it. Nor would I; I was never coming back.

We passed the houses on the outskirts of town and headed into the countryside. There were bomb craters everywhere, scattered across the fields, cows grazing between them.

As we drove onto the *Autobahn* I began to think of home and wonder about Mutti. Was she the same as when I had left her? I knew *I* had changed. When I first arrived at Hadamar I was a only a child. Now I was a fully-grown woman; would she even recognise me? Hadamar had changed my mind too. I had been forced to grow up long before I should have. I didn't know if I would be able to relate to her anymore. Her memories of me must be of a sweet, innocent little girl. Hadamar had taken that from me – and more. How was I going to explain everything that I had seen? How was I going to explain everything that had been done to me?

After a few more minutes of driving through open country, we came across hundreds of American Jeeps, tanks and lines of men stretching as far as I could see. From my vantage point in the passenger's seat, the American war machine seemed immense, insurmountable. Why did Hitler ever think he could win against all of this? The road became clogged with men and equipment, and my driver had to slow down and stop several times as he weaved his way through. Once we were onto clear road again he sped up. Our progress was impeded by the broken roads and remnants of German tanks and artillery guns that blocked our way. What should have taken a little more than an hour took three.

But at last we reached the outskirts of Mainz.

Most of the buildings were completely flattened; those that remained were nothing but thin shells – outlines of what had once been homes and businesses. Piles of rubble lined both sides of the street. People rummaged in and around them, looking for food or anything else they could find of value. We reached the Rhein.

It looked as if the bridge had been destroyed and replaced by a makeshift construction. The driver slowly edged the Jeep onto the bridge, which was a series of side-by-side boats, strung together with rope. Lying across the boats were two tracks, steel grates fitted together to form a road. Scores of American soldiers moved up and down the river, ferrying supplies or men from one bank to the other. We approached the opposite bank and the Mainzer Dom came into view, untouched and standing proudly against the purple and oranges of the evening sky. Free of the bridge, the driver turned left.

'*Nein*; my grandparents live outside of town,' I said to him.

He ignored me. We hadn't spoke for the entire the trip and I wasn't even sure he spoke German. He took several more turns and pulled up to the curb outside my old house. Barely turning his head towards me, he waited until I got out of the vehicle before he put it back into gear and sped off. I stood and looked up and down the street. The random nature of the Allied bombs became all too apparent. Some houses had been annihilated, while others – mine included – were exactly as I had remembered them. I walked through the gate and anxiously made my way to the front door, certain that the Americans had made a mistake. I knocked. There was no answer. I walked back down the garden path and stood on the footpath, wondering what I should do next.

'Ingrid?' I heard a voice say. It was unmistakable. 'Ingrid? Is that you?'

I turned to see Mutti standing in the doorway, her clothes dirty and worn. Her face carried more wrinkles than I remembered, and her hair was beginning to grey. But she maintained the dignity I remembered so well.

'Mutti,' I sobbed as I rushed into her arms.

'Oh, Ingrid!' she cried, wide-eyed with shock. 'I don't believe it!'

We held each other tightly. I was the first to pull away, desperate to ask a question that had plagued my mind for so long. 'Mutti, why did you never come for me?'

CHAPTER 13

'Ingrid, my darling, come inside and I will tell you everything.'

The house was exactly as I remembered it, except that the paint had faded and was beginning to peel. Seeing it sent a shiver down my spine; suddenly Hadamar did not seem so far away. The furniture was still the same but dustier and worn. Mutti set about making some Ersatz coffee and offered me a piece of black bread. I shook my head. 'The Americans fed us well.'

'I'm pleased. People are fighting in the streets over even the most basic of basics.'

There was a question that could not wait. 'Is there news of Vati?'

Tears welled in her eyes as Mutti shook her head. 'Your Vati is dead,' she wept.

'What? How? Are you sure?'

'When the Americans liberated Dachau they found records that your father was there and that he had been killed.'

It wasn't a surprise, but another piece of my soul was taken away with the confirmation that my father was gone. I was determined not to cry but I struggled not to let my grief take over.

With a shaking hand, Mutti poured the coffee. I took polite sips, watching her closely as she sat down across from me. She drank her coffee but kept her head down.

'Ingrid, I had no choice.'

'What do you mean, you had no choice!' I yelled, letting my anger and heartache get the better of me. She began to sob. Minutes passed before she composed herself enough to speak.

'At first I didn't know where they'd taken you, but I heard whispers around the town that mentally ill patients were being taken to places like Brandenburg, Hartheim, Hadamar. Through a doctor friend of your grandfather's, I managed to find out where you were. Ingrid, you don't know how many times I visited the Reich Offices trying to get them to release you – or at least let me visit you – but they refused every time. Opa drove me up there many times, but we only ever got as far as the town before we were turned away. I even took the train once. I made it to the gates at the bottom of the driveway … but the guards wouldn't let me in.

'Can you understand, Ingrid, how painful it is to know your only daughter's only a few hundred yards away – and you can't get to her? Then other parents with disabled children began to get those awful telegrams saying their child had died of tuberculosis or appendicitis. Every day I avoided the mailman, expecting a letter of my own. Then I got one.' She paused and drew a breath. 'It said you were dead.'

I stared at her in shock. 'You received a letter?'

'*Ja*,' she said as she stood up and moved stiffly towards the chest of drawers in the lounge room. She reached inside a drawer and retrieved a piece of paper, came back to the table and handed it to me.

I read it.

Ingrid Anna Marchand.

Day of death: 24 July 1941.

Time of death: 12.30 Uhr.

Cause of death: Pneumonia.

Name of physician: Doktor Alfons Klein.

Place of death: Hadamar Psychiatric Hospital.

I remembered the day they had tried to gas me. I realised that they had decided I was going to die long before they even 'selected' me. They had prepared my death certificate long before my actual death.

'Ingrid, I thought you were dead. I tried to get your body back – your ashes, anything! But no-one seemed to know what had happened to your remains.'

She cried and cried, wiping her eyes with the sleeves of her jacket. I put my coffee down, moved around the table and placed my arms around her. 'It's okay, Mutti, I'm home now.'

She looked up, placed her hands on my cheeks, pulled my head down towards her and kissed me on the forehead. Now that she had explained what had happened, she could look at me in wonder. She'd thought she'd never see me again.

'And I will be forever grateful for it.'

We took our coffees into the living room, sitting side by side like we had so many years ago as we waited for Vati to come home. We sat and talked. She told me all that had happened to her.

'So, what was it like in that place?' she finally asked.

I didn't know where to begin, what to say.

'Wait,' she said as she stood up. 'I think I'm going to need something stronger than coffee before I hear this.'

She rummaged around in the cupboard below the sink and retrieved a bottle of schnapps, blowing the dust off it as she found two glasses. She sat back down and filled them, handed one to me then put the bottle on the table between us. I gulped it down before I poured myself another and drank it just as quickly. We talked long into the night. I had to think carefully about just how much of the truth of Hadamar to reveal. It became harder as the alcohol began to take hold. I looked into her age-wearied face and knew I would never tell her the truth of all I saw; she didn't need that burden. As the first dawn rays came through the windows I finally asked, 'How are Oma and Opa?'

'Ingrid, your Oma and Opa are dead. They were killed in an air raid a few months ago. I was in town visiting a friend about some possible work when it happened. I hurried to an air raid shelter and waited. Once it was over I came home to find that your grandparents' house had been flattened. I found them in the cellar. I *told* them their cellar wasn't enough to protect them, but they didn't listen. You know how stubborn they were.'

I didn't. I didn't even know them. I felt like I should have been saddened by the news of their deaths, but I wasn't. My grandparents had never accepted me and I'd never even met them.

'After I buried your Opa and Oma I didn't know what to do. Luckily our house was still standing, so I came back here. Fortunately, your grandparents left me enough money to get by, for now.'

'We'll be okay, Mutti, the Americans will look after us. They told me to ask for anything I might need. They want me as a witness when they put the nurses and doctors on trial.'

I drank the last of the schnapps before I said, 'Mutti, I have something I want to tell you.'

'*Ja*, Ingrid, *meine Liebschen* – anything.'

'When the trials are done I want to leave.'

'Leave Mainz? But this is our home.'

'*Nein*, Mutti,' I said as I leant forward and took her by the hands. 'I want to leave Germany.'

CHAPTER 14

THE WAR CRIMES TRIALS

Although the American soldiers brought supplies and checked on me every few days, I didn't see Major Bolker for a few weeks. He arrived one evening just as the night settled in. When he knocked and I opened the door, I embraced him as if he was my father before I took his hand and led him inside. When I introduced him to Mutti, I told her that he was one of the men who had saved my life.

'Ingrid,' he said bashfully. 'We both know you saved yourself. I only arrived at the end.'

'Pleased to meet you,' Mutti said as she kissed him on either cheek. 'Thank you for saving my daughter.'

He blushed bright red as he sat down.

'I've come to discuss some very important things with you, Ingrid. Is there a place we can talk?'

'Whatever you have to say, you can say it in front of my mother,' I replied.

Without asking if he wanted any, Mutti set about making him some coffee.

'What is it?' I asked, after what seemed like an age of silence.

He sipped his coffee as he looked around nervously.

'I can put something stronger in that coffee if it will loosen your tongue.'

He nodded and Mutti retrieved yet another dust-covered bottle of schnapps from beneath the kitchen sink. She poured some into his coffee. He drank deeply and Mutti refilled his cup.

'I've come to tell you something before you hear it from anyone else.'

I leant forward expectantly, as did Mutti.

'While I still need you in Wiesbaden to tell your story, the doctors and nurses are not going to be tried for what they did to you.'

'What?' I exclaimed. Deep down, in my heart of hearts, I had always known this was a possibility.

'I've been informed that under international law we have no jurisdiction in Germany. It's like I told you when I did the autopsies on the bodies. We can't try German citizens for what they did to other Germans,' he said as he drained his glass. I did the same. Mutti refilled our glasses before she retrieved a second bottle.

'But they *will* be tried for what they did to the Russians and the Poles?'

'*Ja*, the Hadamar staff will go on trial – but not for what they did to *you*.'

I wanted to be angry, but all I felt was numb. Perhaps it was the alcohol.

'Ingrid, they killed almost five hundred Russians and Poles; they'll still be held accountable for their crimes. The severest of penalties still remains death. They may not hang for what they did to *you* but they'll still hang. I promise you.'

I didn't share his optimism. The war might have ended but Germany was still Germany. Excuses would be made. Justifications would be given. They would escape prosecution. Even then, I was sure of it. Deflated, Major Bolker rose from his seat, finished his drink and said, 'I'll come back tomorrow to take you to Wiesbaden. Thank you for the drinks, Frau Marchand.' He doffed his cap and departed.

For the second night in a row, Mutti and I stayed up late discussing how the trials might be. She drank and drank. I did too, but not as much as she did. When it was clear she had had too much, I helped her upstairs and put her to bed. I went to my old bed and lay back thinking. Every time I closed my eyes, there they were. No sooner had I closed my eyes than they were there, right in front of me – so lifelike I felt I could reach out and touch them. Chief Nurse Huber, Dr Wahlmann, Dr Klein, Nurse Willig, Nurse Ruoff. When I finally rid my mind of one of them, another would take his place. Was this going to be the rest of my life? Had they created such a stain on my conscience that I would never be rid of them?

Unable to sleep, I went back downstairs, sat in a chair and relived everything that ever happened to me in Hadamar. I did not know what Major Bolker was expecting me to do but, whatever it was, I wanted to make sure I had everything clear – that not even the most minute details were forgotten. I knew that even the smallest, the slightest, the most insignificant detail might make the difference between whether they lived free or hanged at the gallows.

CHAPTER 14

Mutti awoke early the next morning, seemingly with no ill effects from the alcohol she had consumed the night before. As we sat and ate a simple breakfast of black bread she asked me if I was okay.

'I dreamed of them all,' I said. 'I can't seem to get them out of my mind.'

'Who?' she asked.

'The staff, the crimes they committed. How *could* they, Mutti? Some of the children were little more than babies. I don't know if I can do it – the trial. What if I freeze up and forget to tell them something important?'

'What is to come is nothing compared to what you've already been through. You spent years in that place. You took everything, *everything*, they could throw at you – and you survived. If you can do that, you can do anything. Remember, Ingrid, they will only ever have control over you now if you let them have it.'

I appreciated her words, but it was easier said than done. My formative years had been spent under their control. The essence of who I had become would be forever intertwined with them. In the excitement and hope of liberation I had convinced myself that I could be free, but now, as the prospect of having to see them again loomed, I wasn't so sure.

A knock came at the door. Mutti answered. It was Major Bolker.

I picked up my suitcase and went to the door.

'We'll take good care of her, Frau Marchand, I promise. Besides, we will only be across the river – she can come home if she needs to,' he said as he stepped aside to let me pass. Outside, he indicated for me to put my suitcase in the back of a waiting Jeep. He held the door open for me, allowing me to sit in the back next to my suitcase, before he hopped into the passenger side. We wound our way out of Mainz, across the temporary bridge and on to Wiesbaden. We stopped outside a single-storey building. Around the entrance the Americans had erected a steel fence. As I waited in the back of the Jeep, I examined the rows and rows of statues in between the windows on the top floor. Above them the roof was a rusty orange shining brightly against the grey, overcast sky. Major Bolker stepped onto the footpath and retrieved my suitcase.

'Is this my hotel?' I asked naïvely.

'*Nein*,' Major Bolker laughed. 'This is the district courthouse. I need to introduce you to the lawyers so you can tell them your story. They may be on trial for the deaths of the Russians and the Poles but your story, and others like it, will help the prosecution immensely.'

Following Major Bolker towards the entrance, my nerves intensified with each step. My mind went blank as we came across two wooden doors, not dissimilar to those at Hadamar. He held one of them open and allowed me to walk through. After closing the door behind him he led me through another series of doors until we came to one final door. Beyond it I heard the muted sound of deep masculine voices. My heart raced. Was it Drs Klein and Wahlmann, Nurses Ruoff and Willig? I felt sickened by the prospect. I knew I had to face them but I didn't think it would be like this.

Major Bolker opened the door and led me inside, indicating for me to sit down opposite seven older men, some dressed in military uniforms, some in black and grey civilian suits. My mouth and throat went dry as they watched me sit down. To my relief, Major Bolker sat next to me. A grey-haired man with a large nose leant forward as he crossed his hands in front of him.

'Ingrid, is it?' he said through a translator on his left.

I nodded.

'My name is Leon Jaworski, Trial Judge Advocate. I will be acting as the Chief Judge in the trials. We understand that you are one of very few people who survived for a long time in Hadamar. This makes you vitally important to our work here. If you think you can handle it, we would like you to tell us everything. Take your time. If you need to take a break, please tell us. Now, if you could start from the beginning.'

I was extremely nervous and I looked to Major Bolker for reassurance. He told me to tell them everything, not to omit even the smallest detail. I began from the day Herr Schleck came to collect me, but no sooner had I begun than Herr Jaworski put his hand up and asked me to go back further. I told them everything, about the teasing, my time at school, the sterilisation, the day they took me. Hours passed, and I had barely reached the time of my arrival at Hadamar. Several times I was sure I must be boring them, but they leant forward, seemingly hanging on my every word. When evening came they asked me to stop and to return the next morning to continue. As the men packed up their files, Major Bolker led me back outside.

'I'm very proud of you, Ingrid. You did extremely well. What you said in there will go a long way to securing prosecutions. You've given us a strong picture of the true nature of the people we are dealing with here. My men will take you to the Hotel Nassauer Hof; this was the main place for Nazis to stay in Wiesbaden and where the French and the Germans decided on the terms of the cease-fire agreement after the fall of Paris.'

I wasn't sure how I felt about this. Would the rooms and corridors be haunted with Nazi ghosts like Hadamar was haunted with the souls of the dead? I did, however, revel in the irony of what Major Bolker had just told me. Hitler and his regime had tried everything they could to exterminate people like me, but my continued existence was living proof they had failed. They had done so much to hide their crimes, to conceal their murders, but it had all been to no avail. People like me had survived and we would get justice for all those who hadn't. I knew that, however small my role, I had a duty to fulfil – a debt to the dead that I needed to pay. A car came to a screeching halt in front of the district courthouse. Major Bolker spoke to the driver before asking me to hop into the back seat.

'You're not coming with me?'

'*Nein*, I have a lot more work to do here before tomorrow. My driver will take you and pick you up in the morning. If you need anything at the hotel just put it on your tab. Everything is on us!'

I sat in the passenger seat, my backside barely touching it before the driver sped off. A short time later he pulled up outside the hotel. He retrieved my suitcase, placed it on the curb, and waited for me to step out. I stood like a lost child, looking at a wide four-way intersection. Beyond it there was a lake with a fountain in the centre; beyond that were trees lining a canal. I picked up my suitcase and turned towards the hotel. It was five-storeys high and had archways running along the ground floor. On top of the flat roof were four flag poles, each one flying the flag of Germany's four new masters. Months earlier Swastika flags would have fluttered high in the night breeze, but now the flags of the United States, Russia, Britain and France flapped back and forth.

The driver walked me as far as the main foyer and spoke to the concierge while I stared around at the Gothic architecture and high painted ceilings. The Nazis truly had spared no expense on this hotel and it was clear why the Americans had chosen to occupy it: all that the Nazis had cherished was now in American hands and the Americans wanted the people of Germany to know it. The extravagance of the hotel repulsed me. I thought back to my mathematics lessons and how Frau Kellner and Fräulein Pletcher had explained that it was we disabled, unwanted, undesirable children who were a financial drain on the Reich. This hotel epitomised the Nazis and their lies.

The driver gave me my key. Room number 18. After he left I walked along the hallway and counted the room numbers until I found mine. The door opened to reveal a simple room with two single beds, a wooden chair and a desk. I put my suitcase down and went to look out the window, finding nothing more than the buildings next door as my view.

My stomach hurt. I realised I hadn't eaten all day. I locked the door then headed out into the hallway and into the dining hall opposite the concierge's desk. When I walked past the first of the tables, the civilian staff looked me up and down, watching me pass by with the same weighty stares I'd received as a child. There were no other patrons around and I became acutely aware of the darkness of my skin. I sat down at a table near to the entrance.

Their party and its leaders may have gone but, as the waiters and other staff began to whisper and point, it was clear to me that Nazism would remain in the mind of the people for a long time yet.

I waited and waited and still no-one came. I stood up, pushed my chair in and was about to return to my room, hungry. Suddenly, as if they echoed off the high ceilings, I heard the shrieks and cries of the starving children in Hadamar, telling me to eat what they could not. Ignorant fascists had starved me once before; I would never let them do it to me again.

'Excuse me!' I said as I coughed loudly. 'Can I get something to eat, *bitte*?'

An older waited slowly edged towards my table but refused to look me in the eye as he said, '*Fräulein*, due to the war we have limited choices. I'm not sure we have anything for you.'

I calmly said, 'If you do not serve me, I will be forced to tell the Americans that you won't. I am their guest here.' This threat immediately changed his attitude.

'My apologies, *Fräulein*,' he said. 'If you tell me what you would like, I will see if we have it. It is late and the chef may have gone home.'

I asked him for *Gemüsesuppe*. I could have ordered anything I wanted … and I chose vegetable soup.

Given the state of Germany at the time, I wasn't sure that they would have anything else. It's a strange thing, but all I had eaten for so many years was stale bread and soup, if you could call it that. I wanted to taste proper bread, proper soup. I don't know. Maybe I was still adjusting to life on the outside and it was a comfort thing. In any case, the waiter disappeared into the kitchen, and returned shortly afterwards with a large bowl of soup which was swimming with vegetables. He placed it down in front of me, along with a basket of bread.

I picked up my spoon and stared at the soup. The tremendous size of the bowl made me feel guilty. Soup like that could have saved twenty children in Hadamar, the bread twenty more. Dipping my spoon in and out of the bowl, I slurped on the soup. It tasted wonderful but the longer I ate, the guiltier I felt. The dead children, emaciated, eyes wide open, who had haunted my dreams now haunted my waking moments. I told myself there was nothing I could do for them now.

I finished my soup and went to bed with a full stomach, determined to get through the ordeal that faced me.

7 October 1945

I was woken early the next morning by loud knocking. I dressed quickly in a dark blue dress Major Bolker had given me and one of Mutti's jackets. I opened the door to be greeted by the same driver from the previous evening.

He gestured at the car.

I nodded.

I followed him outside and soon we were at the Wiesbaden courthouse. I sat for half the day and told them the rest of my story.

'Thank you,' Herr Jaworski said through the translator when I had finished. 'You have done your country a great service. I look forward to seeing you at the trials tomorrow.'

Major Bolker escorted me outside, told me the same and left me with the driver, who took me back to the hotel. With the rest of the day to kill, I decided I would wander the town, exploring as far from the hotel as I dared. By the time I returned, evening had settled in, so I went to the dining hall. I ordered the same dinner, suffered the same guilt, overcame it and finished my meal. Tired from my memories, I went to bed early.

The next morning the driver came to collect me to take me to the courthouse. We seemed to be following a different route. Driving off course, however, allowed me to take in the true extent of the effects of the war. Lines of defeated and broken soldiers marched through the streets as the Americans moved them from one camp to another. Women hurried along clutching loaves of bread they had managed to procure as if they were carrying their own children. Impromptu markets had sprung up with people – mostly women and old men – trading and bartering whatever they could. Some of the shops were open for business too. Despite her defeat, despite the temporary hardships, Germany was beginning to heal.

The driver pulled up outside another hotel where Major Bolker was waiting. I hopped into the rear seat as he sat in the passenger side.

'Good morning, Ingrid!' he said enthusiastically. 'I'm glad you made it! I thought you might change your mind.'

'*Nein*, Herr Bolker. I am ready,' I replied.

As we drove towards the courthouse, he turned himself to face me and told me that he doubted that I would have to testify, given that I had already told most of my story. I was relieved. I didn't think I could have said what I did with Chief Nurse Huber, Dr Wahlmann, Dr Klein, Nurse Willig and the rest of them staring at me.

When we reached the courthouse, the driver came around to help me down from the Jeep and Major Bolker and I made our way inside. Inside, we stopped short of two large oak doors. Next to the doors was a sign that read:

Hadamar War Crimes Case: The United States v Alfons Klein et al.

When we reached the courtroom doors, Major Bolker reached forward, turned the golden brass handle and opened them. In the foyer it had been eerily silent, but as soon as the doors were opened we heard a hubbub – a mixture of loud talking in both German and English. I tried to do a quick count. There was easily a hundred or more people: American soldiers in their dress uniforms, crisp and dark green with their caps tilted slightly to the right; lawyers for both sides dressed in their long, black robes; scores of news reporters. And seated on the right side in a special box: the Hadamar staff.

Major Bolker led me to a seat nearer to the front and sat on my right-hand side, acting as a human shield between me and them. I peered around him to look at them. The men sat together in rows of white chairs, dressed in cheap, ill-fitting suits, their hair clipped short in military style. Their faces were thinner but they looked much the same. They were talking animatedly, but wielded none of the menace, power or authority they once did. An American military policeman stood behind them with his hands stiff at his side. I realised there was nothing to fear from them.

Chief Nurse Huber sat on a white chair in the row in front of the male staff. She waved her arms around angrily as she discussed something with a man with slick hair, thin glasses and a long black gown who stood in the aisle. She wore the same grey woollen jacket with small buttons that she always wore. Her hair was neatly tied back in a ponytail. As she spoke, she pointed to herself again and again. She was clearly nervous and bothered by the prospect of what may happen. It pleased me greatly.

At the front and centre of the room there were nine judges, all of them colonels, many of whom I had spoken with the day before. They were all dressed in long black robes, but beneath them I could still see their military uniforms and silver American eagles on their collars. Herr Jaworski was in the centre with four other judges each side of him. Yesterday and the day before he had seemed so kind, so friendly. Now he had an air of authority. A judge to his left sifted through one of the several piles of papers that sat in between the nine microphones, one for each judge. Herr Jaworski spoke with his companion to the right then looked around the room before he banged his gavel. The room went silent. The accused put their headphones on.

'Here,' Major Bolker said as he gave me a pair. I put them on. I could clearly hear the translator's voice as he relayed Herr Jaworski's words. Herr Jaworski outlined the main points of the case and the authority under which the Americans had convened the court. I watched him intently. His silver hair was slightly wavy, meticulously combed and cared for. His nose was large for his roundish face. He looked Eastern European, like the labouring men who had died in Hadamar. He reached for a leather-bound folder, opened it and began to read. He outlined the powers of the Court, the evidence that would and would not be permitted, and finished by saying that a two-thirds majority vote was necessary for a conviction.

Herr Jaworski talked about the Moscow Declaration of 1943. Of course, being in Hadamar at the time, I had no idea that the Allies and their three leaders had resolved to bring the Axis powers to justice for their atrocities, massacres and cold-blooded mass executions. He clearly stated that members of the Nazi party who had participated in the atrocities would be taken back to the scenes of their crimes to be judged by the people against whom they had committed them. He made it clear that the Allied powers were going to pursue Nazi war criminals to the 'ends of the earth'.

Herr Jaworski continued on for some time, speaking of the finer points of the trial and how it was to be conducted. He made continual references to 'legal ambiguities', but that despite these, the United States Army had the right to pass ultimate judgement. Although the accused were not members of the German armed forces, and even though they were personnel of a civilian institution, they were still guilty of war crimes as they had committed illegal acts against people of a foreign nation.

Herr Jaworski was calm, collected and completely in control. I felt convinced that the Americans had been thorough and the staff had little recourse. I was sure the trial would be short. In the face of overwhelming evidence, surely the staff would have to admit to their guilt. He read out a copy of the order signed by Hitler himself authorising the Nazi euthanasia operation. I learned that it was codenamed 'T-4' after the address in Berlin from which the department operated (Tiergartenstrasse 4), in October 1939. It gave them permission to carry out *Gnadentod.* He then reached for a brown leather folder with golden-edged corners and began reading; the defendants leant forward in anticipation.

Alfons Klein, Adolf Wahlmann, Heinrich Ruoff, Karl Willig, Adolf Merkle, Irmgard Huber and Philipp Blum: all seven of them were charged with killing the Russians and the Poles. This I had expected. What I did not expect was that Herr Jaworski was going to ensure the world *knew* about the ten thousand people they had killed, even though these people could not be charged for their murders.

'Between January of 1941 and the middle of 1944 as many as ten thousand, allegedly mentally ill, were committed to Hadamar and there they were killed. The first bodies were disposed of in the crematorium and the patients were later killed by medications and injections. These bodies were then buried in the institution cemetery,' he said.

I looked around the room. The press and civilian gallery were clearly shocked and horrified by the revelations that children had been murdered. Their hushed whispers soon turned into uproarious chatter. I began to taste the saltiness of my tears. No matter what happened now, no matter the verdicts, their deaths had not been forgotten. Major Bolker took off my headphones and wiped my cheeks with his handkerchief. I watched my former tormentors. They were clearly agitated, their body language nervous and unsure as they conversed with their lawyers. It took several bangs of Herr Jaworski's gavel to restore normality. The last thing I heard before Herr Jaworski continued was the deep, booming voice of Doktor Klein crying out that the Americans had no authority and that the trial should be abandoned immediately.

Herr Jaworski shot him and the others an angry stare before he returned to reading from his folder. Silence ensued. He read out the exact numbers of victims. There were eighty Polish people murdered: forty-six men, twenty-nine women and five children. As for the Russians: three-hundred and eighty were murdered. Two hundred and eight men, one hundred and sixty-three women and nine children. There were another nine men, five women and two children whose nationality they could not determine.

Once they had submitted their pleas, the hearings for that day came to an end. Major Bolker held me back until the defendants had departed. When we walked outside, they were being put into the back of cars to be driven away and returned to their cells. I watched until the cars disappeared from view. I hoped, as they sat and contemplated their lives, that they were preparing themselves to face the hangman's gallows. Their lack of remorse made me angry. I wanted them dead.

When my driver arrived, Major Bolker opened the door for me and said, 'I know it may seem that we didn't get very far today, but be patient; these things take time. The American military and its legal team are well prepared and very thorough. Despite what they did, they have a right to a fair trial and to defend themselves.'

I sat in the car, closed the door and looked up at him. 'The children of Hadamar never had a chance to defend themselves.'

9 October 1945

The next morning at the courtroom I sat in the same seat with Major Bolker right beside me. I wondered if, given a night to think things over, the staff might show some sign of repentance. What I saw was, in fact, the complete opposite. They didn't seem concerned in the slightest. Some even joked with one another as they entered. The talking stopped when Herr Jaworski came in from an adjacent room. Everyone stood up. He said we could all be seated. When he sat down he started flicking through the golden-edged folder. He reminded the defendants of the charges laid against them before giving a brief summary of the previous day's proceedings. He then asked the defence to begin their opening statements.

A tall, elegant man adjusted his robes and pushed his hair behind his ears as he approached the bench. He walked with a slow, confident stride, exuding wisdom. It bothered me greatly.

The defence lawyer referred to a case: *Mitchell v. Harmony*. Perhaps it was the legal wording, or perhaps things became lost in translation, but I wasn't quite sure what he was talking about. He mentioned a case from the war between America and Mexico. An officer had taken something illegally, but argued he had not committed a crime because his superiors had ordered him to act in such a way. I may not have completely understood, but I knew where this was going. During a time of war, he argued, a person was required to follow orders. If those orders happened to constitute a criminal act, then a subordinate could not be held responsible for those actions.

The 'supposed' offences that occurred at Hadamar happened before the Americans had occupied that part of Germany. Because of this, the defence lawyer said, the Americans had no authority because American authority only extended to offences committed during the actual occupation by the conquering forces. I thought this was spurious. They had been killing people right up until the end, and for months before that. As soon as the Americans had crossed the Rhein, they became an occupying force. The only reason the killings stopped was *because* the Americans had arrived and 'conquered' Germany!

However, what he said next repulsed me to my core.

The defence lawyer painted a picture with his words, cleverly describing how these people were 'good' German citizens who were just doing their service, their duty, for their country – and that service was to ensure that mental patients and people like me were 'put out of the way'.

Put out of the way! Thousands of people had died, been murdered, and they reduced it to nothing more than putting us *out of the way*!

Herr Jaworski didn't believe it. He continually yet politely reminded the entire defence team that they did not actually have any definitive evidence to back up their claims, and until they could show some kind of official paperwork with Hitler's or some other high-ranking Nazi's signature authorising all of this, then it remained hearsay. The defence countered by saying that, even though the orders from Hitler had been unofficial, they still maintained their validity because he was *Der Führer*. His power was absolute; his words were the law.

There were several prosecution lawyers, but the main one was a stocky man who clearly liked his food. His full figure gave him an air of authority when he walked back and forth in front of the judges' bench with his hands behind his back. He told the Court that not only did the Americans have jurisdiction but that every country in the war, and indeed the world, had a vested interest in the violations of international law.

He called the judges' attention to a joint declaration by nine of the countries occupied by Germany signed as far back as 1942. In the declaration, those nine countries denounced the murderous actions of Germany towards people of occupied countries and declared the illegality of acts of violence against civilians.

Hearing that nine whole countries had felt the need to denounce Nazi war crimes made me finally realise the depth and scope of Germany's atrocities. I realised I was but one of millions. It made me feel somewhat insignificant, but when the large American lawyer outlined that the Hadamar crimes were shocking to all humanity, I felt better, especially when he argued that the staff's crimes also violated the unwritten rules of war.

He sat down. I was pleased. Even in war there were rules, and the Hadamar staff had clearly broken them. I could not see how the defence team could argue against this, but they did. They argued there was no violation of law because Poland was under German occupation and therefore German law applied. In addition, they said, Russia had not signed the Geneva Convention and therefore to charge the accused of war crimes was impossible because the actions of the accused existed outside the scope of international and American law. This being so, they added, the trial should be conducted in a German court and not an American one.

The thought of it horrified me. The Americans were sympathetic; they were seeking the truth. They wanted justice. If this were a German court, then the judges making the decisions would, potentially, be people who thought the same way as the accused. The Americans would give us a fair trial; I was sure a German court would not. The defence argued, perhaps fairly, that the opposite applied in the case of the accused. Millions upon millions of people had died in the war and everyone was looking to point the finger of blame. They argued that it was unlikely that the Hadamar staff would receive a fair trial.

So what if they didn't get a fair trial? They didn't deserve one. Did Erich get a fair trial? Did Anka? Even Dr Oppenheimer and Mia had been taken away without a chance to plead their cases. Where was *their* fair trial?

Guilt about Mia and what I did to her hit me like a tsunami. I felt faint. The sweat pooled on my forehead. I looked at the defendants in the dock. I pictured myself sitting beside them. I couldn't shake the thought that I should be on trial too, sitting next to them, having to answer for what I did to her. Did my actions constitute a war crime? The staff had done what they did out of a sense of moral duty, however skewed that sense of duty may have been. I did what *I* did out of jealousy. At least they had thought their actions were well intentioned. I knew mine was wrong and I did it anyway. Did that make me worse than them?

Nein, I told myself; they had killed thousands. I hadn't killed anyone. I hadn't put her in an institution nor a death camp. I had not starved her. I had not beaten her. It was *they* who were responsible. I wasn't a criminal; I was just a stupid, jealous little girl. My punishment was to fight my own demons.

The remainder of the day was mired in legal wrangling and arguing over who did and did have authority to try the case. I tried to listen, but I soon became bored. Major Bolker tried, several times, to explain things to me but I just wanted it all over and done with. By the end of the day, I had no idea which side was winning. I returned to my hotel, wondering if this would take weeks, months, or even years.

CHAPTER 15

THE TRIALS CONTINUE

10 October 1945

On the third day, before Major Bolker escorted me in he informed me that today was the day the defendants would give their testimonies. I sat down in my seat. Dr Klein sat, surrounded by three wooden panels, to the left of the Judges' bench. Herr Jaworski entered. We all stood up. Herr Jaworski sat down, opened a folder and began outlining legal technicalities. He asked Dr Klein to stand up before he read out the charges: the murder of more than *four hundred* Poles and Russians. He asked Dr Klein if he understood. Dr Klein nodded and sat back down.

The prosecution began by stating that Dr Klein had already shown his own guilt – or at least some degree of it – by immediately fleeing Hadamar when the Americans entered Germany. He had changed his name to Alfons Klan in May 1945 and carried around forged identity papers until the Americans discovered his true identity. These, the prosecution argued, were not the actions of an innocent man. Now I understood why I had not seen Major Bolker and the others interview Dr Klein in Hadamar.

The stout American prosecution lawyer read from a leather folder. In it was Major Bolker's autopsy report that stated that the deceased seemed well fed and that tuberculosis was not the primary cause of death. Dr Klein stated confidently, and – in my opinion, arrogantly – that Major Bolker's work was flawed and that the autopsy report was incorrect. The lawyer read on; much of what he said I knew because I was there, but there was one extra piece of information that Major Bolker had never told me. His report stated that these people, had they received adequate medical attention instead of poison, might have gone on living for years. How, the lawyer asked, could these be considered 'merciful' deaths if these people were not in danger of dying?

Dr Klein listened carefully as this was all translated. At one point he tapped his headphones, scrunched up his face and pretended there was something wrong with the translation. He asked for a better interpretation. One of the translators went to him. Dr Klein leant to the side, his ear close to the translator's mouth as he listened. When it was finished he smiled, unperturbed. His response was robotic, as if it had been rehearsed a hundred times. The Americans had it wrong, he said. In his and the other German medical practitioners' opinions, the killings had only taken place because they were absolutely necessary.

I doubt that I will ever forget his next words. He said, 'These cases can hardly be regarded as cruel murder, but rather that it was made easier for them to die. The killings were injections of mercy to relieve those poor souls of their incurable and painful suffering.'

Despite his arrogance, Dr Klein wasted little time in trying to shift the blame. He was not the one who was responsible. He took his orders from two men who I had heard of but had never actually seen: Landesrat Bernotat and Gauleiter Springer. All the decisions about who came into the institution and who was to be killed were made in Wiesbaden. Klein sounded less and less convincing, and I realised his arrogance was just a front. He talked about an oath of secrecy they had to take. He said that although he had never seen any law permitting the killings, he had never doubted the existence of such a law.

He was asked to clarify his exact role at Hadamar. He was the chief administration officer. His role, he said, was to organise the food and housing arrangements for the patients. I knew the German deaths did not count towards a conviction in the context of the trial but, in my mind, his admitting to controlling the food supply was an admission of guilt. People had starved. People had died because of his orders.

When pushed about the deaths of inmates, he argued that death orders came from Herrs Bernotat and Springer. In a conference with them in July or August 1944, he said, he'd been informed that the Polish and Russian labourers would be coming to Hadamar. He was instructed to kill these labourers in the same fashion as they had killed the German insane inmates. He tried to argue that he 'protested greatly at these orders'; that if he had disobeyed them he would have been sent to a concentration camp. He admitted he was present at many of the lethal injections, but at no time did he actually participate in the administration of them. He returned, again and again, to the secret oath. There were several former employees, he said, who had broken it. They were immediately arrested by the Gestapo and taken to concentration camps. One former staff member had even died.

I wondered if the staff member to whom he was referring was Dr Oppenheimer! The thought brought me to tears. I thought about Vati. I thought about all the ways the Gestapo might have tortured them. Lost in my thoughts, I stopped listening.

Then something piqued my interest. I watched the prosecution lawyer reach into his folder and retrieve a document. He read from Dr Klein's pre-trial statement. In it, Dr Klein had said that 'personnel were free to leave Hadamar at any time they wished', and that 'nobody was threatened with the concentration camp. Nobody was told not to talk. Everyone worked there voluntarily and was able to resign at any time. If anyone says that he was forced to work there, and was not able to quit, it is a lie.'

Dr Klein feigned confusion, but his face was clearly pained now that the contradictions and holes in his story had been made apparent. He pretended, again, to not understand the translation, before he quickly fumbled a vain attempt to recover his credibility. He tried to clarify that what he actually *meant* was that the *other* staff were not threatened but it had been different for *him*. He finished by saying he *knew* what had been done was wrong – but he'd been given no choice.

Dr Klein's unravelling testimony pleased me greatly. I revelled in watching him squirm. His defence team did their best to recover the situation, but the more he was cross-examined the more he dug his own grave. He was cornered so he became spiteful and defensive. In his closing statement he clumsily tried to argue that he'd inspected all the medical papers for all the labourers and he was certain more than half of them had tuberculosis. The Russians and Poles were an 'immense' danger to all of us inmates. They'd killed the foreigners to protect the Germans. Such lies! They'd killed ten thousand Germans and *celebrated* the fact. As if they cared how we died!

The depth of his self-delusion knew no bounds. He was deranged. He said, 'For fifteen years I had toiled at the sickbed and every patient was to me like a brother. I worried about every sick child as if it had been my own. I fully realise the problem; it is as old as mankind, but it is not a crime against man nor humanity. It is pity for the incurable, literally. Here I cannot believe like a clergyman or think as a jurist. I am a doctor, and I see the law of nature as being the law of reason. In my heart there is a love of mankind, and so it is in my conscience. That is why I am a doctor! Death can mean deliverance. Death is life – just as much as birth. It was never meant to be murder.'

The journalists and onlookers erupted into an unfettered commotion. Herr Jaworski banged his gavel repeatedly, but it could hardly be heard over the noise. Seeing no alternative, he called the day's proceedings to a close. People began to file out. I went to leave too, but Major Bolker's outstretched arm held me back. While we waited for the room to clear I watched Dr Klein being led away. His words rang over and over in my head. *It was never meant to be murder!*

Hadamar was a killing factory, set up for systematic extermination. It only had one reason to exist: murder.

11 October 1945

The next day Dr Wahlmann took the stand. As he walked towards it his frame was no longer imposing; he was hunched over and had somehow developed a limp. His face seemed crumpled, the scar running down the right side of his face deeper and darker. He sat down, his fearful gaze fixed on the judges. Herr Jaworski read from the statement Majors Vowell and Bolker took before he asked Dr Wahlmann to confirm that he was the man in charge of everything but medical procedures.

He replied, 'I was the leading doctor in Hadamar. My primary role was to act as a psychologist, to assess the mental condition of the mental patients. I became the chief physician and the only doctor at Hadamar by August of 1942.'

The burly American prosecutor stood and adjusted his robes as he slowly stepped towards Dr Wahlmann and asked him about the killings. Dr Wahlmann clasped his hands together and placed them on the dock as he leant forward. Despite his feeble body and apparent fear, he had clearly thought long and hard about what he was going to say. He gave the inmates a merciful death. He had relieved their suffering.

Besides, he argued, the masses of mentally 'defective' Germans were a drain on the state; surely even the Americans must be able to see the necessity of getting rid of such people. I hated him, but part of me had to be impressed by the strength of his convictions. Here he was, on trial for his life – and he was still trying to justify what they did! There was little honour amongst the wicked, however; he blamed everything on Dr Klein.

The prosecution asked Dr Wahlmann about the role of Herr Bernotat. Herr Bernotat was the elite guard regimental commander, the SS *Standarten-Führer*. He was responsible for all the orders given out and for the oath of secrecy. According to Dr Wahlmann, anything that wasn't Dr Klein's fault was Herr Bernotat's. A smug look came over his face. In his mind, he was off the hook.

But the prosecution lawyers were having none of it. They made him admit that, in his role as chief physician, he determined and delivered the type and amount of drugs administered to the patients. He had overarching responsibility for the death certificates.

The mention of death certificates reminded me of Dr Oppenheimer. I thought back to the day he saved me and the night when I had seen him writing those same certificates. Why hadn't his name come up thus far in the trials? If he was dead or had disappeared, he would have made an easy scapegoat. Maybe he was alive and had managed to escape; maybe the Americans were still looking for him. Perhaps he'd fled to another country. I hoped, for his sake, that the latter was true.

Dr Wahlmann was sweating now. He reminded the judges that he was under orders from his superiors. If he didn't follow them he would have been sent to a concentration camp. His next words made the bile rise in my throat. He said, 'I have never done anything wrong in my whole life. I am a good-hearted man and I wish you would ask the people in the city, the patients in the hospital and the personnel what they have against me. I have done nothing wrong. I did what my government told me to do during this war and that is all I could have done, and it is a great misfortune that I happened to be unlucky enough to be assigned to this institution.'

Herr Jaworski ordered a brief recess. I went and sat on the stairs outside. I was plagued by uncertainty. Had they said enough to get themselves freed – or were they edging closer to their graves? Major Bolker came and sat with me, slowly smoking a cigarette as he asked me how I thought it was all going. I told him that most of what was being said was going over my head; because I had been taken out of school so early, I didn't think I was very bright. I didn't know if we were winning or not.

'Ingrid', he said as he threw his cigarette down, extinguished it with his foot, and lit another one, 'You may not have gone to school but you're more intelligent than you give yourself credit for. They're digging their own graves. You just need to be patient.'

Major Bolker smoked another three cigarettes, explaining the proceedings before one of his subordinates came to tell us it was time to return. Nurse Ruoff was already in the witness box. He looked much frailer than I remembered him; much older too. Maybe he would be the one to seal all of their fates.

He was first asked about his role during and prior to his time in Hadamar. He began working as the chief male nurse at Hadamar in 1936, he said: about two months after the extermination program began. He was a member of the *Sturmabteilung*. They asked him about his role in the killings. He conceded that he performed the injections, but only because he feared being sent to a concentration camp. They asked him how many patients he thought he had personally injected, including all the Russians, Poles and Germans. He stroked his chin as he thought. The courtroom went silent.

'I would say between four and five hundred.'

I heard soft murmuring behind me.

He was asked to repeat himself. The murmuring turned uproarious. It took dozens of bangs from Herr Jaworski's gavel to quieten things down. Nurse Ruoff looked around the courtroom and immediately started shifting the blame. He was only following orders. He would have been severely punished had he not done so.

The prosecution asked about Herr Bernotat. I wasn't sure why. I guess he was the big fish and he had slipped through their net. Herr Bernotat, Nurse Ruoff said, had fled three days before the Americans arrived, on 26 March. It made me wonder what Herr Bernotat knew that the others didn't. Why did he flee and the others did not? Maybe he knew the Americans were close but, concerned only about himself, fled before he told anyone. His actions didn't surprise me. They talked about doing what was right for the Reich, but it was never about the Reich nor their comrades. It was about *them*. What they could get. How the war, how the killings, would benefit them. They were selfish – all of them. Anybody with even an ounce of empathy would not be able to kill children.

Next the prosecution returned to Nurse Ruoff's role in the fatal injections. He repeated that he had had no choice and that he'd attempted to leave several times. The prosecution immediately seized upon this. They asked him why he had made no previous mention of it. Nurse Ruoff said he was scared of the Americans and it was their fault because they'd never asked. Nurse Ruoff's testimony was coming apart at the seams. Major Bolker was right. I did need to be patient. In time, all of their lies would unravel, no matter how hard they tried to conceal them. Nurse Ruoff was allowed to step down. He returned to the defendant's box on the far side of the room.

His murder companion, Nurse Willig, replaced him in the witness box. He stood up and nervously walked towards it, his body language unsure after his buddy's less than convincing testimony. He told them he started working at Hadamar in 1941 and that his role, like Herr Ruoff's, was to kill the inmates through administering hypodermic injections of narcotics and oral doses of Veronal and Chloral.

Perhaps he thought telling the truth would save him, or perhaps he had finally grown a conscience. Whatever it was, he was very forthcoming. He freely admitted that he had participated in the conferences to decide who would be killed and who would live. He was certain he was required to do this by law. He said he was never threatened with a concentration camp and, although he had asked for transfers, he could not leave because he did not want to jeopardise his pension. His *pension!*

Nurse Willig's testimony made the others' testimonies seem convoluted and contradictory. Much of what he said cast serious shadows of doubt on the key ideas upon which they relied. When they had finished questioning him, the hearing was adjourned.

I returned to my hotel and ate my *Gemüsesuppe*. On the way to my room I picked up a copy of the local newspaper. I took it to my room to read. The trial was big news, sprawled all over the front page and for dozens after that. Everything – absolutely *everything* – that had been said in the courtroom had been reported. I slept soundly that night. It seemed the people of Germany were on my side after all.

CHAPTER 16

VERDICTS

12 October 1945

The next day I arrived flushed with hope. Major Bolker stood outside, waiting for me. He asked if I was okay. I said I was. He said 'good', because today was going to be a big day.

Inside, I didn't see her at first, as she was obscured by the crowd as they settled into their seats. But once everyone had sat down, I saw her in the witness box. Chief Nurse Huber sat quietly, dressed in a brown tweed woollen jacket. Her hair was neatly tied back and it seemed much greyer than before, as if she had aged ten years.

Much to my surprise, Herr Jaworski took the lead in questioning her. Clearly, they saw Chief Nurse Huber as their best chance to get to the truth. She was asked to state her name and her duties, as well as her involvement with the Poles and Russians. She said her job was to clear the wards to prepare for their arrivals. I knew what 'clear' the wards meant, but I knew she was not about to admit to it.

Herr Jaworski informed her that witnesses had said that she had directly participated in the fatal injections. She resolutely denied the accusation, pushing the blame to the male nurses and doctors. Her *only* job was to retrieve the narcotics, she said, and, although she was present at the injections, she never gave them herself.

I wondered why she had implicated herself in the killings. Then I realised. She was trying to garnish sympathy for her plight. I couldn't believe what I was hearing! She was actually trying to portray herself as the *victim*! She pushed the 'I was following orders' line. She talked about how much *she* had suffered in her time at Hadamar. She said she'd even had sleepless nights because of it.

Herr Jaworski was not going to let her off that easily. Now I understood why they'd interviewed me. He said that even if she hadn't participated in killing Russians and Poles she most certainly *had* killed Germans. She admitted that her primary duty was to administer morphine to the female German patients. The faces of girls I knew in Hadamar flashed through my mind. She continued. The way she spoke so matter-of-factly made my skin crawl. I wanted to run to the front of the court and scream out in front of everyone so they knew all of the things she had done. I wanted to paint a true picture of this woman for the Commission. I had to content myself with the fact that I had already done so through my witness statement.

I closed my eyes as she talked. Hundreds of random faces appeared. Some were in pain, others shook with fear, confused as to why they were being killed. Every face I saw had one thing in common: they were all victims of Chief Nurse Huber.

I opened my eyes and stared at her. I hated her. I wanted her punished. I pictured her thin frame dangling from the gallows like a wind chime. I envisaged her body shoved in an unmarked grave.

She argued that the killings *were* merciful. Herr Jaworski kept questioning her, trying to get her to implicate herself in the deaths of the Russians and Poles. That was when she came out with the biggest lie of them all: that she had actually asked to be relieved of her duties rather than deal with the foreign workers, because she didn't feel comfortable participating in the process! It caused a great weight on her mind, she said, so she asked Dr Klein to be relieved and he agreed.

My blood boiled. My face reddened with anger as she tried to play the part of victim. It was unbelievable! Herr Jaworski didn't buy it. He simply reminded her of what she had done and why she had done it. She had made the arrangements for the elimination of these so-called worthless people and, because of this, she was indeed an essential cog in the machine. She nodded solemnly. I thought she was about to accept her fate – to admit her guilt. Instead, she looked around imploringly at the people in the gallery, her eyes and words pleading for sympathy as she demanded the court recognise that the Hadamar staff were doing what was best for the Reich!

Calmly and firmly, Herr Jaworski, told her that murdering people had no justification, no matter what arguments she put forth. She buried her head in her hands and broke into tears. I was sure they were nothing more than crocodile tears, just another ploy for compassion. Herr Jaworski stated he had no further questions, and Chief Nurse Huber, visibly shaken and seemingly fragile, had to be helped back to her seat, still sobbing, by the defence lawyers.

CHAPTER 16

13 October 1945

If she thought it was over, she was wrong. If she thought her performance would make them leave her alone, she was wrong. The following day, Chief Nurse Huber was told to enter the witness box again.

The prosecution lawyers resumed questioning her about her role in dealing with the Russians and the Poles. She said she felt terrible about it; that she was painfully aware that these people had mothers and fathers and that it would have been very hard for them to die in a strange land.

Herr Jaworski rubbed his eyes with his fingers and told her that how she *felt* did not matter. She tried to argue that even though she knew she had done many things that were wrong, deep down she was a good-hearted person. She did what she had to do because she did not want to be sent away.

The defence had their turn. They talked of her good moral character and tried to portray her in an almost saintly light. They referenced all the positive things her co-workers had said about her, particularly focusing on Dr Wahlmann's opinion. It was laughable. How could the opinion of a man like Dr Wahlmann carry any weight? They talked about how much Chief Nurse Huber had suffered. They said she deserved the highest of praise because she had shown nothing but love and understanding for all the patients in her care. As they read out quote after quote extolling her virtues, it bordered on ridiculous. They even tried to say that the proof of her caring nature was in how she brought us cakes and sandwiches and prepared picnics for us.

Sensing they were getting nowhere, the defence team returned to the 'fact' that she had tried to resign from Hadamar on several occasions but SS *Standarten-Führer* Bernotat would not allow it. At last, her testimony finished and she was allowed to step down. She seemed frazzled and shaken. Her testimony had been anything but convincing.

Herr Merkle replaced her. I had never had much to do with him. I had only seen him around the place. He was Hadamar's bookkeeper and it was his job to register the incoming patients and record dates and causes of death. Herr Merkle told of making false entries on both these fronts. He steadfastly denied the accusations that he knew anything of Hadamar's functions.

They had questioned all but one person: Herr Blum. I remembered the interviews in Hadamar. Herr Blum had seemed to be the one most willing to divulge information, and I wondered if this was why the prosecution had left him until last. He took the stand looking bemused and confused. Herr Jaworski asked him to state his name and occupation. He told them his name was Phillip Blum and that he had started working at Hadamar prior to 1940. He was transferred to the Luftwaffe for a short time, before returning to Hadamar in 1941. After 1943 he became the chief caretaker of the cemetery.

They asked him if he was in charge of burials at that time and if he used German inmates like me and Herr Dickmann to bury the bodies. He told them there were too many dead for him to do it by himself. They asked him about the bodies being stacked in the cellars and being left there for weeks. He told the Commission that it took a long time to dig the graves and that he could not bury anyone without

Dr Wahlmann's permission. Herr Jaworski then tripped him up by quoting Herr Blum's own words. In his pre-trial statement, he'd stated categorically that he was the one who gave the orders as to who was to be buried. Herr Blum said he was confused and that, *ja*, he did give the orders.

Then came the key piece of evidence – evidence that *I* had given them. They asked Herr Blum if anyone had ever been buried alive. He denied it, point blank. Herr Jaworski asked him how many bodies he thought were in the graveyard. Herr Blum's response was that he had supervised the burial of at least a hundred bodies or more in mass graves. Then, of his own free will, he offered that he knew when a new 'batch' would arrive and what had to be done.

When pushed for clarification, he freely admitted that he watched the injections and watched the people die, waiting to one side because he knew he would have to bury them. I could feel the disgust filling every crack and crevice in the room; every face in the room (except, perhaps, the Hadamar staff's), stared at him with revulsion. He played with his hands and looked around the room before staring into his lap. Strangely, I found myself pitying him. He may have been a vulture, but at least he had taken the stand and told the truth. He wasn't ashamed of what he'd done, but he didn't understand the severity of his actions either. He wasn't smart enough to understand just how much trouble he was truly in.

Herr Jaworski asked him why he did this particular job. He replied that if he didn't, he would have been sent away to a camp. Herr Jaworski ignored the comment and returned to the mass burials. Herr Blum said he buried eight to twenty people in one grave and that anyone who was buried was recorded in the burial book. I thought of the woman they'd buried alive. I remembered the day when Major Bolker and the other Americans had exhumed the bodies, cutting them open like cattle in an abattoir. Lost in my thoughts, I didn't listen to what was said next, only catching the last question Herr Jaworski asked him: were people buried alive? Herr Blum repeated that they were not.

He was allowed to step down and join the others. Herr Jaworski shook his head before he said that, no matter what Herr Blum argued, he was indeed 'a reaper of souls'.

Now for the closing arguments. The defence blamed Hitler and Fascism itself. They put the blame on Herrs Springer and Bernotat. Herr Jaworski said that, as neither man was present to confirm or deny this – nor was there any legal documentation to prove it – it remained hearsay. He talked at length about the authority of the court and countered arguments that it should be conducted under German jurisdiction.

In one final, desperate attempt to sway the judges, the defence argued that murderers were people who murdered because of a lust for killing, because of sexual perversions or greed. The accused did not fit into the category of 'murderers' simply because they did not hate the people they killed. They did it because they were ordered to – but deep down they were good-natured people who nursed their patients with care for many years. In one last ditch, somewhat bizarre, attempt to save their clients they attacked the judges themselves. They argued that because the judges were American, they could not possibly understand what it was like to be a German under Nazi rule. America was a 'new' continent that had had democracy for centuries; Germans were citizens of an 'other' world: a world the judges would never be able to understand.

The judges were not impressed as they closed the day's proceedings. Major Bolker and I waited for everyone else to file out. I watched the staff as they left, wondering what they were thinking. Were they still deluding themselves that, somehow, all that they had said would save them? I wouldn't have to wait long to find out. Once we were outside, Major Bolker told me that the judges would spend tomorrow collating all the evidence and considering their verdict. I was no longer required to be there; I could go home to Mutti. The day after that, he would send a Jeep for me so I could come back to hear the final verdicts.

15 October 1945

Two days later a Jeep arrived.

As we sat in the rear for the drive back to Wiesbaden, I wondered if the judges would give the right verdict. They *had* to. Nothing the staff had said warranted mercy – a word the staff had used so often.

In reality, today's verdicts meant little. Whether they were punished or not, it wasn't going to change my future. I knew now that I had to be at the trials to confront the Hadamar staff one last time so I could move on with my life. Whatever happened today, I had to leave Hadamar behind. The Jeep approached the courthouse and a sense of calmness washed over me. All that had transpired and all that was to come was beyond my control. Regardless of the outcome, my life would begin again today.

Major Bolker met me outside, as he had done on each day of the trials. By the time we walked in, the defendants were already seated in their box, talking apprehensively amongst themselves, clearly nervous. Major Bolker offered me a brief smile before the proceedings began. The defence lawyers repeated their arguments: that all of the accused had no choice, less they be punished themselves. They finished with the claim that a tribunal led by judges from the United States maintained no authority over German citizens and, therefore, all the charges should be dismissed.

The defence lawyer sat down. The seven Hadamar staff leant forward, anxiously anticipating Herr Jaworski's next words. He shuffled a stack of papers and shifted several folders into a neat pile before he tapped them on the desk. He took a long, measured look around the courtroom. His eyes met the defendants'. His gaze lingered long on them. He repeated what he had said before the trials began: that each of the defendants would find someone to whom they could 'pass the buck', and that each of them would argue that they did what they did under the threat of death themselves. His predictions had come true, he observed. Then he made a statement that revealed the opinions of the American judges.

'I find myself with little recourse but to compare the trial we have just conducted here to the trial given to the victims of Hadamar … let us pause to consider what sort of trial these accused gave to those unfortunate people who appeared before them at Hadamar. There came person after person – weary, heavy-laden, some sick, some quite sick – thinking that they saw upon the horizon the dawn of a brighter day. And what sort of trial was given them? What sort of a hearing, what sort of an opportunity was accorded them at this place where they thought they might find comfort, where they might find some happiness?

'They were brought into the death halls. Were they given medical examinations? No. Were they given any medical treatment? No. Upon them was forced the hush of death. Their bodies were taken to a bleak cellar. They were lumped together and dumped together in a common grave buried without the benefit of clergy. With the ease and readiness that one would extinguish a candle light, so were the lives of human beings snuffed out by them.

'Yes, the Counsel will be pleading for their lives. It's his duty. But before closing I want to say only this to the Commission: what right, what right have people situated as they are to expect that their lives be spared when they would not spare the lives of one of the several hundred that appeared before them? All they can ask is that they be judged as they have judged others.

'This Commission finds that between 5 or 6 June 1944 and 13 March 1945, four hundred and seventy-six Polish and Russian men, women and children were shipped to Hadamar and killed within one or two days of their arrival either by hypodermic injections of morphine or scopolamine, or by doses of Veronal or Chloral. The defendants have repeatedly testified that these fatal injections were given because the labourers were incurably sick with tuberculosis and that they believed these people came under the same laws as those for the treatment of the German insane. But at least one of the witnesses here has said that this is not so.

'The defence has been unable to prove beyond reasonable doubt that there was any such decree of law, much less its real or purported application to the non-German victims. The exhumation and autopsies carried out by American pathologists on six Polish and Russian bodies clearly showed that at least one of the deceased had not suffered from any form of tuberculosis. Certainly none of the six bodies was in any advanced enough state of the disease to warrant a death sentence. The labourers were neither examined nor treated for tuberculosis by qualified doctors; if an examination did take place, it was by a non-qualified staff member.

'To make matters worse in these cases, the victims were deceived into thinking that the injections they were receiving were for the treatment of other communicable diseases. So, under the guise of helping these poor people, they were instead murdered. Their bodies were shown less respect than when they were living, tossed into mass graves.

'These people claimed to be doing the right thing; one must ask why then did they feel the need to falsify the death records of these labourers? When these poor, unfortunate souls arrived at Hadamar, records were made of their names, sex and nationality, along with several other aspects of their lives. However, their cause of death was always falsified so as not to reflect the truth of this matter: that they were, in a calculated fashion, murdered.'

CHAPTER 16

Silence engulfed the courtroom. Each person stared intently at Herr Jaworski. He took an extended pause before he said that, by a two-thirds majority vote, on the charge of murdering Russian and Polish labourers, men, women and children, Alfons Klein, Dr Wahlmann, Nurses Ruoff and Willig, Adolf Merkle and Phillip Blum were all found *guilty*.

Overwhelmed with relief and overcome by excitement, I don't know how I managed to keep my composure. I wanted to leap into the air and cry out with joy. There was, however, one verdict left: the one I was most desperate to hear.

'And as for the last defendant,' Herr Jaworski continued, 'Chief Nurse Irmgard Huber, on the charge of the murder of Russian and Polish prisoners, we find you *guilty*.'

My head spun and swum; I felt dizzy, delirious. I looked over to the defendants' box: some were stunned; others buried their head in their hands. Dr Klein's face carried a look of sheer disbelief as he was sentenced to hang until he was dead. He looked at his lawyers, shocked that he had just been told his life would come to an end. *I don't know why you're surprised,* I thought, *you are a murderer. God has come calling for you.*

Herr Jaworski continued with the sentencing. Nurses Ruoff and Willig were also told they would hang until they were dead. They were as shocked as Dr Klein.

'Adolf Wahlmann,' Herr Jaworski continued. I opened my eyes and looked at the *Herr Doktor*, his face filled with fear now that he had heard the fate of his companions. 'You are sentenced to life imprisonment.'

My heart sank. If the others had received the death penalty, then surely Dr Wahlmann warranted the same. If Dr Wahlmann was escaping death, I feared the others would also. Herr Merkle was sentenced to a non-parole period of thirty-five years. Herr Blum: thirty years. The three men looked at each other, dumbfounded, shocked that the next three and half decades of their life would be spent behind bars – but perhaps equally astonished that they had escaped the gallows. I felt warmed by what I had heard. Now they too would know what it felt like to spend your life locked up behind walls from which you could not escape.

One sentence remained. I was sure she was going to escape Hell, for the moment at least.

'Chief Nurse Irmgard Huber,' Herr Jaworski said, his voice stern and deliberate. I leant forward in anticipation. Chief Nurse Huber did the same.

'You are sentenced to a non-parole period of twenty-five years.'

Yelping with excitement, I leapt from my chair, causing several people, including Chief Nurse Huber, to look at me. My retribution had been delivered. She could only hold my eye for a moment before she began to weep. Major Bolker looked at me and smiled.

I had won. I had survived Hadamar. I had survived *her*. She now sat in the dock looking frail and weak, shaking and crying like the children had done when she marched up and down the wards selecting the next to die. The public gallery erupted. Dozens of people shouted insults as the defendants were led away.

Once they had disappeared, it felt surreal. That was it. I would never have to see them again. *I* may have suffered for years, but *they* would soon either be dead or suffering for a lifetime. I felt a huge weight lift from me. Now, like Germany herself, I would have to rebuild my life. The future was uncertain, but it was my future – *mine*, to live how I pleased.

'Both the living and the dead have their justice,' Major Bolker commented as the courtroom quietened and began to empty. We watched the last of the people leaving. I suddenly remembered that there was one doctor from Hadamar who had not been put on trial.

'Herr Major.'

'*Ja,* Ingrid?' he said.

'Do you remember when we were in Hadamar that I asked you about Dr Oppenheimer?'

'I do.'

'Did you ever find out what happened to him?'

'*Ja*, Ingrid. I did. I was waiting until the trial was over before I told you. I checked around. It took some time, but I came across some records of a Dr Oppenheimer. He was identified by the Russians when they liberated Auschwitz.'

I was excited to hear the news of the man who had saved me. I resolved that when the chance presented itself, I would keep my promise. I would tell the Americans that he had saved me and, hopefully, save him from the same fate as the others. Seeing my excitement, Major Bolker's face turned dire. 'When the Russians took the camp at Auschwitz they found a doctor named Oppenheimer in a house near Oświęcim. He sat at a desk; there was a gun beside him. Ingrid, Dr Oppenheimer killed himself.'

My heart sank. Why would he do that? He must have known I would have saved him, told them the truth. What could make him feel so desperate that he saw no other option but to take his own life?

'Maybe it wasn't him. Maybe it was another doctor with the same name! What did he look like?'

'That may be possible. But I'm afraid I don't know any more at this stage.'

'Can you find out for me, please?' I begged.

'The Russians were pushing hard to get to Berlin first. They arrested any Nazis that they found alive but they weren't interested in the ones they found already dead. For all we know they left him where he was.'

As we started to walk outside I resolved to find Dr Oppenheimer and tell whoever needed to be told that he was the one who saved me. When we exited the courthouse, I stopped at the top of the stairs and took a deep breath as I looked up at the blue sky above.

'Ingrid, in my checking around I managed to find someone else you know,' Major Bolker said as he came and stood beside me.

'Who?' I asked, looking at him, puzzled. He flicked his head towards the bottom of the stairs. Sitting at the base, smiling up at me, was Johan.

'Hello, Ingrid,' he said as he wheeled his chair forward.

'Johan!' I cried as I leapt three, four stairs at a time. He hugged me tightly, kissed me on the cheek then whispered into my ear, 'Now you are free.'

CHAPTER 16

'And this is where I take my leave,' Major Bolker said. 'Ingrid, whatever you do in life from this point on, I wish you health and happiness. Thank you for all you have done for us.'

I turned back to him and stood to my full height. By now, I had grown extremely tall; even so, I had to stand on tiptoes to kiss Major Bolker on the cheek before I hugged him tightly.

'*Danke* to you and all of your men. You saved me. You have given me the chance to live a long life.'

I moved around the back of Johan's chair and placed my hands on the handles as we watched the tall, lanky frame of Major Bolker walk towards a Jeep; and just like that, he was gone.

I never saw him again.

For a moment I stood looking at the columns of the courthouse, the fountains in the park in front of me surrounded by neatly kept lawns. It reminded me of the hospital where they had taken me to be sterilised.

'Ingrid, are you okay?' Johan asked.

'*Ja* – just a memory I don't want any more,' I said as I started to push him across the cobblestones and down the footpath. We moved along the streets and past the terraced buildings until we came to a small café. I pushed Johan into position at an outside table and sat opposite him. We sat in silence and I realised this was my life. The chapters of my life would always come to an end, sometimes happily, sometimes not. It was not for me to determine the outcome.

Being with Johan made me feel exhilarated but awkward at the same time. Part of me wanted to sit next to him, to hold his hand, to pretend we were a couple, but part of me was equally content sitting across the table. A waiter came to take our order.

'*Apfelwein,* if you have it?' I asked. Johan ordered a beer.

'Are you sure you should be drinking that?' Johan asked.

'You still see me as some silly little schoolgirl, a schoolgirl that shouldn't drink, don't you?'

'*Nein*, that's not it at all,' he said as he pushed his hand across the table and tried to take mine. I snatched my hand away.

'Johan, why did you never come for me? Why did you never even call?'

'Going home wasn't exactly like I had expected. Nothing could have prepared me for what it was like,' he said as the waiter arrived with our drinks.

I sipped my *Apfelwein* and stared at him, silent.

'At first, people were nice and treated me kindly, but then they started to whisper and point. My family is my family and they have to love me, but as time went on I felt self-conscious about going out into the streets so I found myself staying home all of the time. As to why I never came for you: I don't know! Perhaps I was drowning in my own self-pity … But you were in an institution run by the SS; what was I supposed to say or do to get you out of there?'

'You are a war hero; surely you have connections,' I accused as I looked at the red bricks of the Market Church on the other side of the Schlossplatz.

'One thing that going home has taught me is that honesty is best. Ingrid, I never came for you … I never tried to get you out because I thought you were already dead.'

He sipped his beer, avoiding my eyes. I didn't feel sorry for him. The war had taken a terrible toll on us all. I didn't pity him. He had made his decisions and now he was living with the results. I was angry that he never come for me but, equally, I could understand his point of view.

'I think,' he said as he sipped his beer, 'that I finally understand where you are coming from.'

'*Nein*, you don't and you never will.'

I didn't say what I said to be mean. I didn't say it to be harsh. He was a German – he could never understand my lifetime of feeling inferior or what it meant to have an entire country hate you. We sat. We drank. I felt the warmth of the *Apfelwein* soothe my soul. We discussed the trials; those that had gone and those that were yet to come. We talked of Germany before, Germany now and Germany in the future.

When the alcohol had given him the confidence to do so, Johan asked, 'Ingrid, can there ever be anything between us again?'

He removed a simple gold ring from his finger and handed it to me.

'Before you answer, I want you to have this.'

I took the ring. On the outside it was inscribed: In gratitude for your service. I paused on it for a moment, before I looked up and stared deeply into his blue eyes and said, 'I don't know, Johan. I just don't know.'

It was the truth. For the latter part of my teenage years and the early part of my adult life I had lived in an institution. My formative years had been taken from me; I'd been kept caged like an animal inside the walls of Hadamar. Whilst there, my life was simple. I just had to try to survive until the end. If I did, my sole goal was to see justice done. Now that I had, I didn't know what I wanted to do, where I wanted to go, who I wanted to be.

How could I give part of myself away to him when I did not know which parts of myself were still my own, or which I had lost forever?

EPILOGUE

5 May 2017

Tears dripped down my cheeks as she told me the last part of her story. I put my pen and notebook to one side before I reached into my pocket, retrieved a handkerchief and dabbed my eyes with it.

'You are an amazing woman,' I told her.

'*Nein*, I am not. I am just an ordinary person.'

She closed her eyes. She was clearly deep in thought. I wondered if she was thinking of my Opa – Johan Kapfler – or all of the people she had loved and lost.

'My heart hurts,' she said. 'I've lived my life as best I could. I've tried to escape Hadamar, but it has never let me. I've tried to push my pain aside, but it never worked. My soul will be forever tainted by what they did to me.'

I felt pained for her, but there were still unanswered questions.

'Wait,' I said. 'What about your Mutti?'

'Miss Kapfler, you are looking at me like so many children have throughout the years when I'm reading them a fairytale and they expect a happy ending. Is that what you're after: a happy ending?'

I nodded a single nod.

'I wish I could give you one. Mutti and I did as I had said we would do – we came to America. As I had always wanted, I came to see Fräulein Rothenberg. We came and stayed with her here in Rhode Island, and it was she who encouraged me to become a teacher. I would have stayed with her forever if I could have, but she had her own family. Eventually Mutti and I found cleaning work and a small apartment. I don't want to bore you with facts but America wasn't all I expected it to be.

'Americans were very concerned about the plight of the Jews in Germany, and Jewish people like yourself had many opportunities. I tried to believe that America was the land of the free, but to many people I was just another nigger. Being white, Mutti found work easily at first, but when people found out she had a black daughter, finding a job became harder. It wasn't much better than Nazi Germany. But then the Civil Rights Movement came; we marched on Washington – Fräulein Rothenberg too – and it was on her recommendations that I got a full teaching scholarship at Brown University. The day I was accepted into university was the happiest day of Mutti's life.'

'Fräulein Marchand, forgive me, but you don't say that very enthusiastically.'

'My success gave Mutti a brief moment of happiness, but it wasn't enough. I supposed she never got over losing Vati. The grief, the pain: it was just too much for her. She drowned herself in drink.'

'What happened to her?'

'She died before her time.'

'And Opa? Can you tell me any more about your relationship?'

'Now, that I will *not* tell you about. Some parts of my story are mine and mine alone.'

I did not try to hide the disappointment in my face, but I knew not to push. Perhaps she would come around in time and tell me when she was ready. Instead, I shifted the conversation to the fate of the Hadamar staff instead.

'Like I said, Miss Kapfler, life doesn't always have happy endings. The three that were sentenced to death were sent to Bruschsal Prison, while the others were moved to War Criminal Prison 1 in Landsburg. After the Wiesbaden trials when the Americans captured people like Herman Goering, the crimes committed at Hadamar, and places like it, seemed trivial when compared to other atrocities committed by the Nazis.

'Dr Klein, Nurse Ruoff and Nurse Willig's wives all petitioned for clemency, but they didn't get it. Dr Klein, Nurse Ruoff, and Nurse Willig all went to the gallows on 14 March 1946.

'Chief Nurse Huber, Herr Merkle, Dr Wahlmann and Herr Blum remained in prison but, year after year, they filed appeal after appeal. The world moved on and wanted to forget about the war and think about the future. People were placated that Nazi war criminals had been punished for their crimes. Germany needed to rebuild herself and the German authorities wanted to take control back. The War Crimes Modification Board started to show more and more leniency.

'In February 1946, and again in 1947, a whole new trial began, but this time it was in a German court. I had to make my way to Frankfurt to sit through what they now call "the Euthanasia Trials". I did it with a mixed heart. On the one hand, the possibility existed that the remaining staff would escape justice. On the other, the American trials had only put seven of my tormentors on trial. The Germans tried all of the staff they could find.

'With Dr Klein dead, Dr Wahlmann was the highest-ranking staff member on trial. There was another man, I don't remember his name. I had only seen him once – on the day I was sent to the gas chambers. Chief Nurse Huber ranked number three. The Frankfurt trial lasted almost two weeks, but there was a lot less public interest. The laws in Germany had changed. They might have put more of the staff on trial, but there were limited things they could be tried for. As I said, there were worse crimes than the ones committed in Hadamar. Between fifteen and twenty-five thousand people had died in Hadamar, but that was almost insignificant compared to the millions that had died in places like Auschwitz. In the minds of the German jurors, injecting and gassing German disabled children was less brutal than the gassing of the Jews. The longer the trials went, the more defendants claimed to have acted on the basis of a secret euthanasia law, which still could not be proven. They told the same stories and used the same defences as they had done at Wiesbaden.

'The trials finished in 1947. Eleven out of twenty-five staff were convicted. The ones who had actually participated in the killings received paltry sentences ranging from two to eight years. The technical and bureaucratic staff were let go because they didn't actually participate in the killings, but to me there was no difference. Hadamar could not have functioned without them, right down to the lowest clerk. It was a factory. Every single one of them had played their part. They all shared the guilt.

'It wasn't all bad news, though. Dr Wahlmann's conviction was upgraded to the death penalty, but under the New Federal Deutsche Republic Constitution, capital punishment was forbidden, so the sentence stayed the same: life imprisonment. In 1950 and 1951, the Office of the Judge Advocate conducted a complete review of the surviving defendants. Merkle – given he'd already served time – was allowed to go free. Dr Wahlmann's sentence was reduced from life to just twelve years! Chief Nurse Huber's sentence was also reduced to twelve years. Herr Blum's was reduced to fifteen years. Then, as if the Americans wanted to rid themselves of anything to do with the war, they changed the sentences again. Dr Wahlmann – a man who was responsible for thousands of murders – had his role in Hadamar diminished to 'clerical' one. They let him go in 1952.

'Chief Nurse Huber had dozens of people file petitions of clemency on her behalf. The first one, in 1946, came from her mother, Philomena. She showed the authorities the 'shocking' letters Chief Nurse Huber had sent her throughout the war. These, she argued, proved how utterly miserable her daughter was during her time at Hadamar. Another nurse, Maria Kuhl, backed up the idea that Chief Nurse Huber wanted to escape. My question always was: why didn't she? If what she did was so deplorable, then why didn't she take the punishment, take death – surely that was preferable to killing children. They killed my friends by "relieving" their suffering and removing us from our "misery". If she was suffering so badly, if she was so miserable, why didn't she give herself *Gnadentod*?

'Her sentence was reduced to eight years, but then the War Crimes Modification Board reviewed the case and she was granted clemency. They reduced her sentence to time already served. She was released in July 1953.

'Herr Blum also had people begging for his release. In March 1950, his sentence was reduced from thirty-five to fifteen years. He didn't serve anywhere near that, but he did have to spend three years longer in prison than he needed to because he misbehaved in prison. He didn't get out until July 1957. I found it hard to believe that this meek little man who had never dared to speak out against anyone in authority would actually cause trouble.

'There it is. Twelve years after the original trial, and not a single of the seven sentenced to imprisonment – not *one* of my tormentors – remained behind bars.

'After all the investigations, both the German and American authorities agreed on a final death count from Hadamar: twenty-five thousand. Twenty-five thousand dead, not counting the lifelong anguish and sorrow of those who had survived. Only three staff paid the ultimate price. Three. The rest, eventually, walked free. Free to live their lives how they chose, free from pain, free from suffering, free from torment.

'Something I will never be.'

TRANSLATIONS

German word	**Meaning**
Allgemeine SS	the Schutzstaffel (SS), paramilitary forces of Nazi Germany
Anschluss	the unification of Austria and Germany
Bitte	please
Blutschande	sexual relations between 'superior' Germans and 'inferior' races, particularly Negroes or Jews
Bund Deutscher Mädel	the League of German Girls or Band of German Maidens, the female version of the Hitler Youth
Danke	thank you
Das Reich	a National Socialist newspaper
Der Führer	Hitler's title as leader of Germany
Deutsches Jungvolk	a separate section of the Hitler Youth, a Nazi organisation for boys aged ten to fourteen
Die schwarze Schande	the black shame
Das Sterbebuch	the Death Book
Domplatz	the central square of the city of Mainz
Ein Krankenbuch	a register of sick patients
Einsatzgruppen	SS paramilitary death squads that committed mass killings throughout Eastern Europe
Erbkrank	'The Hereditary Defective', a Nazi film about genetic defects made in 1936
Ersatz	a substitute for a product, usually of inferior quality
Gauleiter	a political official governing a district under Nazi rule
Gefreiter	equivalent to the rank of Corporal
Gestapo	an abbreviation of Geheime Staatspolizei (Secret State Police), the official secret police of Nazi Germany and German-occupied Europe.

Glühwein	a form of hot red wine
Gnadentod	a 'merciful' death; euthanasia
Heiligabend	Christmas Eve
Jungmädel	young Girls, Hitler Youth
Kriminalpolizei, Kripo	the criminal police department in Nazi Germany
Lebensborn	an SS-initiated, state-supported program aimed at raising the birth rate of 'Aryan' and 'racially pure and healthy' children
Lebensunwertes Leben	a life unworthy of living
Liebschen, meine liebschen	my love, my little darling
Mischlinge	people of mixed race parentage
Oberst	equivalent rank to Colonel
Obersturmführer	equivalent rank to First Lieutenant
Ordnungspolizei	the uniformed police officers of Nazi Germany
Rassenschande	'blood disgrace', racial mixing
Ravensbrück	a women's concentration camp in Northern Germany
Reichstag	the German Parliament
Sonderbehandlung	'Special treatment', a term for euthanasia
Stollen	a fruit bread composed of nuts, spices, and fruit. Usually coated with powdered sugar or icing sugar and eaten during the festive season
Sturmabteilung	Hitler's 'storm troopers', the original paramilitary wing of the Nazi Party
Sturmbannführer	equivalent rank to Major
Unterscharführer	no equivalent rank, a Corporal/ Sergeant
Verboten	forbidden
Weihnachten	Christmas Day
Zwangsarbeitslager	a labour camp